BOOK FIVE IN THE RAIDING FORCES SERIES

GUERRILLA COMMAND

PHIL WARD

A RAIDING FORCES SERIES NOVEL

This book is a work of fiction. Names, characters, businesses, organizations, places, events, and incidents are either a product of the author's imagination or are used fictitiously. Any resemblance to actual persons, living or dead, events, or locales is entirely coincidental.

ISBN: 978-0-9895922-0-8
LCCN: 013943059
Published by Military Publishers LLC
Austin, Texas
www.raidingforces.com

Distributed by Military Publishers LLC

For ordering information or special discounts for bulk purchases, please contact Military Publishers LLC at 8871 Tallwood, Austin, Tx 78759, 512.346.2132

DEDICATION

GUERRILLA COMMAND IS DEDICATED TO LT. GEN. HENRY "Gunfighter" Emerson. On 3 June 68 then Col. Emerson, flying over the Plain of Reeds, inserted A/2/39 of his 1st Brigade to investigate muddy water he spotted in a canal. The unit came under heavy fire. The company commander ordered me, the only other officer on the ground at that point, "Take that tree line." Away we went, fifty-five men on line charging what was later estimated to be 800 to 1,300 Main Force Viet Cong across 150 meters of rice paddy as flat as a pool table. The CO had other pressing matters and stayed behind only to be shot dead when he came up later. Then it was learned we were "outside the artillery fan" and air support was "a half hour away." The VC gained fire superiority indicating they were getting ready to assault. Men pulled knives and laid out grenades standing by to repel boarders. I was wondering if it looked this bad at the Little Big Horn. On the radio all was chaos and hysteria – events spiraling out of control. A voice came up, "Paisley Butterfly 6" (or some such call sign). No response. However, Butterfly 6 was not to be denied – still no joy. Finally Butterfly shouted, "God dammit this is the Gunfighter!" The net went silent. And I knew we were going to win that fight. No officer who has worn the uniform ever had a greater impact on the troops he commanded than Gunfighter Emerson. In Vietnam he was a peerless brigade commander, an innovative tactician and a brilliant combat leader who instilled confidence in the men he commanded. I can testify to that – my last hero.

RANDAL'S RULES FOR RAIDING

RULE 1:   The first rule is there ain't no rules.

RULE 2:   Keep it short and simple.

RULE 3:   It never hurts to cheat.

RULE 4:   Right man, right job.

RULE 5:   Plan missions backward (know how to get home).

RULE 6:   It's good to have a Plan B.

RULE 7:   Expect the unexpected.

RAIDING FORCES

ONGOING OPERATIONS

OPERATION CANVASS
The liberation of Abyssinia. Clear Italian forces from the Red Sea for Lend Lease; ejecting the Italians out of East Africa

OPERATION ROMAN CANDLE (Mission 106)
A mission to ferment a rebellion by raising an irregular guerrilla army to operate against the Blackshirt interior lines of communications to prevent the Italians from being able to rapidly shift their forces from one front to another (in support of CANVASS

1
DEATH VALLEY

SOMEWHERE IN ABYSSINIA

MAJOR JOHN RANDAL, DSO, MC, LAY ON A RIDGE STUDYING the coffee plantation in the valley down below through the Zeiss binoculars he had captured from a Panzer colonel at Calais, France, in what now seemed another life.

The plantation was something the Italians called a Democratic Colonization Project (DCP). The Fascists had the model farms scattered all around Italian East Africa (IEA). The layout of this DCP consisted of a main house, three outbuildings and a tall silo.

The Blackshirts had brought agricultural experts by the thousands to Italian East Africa to operate the model farms after forcibly evicting the previous owners. The projects were intended to be showpieces. "The Leader," Benito Mussolini, wanted to demonstrate to the international community the superiority of the Fascist system of managing an African colony.

The plantations were worked by slave labor, something that Il Duce failed to mention.

Maj. Randal glanced at his black-faced Rolex wristwatch. The lime green digits read 0615 hours. The watch was a present from his ex-fiancée Captain the Lady Jane Seaborn, OBE, RM.

Originally it had been intended as a birthday present for her husband, but he had been lost at sea before she could give it to him ... temporarily lost, as it turned out. This had made Maj. Randal's love life, for lack of a better word, complicated. Though it had been pointed out that Lady Jane was in Africa working to support Force N instead of home in the U.K. with her returned-from-the-dead husband.

Maj. Randal thought about her every time he glanced at the watch. He had been informed by a reliable source that was why Lady Jane had given him the Rolex. If true, it worked.

Also attached to his wrist on a faded olive green canvas strap that matched his watchband was a wrist compass. It was made by Rolex for the Italian firm Panerai on contract to the Italian Navy especially for its elite frogmen. Lady Jane had given the compass to him on the last night he was in Kenya. It was a gift from Commodore Richard "Dickey the Pirate" Seaborn, VC, OBE, who had captured it when he boarded the Italian submarine the *Galileo*.

Now he had two reasons to think about Lady Jane on a regular basis. Not that he needed them.

"Stand by ready," Maj. Randal ordered.

"Roger that, John," Captain "Geronimo" Joe McKoy replied, fiddling with the traversing wheel of the tripod machine gun mount on which a Boys .55-caliber Anti-Tank (AT) Rifle was mounted.

The Boys could not penetrate any known armor and was arguably the worst antitank weapon in history. On paper its cigar-sized, .55-caliber, armor-piercing bullet had a maximum effective range of one mile and was extremely accurate. However, in practice the weapon's loud blast, punishing recoil, and its iron sights limited its actual range to 400 to 600 yards.

Capt. McKoy studied the weapon and saw possibilities. He installed an all-steel, No. 32 Mk1 scope designed for use on Bren light machine guns (LMGs) on a Boys and then mounted the AT rifle on an obsolete 110-pound GP Hotchkiss Omnibus tripod. The result was a deadly accurate .55-caliber rifle effective out to its intended maximum effective range of one mile.

Why no one had ever thought of the combination before was a fair question. Capt. McKoy had created the world's finest long-range sniper's weapons system.

1 Guerrilla Corps (Parachute), Force N had a dozen of them scattered between its Mule Raider Battalions (MRB).

In the early morning light down in the valley, Lieutenant Butch "Headhunter" Hoolihan, MM, RM, could be seen leading a file of his Force Raiding Company troops into position on the south side of the plantation building complex. His Abyssinian Patriots were armed with U.S. M-1903 A-1 Springfield rifles. The men were wearing Tom Mix-style cowboy hats and had bandoleers of .30-caliber ammunition strapped across their chests, making them look like Mexican banditos. The native troops were all barefoot.

In addition to rifles, each soldier was armed with a short sword. Only after a great deal of persuasion had they been convinced to leave their small round shields and spears behind. Abyssinians are miserable shots—mainly because ammunition is currency to them, so they never fired any to practice.

The Force Raiding Company troops were the exception. They had been schooled in the fundamentals of marksmanship when they were No. 3 Company of the 2nd Mule Raider Battalion, "Lounge Lizards" trained in Kenya before being selected to deploy to Force N as the Force Raiding Company.

Regardless of their training, the troops still preferred the spear as their weapon of choice, but eight-foot spears and shields are unwieldy.

Lt. Hoolihan had finally hit upon issuing his men bayonets, and that solved the problem. Bayonets are fairly heavy. More ammunition could be carried if they were left behind. They also took up precious cargo space on the handful of aircraft that supplied Force N. However, having a standard issue (U.S. Army) sixteen-inch bayonet fixed on their rifles which could be used like a spear made the troops happy.

In a small guerrilla army far behind enemy lines, having happy indigenous troops is a good thing.

On the north side of the plantation house, Maj. Randal could see Lieutenant Dick Courtney was already in position with his two former Gold Coast Border Police strikers, X-Ray and Vanish, and a small detachment of Force Raiding Company men. With him was an experienced Green Jacket formerly of the Rifle Brigade and Swamp Fox Force manning a Hotchkiss Mk1 LMG. The LMG was notoriously prone to jamming, but it was hoped that a trained Raiding Forces operator could keep it running.

The Rolex read 0630.

Normally, people on farms are early risers. But this was Africa, and there were a lot of hungry animals out and about with big teeth—not to forget shifta bandits. So, no one on Abyssinian plantations ventured forth until well after daylight. Everyone was still inside the DCP model farm.

Lt. Courtney ordered, "Commence firing."

On his command, the Hotchkiss LMG opened, as did everyone else in his detachment, firing their M-1903 A-1 Springfield rifles.

The result was instantaneous. The Italian nationals and the farm security detail spilled out of the main house and the outbuildings, some half-dressed, and stood to. The Blackshirts manned the fighting positions on the north side of the perimeter in the direction the firing was coming from.

That was a mistake. Lt. Courtney was carrying out a feint. And it worked like a charm.

As soon as the Italians built up their base of return fire directed toward Lt. Courtney's men on the far south side of the plantation house, Lt. Hoolihan stood up and shouted loud enough (he hoped) for the people inside the main building to hear the command every Royal Marine officer secretly longs to give: "Fix bayonets!"

This was a completely unnecessary order since the men of Force Raiding Company never, ever unfixed theirs.

"Move out!"

The Force N troops stepped off in a ragged line formation and, as they had been trained to do, bolted and fired their rifles every time their bare left foot hit the ground. The Patriots were screaming savage war cries as much to build up their own courage as to intimidate the opposition. The crackle of forty M-1903 A-1 Springfield rifles was inspiring even if they were not hitting much, not even their objective— the three-story plantation house.

Italian resistance melted the instant the security detail realized they had fallen for the oldest trick in the book. Those men not already dead or wounded bolted from their fighting positions. A lone sniper remained at his post in the top of the silo and began firing on Lt. Hoolihan's assault line.

BAAAAAROOOOOMMM! Capt. McKoy's Boys .55-caliber AT Rifle spoke. A tiny puff of smoke appeared from the target followed by a small "crunch," and there was no more firing from the silo.

Lt. Hoolihan signaled one of his platoon leaders, Bimbashi Cord Granger, to clear the out buildings while he continued the attack on the main objective.

Lana Turner, one of the two slave girls Maj. Randal had liberated on his first day in-country brought up his white mule, Parachute. Then with the other ex-slave, Rita Hayworth, in hot pursuit, the three made a death-defying ride straight down the steep ridge, racing to get to the plantation house in time to influence the outcome of the firefight.

Waldo Treywick, himself a former slave, and Gubbo Rekash, aka Cheap Bribe, the Patriot commander of Maj. Randal's auxiliary troops and his shifta, came pouring around the mountain on their animals at a dead run. Each man was leading a mule belonging to one of the Force Raiding Company soldiers. The Patriot troops were hoping to get to the scene of the action before all the loot was gone.

In the Abyssinian shifta bandit world, there were only the quick and the broke.

As Lt. Hoolihan's assault line approached the plantation house, Lt. Courtney ordered, "Shift your fires!"

The Hotchkiss Mk1 machine gunner adjusted his point of aim to the main house as planned and swept through it from left to right, then ceased fire. Within seconds the assault troops hit the building. Lt. Hoolihan led them inside with his Thompson submachine gun at his shoulder.

Maj. Randal and the two girls rode up. Cheap Bribe and his bandits thundered into the yard. Inside the house there were a couple of muffled pops, then the *RAAAMP* of the Thompson was heard.

Lt. Hoolihan appeared at the door. "Clear, sir," he reported, Royal Marine cool.

"Nice job, stud," Maj. Randal said. "Secure all the military-type weapons then let Bribe's boys clean out the rest."

When Waldo translated that to the one-eyed bandit chief, the old scoundrel immediately started shouting commands to his men. The established protocol was that he and Maj. Randal would divvy up the take once it had been collected—with anything of military value going to Force N and the bandits keeping the rest.

Gubbo Rekash was a veteran shifta chieftain. He suspected that there was going to be hard money or jewels in the house somewhere, and he was already making plans to strip search his Patriots once they made camp later that day. Any of his men caught hoarding loot was going to be in serious trouble.

Cheap Bribe only had one punishment for major crimes, like not turning in all the captured booty—and that was banishment. To be cast out was a fate worse than death. In a country where murder was the national sport and strangers were viewed as fair game, anyone on his own was in for a slow, painful demise.

The threat of banishment should have been a major deterrent. However, there was always someone in his band willing to take a chance. So Cheap Bribe never did. His policy was to consider every member of his command guilty until proven innocent.

There were no prisoners. Any of the Italians or their minions who had not run away were dead. Force N was fighting a war to the knife. No quarter was asked or given.

Orders had been issued before the action began not to pursue anyone who tried to escape. Captain Hawthorne Merryweather, the Force N Special Warfare Officer assigned from Psychological Warfare Executive, wanted panicked Italians arriving at the nearest Blackshirt base describing the attack.

"You better come see this, sir," Lt. Hoolihan said.

Inside the house, the sack was on with the Patriots frantically tearing through drawers and closets and climbing up into the ceiling. The master bedroom on the third floor was an ugly scene. There was a dead blond woman sprawled on her bed in a pink silk negligée with a bloody head wound and a dead Italian male in his fifties on the floor—also with a wound to the head. A Bodeo 10.4mm service revolver was lying next to him.

"We do that?"

"No, sir. It looks like plantation manager killed his wife to keep her from being captured then shot himself, murder—suicide. I wanted you to see for yourself, Major."

"Roger," Maj. Randal said. "Search this room for anything of intelligence value then let Bribe's boys in to get at the rest."

"Sir, I ..."

"This is guerrilla war, Butch — women get shot like anybody else."

Waldo came in, "Gunroom downstairs, Major. Got some heavy huntin' rifles would 'a come in handy when we was sittin' up for lion every night. Couple 'a right nice over and under Beretta bird guns down there too."

"Secure the weapons we need, Mr. Treywick," Maj. Randal ordered. "Tell Cheap Bribe to hurry it up. I want to move out shortly."

"Shot his wife, huh?" Waldo said. "Wops is real brave when they got the upper hand, not so much when the shoe's on the other foot."

Out in the yard, the Patriots were piling up the plunder. Maj. Randal mounted Parachute as Capt. McKoy came trotting up with the three mules that carried his Boys AT Rifle followed by his security detail.

"Butch did a right nice job," the ex-Arizona Ranger said, pulling out a thin cigar and biting off the end.

"Yes, he did."

Waldo came outside with two of the Force Raiding Company troops, each carrying an armful of weapons confiscated from the gun room.

"We're moving in fifteen minutes, Mr. Treywick."

When Lt. Hoolihan walked outside, Maj. Randal ordered, "There's too many men bunched up here at the house, Lieutenant. Post security."

The orgy of looting continued with Cheap Bribe's men dragging everything that could be moved out on the yard, including overstuffed chairs, sofas, even a slate pool table. It was a mad race between the Patriots to see who could score the most treasure, even if most of it could not be carried away on mule back.

"You planning on playing pool, John?"

"Might be nice to have us a game now and then," Waldo said.

"Hope springs eternal," Maj. Randal said.

Kaldi, the Force N interpreter, reported, "We found a small safe, sire. It was open, but there was nothing in it but documents, some of the manager's personal papers and a handful of cheap jewelry."

Maj. Randal glanced at his Rolex. "Time to go Butch, saddle up."

A detail was driving in the livestock that the raiders wanted to take with them. Exultant bandits were wearing petticoats, colorful men's neckties or curtains draped around their necks. One stuck a lampshade on top of his Tom Mix hat.

A giant letter "N" crudely painted on the side of the silo made it clear who had come calling. Capt. Merryweather was going around and placing a calling card he had recently printed up on his mobile printing press on every dead body. The cards had a large "N" on the front and the message, "If you are reading this you may be next. 1 Guerrilla Corps (Parachute), Force N."

The back of the card read, "If everything is blowing up around you—it's probably us."

As the raiders rode out, all the buildings were in flames.

All across central Abyssinia, the four Force N MRBs were carrying out similar operations following orders to "move fast, hit hard and disappear."

Maj. Randal's private war was in full swing.

2
VOICE FROM THE SKY

MAJOR JOHN RANDAL, CAPTAIN "GERONIMO" JOE MCKOY, WALDO Treywick, and Cheap Bribe were sitting outside at the small camp table in the 1 Guerrilla Corps (Parachute), Force N Headquarters' overnight position located outside of the largest village they had ever encountered. The sun was beginning to fade to golden orange as it went down behind the mountains. Force Raiding Company had been living up to its title. In the last five days they had attacked and destroyed five Italian DCPs.

Maj. Randal was following his own orders to his MRB commanders to "attack constantly." He had no intention of slowing the rhythm of the operations. However, the men and the animals of Lieutenant Butch "Headhunter" Hoolihan's Force Raiding Company needed a short break from the intense pace of the constant attacks. No good would come from grinding them into the ground.

While they stood down briefly, time could be spent on the reconnaissance of their next series of targets—ambushing the few roads in the district and reorganizing—a constant, ongoing process.

Maj. Randal planned to keep hitting the isolated plantations until the Italians reinforced each one with at least a platoon-sized unit. The math was simple. If there were a thousand of the projects in Central

Abyssinia (and there were many more than that) at the rate of one platoon per plantation, the Blackshirts would tie down 30,000-plus troops on static guard duty. Then once that happened, Maj. Randal would not raid the DCPs anymore—until he did.

The Italians were never going to know what was coming at them next.

Waldo and Kaldi had gone into the native village to palaver with the village chief, as was the long-established Force N standard operating procedure. However, the headman was not in. According to the villagers he had ridden off with an Italian patrol three days prior. They had been quick to point out no one had any idea why. The villagers were not Blackshirt sympathizers and the chief, they claimed, hated Italians.

"John," Capt. McKoy said, lighting up a thin cigar and offering one to the one-eyed Patriot chief Gubbo Rekash, "you know I'm gonna' want my own outfit. Liberating Abyssinia is turning out to be the biggest circus of the Twentieth Century. I don't aim to miss out on it."

"You're not missing much."

"This is big country. You can squeeze me in somewhere with my own MRB."

"There's two reasons I can't do that, Captain," Maj. Randal said, holding out his battered U.S. 26th Cavalry Regiment Zippo to light Cheap Bribe's cigar. "You're not in the British Army, and I don't have any command to give you."

"There's recruits pouring in."

"Officers and NCOs," Maj. Randal said. "All the good ones are already assigned. Besides, I need you on that Boys, Captain."

The sound of an aircraft could be heard in the distance. This was of no great concern to the men at the table. The Force N camp was widely dispersed and from the air would appear to be a part of the village.

A green and tan mottled Savoia-Marchetti 73 transport swooped low over the village. Rocking its wings, it then banked around to come back for another pass. To make absolutely certain they had everyone's attention, the Italian aircrew started firing their submachine guns out the open door, indiscriminately strafing the village—*RIPPPP, RIPPPP, RIPPPP.*

A tiny speck detached itself from the fuselage. For a moment it looked like a paratrooper, only there was no blossom of silk.

Then they heard the voice—shrieking.

"What the hell ..." Maj. Randal said.

The falling man screamed all the way. He windmilled down, slamming into the center of the village. The natives milled in a panic. Women were crying hysterically, and men were shouting.

Cheap Bribe jabbered angrily with a wild look in his one good eye and shook his cigar at the departing airplane.

"Looks like the chief just got home," Waldo said.

Captain Hawthorne Merryweather came over to where they were now standing. "My guess is, gentlemen, we have been witness to a working example of the Blackshirt Recalcitrant Village Pacification Program."

"Pacified the chief," Waldo agreed. "Don't know about the rest 'a them people. That kinda' rough stuff generally backfires with Abyssinians."

"Mr. Treywick, you and Kaldi shove off to the village and check things out," Maj. Randal ordered. "Give me a report."

"On the way, Major."

"Stay away from the honey wine, Mr. Treywick. You're riding out at first light."

Capt. McKoy said, "Now John, about that outfit ..."

CAPTAIN MICKEY DUGGAN, DCM, MM, RM, THE FORCE N CHIEF OF Signals, hand-carried a message to Major John Randal who scanned it and ordered, "Have Butch report to me immediately."

"Sir!"

Within minutes, Lieutenant Butch "Headhunter" Hoolihan arrived at Maj. Randal's HQ tent where he, Captain "Geronimo" Joe McKoy and Gubbo Rekash, the commander of the Force N auxiliary forces, were enjoying delicious Abyssinian coffee with their cigars.

"Lieutenant Hoolihan," Maj. Randal said in the command tone he subconsciously slipped into when issuing orders. "Have one of your platoons conduct a day ambush of the nearest road at a location of your choosing. Cheap Bribe and his boys will accompany it. Be prepared to move within the hour."

"Yes, sir!"

"Have your other platoon be prepared to travel with me tonight to mark a landing strip for an aircraft inbound from Camp Croc."

"Any preference as to which platoon you would like for an escort, sir?"

"It's your company—pick one."

"Where do you want me to position myself, sir?"

"Your call, Lieutenant."

"In that case I will accompany the ambush party, sir."

"Before you ride out, Butch, we'll pick out a location to rendezvous in three days' time. Be ready to resume the DCP raids when we marry up."

"Very good, sir."

"Ask Captain Honeycutt-Parker to report to me at his earliest convenience."

When the Royal Dragoons officer serving as the Force N adjutant arrived, Maj. Randal ordered, "Have the Force N Rear ready to move out as soon as possible. Get with Butch and me before you ride out and we'll select a place to link up in three days."

"What about recruiting, Major?"

"We'll sort that out when Mr. Treywick gets back from the village."

"If it actually was the chief the Eyeties tossed out of that airplane, the local's feelings should be running rather high about now. Might be an ideal opportunity to capitalize on, sir."

Ever since Lt. Hoolihan had taken command of Force Raiding Company, the adjutant had assumed his responsibilities as the Force N chief recruiter and training officer.

"Well then, we'll seize the opportunity," Maj. Randal said. "Inform Lieutenant Plum-Martin she can travel with the Rear or accompany me tonight."

"Very good, sir."

The Headquarters 1 Guerrilla Corps (Parachute), Force N began humming with activity. Any move was a major undertaking, but they were gypsies and had been striking camp almost every day for some time now. The native troops and camp followers had the drill down. Everyone knew what to do.

Captain Hawthorne Merryweather hurried by lugging a Hotchkiss light machine gun. "I am off with the Headhunter, sir."

"Planning to win hearts and minds with that LMG?" Maj. Randal called to his Special Warfare Officer.

"Oh, I shall have my bullhorn with me as my primary," Capt. Merryweather replied without breaking stride. "Wops fail to listen to reason—then I go to the gun."

"You've been a bad influence on ol' Hawthorne," Capt. McKoy observed as he took a sip of the local high-octane coffee.

Lieutenant Dick Courtney appeared. "Sir, I've been detailed to be your escort tonight attached to Bimbashi Masters' platoon."

"Inform Bimbashi Masters to have his men ready to pull out as soon as Mr. Treywick returns from the village, Dick."

"Yes, sir," the former Gold Coast Border Police officer replied. "Do you care to advise me where it is we're going?"

Maj. Randal took the flimsy out of his pocket. He handed it to the young officer. "Here's the coordinates. The plane will land on a stretch of the road we mark with kerosene flares. Make sure we have enough tin cans and fuel oil for the ground signals."

Rita Hayworth materialized leading Parachute with Maj. Randal's night M-1903 A-1 Springfield with the ivory post front sight in the boot. His personal gear was strapped on the back of the saddle.

Lieutenant Pamala Plum-Martin, OBE, RM, took a place at the table. "Any idea who we shall be meeting tonight, John?"

"Not a clue," Maj. Randal said. The last time he had been ordered to meet a plane out of Camp Croc it had whisked him away on a counterintelligence operation in Nairobi.

That gave him something to think about.

GG, the Force N cook captured in one of the early ambushes, poured the snow-blond Royal Marine a cup of coffee. She produced a Player's cigarette, which Maj. Randal lit for her.

Lana Turner arrived with Maj. Randal's sand-green parachute smock. It got cold in the mountains at night. She had his 9mm MAB-38A submachine gun slung over one shoulder and her Carcano 6.5mm carbine on the other.

Mr. Treywick and Kaldi came trailing back from the village.

"Chief, all right," Waldo said. "Every fightin' man in the village done volunteered for duty with Force N—to include the dead headman's personal bodyguard. Since they ain't any new boss man to put a stop to it we might make a big haul here, Major—recruitin' wise."

"What do you recommend, Mr. Treywick?"

"Strike while the iron's hot, Major. We ain't gonna' get many opportunities like this when nobody's in charge."

"All right," Maj. Randal said. "Mr. Treywick, you go ahead and move out now on that reconnaissance we discussed. Take a four-man security detail. Get with me before you leave, and I'll show you on the map where to link up with us."

"I like to travel light when I'm sneakin' and peekin'..."

"Take the security, Mr. Treywick."

"Yes sir, Major sir."

"Captain Honeycutt-Parker will be moving out with the Rear so he won't be available to handle recruiting," Maj. Randal said to Capt. McKoy. "I can pull Butch off his ambush to evaluate the recruits, or you and Kaldi could do it."

"I knew you was goin' to let me have my own outfit." Capt. McKoy grinned ear-to-ear. "I'll be proud to handle recruiting, John."

"Sign up as many volunteer Patriots as you can who have a mule to ride and Italian-issue weapons or rifles that fire compatible ammunition. Let 'em bring as many pages as their heart's desire. We'll turn 'em into Bad Boys later—but you don't have to tell the volunteers that out front."

"Love to, John," Capt. McKoy said. "I'll be real particular seeing as how they'll be my men. That's the way you build a crack team—handpick your troops for unit cohesion."

"We'll talk later."

"Kaldi," Capt. McKoy said, "Why don't we mosey over right now and get to work before the locals go and elect themselves a new headman."

"OK, Captain Geronimo," Kaldi agreed. "You should shoot a cigarette out of my mouth to impress the villagers. Or throw your knives."

"Sounds like a plan, son," Capt. McKoy said. "I'm gonna' enjoy this."

3

BLUE BOX

THE HUDSON LANDED ON THE DESOLATE STRETCH OF ROAD approximately 600 miles behind Italian lines at 0225 hours under a full tropical moon. Major John Randal and Lieutenant Pamala Plum-Martin were waiting when the door opened. They climbed aboard to find Major General James "Baldie" Taylor, OBE, all alone—the only passenger.

The twin-engine light bomber had been converted into a plush private transport for Lieutenant General Sir Archibald Wavell. The General Officer Commanding Middle East had loaned the plane to Captain the Lady Jane Seaborn to use in the effort to locate the missing Force N advance party and then allowed her to keep it for the duration of the campaign. Recently all the carpet and most of the theatre chairs had been removed.

Nowadays it was a troop transport, paratroop carrier, cargo hauler and whatever else was required to support Maj. Randal's guerrilla army in the field. Tonight it was crammed with cases of Maria Theresa silver dollars, weapons, ammunition and other military supplies. Bimbashi Jack Masters' men immediately began the task of unloading everything on board

"Evening, General," Maj. Randal said. "What brings you to the other side of the rainbow?"

"Slight change of plans, Major. I wanted to discuss them with you in person."

Maj. Randal and Lt. Plum-Martin took seats in two of the chairs.

"And to tell the truth, I have been looking for a reason to fly up-country to get a taste of being close to the action," the Chief of Station Special Operations Executive Khartoum admitted.

"How's it feel to get out of the office?"

"Great! Managing the personalities I have had to deal with to get CANVASS off the ground is enough to put a man in the loony bin. I need to get back in the field."

When Maj. Randal had first met the SOE operative, he was a down-and-out spy, banished to the obscurity of the Gold Coast—or at least that was what he claimed. Now he held the local rank of Major General and was the man running OPERATION CANVASS, the invasion of Abyssinia. Everyone answered to him—though that was classified Most Secret and would never appear in any history book.

Maj. Gen. Taylor was a hands-on operator who liked to make things go *bang* in the dark and bad guys disappear in the trunks of automobiles. However, being in possession of every piece of classified information worth knowing about the upcoming invasion of Italian East Africa, he had absolutely no business being behind enemy lines. Maj. Randal was not the least surprised to see him. In fact, he had been wondering when the general would show up.

"Lady Seaborn sends her regards. She would have liked to come along tonight, but duty demands she be in Cairo doing what she does best—making things happen."

"What's so important you had to come all this way to break the news, General?"

"When we parachuted Lieutenant Hoolihan's Force Raiding Company into Abyssinia the operation stretched our troop transport air capability to the breaking point," Maj. Gen. Taylor said. "There is no way we will ever be able to drop Terry's entire battalion."

"That's not good."

"Sustaining your Mule Raider Battalions is taking a toll on our aerial delivery resources. This is the first time in history a British field force has ever been entirely supplied by air. And it's not proving to be as easy as it sounds, particularly with the hand-me-down obsolete aircraft we have to do it with."

"I've been counting on Terry and his Lounge Lizards, General," Maj. Randal said. "Not one of our MRBs have more than 250 men. Force N is covering an area larger than France—we're spread thin."

"Once the invasion kicks off," Maj. Gen. Taylor divulged, "you are going to be spread even thinner, Major. That's one of the things I wanted to talk to you about.

"When the balloon goes up, the Kaid, General Platt, will attack out of the Sudan. It does not take a Napoleon to understand how his campaign is going to develop. Initially Platt is going to make a mad dash toward his ultimate objective—the port city of Massawa on the Red Sea."

Maj. Gen. Taylor unfolded a map. "Everything will go like clockwork until he reaches Keren, a mountain fortress the Italians have been fortifying for years. At that point General Platt is going to hit a brick wall.

"To make matters worse, Dudley Clarke conducted a misinformation campaign to convince the Duke of Aosta the Kaid would be attacking with overwhelming force—a joke if ever there was one. The Duke believed every word. He concluded the situation was hopeless, pulled all his troops back from the border and consolidated them at Keren, unintentionally reinforcing the one place we did not want reinforced."

"Really?"

"We still have a lot to figure out about the misinformation game. Dudley says he learned, a little late this time around, that the purpose of the exercise is not to make the enemy 'believe' something. The object is to make the enemy 'do' something. And we got it wrong."

"What does that have to do with Force N?"

"As you may recall, General Platt specifically forbade your guerrillas from operating anywhere near his axis of attack."

"Loud and clear."

"My guess is at some point while he is bogged down in a slugging match in the mountainous terrain at Keren, it's going to dawn on the Kaid that it would probably be a good idea to have someone threaten the Italian's rear."

"Who might that be?"

"You, Major," Maj. Gen. Taylor grinned. "So be ready with a plan when I contact you to ride to the rescue."

"I don't have the men," Maj. Randal said. "I can raise the troops, but all the qualified company commanders are assigned. I don't have anyone to trust with a battalion except Captain McKoy."

Maj. Gen. Taylor arched an eyebrow, "The old cowboy wants troop command?"

"I'm getting ready to let him raise an MRB, but company commanders are in short supply."

"We have half a dozen Operational Centers (OC) trained and ready to go," Maj. Gen. Taylor offered. "Originally they were penciled in for Wingate's Gideon Force, but they can be yours if you want them. Cannibalize them and use the personnel any way you need to."

"Six officers, thirty-six NCOs and one hundred eighty indigenous personnel," Maj. Randal said. "That's almost enough to make up for the Lounge Lizards, but it won't compensate for Terry, General."

"I can send you the OC officers and NCOs, but don't count on the native troops except piecemeal as we can get them in to you.

"And I have more bad news," Maj. Gen. Taylor continued.

"You need to designate a liaison officer to travel with the advance elements of Platt's northern pincer. On top of which I will need to find someone to travel with Wingate and the Emperor's column. Their mission will be to coordinate your Force N guerrilla operations."

"You're not making this easy, General."

"The liaison job is a serious assignment, Major. It requires an officer you can count on—not someone you want to get rid of. I have Terry penciled in to assume the role of Force N liaison with General Cunningham—subject to your approval."

"I've really been counting on having him with me, General."

"He doesn't know it yet," Maj. Gen. Taylor said. "I am going to commission him temporarily as a Lieutenant Colonel in the Sudan Defense Force. Since SDF officers traditionally wear the insignia of the next-higher grade, Zorro will be a full colonel. Sir Terry is going to command a cavalry regiment. That's one of the things Lady Seaborn is arranging as we speak. Did you know the Stone family has its own regiment—the Lancelot Lancers Yeomanry?"

"No, Terry never talks about his family much."

"The LLY is a single squadron regiment. Came out to Palestine with the Cavalry Division only to be dismounted. Since then they have been converted to a searchlight unit."

"How'd that set with Terry's father?"

"Not very well. The Duke moved heaven and earth to get the LLY back in a combat arms role, but no luck. No armored cars are to be had for them anywhere in the Middle East Command, which is bankrupt of armor of any kind. A maharaja in India had three 1924 Pattern Rolls Royce (RR) armored cars built on Silver Ghost chassis stored on blocks in a garage on his estate. Terry's father bought them and had them shipped out to Cairo.

"Then the Duke contacted Lady Seaborn to use her influence with General Wavell to convert the Lancelot Lancers to an armored car regiment. Wavell agreed, and acting on my request assigned the LLY to General Cunningham's East Africa Force."

"A three-car squadron?"

"Cunningham has provided the Lancelots with an additional three South African Dingo armored cars, and Lady Seaborn arranged for a team of South African auto mechanics to convert three more Ford vans into 'fighting cars' by installing oversized truck tires, cutting off the tops and mounting twin .303 Vickers K model machine guns.

"When East Africa Force steps off, the Lancelot Lancers will be leading the charge with Sir Terry in command."

"Good for him," Maj. Randal said. "'Right Man, Right Job,' General."

"I thought you would agree. No officer could have done better organizing things for Force N in your absence," Maj. Gen. Taylor said. "So, Major, who are you going designate as the Kaid's guerrilla liaison officer? Has to be a good man."

Maj. Randal glanced at Lt. Plum-Martin.

"Jack," she said without hesitation.

"Lieutenant Merritt," Maj. Randal said. "Captain Stirling is senior but we need him operating against the railroad, our highest priority target. Really hate to take Jack away from Captain Pelham-Davies, General."

"Lieutenant Merritt impressed me in the short time we worked together in Khartoum before he ran off with Geronimo Joe to go searching for you," Maj. Gen. Taylor said. "I'll commission him a temporary captain in the SDF, which means he will wear the rank of major assigned to command a machine gun car company attached to Gazelle Force."

"Before his commission Jack was a corporal in the Life Guards," Maj. Randal said. "He has a solid cavalry background."

"One more thing," Maj. Gen. Taylor added. "Lady Seaborn had her movie star friend, David Niven, travel out to Camp Croc to evaluate the Force N long-range communications set up a while back. As you may know, Niven is with the super hush-hush Phantom signals organization.

"Phantom's primary duty is to communicate the location of friendly forces in the attack to each other. CANVASS is the perfect live-fire field training opportunity for them since they have never actually done it before. Niven has arranged for a long-range radio team to travel with all three liaison officers and a team for your HQ and each of your MRBs."

"General, you hijacked two of my best officers and deprived me of a total of two battalions worth of trained indigenous troops—what's the good news?"

"Good news?" Maj. Gen. Taylor laughed. "I'm not in the good news business. The best I can think of is that Squadron Leader Wilcox has promised to teach me how to land an amphibian. After the invasion kicks off you will be seeing a lot more of me. I shall be flying a Walrus in support of Force N.

"Oh, there is this," Maj. Gen. Taylor added as an afterthought as he reached into his pocket. He produced a small blue box which he tossed to Maj. Randal.

Inside were a pair of khaki cloth shoulder boards with the crown and three pips of a Brigadier.

"Put those on," Maj. Gen. Taylor ordered. "Don't worry, Brigadier Randal, like everything else in this Alice in Wonderland theatre of operations it's only temporary—think of it as an illusion. That's what I do."

LIEUTENANT BUTCH "HEADHUNTER" HOOLIHAN WAS WAITING IN concealment with his page on a ridge overlooking an S-shaped curve in the road below. On the far side was an Italian Fascist kilometer stone marker carved with the Imperial Eagle, a symbol of the modern Roman Empire in Africa that could be found along all strategic roads. Through binoculars he could see it had a graffiti letter 'N' painted on it—so much for symbolism.

The Headhunter was waiting for Bimbashi Cord Granger to bring his men up to the ambush location they had reconnoitered. Cheap Bribe would be moving into place a little higher up on the ridgeline. They had found an almost textbook-perfect location for a road ambush.

In the distance, the roar of a fast-moving 500cc Moto Guzzi motorcycle could be heard. Lt. Hoolihan detected movement down at the edge of the road. He swung the glasses over to the spot. Two young Abyssinians he had not spotted before were crouched down in the bushes.

What was this?

The motorcycle blazed into the S-shaped curve, engine screaming as the Bersaglieri dispatch rider shifted gears. The motorcyclist was leaning hard into the turns. As if snatched by an invisible hand, the rider became suspended in mid-air. The Moto Guzzi was running on its own doing a wheelie for about twenty yards before crashing over backward and tumbling down the center of the road, screeching tortured metal.

The two young natives dropped the steel cable they were pulling taut and ran out into the road. One pulled a short sword and stabbed the dazed Bersaglieri who was sprawled where he had fallen. The other ripped off the Carcano carbine strapped across the Italian's shoulders, put the gun to its owner's head and pulled the trigger.

CRAAAACK

The two quickly searched the dead motorcyclist, taking anything of value. Unbuckling his pistol belt, they pulled it out from under his body then scurried off into the underbrush.

Lt. Hoolihan looked over at his page, who was staring wide-eyed.

"Bad Boys."

4

THE BOMB

"LET'S SEE IF I GOT THIS STRAIGHT," CAPTAIN "GERONIMO" JOE MCKOY said, "You're A brigadier but you ain't a general?"

"That's right."

"Doesn't make any sense, John. If you're a brigadier that makes you a general—a one star.

"Not in the British Army."

"Well, that's a rip-off—a brigadier is a general in my book."

"Maybe you can explain it to him," Brigadier John Randal said to his adjutant, Captain Lionel Honeycutt-Parker.

"Brigadier is a title, not a rank," the Royal Dragoon officer said. "It is temporary in duration for colonels who command other colonels. When the specific mission, operation or campaign for which the officer was tabbed a brigadier is over, then he reverts back to his permanent grade without prejudice."

"Well, John wasn't a colonel," Capt. McKoy pointed out. "And there ain't any other colonels around here for him to command."

"You're right about that, Joe," Waldo concurred. "Ain't a colonel in sight."

"One would presume General Taylor was anticipating that Force N shall come in contact with elements of British Forces commanded by colonels in the future," Capt. Honeycutt-Parker said. "That would warrant the promotion."

"Tell me again," Capt. McKoy persisted, "what *I'm* going to be."

"A captain," Brig. Randal said, "in the Sudan Defense Force."

"But you just gave me your old major's badges."

"Don't lose 'em. I'm going to need 'em back when ROMAN CANDLE is over."

"By tradition," Capt. Honeycutt-Parker tried once more, "SDF officers are badged one grade higher than the rank they hold."

"Well, that's crazy as a bedbug."

"I'm with you, Joe," Waldo shook his grizzled head. "How's anybody supposed to know who's what and who's not?"

"I think that's the idea," Brig. Randal said. "It's only temporary anyway. I could make you a major in the SDF but we don't have any insignia for colonel."

"I don't care what rank I carry, John, as long as you let me have that mule battalion," Capt. McKoy said.

"You've got it," Brig. Randal said. "Now we have to find company commanders for you ... and that's a problem."

"There was a general one time," Capt. McKoy said, "I can't recollect his exact name ... but he claimed there's four kinds of military officers—clever, diligent, stupid and lazy.

"Most of 'em have at least two of those qualities at the same time. For example, the general said the clever/diligent are good staff officers.

"The stupid/lazy make up about ninety percent of the officer corps of every army worldwide, and we want to avoid those for my MRB if we can, John."

"Back when me and P.J. Pretorius was scoutin' square heads in the last one," Waldo said, "P.J. used to say most brass hats was dumber than dirt."

"Now the stupid/diligent ones," Capt. McKoy continued, "they're dangerous. They'll plot on you.

"But the clever/lazy—they're the best. Good combat leaders— make even better generals."

Brig. Randal said, "You learn that in one of your correspondence school courses?"

CAPTAIN "PYRO" PERCY STIRLING, MC, RODE INTO CAMP. HE GAVE Brigadier John Randal a briefing on the current state of his railroad interdiction program. He had two reinforced "Railroad Wrecking Crew" platoons operational on the northern end and the central part of the line. They were hard at it blowing the tracks and culverts, then ambushing the cuts. These were merely working up operations with a full-scale assault on the rail line planned to coincide with the start of the invasion.

However, the southern part of the line ran through a desolate arid desert region before reaching the tropical, more heavily populated coastal section. Capt. Stirling needed to craft a plan for the best way to attack it before committing his third platoon. He wanted to discuss the situation.

It was quickly concluded that what was needed was an aerial reconnaissance. Brig. Randal saw a chance to kill two birds with one stone. He decided to send Captain "Geronimo" Joe McKoy down to Kenya on a recruiting trip to find the officers he needed. Capt. Stirling would accompany him as far as Camp Croc.

From there Capt. McKoy would continue on to Nairobi while Capt. Stirling conducted his aerial survey of the Italian rail line.

Captain Lionel Honeycutt-Parker coordinated an aircraft to fly in that night to make the passenger pick-up.

Before the party rode out, Brig. Randal quizzed Capt. Honeycutt-Parker about Lounge Lizard officers who had not been deployed yet. And he inquired about any Kenyan colonial officers who might be suitable to recruit for Capt. McKoy's battalion.

"There were several men Sir Terry tried his best to have assigned, but no joy."

"Write their names down," Brig. Randal ordered. "Give them to Captain McKoy."

"Yes, sir," Capt. Honeycutt-Parker replied. "I fear that he will not have much success getting the men released. The Secretary of the Colonial Manpower Office, Captain the Lord Joss Hay, was implacable when it came to allowing Kenyans to volunteer for the 2nd Lounge Lizards or the Force N Operational Centers."

"I don't think that's going to be a problem."

LIEUTENANT CHARLES KEAREY, SOUTH AFRICAN AIR FORCE (SAAF), the pilot of an ancient Vickers-Valentia, had been assigned to fly the first SAAF aerial resupply mission to Force N. Sitting in the co-pilot's seat this first mission was Pilot Officer Gasper "Bunny" Featherstone, DFC, formerly of the Millionaires Squadron, now serving as the liaison between Force N and the South African Air Force.

While Commodore Richard "Dickey the Pirate" Seaborn had been unsuccessful in acquiring additional Royal Navy amphibious aircraft to support Force N's guerrilla war, Plt. Off. Featherstone had been able to convince the South Africans of the value of dedicating a handful of their troop transport aircraft to the mission. South Africans have a tradition of guerrilla warfare going back to the days of the Boer War, and they regarded Brigadier John Randal's mule cavalry raiders as kindred spirits.

The SAAF did not have amphibious aircraft for Force N, but they did have some of the world's best rough-landing qualified pilots. The plan was for them to fly long-range resupply missions to air drop or land supplies on improvised landing strips at night. In exchange, Squadron Leader Paddy Wilcox, DSO, OBE, MC, DFC would train and certify five volunteer SAAF pilots as multi-engine amphibious. He would also put them in the Camp Croc rotation flying co-pilot in the Commodores to gain experience.

The Vickers-Valentia carried a crew of two with a maximum of twenty-two passengers. It was not what would be described as a heavy hauler. The ancient bi-winged airplane had a wing span of eighty-seven feet, which meant it required wide open spaces to land, but for a plane of its size it could touch down and take off in incredibly short distances. In flight, its top airspeed was only a little over one 100 miles per hour.

Plt. Off. Featherstone, a Battle of Britain fighter ace in Spitfires, was not enjoying the flight. At times he wondered if the flying antique was actually making any forward progress at all. He was not fond of the open cockpit configuration of the Vickers one little bit.

On the ground in the distance ahead, a large burning letter N could be seen—kerosene and motor oil torched off in cans. A string of similarly improvised flares in a column formation suddenly lit up for about a quarter of a mile. In between the column of signal lights was a straight stretch of one of the strategic roads of the Romans' East African Empire.

The motorway was a tailor-made clandestine landing strip.

"Do try to get this right, Kearey. Not do for us to be marooned out here," Plt. Off. Featherstone advised. "The VD rate runs in excess of eighty percent."

"Give it my bloody best, mate. You really know how to motivate a man."

The huge flying relic touched down as light as a butterfly. As soon as it rolled to a stop, a swarm of Force N troops arrived out of the dark and began unloading the stores. Captain "Geronimo" Joe McKoy and Captain "Pyro" Percy Stirling came on board.

Lt. Kearey revved the engines and prepared for takeoff. It was not exactly a touch-and-go, but the unloading had gone fast for a guerrilla bush operation. Landing behind enemy lines is one thing. Hanging around on the ground there is another. The Vickers-Valentia was airborne and away in short order.

This first joint Force N/SAAF mission had gone off flawlessly.

Hours later Plt. Off. Featherstone came back and informed his two passengers that they would be landing at Camp Croc shortly. Capt. Stirling went up and rode with Lt. Kearey in the open cockpit while Plt. Off. Featherstone chatted with Capt. McKoy. The beginning of morning, nautical twilight, was streaking silver gold and had a bigness effect that was magnificent. The jalapeno-shaped green Lake Rudolf swam into sight as the Vickers-Valentia clawed its way through the sky.

Lt. Kearey pointed to a mud structure in the distance. "That's a bloody Italian fort. We're flying right past it later this morning when we do your aerial reconnaissance. Pity I haven't a bomb to drop on it."

"I can make you one," said Capt. Stirling.

The Vickers-Valentia landed on the landing strip at Camp Croc—it had been steadily improved over time to handle large aircraft. Sergeant Major Maxwell Hicks, DCM, greeted the plane. The former Grenadier Guardsman had come out from Seaborn House to serve as Camp Commandant. He had the place running with the precision of a Swiss watch.

Capt. McKoy was immediately escorted to a Walrus waiting to take off for the 2nd Lounge Lizard's base outside Nairobi. The ground crew began refueling the Vickers-Valentia. Capt. Stirling explained to the Camp Commandant what he had in mind and was shown to a workshop where he began constructing his improvised bomb.

Around a core of 380 sticks of dynamite left over from the construction of the extension of the landing strip, Capt. Stirling packed a fifty-five gallon drum with a ten-pound can of rusty nails that had been at Camp Croc since long before the war, bits of scrap iron, a tractor differential, a broken sewing machine, and various nuts and bolts. Then he poured in motor oil until it was flush. Last but not least, he cut a one-minute fuse, crimped the blasting cap with his teeth, inserted it in the dynamite and sealed off the drum.

Lieutenant Karen Montgomery, the Force N chief parachute rigger, watched wide-eyed throughout the process, as did Sgt. Maj. Hicks. She had donated the worn-out sewing machine, and he had contributed the differential.

The sergeant major was thinking young Capt. Stirling certainly knew a lot more about demolitions now than he did on the first parachute raid when he blew up the three-story lighthouse with its tank of acetylene fuel, earning himself the well-deserved nickname "Pyro." And scaring the wits out every man on the raid in the process.

Capt. Stirling rolled the drum out to the waiting Vickers-Valentia, removed the door and with the help of the ground crew manhandled it in. The bomb was a tight fit. Mattresses were laid on the floor of the airplane to protect the bombardiers (Capt. Stirling and Plt. Off. Featherstone) from the blast and/or ground fire during the run in to the target.

Lt. Kearey took off, hoping to arrive on station in time to make the attack out of the sun that was only now coming up full bore hot. He set a heading across Lake Rudolf straight toward the Italian fort. With any luck he might catch them by surprise—not likely in an airplane that a motorcycle could outrun.

When the word went around Camp Croc that the South African pilot was going to try to bomb the Italian fort, there was a mad dash to the flat roof of the main building to watch the show. The Canadian pilots, officers and other ranks passing through on their way to their assignments with Force N, female riggers, Royal Life Boat Servicemen and various other camp staff all gathered to see the show.

Binoculars were in high demand.

Coming dead out of the sun when he thought they were about a minute out, Lt. Kearey shouted over his shoulder, "Light off the fuse!"

The South African pilot did not know much about explosives or he would have never done that. Fuses are not an exact science. They do not always burn at the same rate every single time, and it is never a good idea to have one lit and attached to an explosive device inside of an airplane in which you are riding.

Capt. Stirling did know about explosives, having been extensively trained after his shortcomings as a demolitions man on the TOMCAT raid had become obvious. However, the pilot is the aircraft commander, there was no time to debate the issue and an order is an order.

He lit the fuse.

"Anybody see the plane?" called one of the Canadian pilots on the roof of the main building at Camp Croc.

"Yeah, I got it."

"He's making his attack run."

"What altitude?"

"Right about anteater level."

With the fuse burning on the improvised bomb in the back, Lt. Kearey put the Vickers-Valentia down lower, skimming the ground. He was flying below the level of the red mud walls of the fort. Machine guns began twinkling from the towers at the four corners. There was a sharp crack in the cockpit. The South African felt a stab of pain. Blood ran down his forehead from a gash caused by a bullet that splintered on his instrument panel.

"Go, Go, Go!" the spectators on the roof of Camp Croc were screaming.

Lt. Montgomery noticed that the laid-back Canadian and American pilots who normally had nerves of steel were as tense as a coiled spring.

"Look at that crazy son of a bitch go ..."

As the giant bi-winged plane made the approach to target, its flight path was so low it was taking hits from the towers that were slanting down through the roof of the fuselage. So much for the idea of the mattresses on the floor serving as protection.

At the last second when it looked like he was going to ram the red mud fort, Lt. Kearey hauled back on the yoke as hard as he could and the plane zoomed up and over the wall at an altitude of about 100 feet. He glanced down and could see inside. The place was packed with enemy soldiers lying prone.

"Bombs away!"

Capt. Stirling and Plt. Off. Featherstone had been caught off guard by the sudden lurch and thrown backward, as was the bomb with the rapidly burning fuse. The two amateur bombardiers wrestled the explosive device back into place then both men kicked the fifty-five gallon drum as hard as they could. It moved forward and wedged in the door.

"BOMB'S STUCK!" Plt. Off. Featherstone screamed hysterically.

"Hang on," Lt. Kearey shouted, instantly snapping the Vickers-Valentia hard to port so sharply it seemed the wing almost touched the ground, then whipping it back level.

"Bomb's away," called Capt. Stirling from the deck of the plane where he had been pitched after ricocheting off the far bulkhead.

There was an instant detonation. The airplane flashed past the fort. The Vickers-Valentia pitched violently, hammered by the shock wave of the massive explosion.

Lt. Kearey fought the yoke trying to tear itself out of his hands and brought the big airplane back under control. Then the intrepid South African flyer put the plane down so low to the ground they were thundering along blowing up dust off the desert floor. When pilot and crew looked back they could see a massive column of black smoke rising.

The cheering at Camp Croc lasted long after the SAAF aircraft flew out of sight. The fat mushroom-shaped column of smoke was truly impressive. The Canadian bush pilots were a critical audience—there was some disapproval of the low-level aerobatics. The stunt, while flashy and way cool, had seemed unnecessarily dangerous to pilots whose routine missions were considered suicidal by most fliers. The consensus was the crazy South African well might have put the wing into the ground while showing off.

They did not know about the stuck bomb.

On board the Vickers-Valentia, Capt. Stirling and Plt. Off. Featherstone lit up cigarettes with shaking hands.

"How far do you think that bomb was away before it blew?" Capt. Stirling asked in a strained tone.

"I have no bloody idea," Plt. Off. Featherstone said through chattering teeth as he pulled out the silver flask he never left home without. "I think we had an air burst—probably singed the bloody paint on the bloody bottom of the bloody airframe. You need to cut the bloody fuse a little bloody longer in future, Percy."

Capt. Stirling was a 17/21 Lancer, what was known in the service as a "Death or Glory Boy."

"Mark my word Bunny, there *is* no next time."

LIEUTENANT CHARLES KEAREY AND HIS TWO BOMBARDIERS BECAME instant South African Air Force celebrities—living legends. When they landed, it had not been possible to hide the ninety-four bullet holes in the Vickers-Valentia or the gash in Lt. Kearey's forehead.

No medals were awarded. In fact, it was reprimands all around, though none were actually put into writing. Senior SAAF officers had a difficult time keeping straight faces when they administered the multiple chewings out ... they expected their pilots to be bold and daring. Bombing the fort in a Vickers-Valentia with a homemade bomb, however, had been over the top—even by their standards.

Lt. Kearey was the toast of the SAAF, which dubbed him with the nickname "Bomber."

Italian radio claimed the raid was the work of an entire SAAF squadron of modern low-level attack bombers that had been beaten off with severe loss to the attackers.

Lieutenant Colonel Dudley Clarke took advantage of the escapade. Rumor soon spread throughout Italian East Africa that the entire garrison—over fifty men—were all killed by the blast. The story was widely believed.

Even though there was some questions about whether the bomb had actually landed inside the walls of the red fort.

5

LANCELOT LANCERS

MAJOR GENERAL JAMES "BALDIE" TAYLOR DECIDED TO TAKE
advantage of the arrangement Pilot Officer Gasper "Bunny" Featherstone
had brokered with the South African Air Force to support Force N. He
got the former Millionaires Squadron pilot on the phone.

"Arrange to have one of the 2nd Lounge Lizard companies
airlifted to Brigadier Randal."

"The SAAF has only provided us one aircraft to date, General.
It's undergoing repairs at the moment, sir."

"Do it the minute the plane is airworthy, Bunny."

"Affirmative, sir. How many men are in a company?"

"Sixty."

"We can transport a max of twenty-two men per flight, sir."

"Make it happen. Expedite, Bunny."

"Tally-ho."

Three flights represented a lot of priceless cargo space. However,
a fully trained company of indigenous parachute infantry would be of
inestimable value to Captain "Geronimo" Joe McKoy. A commander has
to set priorities when supporting a force in the field completely by air.
Maj. Gen. Taylor was learning by trial and error, certain he would be
doing this again someday in some other part of the world.

As soon as he hung up, Maj. Gen. Taylor had orders cut for Major Sir Terry "Zorro" Stone, KBE, MC, to have one of his three remaining companies begin intensive training in motorized infantry warfare (it would be assigned to the Lancelot Lancers as lorried infantry, though Maj. Stone had no way of knowing their assignment).

Additionally, Maj. Gen. Taylor cut orders to have another company report to Major General Alan Cunningham for special duty—they would be assigned to Lieutenant Jack Merritt's ad hoc machine gun car reconnaissance squadron—also in the role of lorried infantry.

Then Maj. Gen. Taylor arranged to have the last remaining company of the 2nd Lounge Lizards be broken up and sent, space available, to Force N to be assigned where needed. Officers, NCOs and Hotchkiss machine gunners were to be given priority of travel.

Lastly, Maj. Stone was instructed to stand by for a new assignment. No mention was made of him taking command of the Lancelot Lancers Yeomanry (LLY) en route to Kenya or his impending temporary promotion.

That was to be a surprise.

Next, Maj. Gen. Taylor ordered Captain the Lady Jane Seaborn to hand-carry instructions to Maj. Gen. Cunningham to recruit a dozen Abyssinian NCOs from among those known to be currently serving in the King's African Rifles (KAR) and have them flown up to Camp Croc for transport and assignment to Capt. McKoy for his 6th MRB. The KAR were going to squawk, but the indigenous English-speaking NCOs would be priceless assets.

In total, the amount of military support Maj. Gen. Taylor was allocating Force N did not amount to much. The harsh reality was he was giving it everything that he could possibly manage. OPERATION ROMAN CANDLE was and always had been bankrupt of just about everything except improvisation, ingenuity and grit.

THE CONSOLIDATED MODEL 31, FONDLY KNOWN AS THE PREGNANT Guppy, lined up on the giant N burning on the drop zone (DZ) down below. The amphibian was Force N's biggest, fastest, heaviest lifter. It was a state-of-the-art aircraft. Unfortunately for Consolidated Aircraft Corporation, the Model 31 was so far ahead of its time that no military clients had purchased a single one. The cutting-edge plane and crew was on loan to OPERATION ROMAN CANDLE as a demonstrator in hopes the Royal Air Force might become interested.

Tonight was an aerial supply drop. The Consolidated Model 31 was too valuable to risk landing on an improvised airstrip. The supplies would be dropped first; then a small party of jumpers would exit.

The Pregnant Guppy planned to make only a single pass.

Lieutenant Butch "Headhunter" Hoolihan was in command of the reception party on the drop zone. His Force Raiding Company was becoming proficient at establishing clandestine reception parties. They should be—the company was out on average of two nights a week setting them up at remote sites in the Abyssinian highlands.

Up in the night sky at an altitude of 1,000 feet, the big airplane leveled out, flying straight up the line of signal flares. On board in the back the light flashed from red to green, and the door kickers began to frantically deploy the bundles. Parachutes streamed out, one behind the other, looking like swimming octopuses to those below.

The heavy bundles drifted down with their loads swinging back and forth. Down on the ground, predesignated teams picked out one single parachute and chased it as it came floating down. The idea was not to lose any when they landed so they would not need to hang around until daylight to conduct a search.

The Italians would not venture outside their bases at night, but they would be out in force come morning if they learned of the drop. Lt. Hoolihan intended to be miles away before that happened. Though he might leave a stay-behind party to ambush the landing zone (LZ).

Eight men jumped in with the supplies: Captain Lionel Chatterhorn and three of his men belonging to the squadron of the Vulnerable Points Wing of the Field Security Police who guarded the Raiding Forces base at Seaborn House and two sniper teams of Lovat Scouts. As soon as they rolled up their parachutes, the new arrivals reported to Lt. Hoolihan standing at the burning N.

Three hours later with all parachutes recovered and provisions packed on mules, Force Raiding Company rode out.

When the caravan snaked into the Force N Rear encampment later the next morning, Brigadier John Randal was on hand to greet them. The arrival of new men and supplies was always a momentous occasion. For the British personnel there was the chance of a letter from home. For the Abyssinians, under Captain Lionel Honeycutt-Parker's watchful eye, there were weapons to be unpacked, ammunition to be sorted and other military stores to be gone through and evaluated for re-issue later.

And there were always the little care packages made up by the crew at Camp Croc with luxuries to be shared.

"What brings you here, Captain Chatterhorn?" Brig. Randal called. "You won't find any Nazi infiltrators wearing blue boots in Africa."

"One can always hope, sir," the former member of Scotland Yard, Security Branch, responded with a crisp salute. "Lady Seaborn cabled me to send a team out to evaluate Force N security arrangements and serve as advisors to your headquarters' security detail. Thought it best if I came myself, sir."

"I already have bodyguards."

"So I hear, Brigadier."

The security detail was a welcome addition. Every man in Capt. Chatterhorn's Vulnerable Points Wing, Field Security Police had graduated from No. 1 Parachute School and the Special Warfare Training Center at Achnacarry. Brig. Randal had a great deal of respect for their commander's attention to detail, professionalism and dedication to duty.

One Lovat Scout sniper team was assigned to Force Raiding Company. The other consisting of Scout Munro Ferguson and Scout Lionel Fenwick was detailed directly to Brig. Randal. He planned to use the team in conjunction with the .55 Boys sniper system though he did not have the tactics completely worked out just yet. The Scouts had never seen anything like the big tripod scope-mounted rifle.

They were suitably impressed.

Brig. Randal showed the Lovat Scout teams one of the 6.5-06 Springfields that Captain "Geronimo" Joe McKoy had ordered specially built for Force N by rebarreling a dozen U.S. M-1903 A-1 Springfield .30 rifles to 6.5mm for sniping. Each one sported a high-powered civilian riflescope for precision long-range shooting. Every rifle came with loading equipment so that captured Italian 6.5 rounds could be cannibalized to hand load .30-caliber brass.

"Captain McKoy claims it's the flattest shooting shoulder-fired rifle in the world."

The Lovat Scouts turned up their collective noses at the weapons. The men favored their Rigby and Wesley Richard's 7X57mm red stag rifles they had owned since boyhood. All four Scouts had used their personally owned rifles to good effect sniping Nazi pilots during OPERATION BUZZARD PLUCKER.

Brig. Randal said, "Carry what you like."

He had plans for the Lovats. The young Scouts hit what they shot at. As long as they did, for all he cared they could arm themselves with muzzle loading muskets or bows and arrows.

LIEUTENANT JACK MERRITT, MC, MM WAS HIDING IN DEEP concealment along an Italian strategic road somewhere in central Abyssinia. Where, exactly, was not entirely clear. The map he had was sadly lacking, being described as "merely advisory." He had one of his two platoons set up in a close linear ambush on a level stretch of road that lay in the saddle of two fairly steep hills. The other platoon was in hiding on the far side of the road where it dropped off for a sheer 300 feet.

Looks could be deceiving, which is what Lt. Merritt was counting on. There was, in fact, a rocky ledge that ran along the length of the road about three feet below the level of the hardball. His troops were crouched down along the ledge with bayonets fixed on their M-1903 A-1 Springfield rifles, completely hidden from the sight of anyone driving along the road. The Italians would never be expecting an attack from the drop-off side.

This was good ambush country—but then it was all good ambush country in mountainous central Abyssinia.

Italian company-sized outposts were stationed at forty- to fifty-mile intervals along the road. The bases had to be resupplied regularly. The only way for the Blackshirts to accomplish that was by the road. In addition, there was a certain amount of commuting back and forth between the isolated bases.

The odds were good that something would pass by.

The signal for the ambush to be initiated was for Lt. Merritt to throw a No. 36 Mills bomb. The plan was simple, as all good military plans are. When the grenade detonated, the platoon on the heavily wooded cliff side of the road would open and lay down a base of fire on the killing zone. Then when the Italians were distracted and firing back at their ambushers, the platoon hiding in defilade on the drop-off side of the road would spring up and go in with the bayonet.

What Lt. Merritt liked about this ambush site was: 1) the Italians would never be expecting it here; 2) the terrain severely limited the enemy's ability to put in a counterattack; and 3) it channelized his own troops so that they had to attack through the ambush in order to reach the rally point up the mountain where their mules where being held in waiting.

Four hours later when Lt. Merritt had begun to despair that a target would ever show, the sound of gears shifting brought everyone to a high state of alert. A gypsy caravan of trucks came down the mountain on the south end of the killing zone headed straight toward their ambush site. Eleven trucks of a diverse mixture of make and model—some Italian, some British and some American rolled into sight.

The trucks were traveling alone without an armored escort. Since the Regia Aeronautica enjoyed total air superiority over Abyssinia, none of the trucks had bothered to post air guards. Force N had never operated in this part of the country so possibly the Italians were lulled into a false sense of security. Or maybe it was pure denial. Either way the commander of this convoy was criminally negligent.

It was almost too easy.

Lt. Merritt was a highly-trained Life Guards NCO recently commissioned. He was an original member of Raiding Forces. Today was his first independent command.

This ambush was the culmination of years of cavalry schooling, tough commando training at the Special Warfare Training Center, a year's worth of intensive Commando experience carrying out high-risk, small-scale raids, plus an Airborne Forces mindset that it was natural to be operating miles behind enemy lines—and he got it right.

BAAAAMOOOOOM! The M-36 Mills bomb detonated in the still mountain air sounding like a cannon. The platoon on the cliff side engaged with a ragged volley that began to gain intensity as thirty M-1903 A-1 Springfields thundered. The troops were not hitting much, but the roar of the massed rifles was impressive.

Lt. Merritt took the precaution of hosing the cab of the lead vehicle, a mottled green three-quarter-ton Ford, with his .45-caliber Thompson submachine gun. He realized he should have found some way to block the road—a mistake he was not planning to ever make again.

Luck was with him, and he got away with it this time. The shot-up Ford sputtered and died, though it kept rolling for about twenty yards as Lt. Merritt shifted his fire to the engine compartment. Steam spewed from the radiator. When it stopped, the lead truck blocked the rest of the convoy on the narrow road.

The Hotchkiss Mk1 light machine gunner, a Cheshire Yeomanry corporal volunteer for Special Service from the 1st Cavalry Division in Palestine stood up firing his machine gun from the shoulder like a rifle—the way it was designed to be fired –and knocked out the dirt-colored Bedford truck traveling last in the convoy. His quick action trapped the remainder of the trucks in the killing zone of the ambush, though not much actual killing was going on.

Lt. Merritt did not think it possible from the high volume of fire coming from the cliff-side platoon that it was not hitting anything. But that was the case. The Italians, however, were pinned down—only sporadically shooting back.

A shrill whistle blew, the drop-off side platoon rose up screaming, seemingly materializing from out of thin air, and led by their Bimbashi, went in with the bayonet. The Abyssinian troops were trained spearmen from birth, and the wet work commenced.

It was all over in minutes.

Savoring his first victory, Lt. Merritt stood in the middle of the road impatiently glancing at his watch while his men looted the trucks. A messenger appeared carrying a forked stick and handed him the flimsy taped to it.

```
TURN  OVER  COMMAND  OF  YOUR  COMPANY  TO  THE
NEXT  SENIOR  OFFICER.  REPORT  TO  FORCE  N  HQ
FOR  IMMEDIATE  REASSIGNMENT.
      Signed Randal, Brigadier.
      1 Guerrilla Corps (Parachute)
      Force N
```

6

A RAS COMES IN

"I'VE BEEN MEANING TO ASK, CAPTAIN," BRIGADIER JOHN RANDAL inquired as they were having their regular morning coffee and cigars, "is that an Arizona Ranger badge on the grip of your pistol?" The old cowboy had returned from his recruiting trip and completed a briefing on the success of his mission.

Captain "Geronimo" Joe McKoy glanced down at the aged, butter-yellow, ivory-stocked 1911 Model Colt .38 Super he was wearing in a chest holster. "U.S. Marshal's Service, John. After the Rangers disbanded I knocked around down in Mexico for a few years then joined up as a deputy U.S. marshal."

"U.S. marshals carry .38 Supers?"

"Well, some do. But me and Captain Frank Hammer, Texas Rangers, bought one apiece when we were detached on a special assignment together to hunt down a couple o' outlaws who had a bad habit of robbing banks, shooting police officers, then speeding away in their souped-up hot rod. A .38 Super will make a cheese shredder out of the body of a speeding automobile."

"Got your man?"

"And woman. But the BARs did most of the real heavy lifting."

"Now, where would you get Browning Automatic Rifles?"

"The Texas National Guard. They loaned 'em to us—a joint Task Force deal, kinda' off the record."

"You never really scouted for Geronimo, did you Captain?"

"No, the only Indians I ever fought was a couple a drunks who jumped the reservation down around Tempe. That Geronimo story was just something I sorta' threw into my stage résumé to make it more colorful for my Wild West Show."

"San Juan Hill?"

"Oh yeah, only we charged up Kettle Hill. The only man riding was Colonel Roosevelt, and I was leading his horse part way. History got that wrong. Fourteen years old—lied to get in the Rough Riders. The colonel found out and made me his groom. You trying to corroborate my actual age, John?"

"Doesn't really matter at this point ..."

"We got company," Waldo yelled, coming in on the run. "A whole bunch of it, Brigadier."

Lieutenant Butch "Headhunter" Hoolihan appeared with his Thompson submachine gun. "About a thousand men on mules coming up the valley, sir. Not able to confirm any Italians but it may be one of their bandas."

"Mr. Treywick?"

"Can't say for sure, Brigadier. I'm thinkin' more like a big Ras has done decided to drop in and pay us a visit."

"What does that mean?"

"Means we best regard all unknown parties as foes until proven otherwise even if they ain't actual garlic eaters."

"Captain McKoy, you and Butch take your troops and set up a blocking force on the ridge at this end of the valley," Brig. Randal ordered. "Don't let those people ride in."

The two officers immediately returned to their commands, shouting orders. Capt. McKoy had the better part of three companies of the 6th MRB he was in the process of forming plus all the British Army officers, temporary Bimbashis and other ranks for three more—what he described as the "cream of the crop" he had recruited on his trip to Nairobi. Lt. Hoolihan had the Force Raiding Company. All up, Force N's strength was about 200 fighting men in camp not counting Cheap Bribe's Patriots and the Bad Boys.

"Be ready to move on my command, Captain Honeycutt-Parker," Brig. Randal ordered. "But don't strike camp until I give the word."

"Sir!"

Captain Lionel Chatterhorn arrived. "Have your security team standing by here with Thompsons at the ready. This would be the time for them to look as tough as they've ever looked."

"Right away, sir."

The security men from the Vulnerable Points Wing had a motto: *Be professional, be polite and have a plan to kill everyone you meet.*

Lana Turner moved behind Brig. Randal's camp chair carrying his 9mm MAB-38A submachine gun. Rita Hayworth was her bookend on the other side of the chair with his cut-down Browning A-5 12-gauge shotgun.

Gubbo Rekash rushed up, clearly alarmed.

"Tell Cheap Bribe to bring up his men armed and ready, in full sight about fifty yards out," Brig. Randal ordered Kaldi, who translated the command. "No shooting unless we're attacked. Make that clear."

The one-eyed bandit chief jabbered out a quick response. "Beware, sire," Kaldi interpreted. "We have no friends in large groups."

"Bribe ain't wrong," Waldo said anxiously. "Big numbers of anybody ain't good for us. You got yourself a serious reward on your head, Brigadier. Even a friendly Patriot, of which there ain't any, might be tempted by the size of it."

"Mr. Treywick, ride down and make the initial contact," Brig. Randal ordered. "If they're Italians, take your hat off and hold it down on your leg."

"If they are, I'm plannin' to tell 'em you been holdin' me hostage."

"In the event they claim to be friendly, only the headman and a small retinue are to be allowed into camp," Brig. Randal said. "We'll fire on 'em if they all attempt to come in, Mr. Treywick."

"You be sure you do, Brigadier … and be quick about it. Let 'em all ride up they'll swamp you—it's how shifta operate."

When Waldo rode out, Brig. Randal ordered, "Kaldi, break out those proclamations and photos Mr. Treywick uses when he politics with the village chiefs. Tell Lieutenant Plum-Martin to stay out of sight—no sense tempting anybody."

"Immediately, sire."

"Captain Chatterhorn, after this is over I'm going to promote your corporals to Bimbashi. You raise a Force N Headquarters Security

Company, they can be platoon leaders—we can use a little more security."

"Getting ready to suggest something along that line, sir."

"Make it happen."

CAPTAIN "PYRO" PERCY STIRLING WAS LYING IN WAIT ABOUT 100 YARDS uphill of the railroad tracks that made a horseshoe curve around the mountain down below. One of his Railroad Wrecking Crew platoons—the 2nd—was strung out to his left and right. Lieutenant Dick Courtney, along as an observer, was holding the mules out of sight.

Running down to the track was an electric cable that Capt. Stirling had wired to an initiating device. All he had to do was lift up on the handle then twist it to detonate the explosives that were carefully planted along the tracks. Brigadier John Randal had once told him demo men in the U.S. Army referred to this system as a "Triple Nickel Thirty." The charge was specifically designed for blowing rail lines with five pounds of guncotton connected by detonating cord every ten yards for thirty yards. The explosion would take out a thirty-yard section of track, and if everything worked as planned, plunge the train off into the gorge 500 feet or so below.

In the movies it's easy to blow a railroad. A saboteur sneaks up to the rails, evades the lone sentry patrolling in the middle of nowhere, pulls out a prepared explosive device, places it next to the track, scurries off and *KAAABOOOOM,* the next passing train is blown sky high. In real life it takes a lot of explosives, quite a bit of hard work and no little amount of skill to cause a catastrophic derailment of a locomotive.

Capt. Stirling was highly trained in the art of explosives by the Kent Fortress Royal Engineers, a Territorial engineer regiment that specialized in commando-type missions. He also had experience blowing up railroads in enemy-occupied France during OPERATION COMANCHE YELL. Though in those days, the explosive charges he planted had been fairly crude, and he had seldom hung around long enough to see the result of his demolitions.

Capt. Stirling was in his element today, an independent command in the middle of Abyssinia, the classic example of Right Man,

Right Job. All of his extensive commando training and raiding experience had come together to make him a deadly effective guerrilla leader and highly skilled saboteur.

Anticipation was high as the platoon waited looking down at the tracks.

Today, the Railroad Wrecking Crew was not setting up an ambush and hoping a train would show up—the troops knew one was coming … and knew when. They had a copy of the schedule.

Capt. Stirling could hear the engine a mile away. He glanced at his wristwatch. As advertised, the Blackshirts actually did make the railroads run on time.

One school of thought says that it's best to blow up a train in a tunnel. The derailment holds up traffic, and the confined space makes it difficult for the enemy to clear the wreckage. However, a sharp curve is almost as good. If there is a steep cliff on the outside rail it may be even better, provided the demolitions are set properly and cause the train to completely leave the tracks and go off the precipice.

Capt. Stirling had all of central Abyssinia from which to choose a site to make his attack. He had selected a bend on a radical downgrade next to a 500-foot drop off. Today's ambush had the element of surprise, plenty of explosives and the train's forward momentum working for it.

In railroad demolitions, it does not get any better than that.

WALDO RODE IN WITH A PARTY OF FIVE MEN. THE STRANGERS WERE ALL mounted on excellent riding stock, wore the traditional white shamma tunics over their jodhpur-style cotton pants and pearl-gray Tom Mix-style cowboy hats. Bandoleers of mixed calibers of ammunition crisscrossed their chests, little round shields rested on their left arms and four of the five men carried a spear in addition to the rifle slung on his back.

The men were the best-outfitted group of Abyssinians Brigadier John Randal had encountered. He clicked on.

Waldo brought the headman over to the table where Brig. Randal sat smoking a thin cigar. "This here is Ras Yaqut Morjan, a sadistic, syphilitic torturer of captives and murder of innocent villagers. He claims to be the chief potentate of this here entire province, which is an exaggeration. Says he's heard the British are passin' out rifles to loyal Patriots who support the Emperor and want to fight the Italians."

"Tell the man we don't have any rifles to give him," Brig. Randal said, "but he's invited to share a cup of coffee."

The Ras was a short, squat, swarthy individual with a pockmarked face. He had not failed to note that every Abyssinian male in camp was armed with a brand new M-1903 A-1 Springfield rifle.

Ras Morjan also observed the giant, ten-foot lion skin with all the bullet holes in it displayed spread-eagle on a stand next to the table where the young guerrilla commander was sitting. Lion skins were everywhere—on the ground like throw rugs, draped over chairs; one was serving as a tablecloth. He had never seen so many.

A ripped green battle-dress jacket with dried bloodstains was displayed on another rack. On the camp table the Ras could see the ivory-handled horse tickler sporting the silver Imperial Seal of the Emperor on the butt with the black lion's tail whisk. An ivory-stocked Browning P-35 9mm was lying next to a gleaming silver Fairbairn Fighting Knife—the one of legend that the British officer who was not British had used to kill the big man-eating lion—everyone knew that story too, hand-to-hand. It was impossible to ignore the four tough soldiers with the .45-caliber Thompson submachine guns staring holes in him or the two armed, high-grade female body slaves.

Clearly the bearded young officer smoking the cigarillo was a *tillik sau*—a big shot.

Ras Morjan was impressed but not intimidated. He could also see that there were more women and boys in camp than fighting men. You did not reach his station in life in the wild primitive society in which he dwelled by taking no for an answer when the odds were stacked in your favor.

"The man says," Waldo translated, "he wants rifles, not coffee— you have many Springfields."

"We're not giving him any rifles."

"The Ras says he has 6,000 men under his command though he did not find it necessary to bring all of them here today. You need to give him the rifles you have in camp and arrange to have the British airplanes bring more until all his men have one.

"If you don't, Brigadier, he'll take 'em away from you."

"Really?"

"That's what the man said."

"Tell him to go ahead."

Waldo looked like he had swallowed a feather but he followed his orders.

"The Ras says, he'll kill all British Force N personnel, make slaves of our women and use Lana and Rita as his personal whores until he tires of 'em then give 'em to his troops to pleasure if you don't give him rifles."

"Ask him how he plans to get out of this camp alive."

Ras Morjan's eyes flashed surprise and possibly a trace of fear when he heard Waldo's translation. No man threatened him to his face, not when he had 1,000 warriors behind him. This boy must be a fool.

"He says he'll make a woman out of you."

"Wrong answer," Brig. Randal said, shooting the Ras three times with the 1911 Colt .38 Super he brought up out of his lap. *BLAMMM, BLAMMM, BLAMMM.*

The man was dead before his body hit the ground.

"I knew I shoulda' handled negotiations," Waldo griped. "You ain't any better at the art of politickin' than you are at huntin' big cat. No natural aptitude at all."

"Go tell the number two man he's been promoted," Brig. Randal ordered. "Inform him the planes that bring us rifles can also carry bombs.

"Tell the man we know where to find him."

CAPTAIN "PYRO" PERCY STIRLING GRASPED THE DETONATING DEVICE IN his left hand and lifted up the charging handle. The train was coming closer. The clickity-clacking sounds it made were crisp in the thin mountain air. Next to him were his interpreter and his pageboy.

Suddenly, the page screamed, started flailing his arms and dancing a jig, tried to run and fell down. The interpreter shouted a curse, jumped up and started running. Other men were scattering, abandoning their position, shouting and cursing.

A pain that felt like an electrical shock nearly knocked Capt. Stirling off his feet. He thought for a moment he had been shot in the neck.

"What the …"

Then he saw the swarm.

A cloud of hornets was in full attack mode—thousands of them—maybe millions. Unknown to anyone, the mother of all hornet's nests was situated in a bush in the middle of the ambush position and Capt. Stirling's page, moving for a better view, had accidently bumped into it, setting the angry hornets off in full attack mode.

Without cognizant thought and desperate to evade the swarm, Capt. Stirling found himself fleeing out-of-control down the hill full speed … straight toward the tracks. Then the train streamed into sight. It went whizzing past at handshake range scaring him stiff and causing him to pull up sharp—he was standing on tip-toes. He had nearly run onto the tracks into the side of the cars. The vortex felt like it would suck him in, wind whipped his bush jacket and blew off his Australian slouch hat with the ostrich feather in the crown.

The detonating device was back where he had dropped it eighty or ninety yards up the slope.

A small crack sounded, then a sharp explosion as the Triple Nickel Thirty went off. The engine overturned as its wheels dug into the dirt where the tracks had been seconds before. The train derailed right in front of Capt. Stirling's terrified eyes, cars T-boning, slamming into each other, buckling, overturning, sparks flying, metal screeching, and one after the other sailing out into space over the edge crashing into the gorge. The violence and noise was mind-numbing, and it went on and on and on.

Even the hornets were affected. In any event, they had disappeared.

The Kent Fortress Royal Engineers had stressed the importance of having a redundant switch—a contact detonator placed on the track. The precaution was a contingency in the event of electrical failure, the demolitions man being discovered, killed or falling asleep before he could blow the charge.

One of Raiding Forces Rules stipulated "It's Good to Have a Plan B," and that was true. Another was "When the Unexpected Happens, Press On."

No one anticipated being attacked by angry insects.

7

RAID ON EL WOK

"WHAT DO YOU RECKON THE REACTION'S GONNA' BE WHEN YOU tell Number Two he moved up a notch?" Captain "Geronimo" Joe McKoy said as he and Waldo Treywick rode down the hill.

"Hard to say, Rases don't generally never have a chain-of-command with a designated man waitin' in the wings to step up if anythin' happens. Ain't a real healthy idea in Abyssinia. Somebody always gets impatient."

"Think they'll be mad?"

"Not too much, Joe. My guess is a couple 'a these benevolent Christian gentlemen is gonna' see the Ras's demise as a career enhancement opportunity. All hell's gonna' break loose when they get to sortin' it out, but it'll probably take a while to get started.

"That said, soon as you recruit the men you want for your battalion, we need to beat feet outta' here, right quick."

"I'll make it pronto, Waldo."

As the two rode into the banda camp, they passed a big man sitting on a red mule; ripped tunic sleeves showcased his heavily muscled, sun-bronzed arms. He was not armed with a spear, sword, or shield. There was a big ugly Bergmann-Bayard pistol strapped to his chest.

Waldo said, "Frank."

"Waldo."

"You two know each other—he an American?" Capt. McKoy asked.

"Born and bred," Waldo replied. "Ride over and introduce yourself. Frank's a soldier-of-fortune. Come out to fight for the Emperor for pay but stayed on after the coward run off. Commands the late Ras's bodyguard—does the same stuff I used to do 'cept he ain't a slave like I was. Don't get paid much."

Capt. McKoy rode over and right away noticed a faded globe-and-anchor tattoo on the man's left shoulder with "U.S. Marines" stenciled below it.

"I'm Joe McKoy—you a Marine?"

"Frank Polanski," the man said. "I used to be. Did a burst of six—Fighting Fifth, helped keep the grocery stores of America stocked on behalf of the United Fruit Company—a banana warrior."

"Americans do love their fruit cocktail," Capt. McKoy said. "Somebody had to do it."

"Joe McKoy—yeah, heard of you in Nicaragua. You're the one killed Bandito Red Charlie. What were you back then—a major or a colonel?"

"How many men in the Ras's bodyguard, Frank?"

"About a hundred."

"You looking for work?"

"I have a job."

"You had one."

"Ras lip off to the wrong man?" the ex-Marine asked. "Oh well, bound to happen sooner or later. Mouth wrote a check his ass couldn't cash, right?"

"Pick your fifty best men," Capt. McKoy said. "Pays a silver Fat Lady a day per man. You'll sign on drawing a captain's wage."

"Throw in an '03 A-1 like the one in your saddle boot? Left the Corps with few regrets, but I do miss my '03—best precision weapon ever built."

"One goes to every man you bring with you."

"I command them?"

"No," Capt. McKoy said. "You're going to serve as my local expert/ advisor/ interpreter for the mule cavalry outfit I'm putting together."

"A .45 ACP to seal the deal?"

"We don't have any .45s, Frank, but I might be able to scrape up a spare 1911 Model .38 Super."

"Never heard of .38 Super but as long as it's a Colt 1911—works for me."

"It's more of a connoisseur's type handgun," Capt. McKoy said. "What's that cannon you're packing there?"

"9mm Largo."

"A Largo, huh?" Capt. McKoy said. "Don't run across one of those every day."

"Waldo over there breaking the news right now?"

"That's right."

"I'll have the men ready to pull out in twenty minutes," the ex-Marine said. "We don't want to be anywhere in the immediate area once the debate commences."

"I can tell already you're gonna' do real good as my advisor, Frank—how'd you like a Thompson submachine gun?"

"No thanks –I'm an '03 Springfield man. Now if you had an extra one of those campaign hats ..."

BRIGADIER JOHN RANDAL, CAPTAIN HAWTHORNE MERRYWEATHER, Rita Hayworth and Lana Turner were in the back of the Hudson flying south to witness the opening move of the reconquest of Abyssinia. Major General James "Baldie'" Taylor was on board. He briefed the upcoming operation.

"The invasion is ready to launch but we have had several missteps, false starts and near-miss disasters. All the nice neat plans I made with elaborate military moves—Cunningham striking first, the Emperor's column crossing the border up in the far north to draw the Italian's attention to Gondar a long way from where the Kaid will go in from the Sudan—have gone down the tube.

"The moves will all take place ... just not in the sequence planned. You are probably going to have to raid the airfields again. The first effort was very, very effective, Brigadier, but as it turns out—premature."

"I need at least a week's notice, General. Two is better."

"Hopefully I can provide that. Timing is a little tricky. We are dealing with natural obstacles like deserts, lack of roads, no portable water and bush that is virtually impossible to penetrate.

"Not to mention shortages of everything. The Italians outnumber us ten to one, but they are the least of our concerns. Our timetable keeps changing."

"When do you estimate the invasion will kick off?"

"The opening moves have already started. You are being brought in to observe what is officially called the 'Raid on El Wok.' In fact, what you are going to see is a full-scale combined arms attack. The purpose of the exercise is a two-fold deception—to draw attention to the Kenyan border and away from where Platt is ready to launch out of the Sudan, and to mislead the Duke of Aosta about the staying power of East Africa Force."

"Staying power?"

"Dudley Clarke came up with the idea of calling it a raid since its textbook definition is a 'limited military operation of short duration with a *planned* withdrawal.'

"The idea is to condition the Italians to believe His Majesty's Forces are only capable of short-term operations when in fact we are preparing to go in and take down IEA and hold it, at least along the Red Sea corridor—we are simply not quite ready yet."

"Think the Italians will get it?" Brig. Randal asked. "Might be a little subtle for 'em."

"Who is to say? Maybe we need to have Captain Merryweather spell it out, now that you point that out."

"Easy enough," the Political Warfare Executive officer agreed. "I shall make sure the Wops understand our limitations clearly, sir."

"Perfect," Maj. Gen. Taylor said. "The raid is also a live-fire training exercise for the as yet un-blooded South African and Gold Coast troops carrying it out."

"Sounds like a plan, General."

"That it is. The battle will be the second in the area this year. In this part of Africa we fight over water wells. El Wok has one and El Uach has the only other for hundreds of miles in any direction.

"Six months ago when we held El Uach, our fort located there was defended by a King's African Rifles Company, surrounded by barbed wire entanglements and well-fortified with concrete bunkers. However, the water well was inconveniently situated outside the wire."

"I hate it when that happens," Brig. Randal said. "You always know how the movie's going to end."

"Particularly in a desert environment where it seldom rains," Maj. Gen. Taylor said.

"The Blackshirts attacked and after some desultory bombing and an artillery barrage—notable only for the high of percentage of the rounds that hit the fort turning out to be duds—the Italians launched their assault under cover of darkness. The KAR repelled them even though when our troops conducted their counterattack they wandered off in the wrong direction, being disoriented in the night.

"Then the Italians got smart, surrounded the place and waited it out. In the desert it is a given—if a military unit occupies a fort and the only well is outside the walls, and the fort becomes surrounded and laid to siege, then eventually the defenders run out of water."

"That's the way it works in the movies," Brig. Randal said, "every time."

"The KAR was forced to abandon El Uach after five days. To their credit they came out in good order with all their arms. However, they left three riflemen behind, believed to be wounded too seriously to move, two of whom later legged it to safety under their own power."

"Why is it your briefings are always one click short of crazy, General?"

"Because this is Africa—it gets better. Miffed at the blow to British prestige, Brigadier C.C. "Fluffy" Fowkes decided to re-take El Uach immediately with a two-company attack.

"The only air support available was an elderly Rhodesian Air Force Hawker Hart. Fluffy's plan was for it to orbit over the fort after the initial assault to aid in relaying communications since the plane was unarmed.

"Everything that could go wrong did. The Hawker arrived on station on time. The troops crossed the line of departure late. The first the Italians knew they were under attack was when the old plane started race-tracking overhead looking for someone to facilitate communications for."

"A dead giveaway," Brig. Randal said.

"That should have put paid to Fluffy's attack. However, being only a handful of indigenous strikers led by a token number of Italian officers, the Hawker Hart looked mighty threatening. The lads holding the fort decided their best interests lay elsewhere and decamped.

"The assault was a walkover—victory at hand, almost. Instead of shoring up defenses, standing-to and preparing for a counterattack, the hearties of the King's African Rifles immediately fell to looting the place. The troops were hard at the booty—too busy to notice a Blackshirt battalion that had come up undetected from El Wok.

"The Italians attacked and caught the KAR in mid-loot. With the tables turned, the KAR took to their heels. About that time the Hawker Hart's engine conked out, and it was forced to land right outside the fort.

"The Italians found themselves back in their fort and the recipients of a heaven sent photo-op. Mussolini bragged he had beaten back a major British invasion, shot the RAF out of the skies and had the pictures to prove it."

"A bit grim," observed Capt. Merryweather, "from a public relations perspective."

"Quite," Maj. Gen. Taylor said. "After the dust settled, Lieutenant General Gustavo Pesenti decided to reinforce El Wok with 1,000 white-turbaned Somali Dubats backed up by the 191st Native Battalion. And that, gentlemen, brings us to where we are today ... getting ready to 'raid' the place."

"That's a lot of Blackshirts, General—what's the good news?"

"The well is still located outside the fort."

SCOUT MUNRO FERGUSON AND HIS ASSOCIATE, SCOUT LIONEL FENWICK, sat on the military crest of a mountain overlooking an Italian company-sized base camp across the valley on the hilltop below them. The two Lovat Scouts were on their first mission since arriving in-country and being assigned to 1 Guerrilla Corps (Parachute), Force N

Headquarters. Today was a trial run with an eye to developing sniping tactics for future operations.

Both men were astonished to find that the Italians would build a permanent base that was not located on the top of the most commanding piece of terrain in the immediate area. But that is exactly what the Blackshirts had done. The Lovat Scouts could sit up on top of the mountain and shoot across a small canyon straight down into the camp ... approximately 600 yards as the crow flies.

Why would the Italians do something as stupid as that? One possible explanation was the chosen location gave the Italians a better view of the strategic road they were theoretically guarding. Another was the base was easier to construct where it was than higher up across the canyon on the mountaintop.

Whatever the reason, the choice of locations for the small Blackshirt fortification was criminal folly.

Compared to the Most Secret BUZZARD PLUCKER missions they had cut their teeth on sniping German pilots at their landing grounds in enemy-occupied France, today's patrol was a walk in the park. Well, maybe not *that* easy. There were animals about with big teeth and an acquired taste for people, plus the odd shifta looking to score an easy trophy kill. But still, operationally it was pretty easy.

To guard against marauding wildlife and discourage bandits, a ten-man security detail from Force Raiding Company was assigned to protect the Lovat Scouts. Half the Patriots were holding the mules out of sight over the top of the mountain. The other half of the detail was hiding under cover in a loose diamond-shaped perimeter around the two Scouts.

The Lovats felt secure. They had a panoramic view, so no one was going to sneak up on them. Only they did not speak whatever Abyssinian dialect the Patriots did, and none of the Patriots could speak more than a handful of English words. Nothing is perfect. Both men agreed ... all things considered, the security was a nice touch.

Brigadier John Randal had ordered, "Get a feel for the terrain, familiarize yourself with how the Italians operate in their road watch outposts and if you get a chance, shoot the highest ranking bad guy you can."

Looking through their 20X Ross scope, the Scouts could observe a large number of enemy personnel wearing sizeable amounts of gold braid—it appeared as if there was a convention of field marshals to choose from. The only problem—it was difficult to tell which one was the highest ranking.

Not to worry, Captain Hawthorne Merryweather had thoughtfully provided them a small paperback manual with watercolor artist's sketches depicting Italians in different uniforms and headgear. There was also a section on unit insignia and badges of rank.

The two Lovat Scouts sat on the side of the mountain thumbing through the manual. They were eventually able to determine that the troops below were from the 63rd Cagliari Regiment, Assiente Division. After a great deal of scoping, to their disappointment, a mere infantry *tenente* (lieutenant) turned out to be the highest-ranking officer on the base.

"Take the shot, Munro," Scout Fenwick said. A standing man at that range was a chip shot for a Lovat Scout.

BOOOOM. The 7x57 Rigby echoed through the mountains.

Down below, the tenente crumpled to the ground before the "slap" sound of the bullet striking reached the snipers. Panic ensued, men scurried like land crabs in all directions seeking cover. In seconds there was not a soldier in sight ... except for the lieutenant.

No one bothered to check on his condition.

By the time the Lovat Scouts and their Force Raiding Company security detail rode out an hour later, not a single Blackshirt had shown himself. The tenente lay where he fell.

The troops must not have liked him very much.

8

RAID

MAJOR GENERAL ALAN CUNNINGHAM, GENERAL OFFICER Commanding East Africa Force (EAF) had his orders. "Attack and destroy the twin forts at El Wok and El Uach then withdraw." The problem was, every operation he had attempted to date had resulted in an embarrassment and was humiliating to British prestige even when the result was technically a victory. There was some question in his mind if the Imperial Forces under his command had what it took to fight and win. Nothing so far had given him the slightest reason to believe that they did.

Things had become so ugly that Prime Minister Churchill, bypassing the chain-of-command, was personally sending cables urging him to be aggressive—attack, attack, attack, "action this day." When he did, one element or another of East Africa Force suffered a blow to its confidence.

Now given orders he could not ignore, Maj. Gen. Cunningham decided not to take any chances. He was going to "shoot a hare with an elephant gun." For the "raid" (it was a diversion—something no one bothered to tell the troops—they thought it was a battle to the death) he ordered up 1 South African Brigade, 24 Gold Coast Brigade minus one battalion, two companies of the 1/6 King's African Rifles, 1st South African Light Tank Company, two companies of South African Armored

Cars (Dingos), two companies of South African field sappers and three batteries of field artillery.

Seventeen planes of the South African Air Force No. 40 Army-Cooperation Squadron were to fly in direct support.

Major General A.J. Goodwin-Austin was placed in tactical command. Concentrating his troops at the point of attack gave him a six-to-one advantage over the Italians.

Looking at a map, it was clear getting the troops to the start line might be more challenging than the battle. To reach the jumping-off point required some impressive road building by the South African engineers through what the Italians believed to be impenetrable bush. Around Lake Rudolf lies fantastic lava country containing black boulders ranging from the size of a golf ball to a Nissen hut. The terrain is as flat as a billiard table with no discernable features to navigate by. The area is called the "Desert of the Night." No one knows why except the boulders are as black as pitch and when you get lost in the featureless terrain it is like stumbling around in the dark.

The dominating factors were the 106-degree heat, the remoteness, lack of water and the distances that had to be covered. The task of moving Maj. Gen. Goodwin-Austin's force to the line-of-departure was formidable. Others had failed at lesser challenges.

The attack was scheduled to go in on Dingaan's Day, a national holiday dear to the white South Africans but not their black counterparts since it celebrated the battle in 1838 when the Boers wiped out the Zulu Army.

Captain Jack Desmond Taylor and his lion-hunting Airedale dog, Kim, met the Hudson at Camp Croc. Major General James "Baldie" Taylor stayed on board. The plane immediately took off for Maj. Gen. Goodwin-Austin's headquarters.

Captain Hawthorne Merryweather boarded a Walrus and was flown to 40 Army-Coordination Squadron where he planned to observe the operation from one of the South African Air Force aircraft taking part in the raid.

Also representing Force N in the upcoming battle would be its liaison to the South African Air Force, Pilot Officer Gasper "Bunny" Featherstone piloting one of four Hawker Hurricanes recently arrived at No. 2 Squadron, SAAF. Forced to walk with a cane because of wounds suffered in the Battle of Britain, the ace from the 601 Millionaires

Squadron was not a man to be left flying a desk—or in his case more likely the nearest bar—when there was air combat to be had.

Brigadier John Randal, Lana Turner and Rita Hayworth mounted camels and set out for the front accompanied by Capt. Taylor, Kim and an escort of hardy Turkana warriors. The plan was to swing around behind El Wok and link up with Captain Mike "March or Die" Mikkalis, MC, DCM, MM. His 1st Mercs were initially tasked to establish a blocking force then lead the pursuit after the objective was overrun—provided it *was* overrun.

As Brig. Randal had learned from hard experience in Africa, there are no sure things.

EAST AFRICA FORCE'S APPROACH MARCH WAS MADE AT NIGHT UNDER total blackout restrictions; 24 Gold Coast Brigade was on the left with a task force consisting of the Duke of Edinburg's Own Regiment and 4 Field Brigade, South African Army led by A Squadron East Africa Car Company making a wide looping flanking movement with the idea of coming in on the Italian right. If ever there had been a recipe for disaster, this was it—a complicated scheme of maneuver with raw, untried troops making a movement to contact through heavy bush in pitch dark with no terrain features to guide on.

Against all odds, the troops of 24 Gold Coast Brigade executed their movement like a parade ground drill team.

The plan of attack called for Vickers Mark II tanks to lead the advance with instructions to crash through the concertina wire surrounding El Wok in order to open up lanes for the infantry trailing in their wake. The idea was to overrun the fort quickly then move on to El Uach and repeat the process.

It was a good, sound tactical plan—once the troops reached their jump-off position.

Unhappily, sixty-horsepower, Rolls Royce six-cylinder, water-cooled engines power Vickers Mark IIs. Only an optimist would call them anything but feeble. When the balloon went up, the tanks were unable to force their way through the wire. In fact, the tracked tin-cans very nearly got tangled in it.

After experiencing initial near catastrophic failure in their attempt to breach the concertina, the Vickers tanks were limited to racing back and forth outside the wire raking the enemy positions with their single .303 machine guns. While the tankers put on a fine demonstration of martial spirit, they did not inflict much in way of actual damage to the enemy. Nor did they provide any tangible aid to the ground troops making their assault.

For their part, the Italians inside the fort stood-to with a will and laid down a withering return fire pinning down the infantry when it moved up to breach the wire.

Brigadier John Randal was sitting on the back of his camel a distance away watching the action through his Zeiss binoculars. It seemed to him the sun was going to set on the Empire's effort then and there—as it had so often in the recent past. While he observed, a Bangalore torpedo's fuse was ignited and a demolitions team dashed forward to blow a gap in the wire.

The sappers were mowed down in a hail of machine gun fire. The torpedo lay in plain sight on the ground, fuse sparking. A young lieutenant jumped up, dashed forward, scooped the explosive device up and thrust it under the wire.

At the exact moment this heroic act was unfolding, Captain Hawthorne Merryweather arrived over the scene of the battle riding in the back of a South African Air Force Junkers 86 belonging to No. 12 Squadron. The irrepressible Political Warfare Executive operator leaned out the door of the aircraft, loud hailer in hand, and informed the Italian defenders below in flawless Italian that hungry cannibals from the Gold Coast were in the van of the attack hoping to have "Wop liver on today's menu."

The Bangalore torpedo exploded, blowing a massive hole in the wire. The South African and Gold Coast troops rose up and charged in with the bayonet chanting the Zulu war cry, which seemed a bit odd considering it was South Africa's holiday for slaughtering Zulus. Not to be outdone in the theatre of the absurd, Capt. Merryweather was a British officer riding in a German-built airplane, piloted by a South African whose grandfather had been a Boer commando who had fought against His Majesty's Forces.

Being reasonable men, the Italians defending El Wok could not see anything to be gained in waiting around to find out if the officer on the loud hailer was speaking the truth about the cannibals. Resistance ceased immediately. The Blackshirts broke and ran. The panic continued to El Uach, which was also abandoned in the stampede.

The climactic moment of the day's action came when a flight of three Savoia bombers arrived to bomb the Imperial Forces. Circling high overhead Pilot Officer Gasper "Bunny" Featherstone, flying top cover in his Hurricane, spotted them and dived to attack.

"Tally-ho! Purple Leader rolling in."

When he had one of the Savoia lined up in the illuminated pip of his gunsight, the Battle of Britain ace came up on the radio, "Take that, Garlic Breath!" Then he raked the intruder with eight chattering .303-caliber air-to-air machine guns. The Italian plane rolled over and went into the ground headfirst; its tail sticking up in the air looked like an upside down wine glass.

The crash marked the end of the battle.

By 1100 hours the Transvaal Scottish battered their way through the dense brush to cut the road relieving Mikkalis' Mercs who had been acting as a blocking force. First Battalion, 1 Guerrilla Corps (Parachute), Force N then set off in hot pursuit of the fleeing Italians.

Brig. Randal waved a salute to a stone-faced Captain Mike "March or Die" Mikkalis as he trotted past with his "Don't Dance" 10th Lancer lieutenant on a fast-stepping mule at his side. On signal, the young Lancer raised a small hunting horn and sounded the chase.

Brig. Randal almost felt sorry for the Italians.

For his part, most of the battle had been spent lying in a shallow ditch with Rita and Lana being strafed by the trigger-happy South African pilots of No. 40 Army-Cooperation Squadron—their camels had been shot dead in the road. So much for air-ground cooperation with the SAAF. No matter what their name implied, No. 40 A-CS shot first and asked questions later. There was no cooperation to it.

Brig. Randal said farewell to Captain Jack Desmond Taylor who was off to broker a truce between warring tribal factions on the other side of the Italian East African border. Then he and the two ex-slave girls hitched a ride to within walking distance of Camp Croc in the cab of a South African truck transporting a load of Italian prisoners to a POW cage. Standing crowded in the truck bed, the prisoners did not seem all that dispirited.

For them, the war was over.

In the dust-encrusted rearview mirror, Brig. Randal watched the mud walls of the forts near the wells being demolished. Not a single building was left standing as the truck rolled out of sight down the red clay road. Secretly, he felt a sense of satisfaction at their destruction.

El Wok had not been his finest hour.

LOVAT SCOUTS MUNRO FERGUSON AND LIONEL FENWICK WERE BACK on the mountaintop overlooking the Italian 63rd Cagliari Regiment base two days after their last call. The snipers were interested to see if the Italians had done anything to improve their defenses since their last visit. Apparently not—things seemed like business as usual. It looked as if everyone was asleep.

As they watched, a convoy traveling down the strategic road running past the outpost came to a halt. A single truck detached itself from the column and wound its way up the track to the front gate. A man stepped out. Looking through their 20X Ross spotting scope they determined from the badges of rank on his epaulets that he was a tenente. Another soldier climbed from the back of the truck and hauled a metal trunk out from under the tarp covering the bed.

Inside the small fort a formation of troops was hastily assembling. As the tenente entered the front gate, the garrison came to attention. The big soldier standing out in front of the formation snapped a ridged salute.

Undoubtedly the Lovats were observing a change of command ceremony. A new officer arrived to replace the one they had sniped on their first call. This could not be happening.

"Your turn, Lionel," Scout Ferguson said. "Take the shot, laddie."

BOOOOMMM.

9
CAPTAIN McKOY'S ASSIGNMENT

"LET ME GET THIS STRAIGHT," WALDO TREYWICK SAID. "YOUR married ex-fiancée used to be a widder before you went out and rescued her dead husband?"

"Well ..."

"Brigadier, sounds like you're a lot better lion hunter than a Romeo, and you have got to be the all-time worst at huntin' lion in the history of the dark continent."

"That sounds harsh," Captain "Geronimo" Joe McKoy protested. "John has killed a pile of man-eaters and that rescue was a neat piece of work—there's talk of him getting a medal for it."

"Now," Waldo persisted, "your ex has done recruited Rita and Lana into the Royal Marines?"

"That's what I understand," Brigadier John Randal said.

"You can't have Royal Marines for slaves!"

"Lana and Rita aren't my slaves."

"They don't know that. You could get yourself court martialed if the girls go and start talkin' to people. Nobody'll ever believe you. Think you're a slave master—imagine all kinda' lurid details.

"Course I'll testify ... and Butch, he can too, so you ought to get off."

"Let's get back to this map," Brig. Randal said, cutting off the once-and-future ivory poacher. "Captain, you have all your officers— picked men, a full complement of NCOs from some of the best cavalry regiments England has to offer, plus a dozen English-speaking King's African Rifles NCOs. You now have five companies of troops, one of which is made up of paratroopers from the 2nd Lounge Lizards. Your battalion should be prepared to take the field."

"Ready as we'll ever be, John."

"Excellent; what I have in mind for you initially is a two-part mission. Cut the road with ambushes on either side of these five Italian outposts," Brig. Randal pointed with the tip of his Fairbairn Fighting Knife.

Capt. McKoy studied the map laid out on the camp table. "Let's see, that means I'll have my 6th Mule Raider Battalion spread out for about 250 miles. We can do that. What's the second part?"

"Carry out small-scale raids on isolated Democratic Colonization Projects of your choosing within a fifty-mile radius of each of these Blackshirt bases."

"Now we're talking, hoss," Capt. McKoy exclaimed. "Oh, that's downright sneaky, John. You're gonna' have me cut the Wops off, make 'em feel isolated and scared, then force 'em to venture out of the safety of their bases to go rescue the Italian colonial farmers. And when they do, I reckon you're gonna' want me to follow up and harass the Wop's columns on the march?"

"You'll know where the Blackshirts will be coming from," Brig. Randal said, "where they're going and how they're going to get there. Hit and run, over and over."

"Frank," Capt. McKoy said, "you know this country?"

"Oh, yeah," the newest American member of 1 Guerrilla Corps (Parachute), Force N, ex-Devil Dog Frank Polanski, nodded. "I've traveled all over it. As long as you don't stay in any one place for too long the Italians will never catch you in that rugged terrain."

"You have your orders, Captain," Brig. Randal said. (Despite the fact he wore a major's insignia, no one ever called Geronimo Joe anything but Captain). "Move when ready. What are your questions?"

"One request. I want Dick Courtney and his two strikers."

"I have plans for Lieutenant Courtney."

"My guess is you're 'a fixin' to let Dick recruit hisself a company then you'll have two, his and Butch's to go off raising merry hell—fighting your own private war."

"What of it?"

"I need him, John," Capt. McKoy insisted. "I've got Frank, but if I send him off on a reconnaissance I won't have an expert, advisor or an interpreter. Besides, Frank's a former machine gunner; he's not a recon man."

"OK, Captain," Brig. Randal conceded, not sounding happy, "Dick's yours, what else?"

"Just this, you ever hear of the Frontier Battalion, Texas Rangers? Had companies spread from the Panhandle to the Rio Grande fightin' Mexicans, Comancheros and Indians."

"What do the Texas Rangers have to do with Force N?"

"Only this ... Major Fred Jones, the battalion commander, picked one Ranger Company—A Co.—as his personal escort. He traveled up and down the length of the state of Texas inspecting his line of strung-out companies—in the saddle all the time. Saw quite a bit of action that way, I understand."

"Sounds like the man knew what he was doing," Brig. Randal said, locking eyes with the silver-haired cowboy. "Recommendation noted, Captain. Now would you go kill some bad guys?"

"We're moving now," Capt. McKoy grinned. "Keep your eye on Waldo while I'm gone ... he's about half outlaw."

BRIGADIER JOHN RANDAL HAD A SHORT MEETING WITH CAPTAIN Hawthorne Merryweather, his Special Warfare Officer, and Lieutenant Pamala Plum-Martin, his Intelligence Officer.

"Captain Merryweather, I want you and Lieutenant Plum-Martin to be prepared to relocate to N-2. Squadron Leader Wilcox has agreed to station one of the Walruses there for you to use as a flying radio station."

"Radio station?" Capt. Merryweather inquired.

"Ever since you used that bullhorn at El Wok I've been toying with an idea, and now's the time to give it a shot. I want you and Pamala to fly psychological warfare missions over the small isolated Italian bases in our AO at night. Broadcast opera music or whatever to the troops from speakers mounted on the Walrus."

"Capital idea, Brigadier," Capt. Merryweather said enthusiastically. "We may make a PWE operator out of you yet."

"You gave it to me."

"Why should I have to go to N-2?" Lt. Plum-Martin demanded. "Hawthorne can speak fluent Italian as you well know."

"Yeah, that's true, Pam, but his voice announcing the songs won't have the same impact on those lonely homesick Italian troopers as yours."

"We can mix in propaganda leaflet drops," Capt. Merryweather suggested. "I think it's a splendid plan, Brigadier."

"I'm getting ready to split off from the Force N Rear with Butch's company. We'll be on the move all the time," Brig. Randal said. "You can set up a permanent intelligence shop on N-2, Pam, and send me regular reports."

"You simply want me out of your hair," pouted the Vargas Girl look-alike Royal Marine.

"Negative," Brig. Randal said, lighting a thin Italian cigar with his battered U.S. 26th Cavalry Regiment Zippo.

"I'm going to make you a star."

"WHAT DO YOU MEAN, TEXAS RANGERS?" LIEUTENANT BUTCH "Headhunter" Hoolihan demanded.

"That's what the Brigadier said," Waldo repeated, "Go tell the Headhunter—that's you—he's gettin' ready to be my Company A of the Texas Rangers."

The two were headed to Brigadier John Randal's HQ tent. Captain Hawthorn Merryweather and Lieutenant Pamala Plum-Martin were leaving as they arrived. Captain Lionel Honeycutt-Parker walked up at the same time. Captain Lionel Chatterhorn was already there.

"Captain McKoy made a suggestion before he rode out I intend to follow," Brig. Randal said when they were all seated at his camp table. "Force Raiding Company will split off from Force N Rear to serve as my escort as I travel from MRB to MRB to inspect 'em.

"Captain Honeycutt-Parker, you will assume command of the Rear. Captain Chatterhorn, you will have two of your security platoons continue their mission with the Rear and one platoon will accompany Lieutenant Hoolihan. You have the option to move with whichever element you chose."

"I shall travel with you, Brigadier."

"Private instructions from Lady Jane, I presume?"

"Something like that, sir."

"Right," Brig. Randal said. "In that case, Lionel, make arrangements to bring along an extra thirty Springfield rifles. I may have work for you other than strictly pulling security."

"Sir!"

"Any questions? OK, move out gentlemen."

After the officers departed, Waldo said, "You're still kinda' worried about Joe, ain't ya', Brigadier?"

"Could be."

"Let me tell you a little story," Waldo said. "Me and P.J. Pretorius was in between ivory expeditions holed up in Nairobi plannin' our next move when a couple 'o rich Arizona ranchers showed up to hunt the big five. They wanted to hire P.J. and me to take 'em on safari after elephant—wanted heavy ivory. Naturally, we was the men who knew where to find it.

"P.J. said no, we wasn't professional white hunters—meanin' wet nurses. But those cowboys talked money and pretty soon we struck a deal."

"Is this going somewhere?"

"One night we was sittin' around our safari camp drinking their liquor—somethin' real evil called *mescal*—eat the worm in the bottom of the bottle—and we got to sayin' do you know so and so.

"The only person I ever heard of from Arizona before was 'Widows and Orphans' so I said 'either of you boys know Joe McKoy?' Well, things got real quiet around that campfire until finally one of the ranchers said, "Hell, everybody knows Joe."

"Really."

"That's what they said, and then they told me why. Joe was an Arizona Ranger like he claims. One of his buddies—a Ranger named Kidder—fancied himself a pistolero. Couldn't hold his liquor too good and liked to slap Mexicans around when he was drunk. He went across the border into Mexico one night to see a *señorita*, which was against standin' orders to go over there only on official Ranger business.

"Went to the bar where she worked, took her in a back room, and when it was time to leave Kidder noticed his money and watch was missin'. One thing led to another, a bunch of Mexican police with some armed civilians mixed in was conveniently waitin' just outside the door and a fight ensued. Kidder shot a couple of 'em in a runnin' gun battle then went dry on bullets. Those Mexicans stomped and pistol whipped him practically to death.

"Joe got word about it, rushed down and brought his buddy back across the border. Kidder lingered for a day or so, conscious enough to identify who done it. Joe stayed with him until he died."

"Do we have a point here, Mr. Treywick?"

"Joe resigned his Ranger commission, disappeared into Mexico for three years trackin' down every single man in that gang who murdered his friend. Joe killed 'em all."

"How many?"

"Seven or eight, they said. Nobody knew for sure, and Joe wasn't tellin'. The point is, Brigadier, Cap'n McKoy ain't somebody you need to lose much sleep over. The ranchers said the Mexicans still scare their kids with stories about him if they don't be good.

"Joe's a practicin' badass. He can take care of hisself."

CAPTAIN "GERONIMO" JOE MCKOY HAD GIVEN MARCHING ORDERS TO THE FIVE COMPANY commanders of his 6th Mule Raider Battalion. The companies had moved out on their individual missions. Then he and his small thirty-man HQ Company, a platoon of Bad Boys and a platoon-sized element of Patriots under one of Cheap Bribe's lieutenants marched out on their own. Capt. McKoy's idea was to give his company commanders time to reach their assigned areas of operation, make a reconnaissance and commence raiding operations before he interfered with them by dropping in to look over their shoulders.

Today he was doing exactly what he had counseled Brigadier John Randal *not* to do—go freelancing on his own. Capt. McKoy's justification was that he was looking for an opportunity to introduce

Frank Polanski to the joys of the .55 Boys AT Rifle with an all-steel No. 32 Mk1 scope, mounted on a 110-pound Hotchkiss Omnibus General Purpose tripod machine gun mount. All they needed was something to shoot.

Roads were out since he did not want to do anything that might interfere with his company commander's plans. There were no DCPs anywhere close. That left only small isolated Italian military garrisons they could harass. But the only one they could find was a company-sized installation located in a savanna in the center of a large valley two miles from any mountain. The little company-sized fort was theoretically guarding the strategic road that ran by it. In fact, the troops were stagnating behind the wire doing nothing more constructive than defending themselves from enemies—mostly imagined.

The only cover to screen an approach were three cone-shaped kopjes in the valley, one located about three-quarters of a mile from the Italian position. Capt. McKoy left the bulk of his HQ company with all attachments behind in the jungle and rode out into the valley to the kopje with Frank Polanski, the two mules carrying the .55 Boys, two King's Royal Rifle Corps Hotchkiss light machine gunners—both veterans of Swamp Fox Force—and three Patriots to serve as mule holders. Leaving the mules and holders in defilade at the bottom, the men muscled the .55 Boys and the 110-pound Hotchkiss Omnibus General Purpose tripod up the reverse slope of the cone-shaped hill.

Then they dug it in, filled empty sandbags and tamped it down. Frank, a former U.S. Marine who had served six years in a heavy weapons platoon, soon demonstrated that he knew all about the mysteries of traversing mechanisms, elevation wheels and range card preparation. Capt. McKoy pointed out the tall guard towers that the Italians typically built at the four corners of their road guard garrisons, only three of which could be seen from their location on the kopje because of the angle.

"Left to right, Frank. On my command I want you to take them out—one, three, two."

"Can do," said the ex-Marine who was now wearing Capt. McKoy's cherished campaign hat, chewing on an unlit cigar, squinting through the No. 32 Mk1 scope.

"Fire when ready."

BAROOOOM, BAROOOOM, BAROOOOM

Watching through his binoculars, Capt. McKoy saw the guard in tower No. 1 blown over the side and the other two towers visibly shake from the impact of the .55-caliber rounds.

He was in the act of saying, "Nice shoot–" when the gate of the Blackshirt outpost was thrown open and a platoon of mounted native banda led by an Italian officer on a white Arabian horse came galloping out straight toward the kopje they were sitting on.

"Saddle up, Frank. Time to go," he ordered, realizing as he said it they were never going to get the heavy weapon disassembled, down the kopje and packed on the mules in time to get away. "Disregard— stand by to repel borders. Machine guns up!"

The two Raiding Forces Commandos came charging up the reverse slope with their Hotchkiss light machine guns at port arms, reached the top and fell into a prone position. Frank grabbed his M-1903 A-1 Springfield, rolled over and also took up a firing position. Capt. McKoy, who was armed with one of the scoped Springfields converted to 6.5-06 brought the long-range weapon up to his shoulder firing immediately. He emptied a saddle with every shot. Unfortunately, the magazine only held five rounds, and reloading was out of the question in the time available because the scope prevented the use of a stripper clip.

The banda cavalry came on line closing fast, the officer on the white horse stood in the stirrups and brought his saber down to signal the charge, and the platoon transitioned from a gallop into a dead run. At 500 yards, Frank and the two Green Jacket machine gunners commenced firing.

One of the notoriously unreliable Hotchkiss LMGs ripped off six rounds then jammed. The banda reached the bottom of the kopje urged on by the officer on the white horse and started spurring their mules up the slope. By this point Capt. McKoy had emptied the converted 6.5-06 Springfield and had his Colt .38 Super in one hand and one of his Colt Single Action .45 Peacemakers in the other.

Then the other Hotchkiss malfunctioned. Frank was cramming a stripper clip in his rifle. Capt. McKoy got a clear shot and knocked the officer on the white horse out of the saddle—dead before he hit the ground. As suddenly as it started, the charge spent itself, the banda turned tail galloping for the safety of their garrison.

"Round up that white horse," Capt. McKoy ordered the two Raiding Forces Commandos who were tinkering with their disabled Hotchkiss light machine guns. "I may want that officer's fancy saddle."

"That was close," Frank said.

"I never thought those Wops would come for us like that," Capt. McKoy shook his head, realizing he had made an inexcusable tactical error—holding his enemy in contempt.

"We're going to be a tad more careful picking our fights in the future, Frank. Got downright Western for a minute there ... looked like we might be going under."

"*Semper Fi.*"

10
HELLO LOVE

LIEUTENANT JACK MERRITT WAS SELF-CONSCIOUSLY WEARING THE insignia of a major for the first time, fully aware that it was temporary—a lightning advancement for someone who had been a corporal in the Life Guards Regiment serving in Raiding Forces four months previously. He had been plucked out of the field in the middle of a guerrilla operation deep behind enemy lines in Abyssinia and flown first to Camp Croc, then Nairobi and on to Khartoum. Major General James "Baldie" Taylor had his aide pick up Lt. Merritt at the airport and drive him to the safe house Force N used. Most Force N functions were being wound down and transferred to Kenya as the date for the invasion approached. Compared to when he had last been there, the place seemed strangely deserted.

Maj. Gen. Taylor awarded him the surprise promotion, first to acting captain then handed him major's crowns explaining, "You are an acting captain assigned to the Sudan Defense Force which accords British Officers seconded to command its units the privilege of wearing rank one grade higher—making you a major. I shouldn't bother to mention the 'acting captain' part if I were you. Best keep your exact status vague if you get my drift."

"Sir!"

"You are off to command a Motor Machine Gun Company of the 1st MMG Regiment commanded by a wild man, Major RFC "Rhino" Fosdick, 7th Hussars. Expect a real interesting next few months. The SDF considers itself a *corps elite*. Practically saved the Sudan single-handed by racing up and down the 1,200-mile border attacking Blackshirt outposts like a fire brigade. They patrolled so aggressively that the Italians were fooled into believing the Kaid had a larger force than the handful of Machine Gun Companies from the old Camel Corps that he actually had. Rhino was all over the place—you're going to enjoy serving with him."

"The SDF has a splendid reputation, sir."

"You are slated to take over 9 MMG Company. You will have three platoons of tough Sudanese warriors led by British officers lorried in 15 cwt Chevrolet V-8 trucks bristling machine guns.

"One additional Bedford truck transporting an element of Phantom Force will be attached. Phantom is Most Secret—even its name. Between us, it's a long-range communications job—to keep higher HQ in the picture about the location of their units in the field. That's classified, and no one has a need to know. Nothing like it has ever been attempted before. Keep people away from the Phantom team, Major, regardless of rank. Is that clear?"

"Clear, sir!"

"1st MMG Regiment, SDF is the spearhead of Gazelle Force commanded by a polo-playing Indian Army officer, Colonel Frank Messervy. You two ought to have a lot in common; you used to be on the Life Guards polo team, I understand."

"Yes, sir. Our squad and the Blues squad made up the first draft of Raiding Forces when it was initially being formed."

"Colonel Messervy loves to talk polo, so you should hit it off. Gazelle Force is motorized cavalry—it's going to lead the charge when 4 and 5 Indian Divisions invade Italian East Africa out of the Sudan in the next few days.

"You are to have a fighting command, Major, but remember this—you work for me ... still Force N. Is that clear?

"As polished crystal, sir."

MAJOR SIR TERRY "ZORRO" STONE AND CAPTAIN THE LADY JANE Seaborn were onboard the Hudson flying to the Kenyan port city of Mombasa. Also aboard was Brandy Seaborn. The two women knew where they were going and why. Maj. Stone did not have a clue. All he knew was that it was a surprise.

When the plane arrived they were met at the airport by a car arranged for by the local Special Operations Executive Chief-of-Station and whisked to the port facility. Waiting for them dockside was a squadron formation recently disembarked from their troop transport ship, drawn up for inspection. Astonished, Maj. Stone recognized his family regiment, the Lancelot Lancers Yeomanry. When he stepped out of the automobile the command rang out, "REGIMENT ATTENTION!"

Maj. Stone glanced at Lady Jane, "Take the salute, Sir Terry— your new command, Colonel… acting Lieutenant Colonel, that is. But you will be a full colonel since your commission is in the Sudan Defense Force."

"Jane, whatever crimes you may have perpetrated against me in days past—you are forgiven. How in the devil did you ever manage to arrange this?"

"All in good time, Colonel. Now go meet your regiment, Sir Knight."

There was not very much meeting to it. Col. Stone had been commissioned a "Third Lieutenant" in the Lancelot Lancers at age twelve. He had grown up in the unit until receiving his regular commission in the Life Guards. He knew all the officers, non-commissioned officers and most of the other ranks except for a handful of new men recently joined. He was related to more than a few. The Lancers were a single squadron horsed cavalry (Yeomanry) regiment until coming out to the Middle East where, to their horror, they had been dismounted and converted to a searchlight battery.

The highest-ranking officer present was a man he did not recognize—a darkly tanned major wearing the badges of the 11th Hussars *aka* Cherrypickers, and the Military Cross ribbon.

Family tradition dictated that a Stone always command the regiment in time of war. His older brother had been the CO up until this moment. *Now what could he have gotten up to not to be here at the head of the Lancelot Lancers today?*

Col. Stone took the salute.

"Major Black, sir," the officer introduced himself. "The regiment is ready for your inspection."

Accompanied by the Cherrypicker, Lady Jane and the Regimental sergeant-major, in peacetime his father's Master-of-the-Hunt, Col. Stone, did a leisurely walk through inspection of the ranks. The experience was nostalgic—like going back home. He knew nearly everyone, and they were clearly happy to see him—a fact the troops took no pains to conceal even though they were standing at attention.

In the rear rank he found Lieutenant Randy "Hornblower" Seaborn, DSC, RN, one of his sub-lieutenants, eight Royal Navy ratings and a Royal Marine—all members of Raiding Forces.

"What in the blazes are you doing here, Randy?"

"I came out to command the three-pound fast-firers, sir. MGB 345 is undergoing a refit. I volunteered when I found out she is to be out of action for the next four months or thereabout."

"Right," Col. Stone said, not having the vaguest idea what three-pounders he was talking about. "Why not fall out and go visit your mother, Hornblower. Later you can bring me up to speed on all things nautical."

"Yes, sir!"

After the inspection, the troops were returned to the control of the troop commanders to continue with the unloading of the regiment's vehicles and other heavy equipment. Col. Stone, Lady Jane and Major Jack Black stood on the dock and observed the process.

"Terry, let me introduce you to Jack—he has been out in Egypt with the 11th since they deployed three years ago. Officially assigned to East Africa Force as General Cunningham's Armored Car Advisor, but that was simply a ploy to steal him away from his regiment so he could serve as your second-in-command."

"Subject to your approval, naturally," Maj. Black said. "The regiment is deuced unhappy about my running off to East Africa. I can return to unit if you prefer someone else, Colonel."

The 11th Hussars were the lords of the desert, the finest armored car regiment in the world. They had recently covered themselves in glory in the fighting against the Italians at Sidi Barrani.

"Delighted to have you aboard, old stick," Col. Stone said, meaning it. "Now if someone would be so kind as to explain to me what exactly is happening, that would be nice."

"Terry," Lady Jane laughed, "you have been selected to command the reconnaissance regiment for East Africa Force in order to be in a position to serve as the liaison to Force N. Since one did not exist we had to create it for you. It was thought that no armored cars could be spared, but your father located three privately owned Rolls Royce armored cars in India used by a maharajah to hunt tigers from. In the finest tradition of the Yeomanry, he purchased all three at his own expense and had them shipped to Egypt. General Wavell was so impressed he had his staff search high and low and they found three more stored in an RAF warehouse left over from the last war. General Cunningham is going to supply three South African Dingoes.

"Rolls Royce has the guarantee that if you buy one of their cars they will send a repair representative anywhere in the world to repair it if it breaks down."

"Do not believe that applies to military models in time of war, Jane," Col. Stone said.

"Possibly not, but when I contacted the Rolls company, management immediately agreed to put together a team of fitters who volunteered for overseas service with the Lancelot Lancers. Then the firm built another two armored cars from parts left over from the last war. Also, they provided a Silver Ghost chassis they armored and outfitted as your command car."

"Outstanding!"

"When the Bradford Hotel kitchen staff learned John was behind the lines in Abyssinia and needed to be retrieved and you were going to command a regiment of armored cars to go get him, they volunteered *en masse* to come out to East Africa to cook for the Lancers. We picked the ones fit enough and outfitted a Bedford as a field kitchen—you should have the best-fed regiment in the army."

"Are you serious?"

"Jack has been a treasure trove of information. He mentioned in the early days in Palestine the 11th Hussars borrowed fast-firing anti-aircraft three-pounders from the navy. Mounted in five-ton trucks crewed by volunteer sailors, they were very effective. Since his boat is in dry dock, Randy came out to organize a similar battery for the Lancers—his father has salvaged the requisite three-pounders from a ship badly damaged in an air raid at Tobruk.

"Wesley Richards mounted No. 32 Mk1 scopes on the Boys .55-caliber Anti-Tank Rifles organic to the armored cars. Like the ones Captain McKoy had modified for Force N.

"Huge stocks of Italian weapons were captured at Sidi Barrani—I secured 100 of the .9mm MAB-38A submachine guns for issue to your regiment. John swears by them. Also I was able to obtain twenty-five of the Italian Breda 12.5mm heavy machine guns (HMGs). The RAF is phasing out their twin .303 Vickers K model air-to-air machine guns. I requisitioned forty for you to mount on your vehicles. You will have to get the fitters to design gun mounts for them.

"Bunny Featherstone has arranged for a team of South African Air Force air-ground support people from No. 40 Army Co-Cooperation Squadron to be attached to the Lancers to coordinate close air support. Our hero will be flying with the squadron for the duration to ensure you are well cooperated with."

"Excellent ... your idea?"

"No. 5 Company you have been training as lorried infantry," Lady Jane continued ignoring him, "was to be sent to Jack Merritt. Fortunately for us, in a change of plans he has been given command of an SDF Machine Gun Company, which means now it is available to be assigned to the Lancelot Lancers.

"Lastly, our old friend David Niven has brought out a hush-hush Phantom Det from the U.K. to be attached to the regiment. You will be briefed on its mission privately. And that, I believe, about covers it. Jack will fill you in on the rest."

"Jane, I have no idea how to ever repay you—on my word if it takes the rest of my life to come up with something, I shall."

"Bring John back in one piece please," Lady Jane said. "That's all I ask, Terry."

Col. Stone and Maj. Black walked down the dock to observe the unloading. The desert veteran briefed as they strolled, "At full establishment an armored car regiment has twenty-three officers, four hundred eight other ranks and fighting vehicles to consist of thirty-four Rolls Royce armored cars and five Crossleys, broken down into HQ, A, B, and C saber squadrons. Each saber squadron has a HQ and three armored cavalry troops—each built around a battle unit of three armored cars. The Crossleys carry the wirelesses and are distributed among the regimental and squadron HQs.

"The Lancelot Lancers have one understrength squadron, seven officers, one command car, eight prehistoric Rolls Royce armored cars—of which no two are configured exactly alike, three Rhino armored cars, six BSA W-M20 motorcycles painted something hideous called '#3 gas-proof khaki,' six Bedford WL three-ton trucks, half of them to be used as gun carriages for the Navy three-pound fast firers, plus the attachments Lady Jane mentioned. Even with the company of Abyssinian paratroops, sixty-five men as I understand, we are a far cry from anything close to a full-strength armored-car regiment."

"Have to make do, Jack," Col. Stone grinned. "Welcome to the absolute rump end of the Empire supply chain, old stick."

"I thought Palestine was the short end ..."

Sergeant Major Matthew Clive, the man who had taught Col. Stone how to ride a horse, walked up and saluted. "Sir, would you care to inspect the first fighting car unloaded?"

"My pleasure, Sarn't Major."

They did a slow stroll around the vintage Rolls Royce. The tall-turreted car had been painted faded chocolate, pale olive and pink-colored camouflage.

"The Lancers had never been assigned a unit road march identification symbol, sir," Sgt. Maj. Clive said. "Being horsed it was not necessary and searchlights seldom seem to travel anywhere so we had no need of one. Lady Seaborn corrected our deficiency with an insignia she said you had a history with."

When they came around to the front of the Rolls Royce, prominently painted on the bumper was a spread-eagle turquoise lizard that looked like it had been rolled over by a stone crusher.

"The lads love it, sir," Sgt. Maj. Clive said. "Lady Seaborn called it 'a lounge lizard.' "

BRIGADIER JOHN RANDAL, CAPTAIN LIONEL CHATTERHORN, WALDO, Rita, Lana and a Green Jacket manning a .55-caliber Boys AT Rifle w/ No. 32 Mk1 scope mounted were ensconced on a ridge above one of the Blackshirt main strategic roads in the dark of night. Lieutenant Butch "Headhunter" Hoolihan had set up a small perimeter around them to provide security. It was 2100 hours, and the moon was out three-quarters full.

They were located on a spur on about the same level as a small Italian garrison approximately a half mile distant across a deep gorge. Since the Blackshirts did not practice blackout during the hours of darkness, lights were showing in the camp.

Overhead could be heard the faint sound of a small aircraft engine, but the airplane was not visible to the naked eye. From the sky, over an externally-mounted loudspeaker on the airplane, a sexy voice purred, "Hello, Love. This is Pamala Plum-Martin ..."

When it was realized the woman on the loud hailer was speaking English, every Italian soldier on the base manned his weapon and blazed away at the intruder. A stunning array of tracers streaked skyward in an impressive show of pyrotechnics. The gunners did not hit a thing.

The Raiding Forces Commando, a machine gunner from the King's Royal Rifle Corps, peered through the No. 32 Mk1 scope. Using the tips of his fingers with the dexterity of a safe cracker, he began dialing the elevation and traversing mechanism on the Hotchkiss Omnibus General Purpose tripod. He was identifying and marking in the cross-hairs the exact location of the origin of the heavy fire coming from the fixed machine gun positions. When the gunner was on target, he called out the clicks to Waldo who was under a poncho with a flashlight writing the information down on a range card.

The enemy firing did not last long when it was realized Italian Grand Opera was now blaring from the invisible aircraft. When it ended, Lieutenant Pamala Plum-Martin introduced another song. On the third record, voices could be heard coming from the camp as the soldiers began to join in singing as the strains of Puccini and Verdi floated down. Soon the entire camp was awash in full-throated arias.

The aerial broadcast lasted an hour with the hypnotic voice of the woman announcing each new record in flawless Italian. At last she signed off, "*Ciao* ... this is Pamala Plum-Martin wishing you a good night. Be advised—they are out there, watching and waiting, sharpening their knives."

Then there was only silence.

Brig. Randal waited a full half hour before giving the order, "Fire 'em up."

The big .55-caliber Boys AT Rifle boomed five times in measured cadence. Every *BOOOOOM* was followed by the sound of a distinct metal-on-metal strike. Nothing in the way of tangible results could actually be observed other than sparks flying.

As Brig. Randal's party slipped away across the gorge in the night, the Italian garrison was full of unhappy, homesick, scared soldiers stationed somewhere they did not want to be, guarding a strategic road that could not be guarded. Three were dead. Every heavy 12.5mm Breda machine gun on the base had been knocked out by an armor-piercing .55-caliber round as if by the hand of God.

Hunkered down in their bunkers, the troops wondered if Pamala Plum-Martin would ever come back. They fantasized about what she looked like. The troops were so lonely it hurt.

SITUATION REPORT

The Viceroy of Italian East Africa, the Duke of Aosta Amedeo Umberto Isabella Luigi Filippo Maria Giuseppe Giovanni de Savoia-Aosta was in turmoil. Life could be a cruel mistress, and his had been caught in a downward death spiral. One minute he was New Rome's Supreme Commander of its largest colony, commander of a 350,000-man army destined to amalgamate with the colossal Italian Army in Libya and drive the English completely off the African continent. The next it all was slipping away.

Why the reversal of fortune?

Field Marshal Rodolfo Graziani's shocking defeat by Lieutenant General Archibald Wavell at Sidi Barrani meant there would be no link-up of Italian armies in Africa.

At sea, Vice Admiral Andrew Cunningham—the buccaneering brother of Major General Alan Cunningham, Commander of British East Africa Force in Kenya—had crippled the Italian fleet in its base at Taranto. Swordfish torpedo planes flown by intrepid British pilots and aircrew pressed home an air strike that sank the cream of the Italian fleet—three battleships. In a matter of minutes, tremendous damage that would take years to repair was inflicted on the port facility—the Duce's hopes and dreams of naval conquest went up in flames.

The El Wok Affair, as the remote battle of the wells on the southern Kenyan border had come to be known, was described by shell-shocked survivors straggling back as "an attack by a precision combined arms team consisting of air, armor and blood-thirsty cannibals working together like robots." Incredibly, a minor skirmish at a tiny mud fort in the middle of nowhere was having more impact on morale in Italian East Africa than the catastrophic defeats at Sidi Barrani and Taranto combined.

The highly exaggerated story of the battle propagated by the survivors and enflamed with the help of Captain Hawthorne Merryweather demoralized the Italian High Command in Addis Ababa and caused the confidence of Italian troops throughout Abyssinia to plummet.

An outright lie that the fort's commander had fled in a mule cart, concocted in a moment of euphoric military genius by Capt. Merryweather, scored a direct bulls-eye on Italian national pride. It spread by word of mouth like wildfire throughout the country and rocked enemy capitals worldwide by radio. Hitler even inquired if the story were true—then chose not to believe Mussolini's denial.

Privately, the Viceroy was much depressed by the unrelenting guerrilla war raging in the central highlands being carried out by the mysterious 1 Guerrilla Corps (Parachute), Force N led by a renegade American on the pay of the British—Brigadier John Randal. Attacks he was powerless to stop interrupted his communications, paralyzed his rail system, and made travel by road chancy. The guerrillas had everyone looking over their shoulders. The prevailing view was that a Patriot armed with a gun and a sharp knife was hiding behind every bush.

And maybe there was.

The force multiplying effect of guerrilla warfare is that for every man actually attacked 1,000 live in dread of being attacked. According to the Viceroy's daily intelligence briefs (wildly inaccurate overestimates), at any given moment there were 250,000 full-time outlaws at large with another 750,000 part-time bandits roaming the Abyssinian countryside doing random dirty deeds as the opportunity presented itself.

The Duke was convinced the American, Brig. Randal, was in fact coordinating their activities. He was being encouraged daily in that belief by a constant Chinese water torture drip, drip, drip of misinformation crafted in faraway Egypt by Lieutenant Colonel Dudley

Clarke, A-Force, and on the ground in IEA by that diabolical psychological warrior, Capt. Merryweather.

With an imaginary million shifta and a very real handful of small Force N Mule Raider Battalions active in the field, there were a lot of Italians coping with the idea of being the next victim.

To make matters worse, now the military and police tended to blame every unsolved crime, large or small, anywhere in IEA on Brig. Randal, Force N and the Patriots. With Capt. Merryweather staying up nights inventing new notional acts of guerrilla-type devilry, the equally notional one million Patriots had carried out to broadcast over the pirate radio station he had established on N-2, it is no wonder the Viceroy and his Blackshirt minions believed that the guerrillas of Force N owned the countryside.

Even though there were no Patriots.

Then there was the issue of tires. Due to a miscalculation before the war, there was a critical shortage of spare tires in IEA. The last shipment to run the British blockade was aboard a Japanese ship eighteen months previous, but "so sorry," the tires were the wrong size to fit Italian vehicles. After that the Royal Navy tightened the noose on the Red Sea ports, and there was no hope for more tires to arrive. The situation was critical and getting worse.

Thanks to Force N's Bad Boys, every road in the country was littered with broken bottle tops, nails and/or spikes. When a convoy set out it was only possible to travel in spurts because the truck drivers were constantly forced to stop and repair flats. These stops had become so common that for the last two months they had to be routinely factored into the equation of every convoy's time of arrival.

To add insult to injury, the Viceroy's personal limousine suffered at least one flat virtually every day, sometimes more. Everywhere he passed, the Duke saw the graffiti letter *N* smeared on a wall, painted on the side of a building, on a sign or even the trunk of a tree. Once he stepped out of his Alpha Romero and was mortified to see the hated *N* crudely scrawled in the dust on the trunk, making him a mobile advertisement for the rebels.

The sight of that *N* on his own automobile was the exact moment that the Duke first felt real fear deep down in his gut.

Nowadays the Viceroy had to contend with the growing realization that a general uprising by the native population was a real and present danger. The fact that he possessed more troops, more armored fighting vehicles and, in fact, more of everything including combat-experienced officers and men ten times over all the British he faced on all fronts did nothing to make the Duke feel confident. Il Duce, Mussolini, cabled him to hang on until the German General Erwin Rommel arrived to reconquer Egypt, which only accelerated his growing sense of isolation and paranoia. Who knew how long that might take? What if Gen. Rommel did not reconquer Egypt?

An invasion by the British Forces was imminent, coming from the Sudan for certain, and possibly from Kenya. The Duke's ability to ascertain the details of a southern attack, if any, had been wiped out recently when his master spy in Nairobi was recently murdered—by a jealous husband, it was rumored—of all the luck.

Each day the Viceroy's position felt more and more like that of an ancient Roman garrison commander in a far-flung corner of the dying empire, surrounded on all sides by murderous hordes of bloodthirsty vandals. Only *his* modern-day nemesis were called *Patriots*, and they were widely known for their predilection to collecting precious body parts as war trophies. Every single Italian soldier in IEA had that thought in the back of his mind every waking moment, including the Duke of Aosta.

There was one other issue—a dark secret the Duke of Aosta would never admit—not to anyone. He was not sleeping at night. Knowing that 1 Guerrilla Corps (Parachute), Force N was out there commanded by the most dangerous man in Africa was haunting him. When he closed his eyes at night, in his mind's eye he obsessed parachutes were descending. It was Brig. Randal dropping in with a team of the dreaded 10th Abyssinian Parachute Battalion to capture and steal him away in the night as described in *Jump on Bela*. The book had magically appeared all over Addis Ababa. Who knew what fate waited?

He had some very unpleasant ideas.

The Viceroy had come to the opinion the war was one great miscalculation. The Duce had dreams of conquering the English African Colonies so he could have his own army of a "million black bayonets." Mussolini had believed he needed to get into the fighting quickly because it looked like the Germans were getting ready to win it and he would miss out on his share of the spoils. The fool. Great Britain had been an ally, not their enemy, and she was not giving up.

Privately the Viceroy concluded defeat not only seemed like a possibility—it was inevitable.

And just like that—with no fanfare, no sounding of trumpets, no declaration of any kind—the Italian Army in Abyssinia went over to the defensive. The Blackshirts no longer posed an offensive threat outside IEA's borders, even though the Duke still had the opportunity and the means to invade both the Sudan and Kenya at the same time with overwhelming superiority, achieve victory and put the Axis Powers in a position to win the war.

Mentally, the Viceroy had stacked arms.

11
NIGHT FLIGHT

BRIGADIER JOHN RANDAL WAS PLANNING A LIVE-FIRE TRAINING exercise against a real live target that could shoot back. He had issued orders to his five Mule Raider Battalion commanders not to attack any of the small Italian bases located along the strategic roads. Now, tonight he was preparing to do exactly that with one platoon of Lieutenant Butch "Headhunter" Hoolihan's Force Raiding Company and one platoon of Captain Lionel Chatterhorn's company, which the Vulnerable Point's Security Wing's officer had recently formed as an "escort" for Brig. Randal.

What he had in mind was basically an experiment. He wanted to work out tactics that would allow Force N to attack the Italians in their fortified positions and inflict casualties on them without having to expose his troops to a costly direct assault. Brig. Randal's idea was to continue fine-tuning his method until he could come up with a tactical blueprint to pass on to his company commanders that they could use as a general guide.

In the past, only carefully selected Italian garrisons along the strategic roads had been harassed by Force N. Force N only targeted bases where height gave them a tactical advantage over the Italians. Not all the enemy camps were so conveniently situated. In fact, most were built on high ground. Brig. Randal did not intend to allow them to get a free pass.

On the other hand, a full-scale attack uphill on a hardened Italian position was not something he was prepared to attempt with his lightly armed troops. The successful guerrilla commander does not take casualties if he can avoid it. He inflicts them.

That meant Force N had to learn how to attack the road watch bases even when the terrain did not appear to be in its favor without having to pay a price.

The afternoon was spent carefully reconnoitering the target. Brig. Randal, Waldo, Capt. Chatterhorn and Lt. Hoolihan spent an hour on a mountain a mile distant from the Italian company-sized garrison, studying it through binoculars. The enemy position was heavily fortified, meaning it should be able to defeat a ground attack by shifta in any strength.

The Italians built their road watch bases using the cookie cutter method—they all were virtually identical. Standard Operating Procedure called for a low stone wall to be constructed around each fort's perimeter. Outside of the wall a maze of concertina wire 100 yards deep covered a minefield consisting of a belt of anti-personnel mines. In towers at the four corners of each base were observation posts. Artillery consisted of a three-tube 81mm mortar battery sandbagged in individual circular revetments. Buildings were a combination of small wooden structures and sandbagged bunkers.

At this place five Breda Model 37 12.5mm HMG positions were visible.

The plan Brig. Randal crafted was as simple as he could make it. He called his two company commanders together and issued a bare bones Frag Order.

"Lieutenant Hoolihan, work one of your platoons around to the east and move up through the woods until you can observe the enemy position. Have your men lay down in the prone and low-crawl their way partway up the slope. At 2300 hours engage the Italians with rifle fire. If the opportunity presents itself to work some of your people in close enough to engage with hand grenades, do it.

"Continue to harass the target until the signal to withdraw, which will be two green flares from my Very pistol. If for any reason you do not see the flares, pull out by 0200 hours.

"Under no circumstances are you to allow your troops to get committed to the point you cannot break contact. Is that clear?"

"Clear, sir."

"Detach your machine gun teams to Captain Chatterhorn," Brig. Randal said. "Your platoon not taking part in the attack will provide security for the Force N HQ element remaining behind tonight."

"Yes, sir."

"Captain Chatterhorn, I want you to position one of your platoons with both your LMG teams plus Hoolihan's two to the south approximately 600 yards out in the open savanna and engage the Blackshirts once Hoolihan opens up. Have the gunners fire a few bursts, shift positions, re-engage then shift again."

"I understand, sir."

"Split your platoon not taking part in the attack—one squad to provide security for the Boys rifle team and the other to provide security for my command party."

"Sir!"

"Take charge of your companies, gentlemen."

The two company commanders spent the rest of the day taking their platoon leaders, their platoon sergeants and team leaders up on the mountain to conduct their own leader's recon, issuing their operations order and readying their commands for the night's mission.

As dark approached, the three elements of the night's mission set out. Capt. Chatterhorn led his men out first. One platoon of the Force Raiding Company under Bimbashi Cord Granger remained behind to secure the overnight position containing the small mobile HQ element and the Phantom radio team.

Lt. Hoolihan was out next with his attack platoon led by Bimbashi Jack Masters. He was followed by Waldo and the two Green Jackets with the .55 Boys AT Rifle, the three mules it took to carry it and a squad detailed from Capt. Chatterhorn's company to provide security for them. The rest of Capt. Chatterhorn's men came last.

Brig. Randal, Waldo, Rita and Lana sat on their mules and watched the troops trail past then fell in at the rear of the column. The Force N commander's intention was to move to a predesignated position accessible by all three elements of the attack where he could easily be found in the event a messenger needed to deliver a hand-carried communication. And from which he could signal the withdrawal with his Very pistol.

Waldo would guide the .55-caliber Boys AT Rifle team to their firing position on the mountain.

"Mr. Treywick, ride up and tell Hoolihan and Chatterhorn to send me a message when they have their troops in position."

"Roger and Wilco," Waldo said moving out. This was a meaningless order and he knew it. Brig. Randal would have no control over events tonight other than to signal the withdrawal. The information would not do him or the mission one bit of good. On the other hand, it would not hurt anything, and it is always good for a commander to have his subordinate commanders report their actions.

This was a movement to contact, and Brig. Randal felt the old familiar butterflies in his stomach. They were reassuring, and the hard, edgy feeling he got on every mission kicked in early. He was clicked on.

The mules seemed to sense the gravity of the situation, and the column moved along at a fast clip. The night was cool. Brig. Randal was glad he was wearing his sand green parachute smock.

Lt. Hoolihan and Kaldi were sitting on their mules beside the trail waiting for him to come past.

"My men have split off," Lt. Hoolihan reported. "See you when we rally, sir."

"Good luck, Butch," Brig. Randal said. "Don't press too hard. Get the hell out of Dodge quick on my command."

"Understood, sir."

The column moved along for another half hour until Capt. Chatterhorn broke away to lead his platoon into position. His platoon was reinforced with an additional three .303 caliber Hotchkiss M-1909 light machine gun teams, giving him a total of four. From here they would strafe the Italian position once Lt. Hoolihan commenced firing.

Waldo kept marching with the Boys AT Rifle team and their security detail. They had to ride on to the mountain, then up to their pre-selected position and set up. The Green Jackets would be firing at muzzle flashes on the Italian base once the attack began. Tonight they would be shooting at the far extreme of the Boys maximum effective range.

The team had brought a double basic load of .55-caliber ammunition with them.

Brig. Randal, Lana and Rita broke off, navigating by the luminous dial on his Panerai wrist compass, escorted by the other of Capt. Chatterhorn's security squads. They walked their mules to the strategic road at a point where a small intermittent stream crossed it.

From this position, Brig. Randal could not actually see the enemy garrison, which was approximately a half-mile distant—but it was a good spot for the command party to position itself—easy for messengers to locate in the dark. It was also the Objective Rally Point (ORP).

Then they waited. And waited. And waited.

Brig. Randal decided that the waiting was worse than leading an attack element. Tension was intense. He was beginning to have doubts about the wisdom of attacking the Italians in their base. This was Capt. Chatterhorn's first combat assignment. The Abyssinian troops were basically mercenaries serving for the one Maria Theresa Thaler per day—most of Lt. Hoolihan's men had spent time in the Italian Army before deserting to Kenya and joining the 2nd Lounge Lizards. They had friends and family members in the Blackshirt Army.

From their fighting position out in the open it was going to take courage and discipline to shoot it out with an enemy who was safe behind the wire, then disengage and withdraw in good order.

A lot of things could go wrong.

Brig. Randal was pacing back and forth on the crushed stone hardball of the strategic road, swishing his ivory-handled mule tickler against his leg. The lime green luminous hands on his Rolex seemed frozen. He checked it every thirty seconds or so. As usual, every time he glanced at the watch he thought about Lady Jane. Brig. Randal wondered what she was doing tonight.

A mule clattered through the moonlight. The rider leaned down and handed the Force N commander a handwritten note from Capt. Chatterhorn. In the yellow light of his torch he read, "In position 2225 hours."

Moments later another messenger trotted up with a message from Lt. Hoolihan that read, "Ready to commence operations as ordered."

Waldo would not be sending a messenger. The time was 2300 hours—the Rolex wasn't broken after all. Rifle fire rippled through the night muffled by the thin jungle separating the Command Post (CP) from Lt. Hoolihan's platoon. The unsynchronized opening shots were greeted by even more ragged return fire from the Italian base. Then Capt. Chatterhorn's machine guns roared into action.

Through the trees tracers could be seen flashing back and forth as Lt. Hoolihan's troops began to warm to their task and the Italians began to build up their return fire. The Blackshirts were slow off the mark, but once they got into action the amount of firepower they put out was impressive. Then came the crump of their 81mm mortars.

Instantly they were followed by the booming sound of the big .55-caliber Boys AT Rifle operating in the counter-battery role. The Boys team was tasked with trying to knock out the enemy 81mm mortars or their crew, go after the HMGs and then individual rifle flashes—in that order.

Firing came in waves. It would build up to a crescendo and die down from time to time. Then it would start back up again even more intensely than before. The Italians had a significant firepower advantage.

The wind had an effect on the sound of the battle that made the gunfire sound something like a flag rippling in the breeze. There were several distinctive sounds. Capt. Chatterhorn's Hotchkiss light machine guns fired in chattering bursts sounded almost like the rounds were chasing each other. Lt. Hoolihan's riflemen, all armed with M-1903 A-1 Springfields, made a crackling like you would hear on a rifle range. The incoming Italian 81mm mortars made a loud but curiously soft *CRUUUUMP*.

The occasional random burst of Italian machine gun fire that was being fired in the direction of the ORP sounded not unlike a giant metal carpenter's ruler being rattled furiously as it cracked overhead. The ORP was in defilade. There was no way anyone in it was going to be hit by direct fire, but the rounds passing above had an invigorating effect.

The Force N firing crackled. The incoming Italian rounds snapped. There is a big difference to the trained observer. A snap means immediate personal danger and is an angry noise. Because bullets break the sound barrier, the sound of a round or string of rounds snapping by is actually heard from behind the person being shot at. When you hear a bullet snap it has already missed—that, however, does not make it a happy sound.

Brig. Randal gauged the course of the firefight by listening to and interpreting the sounds. After the initial contact, time seemed to speed up. He paced back and forth slashing his leg with the lion's tail whisk. Being in command of a battle he had virtually no control over was even more nerve-wracking than being in charge of one of the maneuver elements in close contact. He had to force himself to remain calm—something he never had to do when leading troops.

Rita and Lana, sensing his tension, stayed well out of the way.

The main concern Brig. Randal had was that his commanders not allow their troops be committed to the point they were not able to break contact when he gave the signal. Not getting pinned down was all-important. The Caproni bombers would be out at first light. He knew if his column got caught in the open in broad daylight before they could escape back into the mountains it would be a massacre.

The Italians built up a heavy volume of fire. And they sustained that rate for two hours though the firing came undulating in waves, from time to time surging as if the Blackshirts were suddenly stricken by a sense of urgency … or maybe it was panic. Brig. Randal had no idea a company-sized base camp would have laid in that much ammunition. Even considering an Italian company was four times the size of one of Force Ns, their return rate of fire was staggering. His lightly armed troops were clearly outgunned.

It was, he decided, a lesson learned.

The enemy 81mm mortars had not fired again after the opening salvo. Apparently the .55-caliber Boys AT Rifle had silenced them—or at least discouraged anyone from wanting to take the chance of firing one. However, the Breda HMGs were still going. Shooting from sandbagged bunkers, the HMGs were almost impossible to knock out barring a lucky shot through one of their firing slits.

Finally, Brig. Randal took the Very pistol off Parachute's saddle, popped the short fat barrel open and plunked in a round. He pointed the handgun at open sky in the general direction of the Italian fortification and fired first one then a second green flare. The big Very pistol bucked and it gave him a sense of satisfaction to actually be doing something positive at last.

Time went back to standing still. The wait was agonizing. Capt. Chatterhorn's orders were to have his party continue providing fire for thirty minutes after seeing the flares, thus providing cover for Lt. Hoolihan to begin moving his men back. The Hotchkiss light machine guns continued firing, but so did the M-1903 A-1 Springfields the Force Raiding Company platoon was armed with—meaning it was not breaking contact and withdrawing.

Finally Lt. Hoolihan managed to get his men in hand, and they ceased firing. After an eternity, the sound of a body of men could be heard approaching. It was one of the Force Raiding Company squads being escorted to the ORP by Bimbashi Masters. The men were walking—leading their mules.

"Give me a report, Jack."

"One man killed, sir, three wounded. None of the wounds appear to be life-threatening."

"Have your men mount up," Brig. Randal ordered. "Move out right now, make your way back independently."

That was a change of mission. Spur of the moment ideas that result in modifying well-thought-out operational plans are to be avoided in most cases. However, in Brig. Randal's mind the importance of getting at least part of his troops back to safety under cover in the mountains warranted it. The Regia Aeronautica was *the* major threat and it would be out in force at first light searching for them.

No sense taking any chances.

The wait for the remainder of the Force Raiding Company platoon to come in was excruciating—seemed to take hours. Could something have gone wrong? Were they lost? Finally the men arrived, marching single file leading their mules. Lt. Hoolihan and Kaldi brought up the rear.

Brig. Randal called out anxiously, "How did it go, Butch?"

"Well, sir," Lt. Hoolihan reported. "The lads got into the spirit of it once they realized the Italians were shooting high down the slope at us. And after the mortars ceased fire."

"Any casualties to add to Jack's report?"

"No, sir—just the four. One of the 81s got them. They were bunched up.

"Not able to advance close enough for hand grenades—Wops put a blizzard of rounds down-range. Bloody fools are still hard at it."

"Change of plans, take your men and make your way back independently," Brig. Randal said. "Jack's already marched."

"I will wait for you, sir."

"Move out, Butch," Brig. Randal ordered. "I'll be along as soon as Captain Chatterhorn comes in."

When the last of the Force Raiding Company troops had disappeared into the dark of the night, the ORP suddenly felt strangely alone. The wait for the remainder of his troops to come in was almost unbearable. Where was Capt. Chatterhorn? Was he disoriented? Captured? Time now seemed to come to a dead stop.

One of the M-1909 Hotchkiss light machine guns commenced firing again in the distance. Had the Italians counterattacked? Not likely,

Brig. Randal thought. The Blackshirts were not about to leave the safety of their fighting positions. Still ...

Men and animals could be heard walking down the strategic road toward the ORP. Bimbashi Airey McKnight, one of Capt. Chatterhorn's men from the Vulnerable Points Wing promoted to command one of the Escort Company's two platoons, came in at the head of the file. For a former security specialist now commanding a guerrilla platoon behind enemy lines he seemed remarkably casual.

"Captain Chatterhorn is right behind us, sir," Bimbashi McKnight reported. "He stayed behind with one gun to discourage any of the Wops from getting their courage up."

"Get your men mounted," Brig. Randal ordered, hoping he did not sound as relieved as he felt. "We're moving the minute he comes in."

Elements of Force N had pulled off a complicated night maneuver with a combination of tried and untried officers and men, fought a pitched battle, disengaged on command, then withdrew in good order—and they had made it look easy.

Much had been learned. Brig. Randal had some new ideas about how to improve his tactics. He was already planning to do it again.

Shortly.

12

PYRO

MAJOR JACK MERRITT REPORTED TO HIS NEW COMMAND, NO. 9 MOTOR
Machine Gun Company, Sudanese Defense Force (SDF), which was
closed up on the start line ready to roll into Abyssinia as part of Gazelle
Force when the balloon went up. No. 9 Motor Machine Gun Co. (MMG)
was expecting him. The men were drawn up in a formation that would
have made his old Life Guards regiment proud. In fact, that's what the
Sudanese soldiers reminded him of—black Life Guardsmen.

The troops were very sharp.

Since the officer he was replacing had been wounded and
evacuated, the change of command ceremony was brief. Nevertheless, it
was carried out with military precision and all due pomp and ceremony.
Assigning Maj. Merritt to No. 9 MMG Co. had been one of those rare
events in the army when a square peg is placed in a square hole.

Thanks to Major General James "Baldie" Taylor, Maj. Merritt's
reputation had preceded him. The recently departed commander had been
a virtual living legend in the SDF—a hard act to follow. However, a
decorated British Commando from one of the most prestigious cavalry
regiments in the Brigade of Guards who had been behind the lines in

Abyssinia serving as a guerrilla leader when tapped for command of No. 9 MMG Co. is not without credentials.

The Raiding Forces officer clearly knew his way around a parade ground—the inspection was as crisp as any the Sudanese had ever experienced. Without anything being said, the men got the message from the start there was not to be any slacking of standards. Professional soldiers from fighting tribes, to a man, the troops collectively heaved a sigh of relief, "everything was going to be all right."

No. 9 MMG Co. consisted of four platoons of 1935 Chevrolet gun-trucks (five gun-trucks per platoon—three rifle platoons, one three-inch mortar platoon x three mortars) plus a HQ element and a small fleet of Ford tenders. A British captain commanded each platoon (lieutenants, since by tradition officers seconded to the SDF wore rank one grade higher). The company was a highly mobile, hard-hitting outfit with a year's experience racing up and down the border of Italian East Africa from one hot spot to another. No. 9 MMG Co. operated like dragoons, mounted infantry that could dismount and go into the fight on foot while the gun-trucks provided support.

There was one additional 15 cwt Bedford truck attached to No. 9 MMG Co. It transported the Phantom Detachment consisting of one lieutenant and two other ranks guarded by two security specialists from Captain Lionel Chatterhorn's Vulnerable Points Wing Field Security Company. The security specialist had traveled out from Seaborn House for the specific task of making sure none of the Most Secret signals equipment or the operators fell into Italian hands. The Phantom truck would travel with Maj. Merritt's HQ element.

Phantom would be reporting directly to Major General William Platt, the Kaid, with copy to Lieutenant General Sir Archibald Wavell in Cairo. No one else other than Gazelle Force's commanding officer, Colonel Frank Messervy, had a need to know the exact nature of what it did. Even he did not have a need to know Phantom's entire mission. The secret radio team would also be in direct contact with 1 Guerrilla Corps (Parachute), Force N—that was classified.

Maj. Merritt's mission statement was simple. Lead the charge—find the enemy, fix him in place and finish him off when reinforcements came up. Then mount back up and continue to march—a dream assignment come true for a cavalryman.

BRIGADIER JOHN RANDAL, CAPTAIN "PYRO" PERCY STIRLING AND Waldo were lying in concealment on a ridge observing a railroad bridge that spanned a giant intermittent river two miles distant in the tan desert-like flatlands. When it rained high in the mountains, a wall of water would cascade downhill and become channelized into the deep-cut riverbed, turning it into a raging torrent in minutes. Most of the time, however, the gorge was bone-dry like it was today.

The bridge consisted of four heavy wooden trestles buried in concrete with an intricate latticework of supporting crossbeams all the way to the top—which looked to be about forty feet. There was an Italian camp located about two miles east of the railway bridge where the tracks crossed one of the New Roman Empire's strategic roads. The Blackshirts sent a patrol down the tracks every day to check for signs of sabotage. Capt. Stirling had knocked out this particular bridge once before. The Italians, being good railway men, had replaced it.

"What are you thinking?" Brig. Randal asked as he studied the bridge through his Zeiss binoculars.

"We have two options, sir," the Death or Glory Boy explained. "Last time, being short on guncotton, we simply constructed a giant bonfire around each trestle and lit it off. The wooden trestles are soaked in creosote, which makes it difficult but not impossible to burn. We finally managed to get a hot enough flame going so it weakened the structure to the point the Wops had to replace it—might do a repeat.

"Or, we could knock it down—require a lot of guncotton explosives to do the job right, but it's more certain—the Eyeties could show up and put the fire out.

"Either way, by the time the Blackshirts reconstruct it sir," Capt. Stirling added, "the invasion will be in full swing."

"Without that crossing the bad guys won't be able to rush reinforcements south to counter Cunningham until they re-bridge the gorge," Brig. Randal said. "This is a strategic target—blow it."

"I can have the explosives here by tomorrow, sir."

"We'll remain overnight on the reverse side of this ridge. Monitor the railroad the rest of the day," Brig. Randal said. "After taking down the bridge, Percy, I want you to blow every culvert and knock out as much of the rail line as possible for twenty miles in both directions. Make the Italians work for it if they want to send troops south."

"With pleasure, sir."

Capt. Stirling dispatched a party to travel to a secret location where he had cached a supply of guncotton explosives. The Railroad Wrecking Crew had clandestine caches located every 100 miles or so from the Chalbi Desert to Addis Ababa. He estimated that the bridge demolition project would require at least 300 pounds of guncotton—he ordered that 500 pounds be brought back.

"Overkill never hurts," Capt. Stirling explained cheerfully.

"Right," Brig. Randal said, remembering a certain lighthouse explosion that had taken ten years off his life. "That's why they call you 'Pyro.' "

Brig. Randal, Waldo and Capt. Stirling stayed up on the ridge until sundown observing the rail line and the Italian garrison in the distance. As dark set in, the men moved back down to the perimeter of the camp that had been set up on the reverse side of the ridgeline. A pleasant evening was being had by all sitting around the campfires customarily built inside the brush boma to discourage the odd hyena or lion. Italian patrols were not a concern—the Blackshirts never left the safety of their bases at night.

The moon was out—rat cheese gold. Tomorrow was going to be a busy day. Anticipation of the mission was running high.

"Hello love, this is Pamala Plum-Martin ..."

"What the ..." Brig. Randal said nearly spilling his cup of delicious Abyssinian coffee.

"That's Pam," Waldo chortled. "Sounds like she's 'a fixin' to serenade the Wop camp over there."

Rita and Lana were looking at each other like they were experiencing some supernatural event. Even for two Zār priestesses this was strange.

Then the music started. Unlike the first Political Warfare Executive operation that Brig. Randal had observed, there was no firing at the Walrus circling over the Italian camp. That could only mean this was not Lieutenant Pamala Plum-Martin's first visit. These Italian soldiers were looking forward to her serenade.

"Let's go take a look," Brig. Randal said.

From the top of the ridge, Brig. Randal, Waldo, Capt. Stirling, Rita and Lana could see the Blackshirt base camp.

The garrison was lit up. Italians did not practice blackout discipline in Abyssinia. The Regia Aeronautica owned the sky. The Royal Air Force did not have a night-flying capability—at least not one they admitted to. These nocturnal music aerial missions were an aberration. Besides, Pamala only played opera—she posed no threat.

The blacked-out Walrus was invisible to the naked eye. Lt. Plum-Martin announced each new song in fluent Italian. Sometimes it sounded like she was talking directly to individual men down below.

Brig. Randal said, "What do you think she's saying?"

"Pam is dedicating records to Italian soldiers in the camp by name, sir," Capt. Stirling replied. "I can understand the language a little. My brother and I had an Italian nanny, but it's been a long time."

"Whatever she's doin'," Waldo said, "it's hurtin' them Wop boys. Listenin' to Pam out here in the middle of nowhere, a long way from home with no chance o' goin' back there anytime soon—has to be cruel and unusual punishment."

After an hour the aerial music show came to an end. A final super-sexy *"Ciao.* Be careful boys—they're out there waiting and watching, sharpening their knives."

And then there was only silence—she was gone.

"Ought to be against the Geneva Convention," Waldo said. "She's hittin' 'em garlic eaters where it really hurts."

They headed back down the ridgeline and when they reached the edge of the boma where there was a gap to enter, a voice challenged, "Halt! Who goes there?"

One of the Phantom radio operators was standing sentry duty. This was his first week in Abyssinia, and he was more than a little anxious being this far behind the lines in a country where every animal wanted to eat you and the natives aspired to collect your most precious private body parts. Phantom took security seriously.

"Halt! Who goes there?" the sentry challenged again, sounding more determined the second time.

"None o' your business, Jameson," Waldo retorted. "Besides, we're coming not goin'."

"Mr. Treywick, is that you?"

"Yeah, it's me. Better not have that Springfield loaded and pointed at me, boy. You do, you'll find out right quick who's a friend or foe. Ain't in no mood to be doin' any advancin' and bein' recognized neither."

"I have a Thompson tonight, sir," the sentry replied. "Will you at least come forward to count your party in through the wire?"

"I'm fixin' to come over there and brain you if you don't cut out this nonsense in the middle of the dark o' night, boy."

"Advance then," the guard said, "all's well."

After they entered the boma and were out of earshot of the guard, Brig. Randal said, "What's the matter with you, Mr. Treywick? He was only doing his job."

"Listenin' to Pam made *me* homesick."

"You don't have a home."

"Yeah."

The mule train carrying the demolitions arrived at 1000 hours the following morning.

Lieutenant Butch "Headhunter" Hoolihan was ordered to dispatch one of his Force Raiding Company platoons to cut the landlines to the north of the Italian garrison and another to cut those to the south. The Blackshirts in Abyssinia did not have radio communications below the brigade level. They depended almost entirely on landline, and now with the lines cut they had no way to report enemy activity—meaning Force N.

Cheap Bribe was instructed to set up an ambush along the strategic road to the north of the Italian camp. He was to allow his Patriots to be seen by the garrison, however, he might catch something moving down the road. This was more of a demonstration than an actual ambush. The idea was to give the Italians something to think about when they lost their ability to communicate.

Captain Lionel Chatterhorn's assignment was to provide porters for the Railroad Wrecking Crew and to set up local security at the bridge site.

Cap. Stirling did an inventory of the blocks of guncotton, detonators and detonating cord on the pack mules. Satisfied, he ordered, "Prepare to move out in zero five."

Every available man excluding the Phantom team and their security detail hurried to mount up. Capt. Stirling led the demolition party down off the ridge into the dry riverbed to screen his approach march to the target. He was planning to do his work in broad daylight.

The fact that the Blackshirts could be able to see the demolition men for at least part of the time did not seem to bother him in the least. He had his measure of his enemy. The Italians would not come out of their fort.

Carrying out a major demolitions project is long hard work. Placing the explosives took four hours. Brig. Randal sat on Parachute, flanked by Lana and Rita, chewing a thin unlit cigar observing as the Railroad Wrecking Crew swarmed all over the trestle and the latticework placing blocks of guncotton, tying it down, inserting detonators and attaching the explosive detonating cord that would link all the blocks of guncotton. Capt. Stirling was mad with lust for more and more blocks of guncotton.

Eventually the demolitions men worked their way to the top of the bridge, and lying prone, crawled along the tracks placing explosives. They had to be visible to the Italians. The Blackshirts chose to take no action. Capt. Stirling's method was to lay the guncotton inside the tracks on both sides, each block with its own detonator, then link them all together with detonating cord. Eventually all 500 pounds of guncotton were used.

"Placement of demolitions complete, sir," Capt. Stirling reported to Brig. Randal. "Move everyone back to a safe ..."

A green and moss-mottled high-wing Caproni 133 twin-engine bomber sailed over at grassroots level, machine guns chattering. People scattered, clambering aboard their mules, men shouting, animals pitching and everyone trying to get to cover quickly—and doing a bad job of it. Although they were down in the high-walled, clay-bank riverbed and relatively safe from the air attack, it would be fair to describe the situation as panic of a high order.

Chaos reigned.

The big, beautifully camouflaged enemy ship made a wide banking turn left and came back around for another run.

"Light it off, Percy," Brig. Randal shouted, trying to keep Parachute under control. "Let's get the hell out of Dodge."

Parachute reared up on his hind legs like the movie star horse Silver in a Lone Ranger picture show. With Brig. Randal holding on for dear life, the mule lit out on the ridgeline at a dead run, heading back up the riverbed for the safety of the jungle.

The Caproni 133 dropped bombs on the second pass. The sound of the small charges on the track could be heard cooking off in sequence—like they were supposed to after the fuse burned to them. However, Capt. Stirling had *not* lit the fuse yet.

"Run for your life!" the Death or Glory Boy screamed. "It's going to blow!"

The Caproni 133 made another pass flying down the track with machine guns blazing. The bridge blew, and the last thing Brig. Randal remembered was leaning hard into a turn as Parachute raced around a bend in the riverbed and a massive explosion coming toward him, blotting out the sun.

The Caproni 133 flew straight into the blast and came out the other side with both engines streaming black smoke. The plane flew low over Gubbo Rekash's ambush position. The jubilant Patriots leapt on their mules and, waving their rifles, gave chase across the plains.

Brig. Randal came to with a worried Lt. Hoolihan, Waldo, Rita and Lana leaning over him. Dimly he recognized he was back in camp on the far side of the ridgeline. Apparently he was still alive. Full body pain from the roots of his hair to the scuffed white tips of his canvas-topped raiding boots confirmed that to be the case.

"What happened?" he croaked.

"Percy damn near got us all," Waldo said. "He *did* get Parachute."

"Parachute?" Brig. Randal struggled to sit up. "What happened to him?"

"You don't want to know," Waldo advised. "'A piece o' railroad track about as big as a lamp shade came screaming over the river bank—if that mule had taken one more step we'd be a-holding services for you right now, Brigadier.

"Parachute's dead?"

"As a mule can get."

"How many men we lose?"

"None, but there's a whole bunch of us askin,' 'what did you say—mind repeatin' that one more time?' "

"I really liked Parachute."

"Well, he didn't share the same warm fuzzy-wuzzys for you—that mule had a stone heart."

"Where's Percy?"

"He's in camp. We may need Rita and Lana to perform some Zār Cult hooey on him though," Waldo said. "The Captn's over by the fire jibberin' away in Italian—accordin' to GG he's askin' for his nanny."

13
SAILOR ON A MULE

MAJOR GENERAL JAMES "BALDIE" TAYLOR ARRIVED TO INSPECT Colonel Sir Terry "Zorro" Stone's Lancelot Lancers Yeomanry *aka* East Africa Reconnaissance Regiment. He had a personal interest in seeing to it Col. Stone was given every opportunity to get his command up and running. The regiment had traveled from Mombasa to Nairobi by train. A brief two-week refit and training period was scheduled, and then the Lancers were off to the border.

Not much time to accomplish all of the things that had to be done to turn a searchlight battery back into a cavalry squadron—in this case a reconnaissance regiment—but in the improvised war in East Africa it was all the time available.

In a chance conversation overheard by Captain the Lady Jane Seaborn between the foreman of the Rolls Royce fitters and Col. Stone, she had learned that the chassis on the Rolls Royce armored cars was the same as on the Silver Ghost luxury automobiles—the armored body could be removed and the car turned into a limousine by merely substituting bodies. This information had resulted in Lady Jane immediately placing a call to Chief Inspector Ronald McFarland.

The policeman contacted the Kenya Bureau of Motor Vehicles to obtain a list of every Rolls Royce in the colony. There were five Silver

Ghosts. Acting on Lady Jane's instructions, Special Operations Executive confiscated them under the War Powers Act.

The limousines were then turned over to Col. Stone to be converted into gun-cars by removing the stylish RR body and installing one the fitters hastily constructed out of flat metal plates and wood with a small truck bed in the back. Field-expedient gun mounts for four of the twin-barreled .303 Vickers Model K machine guns were designed and welded in place, giving the gun-cars the same firepower as a Spitfire.

Oversized truck tires with double wheels installed on the rear axle gave the gun-cars the ability to traverse even the most difficult terrain.

It was noticed that there was an ancient Royal Navy Model Rolls Royce armored car, circa 1915, built on the First Admiralty pattern, parked in front of Government House. A relic from the last war—obsolete even before that one had barely begun. The highly polished dinosaur of a fighting vehicle was standing guard parked next to an inert 75mm cannon. The armored car was not a runner—the engine salvaged long ago—only a martial decoration.

Accompanied by Lady Jane, the Rolls Royce fitters showed up unannounced at Government House. The mechanics removed the battleship-shaped armored body, loaded it on to a flatbed trailer and drove away. Left behind on the manicured front lawn was the skeleton of a machine. A building full of bureaucrats gazed out their windows wondering if that had been authorized.

The fitters installed four additional mounts for twin .303 Vickers Model K machine guns (in addition to the original .303 water-cooled Vickers mount, giving the car a total of nine machine guns). Then the mechanics bolted the ancient battleship-shaped body on the chassis of another Silver Ghost recently arrived in the colony, not on the Kenya BMV list. It had turned up at the Muthaiga Country Club driven by one of its hedonistic wastrel members, only to be promptly confiscated for war service. The stupefied owner was allowed to retain possession of his original RR luxury body, which had been left sitting in the parking lot.

Everyone at the club agreed that seemed a bit over the top—war really is hell.

When Maj. Gen. Taylor saw Lieutenant Randy "Hornblower" Seaborn, a light bulb went off. Here was an officer who worked for, though he was not a member of, both Special Operations Executive *and* the British Secret Intelligence Service running guns and agents to enemy-occupied France. The holder of the Distinguished Service Cross with two bars and the first Royal Navy officer to become parachute qualified. He was the youngest officer of his grade in the senior service.

"Lieutenant," Maj. Gen. Taylor asked, "can you ride?"

"Ride, sir?"

"A horse ... or better yet a mule."

"Never been on a mule, sir," Lt. Seaborn said. "Aunt Jane and I ride to the hounds at every opportunity. The Beaufort Hunt is strict about bloodlines—especially for the animals."

Maj. Gen. Taylor was keenly aware of the exclusivity of the Beaufort Hunt, said to be the most politically powerful social club in England. He had it on good authority Lady Jane was an international competition-class equestrian. If the young swashbuckler was able to keep up with her, he had to be a competent horseman.

"Could we find someone else qualified to command the three-pounders for Colonel Stone?"

"Yes, sir. Sub-Lieutenant Perryweather is capable," Lt. Seaborn said with a note of alarm. "Why would we want to?"

"Because I have a mission for you, Lieutenant," Maj. Gen. Taylor said. "Should you accept, your providence shall be to invade Abyssinia on a mule. Your assignment will be to act as my man accompanying the Emperor, his Patriots and Major Orde Wingate. However, you will be attached to the Frontier Battalion of the Sudan Defense Force commanded by Colonel Hugh Boustead—used to be a sailor himself. Your full duties will be classified ... I shall elaborate later."

"A sailor on a mule," Lt. Seaborn laughed, "on a secret mission with an Emperor. How could I pass that up, sir?"

"Trust me ... you will dine out on this story for the rest of your life. Even leaving out the Most Secret parts," Maj. Gen. Taylor said. "No one is ever going to believe a word of it. Get ready to ride over the rainbow straight into cloud cuckoo land."

CHEAP BRIBE AND HIS BAND OF CUTTHROATS LINKED UP WITH THE FORCE N Command Party two days later. The Patriots had chased the

Caproni 133 until it crashed, looted the airplane, and then on their way back had knocked over a five-truck convoy driving down the strategic road unawares. The shifta chief was having an extraordinary good run.

"Gubbo wants to give you somethin', Brigadier," Waldo announced as he and the old bandit strolled up to the Command Post tent where Brigadier John Randal was in a canvas chair reading the latest dispatches. The Force N commander was still feeling a bit banged up from the fall he had taken when Parachute was killed.

Cheap Bribe was grinning from ear to ear, which was painful to look at since his teeth looked like termites had gotten at them. The wily land pirate handed Brig. Randal a chocolate-colored leather Italian flying jacket with a dark sheepskin collar. A pair of British Parachute Wings was pinned on front where the previous owner's flight wings had been.

The jacket was a magnificent gift—even more so considering that the concept of giving presents was virtually unknown in Abyssinian society. In the shifta bandit world, it did not exist at all.

"What happened to the original owner?" Brig. Randal asked, unable to restrain himself.

"Ran away," Waldo translated gravely. "Must 'a cut hisself in the hurry considering how Rita and Lana spent about an hour getting the blood stains out. Butch put the wings on—Bribe asked him to."

"Does appear to be a Panerai aviator's chronometer Mr. Rekash is wearing on his wrist," Brig. Randal said. "Nice watch, Gubbo."

The jacket was cut slightly oversized when Brig. Randal slipped it on, which would allow for wearing his pistols in shoulder holsters. The leather was supple, silk lined and it felt wonderful. "Tell the man I appreciate this."

"Brigadier, I been in this loony bin country over five years and I ain't ever seen anyone give a straight-up gift before—except for tribute or maybe at the point of a gun," Waldo said.

"Really? Invite Gubbo to sit down and have a cup of coffee," Brig. Randal said. "Inform him I've been working out some tactics and need his wise counsel. Round up Butch, Lionel and Kaldi. You need to sit in on this too."

Brig. Randal laid out his thoughts. From the start, the overall Force N plan as devised by Major General James "Baldie" Taylor had called for a number of Operational Centers (OC) consisting of one officer and six other ranks to be dropped in to Force N. The OCs were to be tasked with recruiting local indigenous warriors to act in a supporting role to the Force N main force.

The problem was that Brig. Randal had never had any idea how to employ the OCs or the troops they raised. At one point he had considered scrapping the OC concept entirely and having the British personnel dropped in and used as extra stiffeners in the Mule Raider Battalions. Since no one had ever raised a guerrilla army quite the way it was being done in Abyssinia, there were no real guidelines on how to go about it. He was making it up in parts as he went along.

Now Brig. Randal had an idea he wanted to run past his indigenous troop commander. His thinking was to bring in the first OC and have it expand Gubbo Rekash's Patriots. The plan was to raise a semi-trained force with an eye to creating a cloud of local fighters who would descend on the small isolated Italian bases guarding the strategic roads and keep them in a more or less constant state of siege— but not under direct attack.

Since there was not going to be much plunder to be had—the guerrillas would be harassing the bases, not overrunning them—they would have to be paid for their effort. The Patriots doing the besieging would need stiffeners—the Operational Centers—to keep them at it.

If the idea worked, additional OCs could be dropped in to all the Mule Raider Battalions to perform the same mission.

Gubbo Rekash was a shifta commander who had survived on his wits in a country where simply staying alive in his career field was considered a major success story. He listened carefully, understanding clearly that Brig. Randal's proposal amounted to a sea change in the guerrilla campaign currently in progress.

Cheap Bribe had one question.

"When these bands are formed," Waldo interpreted, "will they fall under his authority even though they have English advisors?"

Kaldi said, "The Emperor intends to reward those who support him, sire. Loyalty, valor and numbers of troops raised in the Patriotic War of Liberation will count heavily toward the degree."

"What's that mean, exactly?"

"Should a man raise a large enough body of fighting men and personally pledge fealty to the throne, sire, it would not be difficult to envisage the Emperor bestowing on such an individual the rank of Ras."

"Cheap Bribe understand that?"

"Absolutely, sire. The King of Kings has made that perfectly clear many times in the proclamations paving the way for his return. The trouble is most Abyssinians in positions of authority are attempting to treat with both sides until they can determine which one will be the clear winner. No one is taking him up on his offer."

"Tell Gubbo," Brig. Randal said lighting a thin cigar with his battered 26th Cavalry Regiment Zippo, "volunteers for the Force N auxiliary will be required to take a blood oath to him personally."

"Damn," said Waldo. "Bribe's gonna' be a duke."

LIEUTENANT BUTCH "HEADHUNTER" HOOLIHAN SAID, "WHEN GUBBO Rekash's men captured the Italian trucks they found something interesting, sir. I am not quite sure what it is—some type of very lightweight backpack mortar—one man can carry it."

"We could use heavier firepower," Brigadier John Randal said. "You know anything about mortars, Butch?"

"I'm a light infantry Royal Marine, sir," Lt. Hoolihan replied, sounding embarrassed. "Supposed to know every weapon up to four-inch mortars. However, the Marines were underfunded—mortars became the domain of the artillery due to the budgetary restraints."

"I haven't handled a mortar much either," Brig. Randal said. "Except briefly at the Cavalry School—had about a week's training but that was over five years ago—only fired a half dozen smoke rounds."

"My men and I trained on mortars, sir," Captain Lionel Chatterhorn said. "Pretty much limited to firing illumination flares, I'm afraid."

GG came over to pour Brig. Randal a refill for his coffee, "I'm a mortar man. Everyone in an Italian Headquarters Company has to have a military specialty. Mine was the 81mm mortar—I think it is almost an exact replica of the one the U.S. Army uses."

"This is a 45mm job," Lt. Hoolihan said.

"Brixia Model 35," GG rattled off, "Two man crew served, breach loaded, trigger fired, 45mm light mortar. Weighs thirty-four pounds, fires a high explosive contact round, yellow in color with red fins, has a maximum effective range of 580 yards, and a trained crew can get off eighteen to twenty rounds per minute. The gunner, if firing from the prone position in the direct fire role utilizes the mortar's organic leather firing pads or when in the indirect fire role, the gunner sits up with the weapon between his legs—firing method dictated by the terrain.

"Special ammunition loaded in a separate magazine ignites the 45mm round when the trigger is pulled. A trained operator can drop a round on a fifty-five gallon drum at the maximum effective range. It is very accurate."

"Did Gubbo bring in any ammunition?" Brig. Randal asked.

"A couple hundred rounds, sir."

"Outstanding. Butch, get Fenwick and Ferguson over here—let's find someplace to have a live-fire demonstration. GG, you don't have any problem demonstrating this weapon against a real target? You won't have to actually fire it if you do—just show us how."

"Sir, I hate the Fascists for what they did to me—I consider myself an American like you, even though I only lived in the U.S.A. for two years."

"Well, you can be our mortar advisor until we can get someone in here who knows how to handle one."

"No problem, sir."

"Don't worry GG, not a chance of you getting out of being our cook," Brig. Randal said. "I've grown real fond of your chow."

"Me too," Waldo seconded. "Don't go gettin' killed on me, boy."

Lovat Scouts Lionel Fenwick and Munro Ferguson arrived, and a map was produced. "You two men have been checking out the Italian camps along this stretch of road," Brig. Randal said. "I need one we can obtain high ground on less than 600 yards away from the garrison—what do you recommend?"

The Scouts looked at each other. "There is always 'Old Faithful,' sir," Scout Ferguson offered.

"Old Faithful?"

"Yes, sir. We sniped the fort's commanding officer twice. The base is located less than a day's ride from here."

"Right," Brig. Randal said. "OK, let's do it—strike camp. We're moving within the hour."

When the mule column pulled out, Brig. Randal passed the word, "Keep your eyes peeled for Capronis. I've been bombed enough to last a while."

So had everyone else.

The Force N Command Party snaked its way through the mountains. The idea was to push hard, reach the target and do the shoot before nightfall. Then pull out using the cover of darkness to make good their getaway. Brig. Randal was serious about avoiding the possibility of being caught again by Italian bombers—lesson learned.

Force N Command Party set up an ORP a mile from the target. Waldo and the two Lovat Scouts rode forward to conduct a reconnaissance of the firing position. Since the Scouts knew the area, they were back in less than a half hour.

"I don't know mortars," Waldo said. "We'll see how that works out, but this is the best set-up I ever seen for shootin' up a place and scootin'. The garlic eaters at Old Faithful must be real slow learners."

The sun was beginning to sink when the small group comprising the mortar party arrived on the mountain overlooking the Italian garrison. GG was the designated gunner with Lt. Hoolihan acting as his loader. Fifteen of the yellow, high-explosive rounds with little red stabilization fins were taken out of their individual cardboard containers and primed.

"Possible to launch fifteen rounds in the air before the first one hits the ground," GG explained, "when a gunner has his gun drill perfected."

There was no chance of that happening this evening. GG set up the stubby little tube. Then he took up a firing position sitting behind the mortar with it between his legs. Taking his time but not wasting any, he fiddled with the sighting mechanism.

Down below the Italians could be observed going about their daily business blithely unawares.

GG and Lt. Hoolihan rehearsed the loading sequence several times. "Anytime, Brigadier."

Through the Zeiss binoculars, it was possible for Brig. Randal to distinguish the rank markings of individual troops on the objective. He could see their facial expressions. The Italian troops were not paying any attention to the mountain above them.

"Fire when ready."

The mortar made a soft hollow *THUUUUMP* when GG pulled the trigger. There was a slight breeze blowing into the Force N men's faces so it was possible the Blackshirts did not hear the first *THUUUUMP*. The enemy troops should have heard the long string of them that followed and known what they meant. If anyone on the objective did, there was not much in the way of reaction.

The Blackshirts had the experience of being sniped, but they had never been mortared, so they had no idea what was about to take place.

The first hollow *CRUUUUUUMPH* of an incoming mortar shell was immediately followed by a string of *CRUUUUUUUPHS*. Each round's detonation was highlighted by a small black cloud. Lt. Hoolihan's speed as a loader had improved as he ran through the sequence. The 45mm rounds exploded rapid-fire in a flurry at the end— like the grand finale at a fireworks show.

Tiny black clouds danced all over the base.

Italians scattered and went to ground, though some were clearly panicked and ran here and there before deciding on a place to take cover. One of the garrison's wooden buildings caught fire. No one bothered to expose himself trying to put out the flames.

No attempt was made at counter-battery fire. The Blackshirt mortar crews were cowering against the sandbags in the circular gun pits. They were not about to expose themselves in order to man their gun tubes.

As soon as the last round was fired from the Brixia Model 35, Lt. Hoolihan and GG began breaking it down. Not hanging around to observe the results, Force N personnel ran down the backside of the mountain to where their mules were waiting. Within a matter of minutes, the firing party was back in the ORP.

They did not dismount. The troops in the ORP were ready, waiting in the saddle. As soon as the shooters arrived, the Force N Command Party rode out.

"That was good, Butch," Brig. Randal shouted to Lt. Hoolihan. "Six hundred yards is a little close for my comfort. We're going to need bigger mortars—hit 'em from stand-off range. That's my idea of a good time. Wonder who we can find to handle them?"

"I know the man, sir."

"Who might that be?"

"Jock McDonald—been gun captain of the 40mm cannon on the MBG 345 since we came out to Africa. He's in Kenya now with Colonel Stone. Jock's a heavy weapons expert, knows everything there is to know about mortars, sir—'Right Man, Right Job'."

"McDonald—from that day I met you two Marines on the train before OPERATION TOMCAT?" Brig. Randal asked.

"I'll send for him."

14

LIVE FIRE

BRIGADIER JOHN RANDAL WRAPPED UP HIS BRIEFING FOR ALL British personnel attached to 1 Guerrilla Corps (Parachute), Force N Command Party. Included in the group were Captain "Geronimo" Joe McKoy (he had been asked to send one of his 6th Mule Raider Battalion companies but typical for him, he brought it), his company commander Lieutenant Dirk Van Rood and his two platoon leaders; Captain Lionel Chatterhorn and his two platoon leaders; Lieutenant Butch "Headhunter" Hoolihan and his two platoon leaders; Lieutenant Jeffery Tall-Castle, the officer-in-charge of Operational Center 11 who had recently parachuted in-country; Lieutenant Ralph Brothers, the Phantom team leader; Royal Marine Jock McDonald, recently arrived with a three-man 81mm mortar team; the two Green Jackets who manned the .55 Boys AT Rifle; Lovat Scouts Munro Ferguson and Lionel Fenwick; Waldo Treywick; and ex-U.S. Marine Frank Polanski. Gubbo Rekash, Kaldi, Lana and Rita were also present, as was GG.

"Tonight," Brig. Randal said in conclusion, "is a live-fire exercise intended to test our standoff combined arms capability in conjunction with a maneuver element against a fixed Italian strategic road fortification. We are not trying to overrun the enemy objective. Do not allow your troops to become engaged to the point where they cannot withdraw on my command. Do not take unnecessary casualties—the idea is to harass the Italians in a hard way then pull out and go do it again somewhere else.

"We're also attempting to integrate air support for the first time. An armed Supermarine Walrus carrying two250-pound bombs and ten organic .303-caliber Vickers machine guns flying out of N-2 is scheduled to arrive on station over the objective at 2400 hours.

"The scheme of maneuver tonight requires a lot of individual initiative on the part of each of you operating independently, particularly as you're moving your troops into position. Two red flares over the target signal begin your attack—three greens pull out.

"What are your questions?"

There were none.

"In that case, return to your commands and be prepared to move out in one hour—let's do it."

Normally Brig. Randal would have concluded a final briefing to Raiding Forces with "You all know your jobs ..." Not today. He had a lot of new officers and men who may or may not know their jobs, and they had never worked together before.

Also, it would be the first time he had ever commanded a battalion-sized operation, even though each of the three Force N companies involved were only a third the strength of a normal peacetime line infantry company.

Capt. McKoy and his Devil Dog advisor, Frank Polanski, were waiting after the briefing. "Frank's my .55 Boys operator in addition to his other duties advising me. Since you're gonna' be employing the Boys in pairs, that's where he'll be tonight—with the Green Jacket gun team. "I sorta' need to leave Dirk alone to do his job running his company, so I'm at loose ends—where do you want me, John?"

"Why don't you travel with me, Captain?"

"Long as you don't think I'll cramp your style."

"You're listed as No. 2 in the chain of command—something goes wrong I can always send you to take charge."

"Sounds like a plan. Tonight ought to be real entertaining."

"Frank," Brig. Randal said, "I was planning to have Waldo escort the Boys gun teams into place. Since you're going to be one of the gunners, you handle it."

"Can do, sir," the ex-Marine said.

"Unusual weapon you're carrying there," Brig. Randal said. "Never saw one like it."

"9mm Suomi KP-31 submachine gun sir—Finnish design, but this one was Swiss built under license," Frank said. "Got it off a member of the Emperor's Royal Bodyguard—armed and trained by Swiss mercenaries. The guard must have all been good track men—as he was hauling ass a long way away from the front and didn't have any use for an SMG."

"Frank says the Suomi goes *bang* every time you pull the trigger, which is a real important feature when you're mostly always surrounded by people that'll turn on you right quick unannounced," Capt. McKoy said. "About as ugly as that big Bergmann-Bayard 9mm Largo he's wearing on his chest—man's got unusual taste in his personal firearms."

"I noticed that," Brig. Randal said. "Carry what you like."

"Frank has turned out to be a valued advisor. He's a surgeon with the Boys .55 and a natural-born scrounger."

"Looks like he got your hat."

"Pointed out," Capt. McKoy said, "that an ostrich plume wouldn't have the same visual effect stuck on Paris Island type drill instructor headgear, so I went to Australian cut."

"Mosby's Rangers," Frank said. "Semper Fi."

BRIGADIER JOHN RANDAL LED THE COLUMN OUT CROSSING THE LINE OF Departure (LD) right on time. The Force N raiding party had a twenty-mile ride through the mountains ahead of them. It was imperative they arrive at the ORP in time for a short breather, a quick leader's recon and for a final "frag order."

Waldo, accompanied by Lovat Scouts Munro Ferguson and Lionel Fenwick, had departed ahead of the main body to provide point security. Brig. Randal was not taking any chances. Any daylight movement might result in a meeting engagement with one of the Italian-officered bandas that patrolled the countryside from time to time. Everyone kept their eyes peeled for Caproni bombers or anything else that flew.

The movement to the ORP was not expected to take more than four hours.

Once the column was moving, Brig. Randal turned the lead over to Captain "Geronimo" Joe McKoy. With Rita and Lana as his shadows, he dropped back to ride along with Royal Marine Jock McDonald's mortar section to get an update on the new Force N mortar section.

"I would have liked a few U.S. 60mm mortars sir," the young Marine briefed. "I had heard some were purchased for use by the Cavalry Division. They have about the same maximum effective range as a Boys Anti-Tank Rifle, and we could have paired them up without sacrificing either one's tactical advantage.

"None were available. In fact sir, *no* mortars were. Lady Seaborn resorted to flying in captured Italian Model 35 81mms from the stockpiles of enemy weapons taken at Sidi Barrani.

"The Italian 81mm mortar is broken down into three component groups—tube, baseplate and bipod; each weighing slightly less than fifty pounds, which makes it easily portable in three equal mule loads. Effective range is determined by the weight of the round, sir. With the light high-explosive round, weighing 7.2 pounds, we can reach out approximately 4,400 yards—with the heavy H.E. round weighing 15.1 pounds, about 1,600 yards.

"After discussion with Squadron Leader Wilcox and myself, Lady Seaborn made the decision to only fly in the light bombs—said you always believed in the 'P for Plenty' formula and thought you would want the longer range."

"She's right about that," Brig. Randal said.

"Initially we only brought one tube with us, sir. Lady Seaborn asked me to inform you that if the Model 35 works out to your liking there are enough 81mm mortars prepositioned at Camp Croc to supply one to each company in Force N. She has specialist personnel— experienced mortar personnel from the volunteers from the Cavalry Division standing by to man them—both the 45mm and the 81mms."

"Very good," Brig. Randal said. "Now, tonight what I want you to do, McDonald, is catch the wooden buildings on fire—can you do that?"

"If the Wop bases are not blacked out as briefed and we set up line-of-sight—if I can see the building I can hit it, sir."

"Light 'em up tonight, Jock, and you can put sergeant's stripes on tomorrow."

"Sir!"

The 4,400-yard maximum effective range of the Italian Model 35 mortar meant that there was virtually no target Force N could not find some place where they could set up and fire on an enemy encampment with relative impunity. Brig. Randal now had possibilities available to him undreamed of before—a development that did not bode well for Blackshirts sitting in fixed fortifications throughout mountainous central Abyssinia.

The Force N Command Party with attachments arrived at the ORP and set up a perimeter. Brig. Randal led a party consisting of each of the major element commander's forward to make a Leader's Reconnaissance. He was doing it by the book.

They dismounted below the crest of the mountain overlooking the target and moved to the top on foot. The enemy base camp was the typical company-sized Blackshirt fortifications to be found every fifty miles or so guarding strategic roads. Located on a mountain that gave it a view of the road that snaked past, the camp sat on high ground but not commanding ground. The mountain the Force N leaders were laying on as they studied the fort through their binoculars was more or less level with it, across the valley in between, about a mile away.

Brig. Randal glanced at his black-faced Rolex. The time was about an hour until sundown. He used every minute available pointing out step by step to each of his subordinate unit commanders exactly what was expected of them.

The plan was for Lieutenant Dirk Van Rood to lead his company of 6th MRB down around and behind the mountain that the Blackshirt camp was on and to make a demonstration on the far side to give the Italians the impression they were surrounded.

Captain Lionel Chatterhorn was to take one platoon of the Escort Company with the Force Raiding Company's two machine guns and the two machine guns from No. 11 Operational Center attached down into the valley, advance on the Italian position and take it under fire.

Lieutenant Butch "Headhunter" Hoolihan was to send one platoon of Force Raiding Company down the road and infiltrate past the camp while his other platoon operated to the near side of the camp. At precisely 2330 hours, working away from the Italian base, they would burn every telegraph/telephone pole that ran along the road in sight of the base. As for those Italian troops sitting inside the wires, it was not going to do their morale any good to watch the poles go up in flames one at a time, knowing they were now cut off from the outside world and surrounded by Patriots.

Lt. Hoolihan had a suggestion, "Sir, why don't I take a party and build a series of bonfires shaped like a giant arrow pointing straight at the camp? Provide Squadron Leader Wilcox something to vector on and *really* give the Wops something to think about."

"Do it, Butch," Brig. Randal said. "Merryweather would be proud of you, stud."

GG was going to take the 45mm mortar to a position down in the floor of the valley where he could set up and fire fifty rounds into the camp, pack up and return to the ORP. The signal for him to open fire would be the Boys .55-caliber rifles engaging the Italian's three 81mm mortars in their circular sandbagged revetments.

Frank Polanski would take the two Boys .55-caliber rifle teams and set up on the tip of a ridge that pointed like a finger at the enemy fort.

RM McDonald would set up his 81mm mortar down the ridgeline on the mountain not far from where the leader's reconnaissance was taking place. He was going to put fifty rounds on target then pack up and return to the mule holding point just below the ridge.

Lieutenant Jeffery Tall-Castle would observe the operation and be prepared to stay behind with No. 11 OC, Cheap Bribe and his Patriots when the Force N Command Party pulled out. His mission was to ambush the enemy relief column that would be moving down the strategic road to relieve the fort the next day.

"They'll be coming in force," Brig. Randal said. "Establish a far ambush—harass the column then break off, move to a new location down the road and set up to re-engage. Hit and run."

"Quite right, Brigadier," the former Yorkshire Dragoon Yeomanry officer replied. "Strafing attack, that's the ticket. My two Yeomanry troopers wrote the book on the Hotchkiss LMG, rotten as it is—cavalry weapon, trained with it for ages. If anyone can keep the guns going, they are the lads."

"Don't expect Cheap Bribe's boys to hit anything," Brig. Randal said. "Your machine gunners will have to do what damage is done."

The Leader's Recon made its way back to the ORP. The leaders returned to their commands and made ready to move out on their individual missions. Lt. Van Rood departed first, followed by Lt. Hoolihan, Capt. Chatterhorn, GG accompanied by a security element from the Escort Company, Frank Polanski and the Green Jackets, and last Brig. Randal and Capt. McKoy leading RM McDonald's mortar section to their position. Gubbo Rekash's Patriots with part of one platoon of the Escort Company remained behind to secure the ORP.

The mules were left at the base of the mountain with a security detail. The night was cool and clear with a three-quarters moon. RM McDonald's men muscled the mortar and the fifty rounds of 81mm mortar up to their position and began to set up just below the crest where they could see the enemy base but not be fully exposed.

Brig. Randal and his observers moved up to the high point on the crest where they had a ringside view.

In his mind's eye, he could visualize each of the elements making their movement in the dark to the point where they would initiate contact at the appointed time. This was guerrilla war at its best. Force N was going to hit an enemy who could hit back with superior firepower but would *not* counterattack or pursue—at least not in the dark.

Knowing that information gave Brig. Randal an enormous tactical advantage.

Out of the sky, unscheduled and unexpected, "Hello love, this is Pamala Plum-Martin ..."

Brig. Randal glanced at the glowing lime green hands on his Rolex... 2230 hours. Everyone wanted to get in on this one. He wondered who was flying the plane since Squadron Leader Paddy Wilcox was going to be piloting the field-expedient Walrus gunship tonight. He would have been surprised to learn that Lieutenant Pamala Plum-Martin was at the stick. Tonight was her maiden combat mission as a pilot.

"As a special treat I brought my girlfriend along to keep you company this evening—you're going to like her, boys. Take it away Lady Jane."

A husky female voice announced, "Tonight's first song is dedicated to Brigadier John Randal—I know he's listening ..."

So much for the element of surprise ... but then it did not matter much. The idea was to pound the Italian's morale into the dirt. Telling your enemy you are coming, when you actually are and there is not one thing he can do about it was psychological warfare taken to a new level—particularly a macho enemy like Italians. Using women to rub it in— Captain Hawthorne Merryweather had to be behind this.

"Lady Jane," Waldo cogitated. "Ain't that the name o' your former ex-fiancée? How's she workin' on *your* morale, Brigadier?"

The two girls serenaded the base for an hour. The aerial performance was the perfect distraction for the Force N elements creeping into position. Not one Italian in the camp was doing anything but singing along with the songs, oblivious to everything else.

"*Ciao*, boys. Before we go we have one last treat—stand by," Lt. Plum-Martin rolled in on a low-level leaflet drop over the base. The Walrus showered the troops with autographed photographs of the two girls in their swimsuits taken when they were doing their advanced reconnaissance of the Island of Rio Bonita before OPERATION LOUNGE LIZARD.

It was purely coincidence that the leaflet drop was took place at 2330 hours—the exact minute Frank was to open on the mortar revetment, when GG was scheduled to begin his fifty-round barrage of the Italian camp with his 45mm mortar and the telephone/telegraph poles started bursting into flames. The timing could not have been better. Soldiers were caught out in the open scampering around chasing pin-up photos when .55-caliber Boys rounds began to strike the three 81mm mortar tubes in their revetments and the first of GG's 45mm rounds came raining in.

Chaos reigned on the Blackshirt mountaintop camp. The thunderous barrage was short, over in minutes. But it had a good effect. Casualties littered the ground. No counterbattery fire was initiated.

After the last 45mm round exploded there was only silence. Finally, enemy soldiers began to peek out from where they had taken cover. That was the moment when the Blackshirts first saw the burning telephone/telegraph poles along the road. And in the valley down below a giant flaming arrow—pointed directly at their camp.

"Can't be a good feelin'," Waldo observed, "to be sittin' there in the dark o' night thinkin' you're surrounded by a million bad guy natives, sharp knives 'n all a-hankerin' to collect your most precious body parts with a big burnin' arrow pointin' right at ya."

"Ole Butch flat outdid hisself tonight," Capt. McKoy agreed. "Those Wops' morale hasta' be lower than whale defecation right about now."

The Italian soldiers did not have long to reflect. High in the sky overhead, Sqn. Ldr. Wilcox and Major General James "Baldie" Taylor arrived on station in the recently converted Walrus gunship and rolled in on the target. The little amphibian was a pusher type, which meant it had a hollow nose. Four twin-mounted .303 Vickers K model machine guns had been mounted in the hollow space to augment the two .303 external guns in pods on the outside of the fuselage, giving it a total of ten—more forward firing machine guns than a Spitfire carried.

In addition, the plane had hard points under its wings to support a pair of 250-pound bombs.

The two officers onboard had been briefed to expect the burning telephone/ telegraph poles, but the sight of the giant burning arrow pointed straight at their target sent them into paroxysms of laughter.

At 2400 hours Sqn. Ldr. Wilcox cut the motor and nosed down in a glide. The Walrus had been designed for launch by catapults from Royal Navy cruisers—originally intended as an artillery spotter. The airplane had an extremely strong airframe to withstand the rigorous shock of the launch. The dive was not much of a strain. Barely whispering, the ugly little amphibian swept down. Sqn. Ldr. Wilcox pickled one bomb. Then he switched the motor back on and climbed to gain altitude for a second run.

A 250-pound bomb is small as far as bombs go—unless, of course, you are the person being bombed with one.

Since the Regia Aeronautica owned the skies over Abyssinia, not one soldier in the camp had ever been on the receiving end of an airstrike. Before it could register on them exactly what had happened, Sqn. Ldr. Wilcox swooped in again and dropped his second bomb. On the second pass the Blackshirts figured it out.

All other chaos was insignificant to the panic that swept over the base after the second bombing run.

Sqn. Ldr. Wilcox spent the next fifteen minutes strafing the camp.

Brig. Randal glanced at his watch, aimed his Very pistol in the direction of the Italian base and fired a red flare. Then, as quick as he could reload, he fired one more.

On seeing the second flare, Frank Polanski re-engaged the Italian mortar emplacements.

RM McDonald dropped his first 81mm mortar round down the tube.

Capt. Chatterhorn's six .303 Hotchkiss LMGs commenced firing. He kept them under tight control. A pair of guns operating as a team would shoot a magazine, reload and relocate.

Lt. Van Rood's company opened with M-1903 A-1 Springfields and its two .303 Hotchkiss LMGs. His two platoons maneuvered using fire and movement—not following through, simply making a demonstration.

The Italian reaction was instantaneous. The troops let loose with every direct fire weapon on the base. However, the men were not aiming at anything and were not compensating for the downhill slope of their mountain location. The Blackshirts were not compensating for anything. They were simply burning up an enormous amount of ammunition as fast as they could work their weapons.

The Italian's 81 battery, not being in a covered position— overhead clearance being a requirement for a mortar because of its high angle of fire, did not get off a single round. The gun crews had suffered several casualties during the initial .55 Boys fire and 45mm mortar barrage. One tube of the three-mortar battery had been hit and damaged by an armor-piercing round. Now the mortars were taking even more hits.

The Force N 81mm mortars were pounding the base. RM McDonald walked the rounds up to the wooden structures then fired for effect. It took a while, but eventually he had all the buildings on fire.

Brig. Randal let the battle run the full two hours as briefed. Then at 0200 hours he fired three greens. The flares were the signal to rally.

"We've come a far piece, Brigadier," Waldo said as they made their way back to the ORP, "from that day when you, me and Butch took on an entire village of bad natives with a handful o' unpatriotic Patriots and a bunch of fake dummies."

In the distance on the far side of the mountain the Italians were fighting for their lives. Or so the Blackshirts thought. They were wrong.

Force N had cleared the area.

15

GIDEON FORCE

THE HUDSON BOMBER LEVELED OUT STRAIGHT AND STEADY. THE PILOT came on the intercom, "Ten minutes until green light."

Lieutenant Randy "Hornblower" Seaborn was sitting with Captain the Lady Jane Seaborn in one of the soft theater seats in the front of the aircraft. All of the plush seats behind them had been stripped out so that the aircraft, once the personal plane of the recently-promoted Middle East Commander, Field Marshal Sir Archibald Wavell, could haul air cargo and parachutists. The Hudson was on loan to Lady Jane to use to support 1 Guerrilla Corps (Parachute), Force N.

The field marshal was never going to get his airplane back. It was listed as having crashed in Abyssinia. The Hudson no longer officially existed.

"Randy, do you have your High Standard .22?"

"Yes, Aunt Jane."

"Silencer?"

"Yes, Aunt Jane."

"I have purchased two sound mules and hired a groom named Ali to accompany you. They have been trucked from Khartoum to the Frontier Battalion and will be waiting for you."

"Thanks, Aunt Jane."

"In your parachute bag is an Italian MAB-938, only everybody calls it a MAB-38 for some reason—a 9mm submachine gun. John swears by it. You brought your Colt. 38 Super?"

"I did."

"There are three sets of spare lightweight bush jackets and long twill trousers in the bag also. Your shaving utensils ..."

"We have already gone over the checklist three times, Aunt Jane."

"Quite right. Sorry, Randy. Do be careful—you know I love you."

"I love you too."

"General Taylor wants to give you one last briefing, so this is goodbye for now. Give me a kiss. Your mother told me to give you one for her."

Major General James "Baldie" Taylor was waiting in the back of the airplane. The door was open, and the sound of the air rushing in filled the fuselage. Lt. Seaborn scooted back in the approved airborne shuffle—never picking his feet up off the floor making it impossible to trip. He was wearing an X-type parachute.

"Your mission is classified Most Secret," Maj. Gen. Taylor shouted over the roar of the wind. "We are not having this conversation. Is that clear?"

"Yes, sir!"

"In the special pocket stitched inside your bush jacket—there's one sewn in each of the spares in your kit—is a waterproof containing two envelopes. You already know what they say, but I'm going to go over it one more time."

"Roger."

"In the event Wingate attempts to relieve Colonel Boustead for any reason, you are to produce envelope A and give it to Boustead—it promotes him to Brigadier, places him in command of Gideon Force."

"I understand, General."

"In the event Wingate is killed in action or incapacitated, you are to give envelope B to the Emperor. It promotes Boustead to Brigadier and puts him in command of Gideon Force. Is that clear?"

"Yes, sir."

"Now, there are only two envelopes and they both do the same thing—however there is one more contingency we need to cover. I have a direct order for you, and it's not in writing. In the event Wingate tries to relieve Boustead and ignores the orders or destroys them, you are to terminate Wingate."

"You mean assassinate him?"

"Kill the bastard—make it quick," Maj. Gen. Taylor snapped. "Is that clear, Lieutenant?"

"As it gets, sir."

"Questions?"

"What do I do if Colonel Boustead is killed, sir?"

"Boustead is bulletproof—nothing is going to happen to him. But if something should, contact me immediately using the Phantom radio. I will go back to the drawing board. Might even come in myself and take over.

"Under no circumstance can Wingate be allowed to run loose unchecked. He is not to take the Emperor to Addis Ababa until he is given permission. Wingate has been given verbal orders to that effect by the Kaid, Lt. Gen. Platt—in my presence.

"If for any reason Boustead is out of the picture and Wingate attempts to disobey those orders and drive on to the capital, you are to execute him immediately. The Emperor is not to arrive in the capital until I say so. Is that clear?"

"I understand, sir."

"One more contingency could arise. If Wingate attempts to seize the Phantom radio for his own use, you choose whichever option suits your fancy—written or verbal."

"Yes, sir."

"Hook-up and check your equipment."

"One minute," the pilot announced over the intercom.

Maj. Gen. Taylor hooked up his safety line, wedged one of his boots on one side of the door, the other on the far side, grabbed the rim running around the inside of the door with the tips of his fingers and arched his body out to make his jumpmaster check. The wind from the speed of the aircraft distorted his facial features radically. He swung back inside and commanded, "Stand in the door."

Lt. Seaborn shuffled up with his leading foot halfway over the edge in space and slapped his hands outside and flat against the skin of the aircraft. The young navy officer glanced over his shoulder at his aunt—she flashed him her heart attack smile. Then he stared straight ahead out at the horizon waiting for the next and final jump command.

"Go!"

THE EMPEROR AND HIS ENTOURAGE SET FORTH AT LONG LAST TO reclaim his throne. Escorted by a flight of three South African Hurricanes under the command of Pilot Officer Gasper "Bunny" Featherstone, the antiquated Vickers-Valentia carrying the Royal party made a bumpy landing on an improvised dirt airstrip at Um Lidia, somewhere near the Sudan/Abyssinian border.

Upon landing, the Emperor symbolically knelt down and kissed his native soil amidst a blaze of popping flash bulbs.

"Bloody fool," Colonel Hugh Boustead, MC, said out of the side of his mouth to Lieutenant Randy "Hornblower" Seaborn. "Considering the quality of the maps in this area, it's not 100 percent certain we are actually *in* Abyssinia."

One of the press members present—Leonard Mosley of the *Times*—reported, "The Abyssinian troops were ragged in their drill, the smell of camel dung was heavy in the air, the bugler collapsed from sunstroke halfway through his recital and someone had forgotten to bring the bottles of champagne from Khartoum to celebrate the event."

Not to worry, one of the British officers produced half a dozen bottles of warm beer to toast the joyous occasion.

"Never good form to hold a press conference in *advance* of a secret military operation, sir," Lt. Seaborn said, "particularly one you are going on."

"Right you are, Randy. Lucky for us we will be operating independent of this mob," Col. Boustead said. "If Wingate was half the military genius he claims to be, the fool would realize this charade with the Emperor is nothing but a distraction."

Gideon Force, as the column had been christened, led by Major Orde Wingate, DSO and the Emperor moved out and headed inland. Both men were wearing ridiculous, oversized pith helmets of the type cartoonists like to draw on Colonel Blimp characters—on the insistence of the major. His idea was to set the two of them apart. In that he succeeded. The pair looked like complete idiots.

Traveling with the Imperial party were the Crown Prince, the Duke of Harar; his sons; the warlord Ras Kassa; a bevy of deadbeat noble hangers-on; six alcoholic Australian NCOs; a handful of adventurous subaltern volunteers for Special Service from the Cavalry Division; and an equal number of British "hostilities only" officers from the African colonies intended as stiffeners and a host of illustrious members of the press.

"What a freak parade," Col. Boustead said.

The long anticipated, highly publicized re-conquest of Abyssinia was finally underway. The Emperor was going in. Not making the trip was the brand new Royal Umbrella.

The official state sunshade had been special ordered, handmade to strict specifications. It was covered in sequins and semi-precious stones and enough gold braid to outfit the Admiralty. It cost a king's ransom to have made and flown out from India.

For reasons not clear, something to do with paganism, Maj. Wingate took violent offense to the imperial sunshade. He demanded it be left behind.

Crossing a monarch who believes he is the direct descendant of Solomon and Sheba with a long memory and a history of payback is never a wise career move. Maj. Wingate did not realize it, but he had cut his own throat politically before the operation ever began.

A caravan of 25,000 camels supported Gideon Force. Maj. Wingate knew nothing about camel management. Col. Boustead, having commanded the Camel Corps of the Sudan Defense Force before the war, knew everything there was to know on the subject. Naturally, Maj. Wingate paid not the slightest attention to Col. Boustead's advice to engage only experienced Sudanese cameleers.

Instead, Maj. Wingate had hired street Arabs out of the slums of Khartoum who did not know any more about the care and maintenance of camels than the average London cab driver—but they worked cheap.

The first camel dropped dead as Gideon Force crossed the start line.

"Fool," snorted Col. Boustead, slapping his crop against his heavily polished riding boots. "Come along Randy, my boy.

"Let's go find our own war to fight."

LIEUTENANT JEFFERY TALL-CASTLE WAS IN POSITION ON A RIDGELINE overlooking the Imperial Empire's strategic road that ran past the small fort Force N had attacked the night previous. He had Gubbo Rekash's men in fighting positions from which they could see the road, but it was too steep for them to be tempted to rush down into the killing zone of the ambush if their lust for loot got the better of them.

More importantly, the Italians would not be able to dismount their vehicles and assault into the ambush.

The Yorkshire Dragoon's Yeomanry officer had chosen well. His two Hotchkiss light machine gunners could strafe at long range with little chance of effective return fire. The Blackshirts would have to dismount their vehicles and find another longer way up the mountain if they chose to counterattack.

Two other advisory teams from No. 11 Operational Center (Yorkshire Dragoons Yeomanry), each with a ten-man security detail of Cheap Bribe's Patriots, were in other positions on similar ridgelines spaced down the road with approximately a mile in between each of the three positions. The No. 11 OC men had reconnoitered the fallback ambush positions and were occupying them in anticipation of Lt. Tall-Castle executing his ambush then retreating down the backside of the ridge and bounding to the next ambush site.

Lt. Tall-Castle and the men of No. 11 OC intended to make a good showing in their first action.

The Blackshirts were en route and they were not taking any chances. From the panicked initial reports coming in from the road security base under attack, it sounded as if the entire countryside had risen. The 3rd Battalion, 12 Alpini Regiment with a troop of three Lanica armored cars reinforced by a troop of three L3 tankettes was dispatched to sort out the situation.

All up, over 1,000 Fascist troops were riding to the rescue.

The men were directed to "be prepared to fight to the death" by their regimental commander who, due to pressing administrative matters, was unable to accompany the relief column.

Lt. Tall-Castle had been a member of the Yorkshire Dragoon Yeomanry since he was 15 years old. He was a cavalryman down to the ground, with active-duty experience with the Cavalry Division in Palestine. He had read the condensed *Colonel John Mosby: Gray Ghost of the Confederacy*. And he had memorized Raiding Forces Rules for Raiding.

'Rule #1: The First Rule is There Ain't No Rules' was his personal favorite.

Today he had no intention of fighting fair. His plan was simple. Shoot up the convoy from long range, make the enemy troops dismount and climb the ridge while he was moving his men to the next preplanned fallback position. Lt. Tall-Castle's stratagem was to inflict as many casualties as possible on the Blackshirts and harass the rest by forcing them to dismount and climb mountain after mountain chasing will-of-the-wisp Patriots who would never stand and fight.

The first indication that action was imminent was a Caproni 133 sweeping low down the road. Cheap Bribe's men had been cautioned never to fire at Italian aircraft—not ever. The Patriots did what they always did when one appeared—froze perfectly still. Unless they moved or fired on the Caproni, there was almost no chance of being spotted from the air.

Gubbo's shifta were experts at becoming invisible from long experience sneaking up on unsuspecting victims. They had seen what the Capronis could do. No one moved a muscle.

In the distance came the sound of motors and, in particular, the distinct sound of Lancia IZ armored cars. The armored cars led the procession of troop-carrying trucks. Interspaced in the column were the three open-topped L3 tankettes.

When the column snaked its way into the killing zone, Lt. Tall-Castle gave the order to his two machine gunners, "Fire when ready."

The two Yorkshire Dragoon troopers manning the LMGs had drilled on the Hotchkiss light machine gun in the Yeomanry for ten years each before being mobilized and they knew the weapon's idiosyncrasies. The gunners began firing down into the open-topped troop trucks in short, professional bursts of six rounds.

Operating in pairs, the .303-caliber weapons strafed their way down the line of enemy vehicles hammering the column. Taken by surprise, Fascists were screaming and baling out over the sides of the moving trucks while being chopped down.

The convoy screeched to a halt, blocking the road, preventing the L3 tankettes spaced out in the column from rushing to the front. What they would have hoped to accomplish if they could have moved was debatable. There was no way the turretless mini-tanks could possibly elevate their two 8mm machine guns high enough to fire on the ridge.

Cheap Bribe's men opened in a ragged volley then gradually built up an impressive volume of fire. The Patriots quickly got into the spirit of shooting up a helpless enemy. This was their kind of fight—only, as usual, the Patriots were not hitting much.

After fifteen minutes, which was a very long time (generally ambushes are over in just a few short minutes), Lt. Tall-Castle signaled Gubbo to have his troops pull out. Requiring little encouragement, the Patriots scampered down the reverse slope of the ridge to their mules. The Hotchkiss gunners kept firing in measured bursts covering the guerrilla's withdrawal then packed up and pulled out.

According to plan, No. 11 OC and all native personnel beat a hasty retreat to the first preplanned fallback position. Behind them the Blackshirt convoy was still firing at the abandoned position. The Patriots had not taken one single casualty. Morale was high.

The men rode until they came to the location where half a dozen Patriots were waiting at the base of a mountain to direct them up to the second ambush site. Leaving their mules in care of the Patriots, No. 11 OC and the bulk of Cheap Bribe's men scrambled up the ridge and moved into position.

The two Yorkshire Dragoon Hotchkiss gunners spent what time they had breaking down and cleaning the two light machine guns before their next engagement. The notoriously unreliable weapons were prone to jamming unless meticulously clean. Sometimes they jammed even when perfectly maintained. Being experienced men, the gunners were not taking any chances.

The Patriots were eager at the prospects of shooting up the motorized column again. The semi-reformed bandits had no prospects of loot but had been promised an issue of two rounds of ammunition for every one they fired—a magnificent windfall profit for little risk.

From the ridge, the men had an unimpeded view of an approximate 700-yard stretch of the winding strategic road at a distance of approximately 500 yards.

The Caproni 133 appeared and began bombing the ridgeline they had just abandoned. Blackshirt troops began to form up and assault up the steep incline as soon as the bomber made its last run. The men were not really doing much more than climbing hand over hand, crawling up the steep incline. Mortar fire was being directed at the top of the ridge.

The 3rd Battalion 12th Alpini Regiment put on a fine demonstration of a combined arms attack—only it came about half an hour late.

Once the ridgeline was achieved, the Italians milled around for a while. Apparently satisfied they had put the enemy to flight, the Fascist troops returned to their trucks. Lt. Tall-Castle signaled Gubbo Rekash to get his men down under cover when the column began to move out again.

The Caproni 133, however, had disappeared and did not return.

The Italian military's almost total reliance on landline communications meant mobile units on the ground had no way to coordinate tactical air support once they were in contact with the enemy. As a result, while the Blackshirts had achieved total air superiority they could not take tactical advantage of it. The lack of radios was a deficiency in the Fascist's communications system. There was no easy way for them to correct that deficiency, and it checkmated their advantages.

The convoy rolled into the second killing zone. The Yorkshire Dragoon machine gunners ignored the Lancia IZ armored cars. Instead, they caught the thin-skinned troop carriers in a deadly cone of fire tapped out in short six-round bursts. For unreliable weapons, the LMGs were performing like Swiss watches.

The Patriots engaged, though as usual they were more sound and fury than effect.

Lt. Tall-Castle allowed the firing to continue about as long as the first ambush before ordering the planned withdrawal.

Moving like a precision drill team, Cheap Bribe's men pulled out of their fighting positions, ran down the reverse slope and mounted their mules. Breaking contact was one of their best maneuvers—perfected over years of banditry. At a gallop, Lt. Tall-Castle led the Patriots in the direction of their third preselected fallback ambush position. The site, which was on the opposite side of the strategic road, formed the base of an *L*, which meant this time the killing zone would be vertical lengthwise up the enemy column in enfilade.

The Patriots loped parallel to the road until they came to an intermittent stream bed that ran underneath the road and led around the far side of the mountain to their ambush site. They ran their mules up and over the road and back into the sandy creek bed.

As the riders came tearing around the base of the mountain, Lt. Tall-Castle almost ran headlong into Brigadier John Randal. He was sitting on a big blue-grey mule in the middle of the sandy stream bed smoking a thin cigar with Waldo, Rita and Lana flanking him.

Brig. Randal said, "You didn't really think I was going to leave you out here all by yourself did you, T-C?

16
BARBEQUE

ON THE KENYAN FRONT LIEUTENANT GENERAL ALAN CUNNINGHAM, also recently promoted like his counterpart in the Sudan, the Kaid, was in the final stages of moving up to the Italian East African border prior to the invasion. Before the launch the plan called for one last tune-up operation to blood more of his troops before the big push. Major General George "Daddy" Brink, 1 South African Division, was ordered to make yet another feint with the secondary objective of motivating the Abyssinian Rases to finally rise up in their long hoped-for and much advertised Patriot rebellion to the Italian occupation.

Since there were no Patriots, and the Rases were being cagey by playing both ends against the middle, an uprising was never going to happen. But hope springs eternal for rear echelon staff wallahs who are miles from the front earning their living sticking pins in maps and making bold estimates of the situation.

The Natal Mounted Rifles were tapped to carry out the attack. The objective was the remote water wells located at El Yibo. After a long approach march across the Chalbi desert in their dull green troop carriers, the Rifles arrived late. They were slow going into action because they became disoriented and could not find the wells.

When the Natal Mounted Rifles finally did pinpoint the Italian position, the element of surprise had been lost. The South Africans launched an attack; however, the maneuver element immediately became pinned down. The on-scene ground commander started sending back hysterical signals demanding additional artillery, air and troop support or permission to withdraw. No one bothered to inform the troops this was a demonstration to motivate some nonexistent Patriots to rise. The men believed the fate of the Empire rested on this one action.

Denied.

The battle lasted three days in the scorching hot desert sun. Troop morale was not helped when the water ran out on the first day. The armored car crews roasted in their vehicles in what they claimed was 150-degree heat. Defeat was at hand. The South Africans were ready to withdraw.

Maj. Gen. Brink arrived to personally take charge. In the heat and all the excitement of battle, he too seemed to forget the operation was merely a demonstration. The general ordered his troops to make a suicidal frontal assault. The men made their peace with their maker, said their goodbyes to their mates and went in with cold steel gleaming in the bright African sunlight.

The attack was unopposed. The Blackshirts had abandoned their position and fled.

Enemy casualties: two dead askaris, one Italian national lieutenant killed by artillery.

Friendly casualties: zero. Friendly wounded: zero

Not one casualty of any kind was inflicted on a single South African soldier in the entire three-day battle. A number of cases of sunburn were reported. The only thing injured was South African pride.

The El Yibo casualty report—or lack of—was hard to rationalize considering the amount of ordnance expended by both sides trying to kill each other at close range—including air strikes. Especially since the Natal Mounted Rifles thought they were losing the battle for most of the three days.

There was much finger-pointing. Lt. Gen. Cunningham questioned if his troops could operate in the semi-arid desert. Unspoken but much on every senior officer's mind was the question lingering since the dark days of Dunkirk ... whether or not the King's soldiers had the requisite will to fight.

There were those who thought not.

East Africa Force's three tune-up battles—all victories on paper—had in fact been failures. The Empire's combat arms had performed miserably. The only bright spots were the South African engineers and Captain Hawthorn Merryweather's Political Warfare Executive detachment.

There was no reason to expect things would improve. However, time was up. The invasion of Italian East Africa was imminent.

AT THE TIME OF THE GIDEON FORCE BORDER CROSSING CEREMONY, Major Orde Wingate had recently returned from a meeting with Field Marshal Sir Archibald Wavell in Cairo. He had developed a habit of going outside the chain of command. The mad major had been bombarding FM Wavell's headquarters at Grey Pillars with signals and memoranda criticizing his immediate superior, Colonel Dan Sanford, who had rejoined at long last after having been on the run in Abyssinia for months.

Maj. Wingate wanted his boss's job.

FM Wavell had more important things to occupy his attention than an ambitious staff major with an oversized sense of self-importance in a minor sideshow. German Lieutenant General Erwin Rommel's Afrika Korps had appeared on the scene in the Egyptian desert, Prime Minister Churchill had ordered him to dispatch precious troops he could not spare to Greece in the forlorn hope they could stave off the Nazis fighting there, and the Nazis were rattling their sabers threatening to invade Crete.

He kicked the Wingate/Sanford problem back down to the on-scene commander, Lieutenant General William Platt.

The Kaid had his own problems. He was closed up ready to launch his attack into Abyssinia. The Italians had withdrawn most of their forces from the border to the impregnable mountain fortress at Keren and were dug in there—waiting for him. Faced with what he described as an impending "ding-dong battle to root them out" in the most difficult arid mountainous terrain that any battle has ever been fought, Lt. Gen. Platt turned to Major General James "Baldie" Taylor for advice on how to solve the "Wingate problem."

"Promote Sanford to brigadier and make him the Emperor's "political advisor," Maj. Gen. Taylor counseled, having foreseen this exact scenario playing out. "Then promote Wingate to acting colonel."

"Why would I want to promote Wingate? I hate the nudist— want him out of my command!"

"Divide and conquer," Maj. Gen. Taylor said.

"We are going to lose our ability to exercise any control over Wingate the deeper he travels into Abyssinia. There is no plan to support Wingate in the field. Gideon Force, as he is now calling Mission 101, is nothing more than a diversion. Unless he starts having some success. Then you will be forced to divert some of *your* war material to Gideon Force."

"Not bloody likely!"

"Promote Sanford to brigadier and Wingate to acting colonel. Sanford will be senior, but Wingate will be in tactical command. It's a dog's breakfast. A split command is a guaranteed formula for poor performance at best and mission failure at worst.

"Either way we accomplish our object of diverting the Italians."

"Cut the orders," Lt. Gen. Platt ordered. "I will have Sanford and Wingate flown to my HQ at once to deliver the happy news—another photo opportunity for the glory hunter. You make sure Gideon Force is never, I say again—NEVER—a drain on my resources."

The new Gideon Force commander took his promotion as divine intervention direct from God. He was finally getting the respect he deserved from the "military apes."

Why Wingate believed he was qualified to be the commander of the Emperor's column was open to question.

Colonel Orde Wingate had never commanded in combat though he had been awarded the Distinguished Service Order for his work with the Jewish Night Squads in Palestine. Even then he had not been in command, he had merely been an *advisor*.

Col. Wingate was self-centered, egotistical and hardheaded. Not necessarily fatal flaws as self-confidence, resolve and determination to succeed in the face of overwhelming obstacles are generally considered desirable traits in men tapped for independent command. However, combat commanders—even the egotistical, self-centered, hardheaded ones—need to gather information, listen to subordinates, query experts, evaluate the situation then weigh the pros and cons before making a decision.

That is called leadership.

Col. Wingate neither listened to his subordinates nor sought out the advice of experts. The only opinion he valued was his own. He was no respecter of man or beast, and those who served under him soon came to find that out the hard way.

The new Gideon Force commander and Colonel Hugh Boustead, the commander of the Frontier Battalion, had a terrific row over Col. Wingate's plan to drive Bedford trucks in the column. Col. Boustead argued it was simply not feasible—the terrain was simply too rugged.

Mules that were supposed to be waiting inside Abyssinia were not forthcoming. The country's second leading commodity after nubile slave girls was mules, but the citizens would not sell any to Col. Wingate or the Emperor—mules, that is. Gideon Force could have bought all of the slave girls it desired. That should have been a red flag that Patriot cooperation was a pipe dream.

Camels were now Gideon Force's only means of transport. Col. Wingate had not taken Col. Boustead's advice on hiring experienced camel handlers either. The first camel died at the start line. They kept on falling dead virtually every step of the way. It was almost as if the animals wanted to die in protest.

A carpet of dead camels littered Gideon Force's line-of-march. Follow-on caravans had no need of a map or compass. All they had to do was follow the trail of dead carcasses.

Then Col. Wingate ordered a night march. Operations behind enemy lines during the hours of darkness are easier said than done—particularly with a mixed command consisting of mostly amateurs who had no experience working together.

To navigate, two signals would be used: 1) whistles—men spread out along the route would make a bird whistle to indicate the line-of-march; and 2) bonfires, to serve as beacons.

Col. Wingate was about to prove that it is *not always*, "Good to Have a Plan B."

The advance element dropped off the Sudanese bird whistlers and built bonfire beacons as they marched. Problems arose almost immediately. The weather was hot, dry and no one asked the Sudanese if they could whistle.

They could not. When the men tried, their throats soon became parched, and no water bottles had been supplied. Besides, not one whistler had ever heard the sound of an "English Meadowlark."

The night was dark, the elephant grass was tall and the time of the year was arid. Gideon Force was crossing a wide, grassy escarpment. The reason for the night march was to keep the Italians in the mountains from being able to see them. (Col. Wingate seemed to forget he had ordered bonfire beacons).

A high wind came up.

Since orders had not been issued to post fireguards, the signal beacons soon flared out of control. Massive grass fires raced across the plains. The flames caught men and animals. It became a death march.

Traveling independently, the Frontier Battalion watched in amazement from their overnight position high on a hill twenty miles away. In the distance the fires spread across the horizon. The plains were ablaze for miles and miles.

While observing the unfolding events, Col. Boustead and Lieutenant Randy "Hornblower" Seaborn were dining on a camp table covered with a white tablecloth, complete with crystal and sterling silver tableware attended by a full complement of military servants. The colonel, a seasoned campaigner, saw no reason to compromise on standards simply because one was in the field on active operations.

"Twenty-five thousand camels marching nose-to-tail stretch out for at least sixty-five miles," Col. Boustead said, taking a sip of brandy that had been poured from a decanter by one of the servants. "Signal fires spread out along a column that long make for a jolly big fire, Randy."

The Phantom radio team sent out messages describing a scene out of Dante's inferno. There was no way to exaggerate the disaster. The transmissions were read in disbelief in Cairo, Khartoum, Nairobi and at 1 Guerrilla Corps (Parachute), Force N Headquarters deep in the central Abyssinian mountains.

"Lunatic," Col. Boustead said. "Bet it's scaring the bloody Wops though. Probably looks like a million man army marching on Addis Ababa burning everything in their path."

"Reckon he intended that sir?" Lt. Seaborn asked.

"Lad, what you are witnessing is military folly on a colossal scale—incompetence of the highest order—nothing less. Criminal, in a word."

"One would think Colonel Wingate should have known fires would spread on the savanna in these weather conditions," Lt. Seaborn said.

"Wingate is mad as a hatter," Col. Boustead said. "But even a blind boar in the forest stumbles across a truffle on occasion."

"YOUR CAMEL," CAPTAIN "GERONIMO" JOE MCKOY PONTIFICATED, "IS a large tylopodous ruminant of the genus Camelus, having a humped back."

"Yeah," Waldo Treywick said. "There's one-humpers and two-humpers. What kind you reckon they're barbequing up north, Joe?"

"One humpers, Waldo, called Bikaners—out of Egypt."

"You know camels, Captain?" Brigadier John Randal asked.

"Some … after I got done chasing Pancho Villa down Mexico way the Great War had broke out full and a bunch of us shipped out to Africa to work with General Allenby and his Cavalry Corps against the Turks. The plan was the U.S. Army was going to transfer the First Cavalry Division to the desert instead of over to France. We was what you might call the advance party—only the rest of the boys never did show up."

"You was with Allenby? I never knowed that," Waldo said.

"I operated some with the Imperial Camel Corps, only we was in armored cars ourselves at the time."

"You served in armored cars?" Brig. Randal inquired.

"Not exactly, John. You see, the cars weren't armored. They was just plain Model As with the tops chopped off and a couple of water-cooled Browning .30-calibers bolted on 'em. We had a lot of fun riding around the burning sands in those Ford automobiles shooting up bad guys with our Browning .30s.

"Beat the tar out of getting gassed in the trenches over in France."

"Captain, I'm ordering Operational Centers dropped in to all the battalions to expand the Patriots," Brig. Randal said, changing the subject. "When you get back, the 4th and 5th MRB commanders will be waiting at your HQ. I want you to pick out an Italian road guard fort and demonstrate to them how we conducted our attack."

"Sounds like a plan, John."

"I'll visit the 3rd MRB and do the same for them," Brig. Randal said. "What's your opinion on working in close to the wire and throwing in grenades like Butch did on the first fort?"

"Don't see the sense in it," Capt. McKoy said, taking the cigar out of between his teeth to point for emphasis. "Too easy to accidentally step on a land mine or take gunshot casualties for not much gain."

"Agreed," Brig. Randal said. "Fire 'em up, demonstrate, maneuver and make feints so the Blackshirts *believe* they're being assaulted—but let's concentrate on standing off using our mortars and Boys rifles."

"Now you're talking."

"Have the Patriots ambush the relief column—hit and run. Keep the bad guys off balance."

"Real smart tactics," Capt. McKoy said. "Ain't any reason to run any chances getting in too close to the Wops."

"No need to," Waldo said. "Pam and Lady Seaborn's already done drove a knife through their hearts."

17

THE FRONTIER FALLS

HIGH COMMAND IN ADDIS ABABA WITHDREW ITS FORCES FROM THE Sudan border. Lieutenant Colonel Dudley Clarke had conducted a misinformation/deception campaign, his first, without really having a clear idea of exactly what he wanted to accomplish other than to intimidate the Italians. It worked—better than expected with unintended consequences.

Believing that the Empire Forces had massed overwhelming strength for their much advertised, long anticipated invasion of Abyssinia, the Duke of Aosta decided to pull his troops on the Sudanese border back to the mountain fortress at Keren. Now Keren was even more impregnable than before—if that were possible. That was not part of the plan.

Learning from the experience, Lt. Col. Clarke ruefully wrote his first rule of deception: "The purpose of the exercise is not to make the enemy *believe* something—the goal is to make them *do* something." He realized, too late, the idea is to influence the other side to do what *you* want them to—not draw their own conclusions and act accordingly.

Notified of the Duke of Aosta's order to pull back (gleaned from Y-Service radio intercept), Lieutenant General William Platt, the Kaid, pushed up zero hour, and the invasion was on.

Gazelle Force led by Major Jack Merritt's No. 9 Motor Machine Gun Company, Sudan Defense Force was pounding after the withdrawing Italians of the 43rd Brigade. The Blackshirts—following orders to withdraw from Kassala, fall back to Keru, then "stand and fight to the last man"—had no idea the British would be after them as quick as they were. The Fascists had not counted on polo-playing cavalryman Colonel Frank Messervy's Gazelle Force coming for them like it had been shot out of a cannon.

Nobody in the Italian Army was going to be doing any fighting to the last man. Gazelle Force did not intend to give them the opportunity. They never gave the Blackshirts a chance to stop and set up.

Maj. Merritt, operating in the van, unleashed his Sudanese and they put the pedal to the metal of their Chevrolet gun-trucks screaming after the Italian rear guard. After overrunning it, they then overran the tail of the retreating column as the Blackshirts were streaming toward Keru.

No. 9 MMG Co. was conducting the classic "cavalry in the pursuit"—dreamed about by all cavalrymen, experienced by few. Maj. Merritt was doing what he had trained for all his adult life, running a fleeing enemy to ground. The speed and violence of Gazelle Force (possibly the worst-named military unit in history—gazelles being gentle creatures) threw the Blackshirts retrograde operation into chaos.

Maj. Merritt was standing on the road to Keru with his 9mm MAB-38A submachine gun hanging loosely in one hand. The barrel was still smoking. A pile of dead Fascists were laying where they had fallen behind the barricade constructed across the strategic road. A squad of his Sudanese troopers dismounted from their gun-trucks and began clearing the obstruction by hand.

Col. Messervy, the hard-charging commander of Gazelle Force, raced up at the wheel of his personal Ford truck shouting out the rolled down window, "Bum on Jack, bum on!"

No one in Gazelle Force had a clue what "bum on" meant. It was the source of speculation among the troops. Nobody was about to ask. The colonel said—or more accurately, shouted—the phrase constantly when on the move, which was most of the time. And always when he wanted whomever he was shouting it at to hurry up.

"GRENADE!"

One of the "dead" Italian askaris raised up with an M-35 "Red Devil" grenade in hand to throw it at Col. Messervy's truck.

BRRRRRRP! Maj. Merritt's 9mm MAB-38A submachine gun ripped, knocking the Blackshirt backward. The round, red grenade flew straight up in the air then came right back down and exploded with its distinctive *CRAAAAAAAK.*

"Bum on, Jack!"

Tires spitting gravel, the Ford command truck wheeled around the clutch of startled Sudanese troopers of No. 9 MMG Co. laboring to clear the road, leaving them behind in a cloud of dust as Col. Messervy roared off, leading the charge.

Maj. Merritt's First Platoon Leader said, "Sir, the skipper's truck is unarmed, he's all alone and there is nothing out in front of us but Blackshirts."

"Best be after him then," Maj. Merritt ordered. "Someone else can finish this job. Bad form for the Colonel to be killed on your watch, meaning mine—don't let it happen."

BRIGADIER JOHN RANDAL HAD BECOME FASCINATED BY THE ITALIAN 45mm Brixia Model 35 light mortar. GG had been giving him lessons on how to operate the little weapon. It could be fired as a conventional mortar on its tripod or folded and fired from the standing position with the leather pad against the mortar man's chest.

However, Brig. Randal was not satisfied with the Italian method. He discussed his idea of a modification with Captain "Geronimo" Joe McKoy before he departed for his 6th MRB. The ex-Arizona Ranger listened carefully, examined the mortar and said, "No problem, John."

Capt. McKoy disassembled the mortar tube from the tripod and leather chest pad. Next he sawed the stock off a beat up Carcano rifle about three inches in front of the pistol grip. Then he mounted the cut-down stock on the butt of the Brixia Model 35 in place of the chest pad using a couple of shallow drilled bolts. Taking out the saw again, he cut the butt of the stock off just behind the pistol grip, drilled two holes through the underside of the pistol grip and bolted the butt back higher up on the small of the stock so that when looked at from the side, the line of the finished product was level with the tube but there was a deep 'V' at the pistol grip.

"You need as straight a stock line from muzzle to shoulder as possible to reduce recoil," Capt. McKoy explained. "Don't want any drop at all."

Last, a canvas hand protector was laced tightly around the tube.

The end result was not pretty, but it was rock solid. The Brixia mortar had been transformed into a sawed-off, 14-inch, single-barreled, breech-loading, shoulder-fired weapon. It was about two and a half feet long, weighing six and a half pounds loaded and launched a 45mm high explosive mortar round out to maximum range of 585 yards. There were no sights, but since it was possible to observe the round in flight, aim was a simple matter of watching the trajectory and explosion of the first shell then adjusting the aiming point.

Brig. Randal loved it.

"You'll have to play with it, John, using Kentucky windage," Capt. McKoy said. "Kicks about like a ten-gauge shotgun, but you get a real big bang on the other end –she's a thumper."

"Wish we'd had one," Waldo said, "when you and me was sittin' up for bad lion nearly every night. Wonder how it'd work on big-toothed elephant?"

Capt. McKoy rode out that afternoon. As the old showman was mounting his tall blue mule, Georgie, Brig. Randal said, "Keep your eyes on the Kenya border. When General Cunningham kicks off, we may have to raid the Regia Aeronautica landing grounds again."

"I'll go ahead and recon three or four, John," Capt. McKoy promised. "My boys 'll be ready. You say the word, and we'll take 'em down."

"Pass instructions to Captain Shelby and Captain Pelham-Davies to do the same," Brig. Randal ordered. "I'll tell Captain Corrigan when we go to 3rd MRB. If orders to attack the airfields don't come through, we'll hit 'em later on our own."

"See you when I see you, John."

"Roger that," Brig. Randal said. "Take it to 'em, Captain."

WALDO CAME HURRYING UP, "BIG BUNCH OF ABYSSINIANS RIDIN' UP THE valley just south of here."

"Captain Chatterhorn, Lieutenant Hoolihan—take charge of your companies and stand by to repel boarders."

The Escort Company and the Force Raiding Company commanders quickly moved out to their commands calling orders as they went. There was a bustle of movement as the Command Party prepared for the unknown. Unexpected, uninvited visitors in Abyssinia were rarely a good thing.

Rita and Lana appeared with Brigadier John Randal's personal weapons, the cut-down A-5 Browning 12-gauge and MAB-38A. The girls took up a position flanking the canvas camp chair where he sat smoking a thin cigar while awaiting developments. The M-35 Brixia 45mm was on the camp table with a half dozen of the fat little mortar rounds scattered next to it.

The weapon was an attention-getter. The stubby 45mm barrel made the gun look like it might have been originally designed for hunting dinosaurs.

Kaldi arrived with a concerned expression on his face. This was the second time a large body of Abyssinians had come calling. The last visit had ended in gunplay.

Brig. Randal sat idly swishing the black lion's tail on his ivory-handled mule tickler against his leg.

The two Lovat Scouts, Munro Ferguson and Lionel Fenwick, wrapped their arms through the slings of their Wesley-Richards 7X57mm red stag rifles and lounged against a big tree where they had an unobstructed view.

"Same bunch as last time," Waldo called out, studying the riders though his binoculars. "The one who's Ras you shot. Wonder what they want?"

"Why don't you walk down there and ask 'em?"

"Not a chance," Waldo said, never lowering the glasses while keeping his eyes on the column of riders snaking their way up the valley. "We don't have any idea who the new headman is. Could be the deceased Ras's favorite nephew who worshipped his uncle looking for payback."

"What do you think, Waldo?"

"We got position on 'em, but they outnumber us real bad. Don't look great, Brigadier, if they're hostile. Might be they'll try to swarm us."

Cheap Bribe arrived with Lieutenant Jeffery Tall-Castle. The two Yorkshire Dragoon Yeomanry Hotchkiss machine gunners were trailing them carrying their LMGs at the port arms.

"Have your machine gunners report to Captain Chatterhorn," Brig. Randal ordered the No. 11 Operational Center commander.

One of Sergeant Jock McDonald's mortar men, a volunteer for Special Service from the North Somerset Yeomanry, dashed up. "Sergeant McDonald sends his compliments sir, the 81mm mortar team is standing by for a fire mission."

"Tell Jock I want him ready to start putting out rounds on my command. Come back here on the double to act as my runner to the mortar."

"Sir!"

"You two Green Jackets ready?" Brig. Randal asked.

"Yes, sir," Rifleman Ned Pompedous responded, unruffled. The two former Swamp Fox Force men were manning the scoped Boys .55 AT Rifle positioned on a narrow finger that ran behind the CP tent. The tripod-mounted gun was fifteen feet higher up the slope than the top of the tent, but the Raiding Forces Commandos were close enough that they could speak to the Force N commander in a normal tone.

"See those riders on the white mules?" Brig. Randal said. "If this goes wrong—kill 'em."

"With pleasure, sir."

What looked to be at least 2,000 armed men rode up the valley. They came to a halt about half a mile from the Command Party camp. A single man rode forward holding up the traditional forked stick that identified him as a messenger.

"I'll go find out what the deal is," Waldo said. "You boys keep me covered."

"Try to stay out of our line of fire, Mr. Treywick," Rflmn. Pompedous said.

"You make sure to keep your finger curled on that .55's trigger, boy. Fenwick and Ferguson, same goes for you with those deer guns o' yours."

Waldo came back shortly, shaking his head, "You ain't gonna' believe this, Brigadier. The new *tillik sau* of this here bunch has come to pledge his allegiance to the Emperor. Now, he ain't a Ras 'cause only the Emperor can make you one, and the King o' Kings ain't around presently to be makin' any—but the jungle telegraph has been passing the word he's comin' back.

"Our man here wants to get on board with Force N, seein' as how you're the Conquerin' Lion o' Judah's man so he'll be in line for the Emperor to grant him a title when he gets here."

"He'll have to report to Gubbo Rekash," Brig. Randal said. "You tell him that, Mr. Treywick."

"I did," Waldo answered. "That's OK by him as long as we promise to let the Emperor know he brought us 2,000 fightin' men, Patriots all."

"What happened to the 6,000 men his predecessor claimed?"

"Must'a lied."

"Looks like you've got your work cut out for you T-C," Brig. Randal said. "Two thousand men is nearly two times all our MRBs combined—they'll need to be whipped into shape."

"Jolly good sign, sir," The No. 11 OC commander said. "A local warlord choosing to align with Force N, quite!"

"One more thing," Waldo added. "Mr. Big Shot says he's heard your favorite mule met an untimely demise. As a token of his respect and a symbol of his undying loyalty to the Emperor's designated man, he's done brought you a pair o' new saddle animals as replacements—top quality ridin' stock with royal blood lines as befits a *tillik sau* of your stature."

"Really?" Brig. Randal said. "Explain all the parts of this conversation that matter to Cheap Bribe. Then you, T-C, Kaldi and Gubbo sit down with Mr. Big Shot and work out the details. Once that's done I'll meet with him."

"Good idea, Brigadier, you ain't exactly what I'd call a master of the art of the deal," Waldo said. "Mr. Big Shot *was* a tad hesitant about ridin' on in and sittin' down and discussin' terms, considerin' what happened to the last man tried his hand at negotiationin' with you."

"Ladies," Brig. Randal said to Rita and Lana. "Let's stroll down and take a look at those mules."

THERE WAS NO MOON. IT WAS PITCH DARK. THE BLUE-BLACK SKY WAS flecked with tiny silver stars. Brigadier John Randal stood on a ridge looking across the savanna at the Italian road watch fort on a hilltop about three quarters of a mile away. The place was lit up with strings of lights. Other yellow light was coming from the windows of the handful of wooden buildings scattered around the perimeter.

Strung out along the L-shaped ridge he was standing on were the men of Force N Command Party, Cheap Bribe's Patriots and Big Shot's 2,000 new recruits. They were spaced out for nearly a mile all the way to the end of the bottom of the L. Every man had been instructed to bring his small homemade tin candleholder that was part of every Abyssinian's kit. Brig. Randal had plans for them later.

"You sure you're gonna' do this?" Waldo asked. "We've done some crazy stuff Brigadier, but what you're talkin' about tonight caps it off."

All the key Command Party players were clustered around Brig. Randal in a commander's call.

He ignored Waldo's remark. "Have your people take up position. Green Jackets, target the Italian's mortar position with your Boys. Don't let 'em engage. When I fire two red flares that's the sign to light the candles. Two greens—Sergeant McDonald, you start dropping 81mm rounds on the base.

"Any questions? OK, let's do it."

Brig. Randal shouldered a heavy pack that contained fifty 45mm rounds, slung his Beretta 38 submachine gun over his shoulder and, with his Brixia M-35 shoulder-fired mortar in hand moved down the ridge line. The ground was rough, and with no moon visibility was limited. He managed to stumble and slide his way to the bottom without falling.

His plan was to move across the open savanna to a small intermittent stream that was located approximately 450 yards from the Italian base. Waldo and the two Lovat Scouts had made a reconnaissance of the area and reported that the Blackshirts defensive minefield began on the far side of the stream bed. Brig. Randal had no intention of crossing it.

There would not be any mines in the creek because the flash floods that came out of the nearby mountains would have washed them away. The Italians had a bad (depending on your point of view) habit of installing minefields and not maintaining them. Their attitude was: "who would want to go into a minefield to check on the mines?"—which was actually not so unreasonable—who would?

Brig. Randal was breathing hard from the climb down the ridge. He paused to catch his breath and to get his bearings. The adrenalin kicked in, and he was clicked on—very aware.

Tonight was a tactical experiment. Economy of Force was an ancient principle of guerrilla warfare. He wanted to see how few people he could use to attack one of the company-sized road watch bases.

Brig. Randal also wanted to try out a psychological warfare trick he and Captain Hawthorne Merryweather had discussed a while back but never had the opportunity to test.

The Italian camp on the top of the hill was directly to his front. From the floor of the valley it seemed to be way up high. The strings of lights gave the camp a festive look, like a Mexican restaurant back home in L.A.

After a few minutes, Brig. Randal began moving toward the dry stream. When he reached it he climbed down the four-foot bank and walked along the sandy, pebble-strewn bed. Rising up on top of the hill was the Italian fort. Almost straight up from where he was, the position looked monstrous.

When he reached a point that felt right, Brig. Randal unslung the pack and opened it. The fifty stubby little 45mm mortar rounds were packed neatly. There were another five rounds in one of the billows pockets of his faded green bush jacket. The other pocket held the 9mm igniter rounds for the M-35 mortar.

Brig. Randal reached in and took a 45mm round out of the pack, loaded it into the barrel then bolted an igniter round. The way the Brixia M-35 operated, the bolt action 9mm round was fired into the primer of the 45mm mortar round, causing it to ignite and launch the shell. With the shoulder stock mounted, firing the Brixia M-35 was like shooting a sawed-off shotgun.

Walking up the stream a short distance, Brig. Randal put the Brixia M-35 to his shoulder and squeezed off a round. The explosion of the 9mm round and the 45mm mortar round was almost simultaneous and surprisingly quiet. The sound was *BLOOOOOP*.

Even as the round was in the air, Brig. Randal was reaching in his pocket and pulling out another to reload. He was working automatically by feel, going through the manual of arms to reload without looking down, watching the fort on the hill. After what seemed a long time there came a flash, a satisfying *BLAAAAM* and the sound of men shouting and screaming.

Immediately, Brig. Randal triggered a second round. Then he walked a short distance along the stream bed and fired another. His rounds were impacting the camp. He could see the small clouds of smoke from each detonation, gray-white in the night. But at that distance and because of the angle of the slope, it was hard to determine exactly what he was hitting or if he was causing any destruction.

On the fourth detonation the camp exploded in return fire. Only the Italians did not know where the rounds were coming from. They were simply firing a full 360 degrees around the perimeter into the dark. Some gunners were firing straight up thinking the fort might be under air attack.

The sound and light show was tremendous. The Blackshirts had an extraordinary number of automatic weapons and apparently an inexhaustible supply of ammunition. The Italians truly did live in fear of being overrun by rebel bandits. They were well equipped to fight off attack. And the defenders were not bashful when it came to firing their weapons, although most of the shooting was spray and pray.

Brig. Randal crouched down below the bank and reloaded. He quickly realized not much of the firing was coming his way. With the slope of the hill plus the drop off into the intermittent stream, it was all going overhead about twenty feet high. He popped up and fired off another round.

The sound of the rounds cracking overhead was incredibly loud but they were not doing any harm.

Few things are more exhilarating than being shot at and not hit. Brig. Randal worked up and down the creek, firing the Brixia M-35, trying to give the entire base the benefit of a round or two.

The weapon was supposed to kick like a ten-gauge shotgun, but in the spirit of the moment he did not feel the recoil. Watching the flashes from the detonations, Brig. Randal began to get a feel of where the rounds were landing, and he made adjustments.

The .55 Boys AT Rifle fired from the ridgeline behind him from time to time to pin down the Italian 81mm mortar crew. The Fascists never got off a single mortar round. The problem with mortars is that they cannot be fired from a covered position. The gun crews are always vulnerable to plunging fire. And unless protected by a tall revetment of sandbags around their circular pits, mortar men are exposed to small arms and shrapnel.

Since the forts had never been mortared from the time Italy had conquered Abyssinia until now, the Blackshirts never got around to constructing the sandbag protection.

For all their faults, the Italians were quite good with their mortars. If the crews could pinpoint the source of Brig. Randal's 45mm mortar barrage and man their 81s even briefly, they could make things hot for him.

Brig. Randal's plan was for the direct fire from the .55 Boys AT Rifle to convince the Blackshirt mortar men the idea of attempting to man their tubes was suicide. In the event that failed and the Italian mortars opened, then Sergeant Jock McDonald was cleared to engage immediately.

Working his way up and down the creek blooping out 45mm rounds, Brig. Randal lost track of time. He was totally wrapped up in his own private war—a modern-day gunfight. Eventually returning to the pack to resupply, he found only a few rounds left.

Time to go.

He glanced at the Rolex. To his surprise he had been fighting for almost two hours. Seemed like about twenty minutes.

The last rounds were fired off. He took his Very pistol out of the canvas holster strapped to the pack and launched two red flares. Nothing happened for a while—except the Italians blazing away. Then up on the ridge candles came on sparkling in their holders, which typically had a small round tin reflector. The lights lit up for nearly a mile in an L-shape.

It looked like there were a million of them.

When the candles lit up, the fire from the fort slacked for a moment then stopped altogether. The ceasefire lasted a heartbeat, and then Brig. Randal fired the two green flares. The firing picked back up— only the enemy was firing faster than ever before.

The candles on the L-shaped ridge made it look like the camp was partially surrounded. The Blackshirts became obsessed with the idea they were fighting for their lives. The hills were teeming with shifta. The volume of fire reached a fever pitch.

Brig. Randal ducked down below the bank and worked his way to a point where he could exit the stream bed; running hunched over, he moved back in the direction of the Force N Command Party. He wondered if he had done much damage. The little 45mm mortar rounds were not known for fragmentation.

As he ran, Sgt. McDonald's 81mm mortars were raining down on the Italian base behind him. They *were* known for their explosive power. Any significant destruction to the Italians, aside from hurt morale, was being done right now.

Brig. Randal climbed the ridge and was greeted by Rita and Lana when he reached the top.

"David and Goliath," Waldo exclaimed. "I do wish P.J. Pretorius could'a been here to see that show!"

Brig. Randal said, "Let's get the hell out of Dodge."

TWO DAYS LATER WORD ARRIVED AT 1 GUERRILLA CORPS (PARACHUTE), Force N that the base had been abandoned. Apparently the Blackshirts came to the conclusion it was indefensible. The Italian Army did not have the stomach to be surrounded.

It was a lesson learned.

Only next time instead of candles, Cheap Bribe was going to have his men make small fires. Brigadier John Randal wanted the Italians to *really* feel surrounded.

18
EAST AFRICA
RECONNAISSANCE REGIMENT

EAST AFRICA RECONNAISSANCE REGIMENT, CONSISTING OF THE reinforced Lancelot Lancers Yeomanry Regiment *aka* Lounge Lizards, was driving hard toward the Kenyan border. The regiment was en route to take up their assigned position as the tip of the spear gathering to attack into Italian East Africa. They were traveling at night over the final stretch of the 900-mile dirt road South African engineers had hacked and bulldozed through the waterless track in140-degree heat at a rate of one mile per hour. The regiment was running in complete blackout. The lead Rolls Royce armored car had nothing to guide on—but it did have the advantage of not driving through the billowing cloud of red dust that the trailing cars had to navigate.

The drivers followed the glowing cigarettes of the men in the vehicles in front. The caravan was strung out along five miles of road. It closed up in the dark jungle stretches, then sped up in the moonlit open spaces, opening up the column.

Colonel Sir Terry "Zorro" Stone was leading the convoy in his command car—an armored Rolls Royce of WWI vintage assembled from spare parts. The car had four Vickers K Model .303-caliber machine guns mounted on improvised mounts plus a pair of water-cooled M1917-Browning .303s on the main mount. No two Rolls Royce armored cars in his command were of the exact same model, configuration or armament. Three of the cars had been privately owned by a maharaja who used them for hunting tiger. Others had been improvised using wooden bodies with field-expedient armor plates bolted on, mounted on standard civilian model Silver Ghost chassis.

The Lancelot Lancers had been one of, if not *the* smallest Yeomanry Regiments on the Territorial Army list consisting of a single squadron. Upon arriving in Middle East Command, much to its dismay, the LLY had been converted into a searchlight unit then posted along the Suez Canal. Col. Stone's father, the Duke, acting in his capacity as the regiment's Colonel-in-Chief (it was the family regiment) had moved heaven and earth to get the Lancelot Lancers converted back into a fighting formation. Even going so far as to buy the three armored cars owned by the maharaja and having them shipped out to Cairo—which did the trick.

Family and regimental tradition held that a Stone always commands during time of war. The Duke had naturally expected his elder son and heir, Reginald, to remain as the commanding officer. Major General James "Baldie" Taylor had other ideas.

After reading the medical appraisal—most specifically the eighty-five percent syphilis rate of Abyssinian women—Reginald leapt at the opportunity for a job in deception at Middle East Command Headquarters. There he commanded a dummy/decoy tank brigade consisting of blow-up rubber tanks. In reality he was working for Lieutenant Colonel Dudley Clarke's A-Force ... but not cleared to know that piece of information.

East Africa Reconnaissance Regiment had undergone intensive training during the short time it had before setting off on its trek to the border. The road march was a last shakedown cruise before the Lounge Lizards (no one called them the Lancelot Lancers anymore) undertook their first combat mission. Two days before the invasion, they would slip cross the border and spy out the lay of the land.

Lieutenant General Alan Cunningham issued orders to the officers and men of East Africa Force, "Hit them, hit them hard and hit them again."

Bold talk for a commander whose troops still had yet to win their first clear-cut victory.

As the Lounge Lizards closed on the border, they began to drive past elements of the two brigades spearheading the attack. Some of the troops had been living in the field for up to four months waiting to go. One regiment, the South African Transvaal Scottish, had endured eleven straight days of bombing by Caproni 133s.

When South African Air Force fighter pilots scrambled in response to the daily air raids, they always arrived too late. Their home airfield was located too far away from the front to allow them to respond in time. The EAF ground troops had grown more and more bitter, demanding, "Where is *our* air force?"

Force N's liaison officer to the SAAF, flying alcoholic Pilot Officer Gasper "Bunny" Featherstone, finding his staff duties onerous, borrowed a Hurricane and took off alone on an unscheduled fighter sweep. By chance he arrived over the Transvaal Scottish Regiment at the exact moment a flight of six CA 133 bombers escorted by a pair of CR-42 fighters came calling.

The former member of the now virtually extinct "Millionaires Squadron," decorated ace and survivor of both the aerial Battle of France and the Battle of Britain, did not vacillate. His eyes narrowed, his fangs came down, and he rolled in to attack—only the CR-42s were nimble. Both enemy fighters turned into him, flying in trail with the front plane's machine guns spitting fire.

Plt. Off. Featherstone shot them both down—point blank—in a single head-on pass—first the lead, then the CR-42 in line astern.

The South African troops on the ground were cheering and waving their caps –standing on their trucks to get a better view of the aerial dogfight. Plt. Off. Featherstone's Hurricane came back around, and the fight was on as the Italian bomber pilots panicked, jettisoned their bombs harmlessly in the scrub brush and made a run for home. The ex-"Millionaire" was relentless. One by one the fleeing Capronis crashed—shot down by his Hurricane's eight chattering .303 machine guns. All, that is, except the sixth bomber.

Its crew bailed out—even the pilot.

The Duke of Aosta cabled Rome, "On this day I have lost two CR-4s and six CA-133s. However, we shall carry on undaunted to the death."

ON THE THIRD DAY OF LIEUTENANT GENERAL WILLIAM PLATT'S offensive attacking into Abyssinia out of the Sudan, Major Jack Merritt's No. 9 Motor Machine Gun Company, Sudan Defense Force was still out front of Gazelle Force leading the charge. The Italians were routed. No. 9 MMG Co. was not allowing them the time to catch their breath, regroup and put up a defense.

They were "bumming on"—whatever that meant.

When the lead element of the company *did* encounter resistance, it simply machine-gunned the enemy from their trucks with their organic weapons, creating a base of fire. The follow-up platoon maneuvered to flank the Blackshirt position and the Sudanese deployed, going in online with the bayonet. Those Italians who did not flee or drop their weapons and surrender immediately were shot at point-blank range or had the cold steel put to them.

Native troops are best led from the front. Maj. Merritt, doing it by the book, always traveled with the maneuver element. That meant he was in the thick of the fighting. The Sudanese of No. 9 Co. had seen long, active service prior to the invasion, previously commanded by an officer who had become a living legend during the border skirmishes. But they never had a commander who joined in the final assault with them—leading the way.

The retreating Italians blew the bridge over the Gash, but No. 9 MMG Co. got across and stormed ahead. Finally the Sudanese troops came up to the mouth of the Keru Gorge, a long, narrow valley that ran for a mile and a half through the high, rocky hills to the front of the mountains. Automatic weapon's fire sparkled from the hills. The Italians had managed to assemble all five battalions of the 41 Colonial Brigade to defend the natural barrier created by the gorge, and they were planning to stand and fight.

All of a sudden, Gazelle Force screeched to a halt—pinned down by heavy fire.

Underestimating the opposition, Colonel Frank Messervy quickly brought up his field battery of twenty-five pound guns from the 25th Field Regiment, Royal Artillery, and sent his 4th Battalion of the 11th Sikh Regiment forward. The Indians ran into a buzz-saw and sustained 150 casualties, which temporarily put a stop to the "bumming on."

Elements of Skinner's Horse mechanized reconnaissance regiment arrived. Even with the better part of Gazelle Force up, the situation at the front was still unstable. No 9 MMG Co., Skinner's Horse and the 4/11 Sikhs mechanized infantry were pinned down while the Royal Artillery was taking small arms fire.

Col. Messervy and Maj. Merritt, the commanding officer of Skinner's Horse and commander of the 4/11 Sikas, met with Captain Douglas Gray, the 25th Field Regiment's RA battery commander to discuss what to do next. While their attention was fixed on the action to their immediate front, the battery was charged by a reinforced platoon of Abyssinian Banda Cavalry that appeared out of nowhere.

Led by two Italian lieutenants mounted on white chargers with their horsetail banner and the tricolor with the Cross of Savoy waving gaily, the horsemen had come round from the north—almost to the battery's rear.

No one could believe what they were witnessing. The artillery battery they were standing in was about to be overrun by *horse cavalry*— and right now! The Blackshirts were closing fast, sixty determined men riding full-tilt, straight at them.

Several things happened more or less at the same time. Col. Messervy, unarmed (in contravention of standing orders *he* had issued that "all members of Gazelle Force carry a weapon on their person at all times") tried to wrestle a .303 SMLE rifle away from one of the British soldiers standing nearby. The British soldier fought back and refused to let him have it. The gunners swung the trail of their twenty-five pound cannons around and rapidly began cranking the barrels down preparing to fire over open sights. Maj. Merritt emptied his 9mm MAB-38A submachine gun into the front rank of the charging cavalrymen. Meanwhile, the handful of Skinner's Horse personnel present engaged with whatever individual weapons were at hand, primarily side arms.

Then the twenty-five pounders opened at point blank range, banging furiously rapid fire. The charge stopped like it had slammed into a brick wall. The Italian cavalry reformed and charged again.

The initial element of surprise now over, the gunners and other personnel calmly shot the Blackshirt troopers out of their saddles as they came. Twenty-three enemy combatants were dead on the ground with another sixteen wounded—not counting enemy injured who were able to ride away. One of the Fascist lieutenants had been killed by a twenty-five pound armor piercing (AP) round that decapitated him. The other was wounded.

The charge ended in a massacre of the cavalry, but it had been a near thing. It was a lesson learned: these Italians were made of a different cut of cloth—they would fight.

Noted by Capt. Gray of the 25 Field Regiment, RA: armor-piercing rounds against horse cavalry in the mounted charge were not much more effective than "flinging musket balls—what was needed was grape."

BRIGADIER JOHN RANDAL WITH HIS IMPROVISED 45MM BRIXIA M-35 shoulder-fired mortar was out again against one of the Italian company-sized forts found along the strategic roads. This was the fifth night in a week he had carried out his one-man attacks. Actually, there was more than one man doing the fighting, but as he refined the technique after each mission, the numbers of people involved were shrinking.

The idea was to keep pressure on the Fascists while exposing as few of his men as practical to the possibility of becoming a casualty. The little 45mm Brixia M-35 with its 575-yard maximum range was ideal for the job. Brig. Randal could work in close, but far enough away to stay out of the Italian's defensive mine fields (advance reconnaissance was a must), drop rounds into the fort, move to another location, fire the enemy up with a few rounds then relocate and do it again and again.

In military terms this was called "Economy-of-Force"—obtaining the maximum result with a minimum of men.

Brig. Randal had sound reasons for what otherwise might seem like death-wish madness: 1) create a constant state of fear—degrade the opposition's morale; 2) inflict casualties; 3) cause the enemy to expend his seemingly unlimited supply of ammunition.

Reason #1 was important because guerrilla war is waged against the enemy's mind as much as against his troops or material. Reasons #2 & #3 had dual purposes: Reason #2 reduced morale because of the fear associated with being attacked—and it produced casualties—causing a need for evacuation; reason #3 caused the enemy to deplete his ammunition supply—which required restocking.

Evacuation of casualties and ammunition resupply could be accomplished only by road. Neither wounded nor depleted ammunition bunkers could afford to wait. Convoys would come the next day. Knowing that, provided 1 Guerrilla Corps (Parachute), Force N everything it needed to set up an ambush—what, where and when.

The troops from nearby Italian forts who were forced to respond after the night attacks suffered additional casualties in the ambushes and lost irreplaceable truck transports filled with supplies. The tally of killed and wounded, and loss of material mounted resulting in lowered troop morale, need for additional medical evacuation, resupply, etc.

Brig. Randal was dictating an escalating cycle of violence at a time and place *he* selected—600 miles behind enemy lines.

The Italian High Command was learning the hard way what Brig. Randal had come to realize as a young lieutenant in the U.S. 26th Cavalry Regiment in the Philippines when he was operating against the Huks. Specifically—"never fight guerrillas when guerrillas want to fight you."

Now he was crouched behind a giant boulder in a small valley approximately 500 yards outside the perimeter of a company-sized Italian fortification located on a hill overlooking a strategic road. The Italian defenders were blazing away with everything they had as fast as they could operate their weapons. There was a continuous roar of weapons firing and bullets cracking overhead, thousands of rounds. The tracers streaking overhead made for a spectacular light show.

One thing the Italian Army did not seem to have any shortage of was small arms ammunition, and their troops were not reluctant to use it. The Fascists exercised absolutely no discipline. Shooting downhill, their angle-of-fire was invariably high.

But, as Waldo had pointed out, there "wasn't any guarantee on that."

Brig. Randal leaned around the side of the boulder and triggered the Brixia M-35.

BLOOOOOP.

In a few seconds the solid *KERCHUUUMPH* of a 45mm mortar round exploding at the top of the hill could be heard over the frenzied crackle of the firing.

The only weapons the Italians had in their arsenal that posed any significant threat to him were the three-tube 81mm mortar batteries found at each of the company-sized garrisons. Brig. Randal had two ways to neutralize the mortars. Tonight he had placed his .55 Boys AT

Rifle team on the side of a mountain with a preregistered range card targeting the Italian's 81mm tubes.

Periodically his gunners fired an interdicting armor-piercing round at the mortar battery. With any luck the Green Jackets would be able to knock the tubes out. Even if not, .55-caliber AP rounds the size of cigars zinging through the position from time to time had to have a discouraging effect on the Italian gun crew.

Secondly, he had his own 81mm mortar set up on another mountain a mile and a half away. It had line of sight to the target and was registered on its opposite numbers gun pits. Sergeant Jock McDonald had been laying down interdicting fire of two to three rounds every ten minutes since Brig. Randal had opened with his Brixia M-35.

The combination proved highly effective. The Italians had not gotten off a single round out of their 81mm mortars.

The only other Force N troops directly involved tonight were security elements provided by the Escort Company for the .55 Boys AT rifle and 81mm mortar teams and the Bad Boys who had taken on the mission of burning the telephone/telegraph poles, freeing the Force Raiding Company to carry out other operations elsewhere. Even that task had a new wrinkle—the Boys burned only the poles which ran along the strategic road past the fort in *one* direction.

The concept of the operation was to lure a convoy to be ambushed tomorrow, so it was a bad idea to knock out all communications—the bad guys needed to be able to call for help.

There was no attempt to coordinate Brig. Randal's missions with Squadron Leader Paddy Wilcox in order for him to participate in the attack with his Supermarine Walrus gunship/bomber or Lieutenant Pamala Plum-Martin to deliver one of her aerial serenades. The Phantom radio operators transmitted the coordinates and scheduled time of each attack to Camp Croc. If it were possible for either of the two to respond, that decision was left up to them to make at their discretion.

So far, Sqn. Ldr. Wilcox had been on station every night ready to work over the target the instant Brig. Randal signaled with his Very pistol that he was breaking contact.

Lt. Plum-Martin had been a no-show. She had a target list of Italian bases she was visiting on a rotating basis and had kept to her appointed rounds—though she mixed the sequence up so as not to set a predictable pattern. The Vargas Girl look-alike Royal Marine would not have put it past the Italian High Command to have a night fighter waiting if they ever knew where she was going to be at a certain time and place.

When a cloud passed over the moon, Brig. Randal decided it was a golden opportunity to move and made a dash for another boulder twenty-five yards away. That precaution was pure melodrama right out of Hollywood. There was no way the Italians could see him in the dark at this range, much less engage him. Besides, he was in defilade.

The Blackshirts were not really trying to hit him. Firing downhill would require someone to stick his head up above the berm, lean over and shoot downhill. No Italian soldier in his right mind was about to do anything as remotely stupid as that.

After pausing to catch his breath, Brig. Randal launched another 45mm round up the hill. When the shell detonated, to his delight a loud, satisfying secondary explosion instantaneously followed it, and a ring of fire spiraled skyward. A lucky hit on one of the 81mm mortar pits set off the powder charges stacked in it.

Deciding he had done enough for one night, Brig. Randal slung the Brixia M-35 over his shoulder and put up red over green flares from his Very pistol.

As he was executing the move popularly known in Raiding Forces as "getting the hell out of Dodge," both the Green Jackets and Sgt. McDonald were engaging all out. The measured *BOOM* of the Boys .55 AT rifle and the heavy *CRUUUUUMPH* of the 81mm mortar were very reassuring. The Italians went completely to ground when the big mortar rounds started impacting the camp.

Right on cue, Sqn. Ldr. Wilcox glided in and dropped a 100-pound iron bomb square on target. The Walrus carried three more just like it. Sqn. Ldr. Wilcox had gone to the smaller 100-pound bombs because he could carry more of them. He took his time putting them in, wanting to draw out the suspense. Next, the squadron leader strafed the base with the eight Vickers K model machine guns mounted in the nose of the little pusher bi-plane plus the two machine guns mounted on pods on the side of the fuselage.

Satisfied with his night's work, all ordnance expended, Sqn. Ldr. Wilcox headed home.

When Brig. Randal arrived at the ORP, Waldo Treywick was waiting with Rita Hayworth and Lana Turner standing by holding the mules.

"You've been reached out for," the ex-ivory poacher informed him. "Plane comin' in to pick you up tomorrow night at 2300 hours."

"What's it about?"

"Gen'rl Taylor flyin' in to chew your ass, personal," Waldo said, "for takin' too many chances."

19
THE COLONEL

"WHEN I WAS A BOY THE IDEA OF GOING TO SEA FASCINATED ME," Colonel Hugh Boustead said to Lieutenant Randy "Hornblower" Seaborn as the Frontier Battalion marched into the heart of Abyssinia. The two were plodding along on their mules. "Join the Navy and sail the seven seas ... that was the life for me!

"Arrangements were made, and I went to all the right schools— same ones you did Randy lad, Dartmouth in the end. Only after a couple of cadet cruises it occurred to me loud and clear I bloody despised being on a ship—grease, grime and hot as Hades down in the engine room and the sound of the guns ... well let's just say it was a bad fit—hated engineering and being seasick. Loved horses and realized the cavalry was where to serve."

"So you left the Navy, sir?"

"No, not then. Parents intervened, convinced me to stay and give it a chance. So I was commissioned a Midshipman aboard the old HMS *Hyacinth* stationed off the Cape Station about the time the last war broke out.

"After a year with no action I'd volunteered for the Naval Air Service, but the admiral turned it down. One day while ashore I saw a poster announcing a South African Brigade was being formed in the

Transvaal for service in France. That was all I needed. Jumped ship, joined the South African Scottish as a private under an assumed name and ended up in the trenches in France on the Western Front."

"Must have been a real experience, sir."

"Whisbangs and snipers laying out in the flowers were the real problem—became a sniper myself ... less confining out between the lines than in the trenches. Winston Churchill, our present Prime Minister, commanded the Royal Scots Fusiliers, one of our neighboring units— saw him once three years before when he was the First Sea Lord."

"The Prime Minister commanded a battalion in the Great War?" Lt. Seaborn asked.

"After he got fired for the Gallipoli fiasco. Fairly quiet sector; then the South African Brigade attacked Delville Wood. In a matter of four days my regiment had over 900 men killed and wounded out of a thousand. I came out of it without a scratch and a commission. The life expectancy of a second lieutenant in the South African Scottish was estimated to be three weeks. Being a brand new officer was not much of a reward.

"After commanding an infantry platoon, I ended up taking over the brigade Sniper & Intelligence platoon, a picked crowd of men. Managed to get wounded some many months later, invalided back to England and awarded the Military Cross. A bit of a scandal—not supposed to award decorations to deserters, what?"

"Sounds like it could have posed a problem, sir," Lt. Seaborn said.

"Did; they say I'm the only officer ever given the King's pardon and a medal the same day."

"Amazing story," Lt. Seaborn marveled. "Is that when you joined the expedition to climb Mt. Everest, sir?"

"Actually, no—that came later. First it was off to Russia to advise the White army against the Reds ..."

Shouts came from the front of the column and the Sudanese were pointing at a lone rider on a jaded horse who had suddenly appeared as if conjured up.

"Blast," Col. Boustead spat. "That's Wingate. Looks like a bloody transient in uniform."

Colonel Orde Wingate had a number of strange peculiarities. When in the field he believed in living "rough." His definition of rough was to neither bathe, shave nor brush his teeth and to simply lie down on the ground to sleep. He carried raw onions in his bush jacket pockets and munched one constantly. No one much liked to be up close to him.

The horse limped up to where Col. Boustead and Lt. Seaborn sat on their mules wearing fresh, crisp uniforms that had been laid out by their Sudanese batmen that morning– as they were every morning. "I have come to tell you, Boustead—you were absolutely correct. This is no ground for trucks."

"Wingate, you ass. You rode fifty miles unarmed through enemy territory to tell me something I already knew?"

"The improvised landing strip we built was so rough," Col. Wingate added, "the pilot who picked me up to fly to a meeting with Sanford and Platt in Khartoum was awarded an immediate DFC. No more trucks or landing strips on this expedition. The Emperor was nearly done in a truck wreck."

Then without another word Col. Wingate turned his horse around and plodded back in the direction he had come.

"Sir," Lt. Seaborn said, "you reckon the colonel is all right?"

"No, Randy. The man's cloud cuckoo—needs to be in the glass house somewhere," Col. Boustead said. "French say the most important quality a commander needs to have is *les sens practable*—common sense. Wingate does not have the first drop. Claims to be a military genius. People actually believe him… what rot!"

"Sir, don't you think we should at least provide him a soldier escort?"

"No, lad. The colonel failed to request one. Not voluntarily risking any of my men on a fool's errand. Be best for everyone in Gideon Force if the shifta took trophy."

"Trophy?"

"Randy, my boy … maybe it's time I explain the Abyssinian predilection for …"

MAJOR GENERAL LEWIS "PIGGY" HEATH, HAVING MANAGED TO AVOID crashing his car into anything lately, detached the Highland Light Infantry (HLI had replaced the unfortunate Essex battalion that had fared so badly in Brigadier William "Bill" Slim's 10th Brigade at Galabrat) and the 2nd Motor Machine Gun Group, Sudan Defense Force and sent it racing down a sidetrack from Aicota to loop around behind the Italian positions at Keru. On loan from Gazelle Force, Major Jack Merritt's No. 9 MMG Co. was out front leading the way. Machine gunning their way through a difficult pass, they cut their way across the Italian rear. Gazelle Force's 4/11 Sikhs went in with the bayonet, catching the Blackshirts in a steel pincers.

Cut off and threatened from the rear, the greater part of the Italian Colonial 41st Brigade—deciding discretion to be a better part than valor—abandoned its positions in Keru and escaped cross-country in complete disarray. Left behind was the brigade commander, his staff, guns and 1,200 troops who all went into the bag. In one bold operation, one-sixth of the Italian Frontier Force facing Lieutenant General William Platt, the Kaid, had been taken prisoner.

The Italian High Command realized the extent of the danger facing them. It ordered the 43rd Colonial Brigade at Um Hagar and four additional battalions in the Walkait tableland to make a run for Barentu. The Italian Northern Front Command moved up to Agordat. In addition, the garrison was reinforced with the best Colonial Brigade in Italian East Africa— the 2nd. This was a unit that claimed an unbroken string of victories dating back to the 1890s.

Barentu and Agordat were designated "fight to the last man" bastions. The twin garrisons guarded the approach to the impregnable citadel of Keren. The mountain city fortress was where the final Italian last stand in IEA was planned—though it had been hoped Lt. Gen. Platt would have been stopped far short of there.

Maj. Merritt's No. 9 MMG Co. was released back to Gazelle Force and once again was on the move—pounding up the Biscia road hot on the heels of the fleeing Italians.

Colonel Frank Messervy was pushing his "tin cavalry" hard, screaming out the window of his personal Ford truck, "Bum on!" The column raced eighty miles deep into Italian East Africa and occupied Sciaglet Wells unopposed. Three hours before nightfall, Gazelle Force was within five miles of Agordat.

"Jack," Col. Messervy ordered, "take your company, strike cross-country and cut the line of communications between Agordat and Barentu. Do that and we shall put them all in the bag. Bum on, regardless!"

No. 9 MMG Co. swung around ninety degrees and thundered toward their objective. Caproni 133s appeared in the sky overhead, but Maj. Merritt ignored them and pressed on. The Italian bomber pilots, being experienced veterans, had far too much respect for the firepower mounted on the gun-trucks to attempt anything other than a high-level attack. Bombs screamed down, the gun-trucks raced on, zig-zagging. The detonations were tremendous, with massive mushroom-shaped clouds of dirt and smoke rising from the scrub brush. However, it's not easy to hit fast-moving trucks.

None of the bombs landed within 200 yards of the column.

By nightfall Maj. Merritt's No. 9 MMG Co. was sitting astride the road connecting Agordat to Barentu. The former Raiding Forces officer did not realize it yet, but his troops had cut off the Italian Northern Front commander who was up from Agordat on an inspection. Trapped with him in Barentu was his escort company of a dozen tanks.

Early the next morning Maj. Merritt found out about the Italian armor. Five obsolescent L5/30 tanks armed with two 6.5mm Breda machine guns waddled out of the mist shortly after sunrise. Obsolete or not, the L5/30s were capable of crushing his gun-trucks into scrap iron. The Sudanese's .55 Boys Anti-Tank Rifle teams engaged with armor-piercing rounds. The AP rounds, not being able to defeat any known armor no matter how outdated, dented the Blackshirt tanks causing paint to fly but "CLAAANKED" off harmlessly, ricocheting into the sky—which did nothing for No. 9 MMG Co. troop morale.

Fortunately, Col. Messervy had the foresight to attach a platoon of Bofors 37mm anti-aircraft guns to the SDF Company prior to sending them on their mission. When the Italian tanks appeared, the Bofors anti-aircraft gunners quickly transitioned into the anti-tank role. Firing their 37mm guns as fast as they could be loaded, the anti-aircraft artillery knocked the treads off two of the L5/30s. The other three, discouraged by the sight of their mates' plight, pulled back in the direction from which they came.

Maj. Merritt gave orders to have the two knocked-out tanks hauled to his position and dug in. Their turrets could still rotate, and the 6.5 machine guns could still fire. The Italian L5/30 model tanks may have been the world's most poorly-designed armored fighting vehicles; nevertheless, they made excellent improvised steel pillboxes.

He was on his objective, had established a roadblock, fought off a counterattack and intended to stay—but it had been a close run.

The former polo-playing corporal from the Life Guards was learning on the job how lonely command could be. Surrounded by fighting men, he was not lonesome … but he was very much alone. Since taking over No. 9 MMG Co., he had developed a whole new respect for Brigadier John Randal. Raiding Forces had always been assigned independent missions. Maj. Merritt had never given much thought to the weight carried by command responsibility, even though No. 9 MMG Co. was his third command.

He did now.

THE BLOND ITALIAN HERO, GENERAL ORLANDO LORENZINI "LION OF THE Sahara" was placed in command at Agordat. Orders in writing signed by the Duke of Aosta's own hand exhorted him to dig in and fight to the last man "because at Agordat would be fought the battle that sealed the fate of Italy in East Africa." Clearly an exaggeration—fortress Keren was where the fate of IEA was going to be settled, and everyone on both sides knew it.

The Duke promised a daily *minimum* of ten Caproni 133 bombers flying out of aerodromes at Asmara and Gura bombing the attacking British troops.

The British Y-Service was able to intercept, decode and read this message almost as fast as General Lorenzini. They passed the news to Lieutenant General William Platt, the Kaid.

He did not take it well.

"WE AVOID ATTACKING THE BIG CITIES," BRIGADIER JOHN RANDAL SAID. "Stay away from the battalion-sized and larger garrisons along the strategic roads too."

"Why?" Major General James "Baldie" Taylor inquired. He knew the answer but wanted to hear what the commander of 1 Guerrilla Corps (Parachute), Force N would say. (Every time he heard that title he chuckled—the idea of a corps of mule-riding Abyssinian parachutists was ludicrous.) The two officers were sitting inside the lighted compartment of the Hudson looking at a map while Escort Company personnel were off loading the supplies on board.

"There's no profit in it," Brig. Randal said. "We could raid the big cities or the larger military bases, but it wouldn't accomplish much. The Italians wouldn't send any additional troops to reinforce 'em. We hit the smaller isolated outposts, and they have to send help."

"You have guerrilla warfare down to a science," Maj. Gen. Taylor commended. "Must have been paying attention in those briefings I gave you. But now, Brigadier, we have need for you to raid the Caproni bomber bases at Asmara and Gura—major cities.

"The question is, can you do it? We only have three days."

"Shelby's battalion operates the farthest north," Brig. Randal said, looking at the map. "Even so, it'll take Harry three days to reach the nearest of the two airfields. There's no way to ride to the other target in time—much less raid it."

"Phrasing it mildly, General Platt is troubled about the prospects of ten Italian bombers per day attacking his troops," Maj. Gen. Taylor said. "You have observed firsthand how the Kaid reacts when he's troubled. Anything Force N can do will be much appreciated."

"We can hit 'em," Brig. Randal said. "I'll signal Captain Shelby to get one of his companies started north tonight. All he's going to be able to do is a mortar attack on the Capronis on night three. MRB companies only have one 81mm, so to achieve best results I recommend you arrange to drop Sergeant McDonald in to him with his mortar team as reinforcements."

"Should be able to do that. I need to check to confirm," Maj. Gen. Taylor concurred. "What about the other objective?"

"I'll jump in with a small team," Brig. Randal said. "The best we can do is work in close enough to hammer the bombers with my shoulder-fired 45mm mortar. There isn't time to perform the detailed reconnaissance to carry out a commando raid on either of the targets, which is what is really needed."

"All you need to do is damage the Capronis," Maj. Gen. Taylor explained. "The Regia Aeronautica workshops are down to using horse-drawn vehicles with patchwork harnesses commandeered from civilians. By the time the Italians are able to effect repairs, the campaign will be over."

"Good," Brig. Randal said. "The 45mm round makes a big bang when it hits but doesn't produce much shrapnel."

"How do you intend to get back?" Maj. Gen. Taylor probed.

"We'll have to buy mules, steal 'em, or walk out."

"Parachuting in blind," Maj. Gen. Taylor shook his head. "No exfiltration plan—pretty bare bones."

"Best we can do, General," Brig. Randal said. "It's your call."

"Oh, hell," Maj. Gen. Taylor sighed. "Imagine how it will go when I have to break the news to Lady Seaborn you parachuted into northern Abyssinia and are essentially MIA again—which you will be from the time you exit the aircraft."

"Don't tell her."

"Now how do you believe that would work out, exactly?"

"You'll think of something," Brig. Randal said.

"Your tortuous love life has been an ordeal for us in the rear," Maj. Gen. Taylor grumbled. "For all of our sake, consider going back to chasing women again with your pal Zorro after this show is over."

"Roger that," Brig. Randal said, lighting a thin cigar with his old 26th Cavalry Regiment Zippo. "I'll give it some thought."

"A fool for love," Maj. Gen. Taylor said. "Aren't we all—ask my three ex-wives."

"You could try saying Command Party was temporarily experiencing radio problems," Brig. Randal suggested.

"Maybe I can bribe someone else to brief Lady Seaborn," Maj. Gen. Taylor said. "Do not even *think* about getting killed. That's an order!"

20
GOING NORTH

"I NEED THE GIRLS TO TALK TO ME," BRIGADIER JOHN RANDAL SAID TO Captain the Lady Jane Seaborn.

"They do not speak English to men, John," Lady Jane replied. "You know that."

They were aboard the Hudson headed north, flying deep into Italian East Africa past the enemy capital, Addis Ababa. In the back of the plane were the two Lovat Scouts, Munro Fenwick and Lionel Ferguson, along with a highly nervous Waldo Treywick and the two ex-slave girls, Lana Turner and Rita Hayworth.

Captain Roy "Mad Dog" Reupart was on board giving some last-minute instruction to Waldo about the upcoming parachute jump—his first ever.

"They talked to Mad Dog."

"Captain Reupart was their parachute training instructor. "

"Well, not only am I their commanding officer," Brig. Randal said, "technically, I *own* them."

"How nice for you," Lady Jane replied. "I shall ask them again."

Squadron Leader Paddy Wilcox came back from the pilot's cabin. He laid out a map as Lady Jane went back to have a word with the two girls.

"Two nights hence I'll be airborne, orbiting over this stretch of road between 2400 hours and 0200 hours," Sqn. Ldr. Wilcox pointed to a long straight road. "If I see a letter *N* signal burning on the road, I'll land and pick you up."

"Roger."

"If you do not make that extraction deadline, I'll be back the next night same time. After that you're on your own hook, Brigadier."

"We'll do our best, Squadron Leader," Brig. Randal said. "It's a long walk home."

"Ten minutes," Sqn. Ldr. Wilcox informed him.

"TEN MINUTES!" Brig. Randal stood up and shouted to the five parachutists in the back of the aircraft. He held up the palms of both hands with fingers splayed to indicate the time remaining before the green light.

"Good luck, sir," Sqn. Ldr. Wilcox said.

Lady Jane came forward, "They are not talking, John. Particularly not to their *master.*"

"Mr. Treywick has to jump then."

"Afraid so," Lady Jane flashed her heart attack smile. "Girls can be difficult ... particularly Zār priestesses."

"Thanks for coming to see us off," Brig. Randal said awkwardly.

"You are not getting off that easy, sailor," Lady Jane threw her arms around him, which was not that easy with the parachute harness, pistols, knife and other fighting gear in the way.

Time seemed to stand still until Sqn. Ldr. Wilcox came on the intercom, "Six minutes, Brigadier."

Breaking free from the embrace, Brig. Randal gave the command "SIX MINUTES!"

Then he turned back, "Jane, I ..."

She put her finger on his lips, "Come back safe. I love you, John. I always will, no matter what."

Brig. Randal shuffled to the tail of the airplane.

"HOOK UP AND CHECK YOUR EQUIPMENT!"

Waldo was first in the stick followed by Lana, Rita, Fenwick and Ferguson. The Lovat Scouts were the pushers in case anyone hesitated in the door. Brig. Randal would be the last out.

The ex-ivory poacher was looking pale around the gills. He had spent a day being coached by Lieutenant Butch "Headhunter" Hoolihan in the gentle art of the parachute landing fall (PLF)—the sum total of his airborne training. Volunteering ... *demanding*, in fact, to be allowed to accompany the team had seemed like a good idea at the time. Not now. This was worse than the time he and P.J. Pretorius had snuck onboard the German cruiser *König* while scouting for the Army back in the last war—one of the dumbest things he had ever done.

"Just go limp after you exit the aircraft, Mr. Treywick," Brig. Randal shouted in Waldo's ear over the roar of the wind howling past the open door. "Keep your elbows in, knees unlocked, stay totally relaxed and everything will be all right—we'll get your parachute."

"Relax? Easy for you to say, this ain't your first ..."

"ONE MINUTE!"

"CLOSE ON THE DOOR!"

Brig. Randal arched his body outside the aircraft—spread eagle, fingertips hanging on the inside edges of the door, canvas-topped raiding boots braced wide and jammed against the frame. Directly up ahead he saw their DZ—a small open clearing located on a tabletop ridge of the mountain.

Swinging back inside he nodded at Capt. Reupart who immediately moved up behind Waldo. They had decided not to have a first jump paratrooper stand in the door. That was asking too much. The jump light indicator flashed from red to green.

"GO!"

He and Capt. Reupart shoved Waldo out the door before he realized what was happening. The girls danced out, followed by the Lovat Scouts, and then Brig. Randal was outside the aircraft being tumbled by the Hudson's prop blast.

The X-type parachute deployed perfectly—no twisted risers or lines were looping over the top of the canopy forming the malfunction known to paratroopers worldwide as the *Mae West*. In front of him he could see a string of parachutes floating down, silently drifting toward the DZ. Below each of the jumpers was a lowering line that contained what little weapons and gear they had brought with them. One additional chute followed the stick out. It contained fifty of the 45mm rounds for his Brixia M-35 shoulder-fired mortar.

Coming in backward as usual, Brig. Randal crumpled into a picture perfect PLF, jerked the safety snap off his quick release on his chest, slapped it hard, quickly pulled the slipknot on his lowering line, jumped up and raced to where the Lovat Scouts were already helping Mr.

Treywick out of his harness. Everyone was down, no injuries and no equipment lost.

Waldo was euphoric at still being alive. "I ain't never doin' that again the rest of my life! Don't ask. Don't even think about it. The answer ain't no, it's HELL NO!"

"You OK, Mr. Treywick?"

"Are you crazy? I just jumped out of an airplane—no I'm *not* OK!"

Without wasting any time, the team wrapped up the parachutes, packed them in their lightweight parachute bags, gathered their equipment and the additional 45mm mortar rounds and started moving up the mountain to high ground. They were careful not to leave behind any sign that they had dropped in. So far, this was a textbook-perfect operation.

That ended the next morning when the sun came up on their overnight position on the crest of the mountain. Directly below them the team could see the Regia Aeronautica airfield about a mile away. Brig. Randal immediately realized that he had made a mistake.

The Italian base commander had neither dispersed his dozen Caproni 133s to protect them from aerial attack—he had no reason to suspect such an attack at this distant location since Regia Aeronautica ruled the skies over IEA—nor had he parked his airplanes closely together to make them easier to guard against a ground attack—which he also had no reason to fear. The locals, while not overly friendly, had never ever been a threat due to the heavy military presence in the town next door.

The dozen Caproni 133 bombers were confined to one area of the large bomber airfield and parked in a row—neatly lined up along one side of the runway with approximately fifty meters between aircraft.

Brig. Randal had expected to find the enemy aircraft all in one nice, tight, easy-to-guard cluster parked wingtip to wingtip. Every other Italian base commander had always done it that way. It was a fatal miscalculation on his part. He needed the airplanes to be concentrated for his plan to work.

The improvised shoulder-fired Brixia M-35 was an area-type weapon. It did not even have sights. The odds of him achieving a direct hit on one of the planes were slim. The little 45mm rounds made a big bang but produced very little shrapnel effect, and its bursting radius was no more than a few feet.

Brig. Randal knew he was not going to be able to knock out or damage enough of the Capronis with his shoulder-fired mortar to be of any significant assistance to Lieutenant General William Platt. Although "Poor prior planning produces poor results" was not one of the Raiding Forces mantras, the proverb was widely quoted in the unit. So much for his planning, or for this plan to work out. There was not a chance.

To make matters worse there was no Plan B. At least he had not jumped in with one. And the old exhortation taught in the U.S. Cavalry School, "A bad plan executed vigorously right now is better than the perfect plan tomorrow," definitely did not apply in this situation.

"Mr. Treywick, move out and buy mules from that small village back in the mountains like we planned—take one of the Scouts with you."

"I should be back in about four hours," Waldo said, racking a 12-gauge round into Brig. Randal's chopped Browning A-5 that he had pretty much appropriated as his own personal weapon. "If I ain't, you should get worried. Ferguson, you're on me."

As Brig. Randal raised his Zeiss binoculars to take another look at the airfield, Waldo asked, "Can you hit them planes in the dark with your mortar gun—all spread out like that?"

"Negative."

"Jumping outta that airplane has done got me to thinkin' about P.J. Pretorius again," Waldo mused. "It looks to me, Brigadier, like you done violated ole P.J.'s number one principal for military work."

"What might that be?"

"'Never assume nothin.' Why, you might ask. Well, it's right there plain to see. When you break the word down, spellin' wise, it makes 'a ass outta you and me—least that's what P.J. always claimed."

"Go get the mules," Brig. Randal said through gritted teeth.

Brig. Randal's options were limited by the things the team could *not* do. He did not believe he could accomplish his mission as planned with his Brixia M-35. The team did not have explosives because they would have been too heavy for the team to manage on the jump and move to the ORP, so they could not infiltrate the airfield, plant demolitions and exfiltrate unnoticed. The team was not large enough to launch a raid and shoot the planes up with their small arms.

"OK, ladies," Brig. Randal said to Rita and Lana as he lowered the Zeiss glasses. "Go down and locate the back door to the base—the one where the airmen sneak in the hookers and contraband at night.

When you come back, bring me one of those toga overgarments men wear."

The two Zār priestesses looked at each other then silently replaced their big silver loop earrings they had removed for the jump. They unslung their MAB-38A submachine guns and placed them against a rock. Taking off their pistol belts, they removed the small Beretta .380s from their holsters and tucked them in under their short tunics, behind their money belts, in the back of their jodhpurs. Both were wearing wicked-looking rhino-horned knives at their waist.

Jewelry, guns, money and blades—the girls were good to go.

"Any questions? Now would be the time."

Rita and Lana flashed brilliant smiles but said nothing.

It had taken Brig. Randal less than three minutes to come up with a new plan of action—about three times longer than he had spent on the original concept of the operation. He hoped it was three times better.

Waldo arrived back in the ORP to find Brig. Randal sprawled out taking a nap under a tree while Scout Fenwick stood guard. "No mules," he announced. "The bastards had mules, but they ain't selling any mules. Told me to take my Fat Ladies, the Emperor's proclamation and go to hell!"

"Don't worry about it," Brig. Randal said, pulling his cut-down bush hat back down over his eyes.

"Worry? Ain't nothing goin' right. We're 400 miles from where it's 600 miles home. I sure ain't walkin'—let's just go *get* the mules.

"We'll put the Lovats up on the ridge overlookin' the un-Patriotic village, let the lads snipe eight or ten of 'em to give 'em somethin' to think about. Then you and the girls can work in close with your submachine gun's magazines loaded all tracers and fire up the hut's straw roofs downwind side. Get the place burnin' real good to distract 'em while I ..."

"Lighten up, Mr. Treywick. Catch a few zzzs," Brig. Randal said from under his hat. "Long night ahead of us—we don't need mules."

The girls trailed in a while later. The two had the satisfied look of a pair of sleek pussycats that had eaten the canary. Brig. Randal had seen them wearing that identical expression before. He did not have to ask if they found what they were looking for. Lana gave him an off-white, three-quarter-length, shamma wool garment, typical of those Abyssinian men wore over their pants.

Brig. Randal called a council of war, and everyone gathered around to hear his frag order. "Mr. Treywick, you take Fenwick and Ferguson down to the front gate armed with my Beretta M-38 submachine gun. By 2200 hours be in position where you can take the sentries manning the gate under fire. Rita, Lana and I will affect entry to the airfield from another location and be coming out the front where you are.

"I'll be driving a 3-ton Dovunque 4X6 all-terrain truck. Don't shoot us, we'll be moving fast. Don't get too close to the gate—I intend to mortar it before we come out. What are your questions?"

"Takin' that truck to the pick-up point, are we?"

"That's right, Mr. Treywick—beats riding a mule," Brig. Randal said. "Your job is to provide us cover coming out the front gate. Be ready in case any of the Italians try to be heroes and don't take cover from the mortar fire."

"How you plannin' on immobilizin' those Caproni 133s?" Waldo asked.

"Southern California style," Brig. Randal said, lighting a thin cigar. "The surf is up."

RITA, LANA AND BRIGADIER JOHN RANDAL MADE THEIR WAY THROUGH the city taking the back streets. There were not many people out. Abyssinian towns were not safe at night. In a country of criminals, most people tended to stay home nights. No one paid them the least bit of attention. Not even the occasional Italian soldier they passed.

Then they turned a dark corner, and out of the shadows stepped three evil-looking shifta showing long blades and a bad attitude. Rita and Lana recoiled, reaching behind their backs for their Beretta .380s. Brig. Randal stepped around them and shot all three bandits in the face with his silenced .22-caliber High Standard. *WHIIIICH, WHIIIICH, WHIIIICH.*

The pistol made a sound no louder than a wooden match being struck. Normally, he would have followed his policy of two shots to the head, but tonight he did not care if the three were dead or not. What were the robbers going to do—call the police?

Barely breaking stride, Rita and Lana stepped over the prostrate wanna-be muggers and around another corner. After a short distance, they came to a dead-end in the road, which ran straight into a small gate in the fence of the airfield. This was where the contraband and women passed onto the base. The gate was guarded, but the two guards were not expecting trouble. They were expecting unscheduled visitors wanting entry from time to time.

Rita—or maybe it was Lana—called out, and the gate was quickly opened. The guards were laughing, teasing the girls about a strip search when Brig. Randal shot them both twice with the silenced .22-caliber High Standard. Then with the two airmen down on the ground he shot them each once more in the head … just to make sure. He was not taking any chances on one of them coming to and raising the alarm.

After dragging the two Italian airmen out of the gate and into the shadows, they went back inside the fence and padlocked the gate. Any inspector making his rounds would find the post deserted but not be alarmed for the security of the airfield.

The gate was locked—no problem.

Brig. Randal took the lead and moved straight across the airfield until he came to a parked three-ton Dovunque 4X6 all-terrain truck. It was a giant twelve-wheeled Cab Over Engine all-terrain vehicle he had spotted from the mountain ORP earlier. The truck was equipped with a canvas top and a steel beam for a front bumper with a winch mounted on it.

He took off his heavy pack with the 45mm mortar rounds inside and placed it in the cab. Then he unslung the short-barreled Brixia M-35 and laid it on the seat. The two girls went around, climbed up on the running board and crawled into the passenger side.

Like all military trucks, the Dovunque was keyless. Brig. Randal slid in behind the wheel. It cranked up and broke into a throaty roar on the first try. He put it in gear and let out the clutch.

"Hang on, ladies," Brig. Randal said. "Time for a little Demolition Derby."

The huge truck rumbled down the airstrip past the twelve parked Caproni 133 bombers. When Brig. Randal drove past the last one, he pulled off onto the grass and did a U-turn. He put the truck in neutral, extracted ten of the 45mm mortar rounds out of his pack, loaded one in the chamber of the Brixia M-35 and pointed it out the window toward the cluster of steel aviation fuel tanks down at the far end of the runway.

BLOOOP, BLOOOP, BLOOOP ... He fired all ten rounds then slammed the truck into gear. When the mortar shells began exploding, one of the tanks exploded and a mushroom-shaped fireball of high-octane aviation fuel erupted skyward. A siren sounded and every anti-aircraft weapon on base opened fire skyward. It looked like millions of tracer rounds were streaking into the air.

Naturally, the Italians thought they were being bombed. Everyone heard the bombs explode. The fact this airfield had never been subjected to an aerial attack contributed to the confusion. It had never been mortared either.

The big three-ton truck bore down on the first of the Caproni 133 bombers. Brig. Randal held steady on and clipped the tail completely off the airplane with the steel beam bumper. The impact barely had any effect on the heavy truck and hardly moved the tethered bomber.

Lana and Rita both turned and looked at him round-eyed as he steered toward the next bomber fifty yards ahead. He clipped its tail like the first. The Dovunque was designed to go "Off Road—Anywhere." Running over the aluminum tail section of a tied-down airplane was child's play compared to what it was engineered to handle.

The truck rumbled down the length of the parked bomber formation crumpling the tails of the planes one after another as they rolled. All around them, the firing intensified. No one paid the slightest attention to the Dovunque. The anti-aircraft gunners were hard at work firing on nonexistent enemy airplanes, fighting for their lives against aerial invaders. Italians not manning anti-aircraft guns were cowering in bomb shelters.

If anyone did notice the truck, they probably thought it was some driver trying to flee the incoming bombs.

Brig. Randal turned toward the front gate. When he was about 300 yards away he started firing the Brixia M-35 out the window one-handed. Most were random shots to keep up the impression of bombs falling, but the last five rounds were aimed straight at the gate.

When the truck arrived, no guards were anywhere in sight. The Italian security airmen had all taken cover. Who could blame them?

Brig. Randal crashed through the gate without slowing and flipped on the headlights. Waldo and the Lovat Scouts jumped out in the road waving both hands. The Dovunque came to a gravel-crunching halt long enough for the three men to scramble in the back. Then it was pedal to the metal—they were "getting the hell out of Dodge."

As they rolled into the night, the firing behind them reached a crescendo.

The next morning, the South African Air Force sent a squadron of Hurricanes equipped with long-distance drop tanks to strafe the field. Anti-aircraft fire was unexpectedly light when the fighters rolled in on the target. The pilots reported they saw no signs of a ground attack by the Force N team though one of the aviation fuel tanks was burning. A dozen Caproni 133 bombers were lined up neatly along the airstrip prepared for takeoff. The pilots claimed all twelve of the enemy bombers destroyed.

Several were recommended for decorations.

21
PREPARING THE BATTLEFIELD

BOTTLED UP IN THE DIRTY WHITEWASHED TOWN OF AGORDAT WITH General Orlando Lorenzini, "Lion of the Sahara," were 12,000 infantry, 19 troops of artillery (76 guns) and a company of medium and light tanks—minus the two medium tanks Major Jack Merritt's No. 9 Motor Machine Gun Company had knocked out. Some of the tanks were manned by Germans who had been on ships that were trapped by the Royal Navy blockade at Massawa. Had the Blackshirts come straight at No. 9 MMG Co., they could have rolled right over it.

Alas for the Italians, they did not.

Lieutenant General William Platt, the Kaid, left Gazelle Force to screen while he carried out a brilliant flanking movement with his main force up the hills to the rear of Agordat. A vicious seesaw battle ensued, with the 3/14 Punjab Regiment leading the way up Cochen Mountain. There they found the summit was a wide plateau covered by thick shrub and occupied by five Italian Colonial battalions.

The 5 Indian Division reinforced the 3/14th with the 1/6 Rajputana Rifles. Unfortunately, both the battalions were minus one company because the only mountain transport was mules—and they did not have any. So one full company from the Punjab's and one from the Rajputana Rifles plus one platoon from the Indian Miners and Sappers were detailed as porters hauling ammunition, rations and tins of water up the rocky mountain in the boiling heat.

When the Italians counterattacked, the Empire troops were driven back by their vastly superior numbers. At the crucial moment, the Miners and Sappers threw down their picks and shovels and went in with the bayonet. The Blackshirts were beaten back … barely. Imperial Forces hung on grimly through the night then met success the next morning when they renewed the attack.

The Camerons and 1st Royal Fusiliers followed through on the plain below led by four of the invincible "I" tanks. With no sharp rocks to slice the rubber connectors on their tracks (like they had encountered at Gallabat), they massacred the Italian armor, six medium and five light tanks. It was all over in a matter of minutes.

The Italians caved in.

Later, under cover of nightfall, the garrison of Agordat fled cross-country in disarray, leaving behind 1,000 prisoners, forty-three guns and fourteen destroyed tanks. Barentu fell the next day. The Blackshirts, retreating through the gorge before Keren, were forced to abandon all of four infantry brigade's guns, tanks and motor transport. The total haul for the two weeks of fighting was 6,000 Italian troops, 80 guns, 26 tanks and 400 trucks.

Maj. Merritt and No. 9 MMG Co., once again back out in front of Gazelle Force leading the pursuit, came upon the steel Mussolini Bridge. It was blown. The magnificent Indian Miners and Sappers moved up and fell to with the will of demons, but it took eight hours hard effort to clear the gorge. While they were working in the heat amid the booby-traps and mines, the Italian demolition engineers blew down 200 yards of cliff on the far side, closing the tunnel and bottling up the approach to the impregnable mountain fortress.

The result was like a castle that had pulled up its drawbridge at the last second. There was now no choice. The siege and battle for Keren was on.

Colonel Frank Messervy and Maj. Merritt stood staring up at the ugly black mountain cut with countless razor sharp ridges of solid rocks simmering in the heat.

"No one in the history of organized warfare has ever been tasked with attacking anything more impossible than Keren," Col. Messervy blurted. "Never imagined anything like this existed—Mt. Everest without the snow with a medieval fortification perched on top."

"No more 'bumming on,' sir."

"We are in real trouble, Jack."

EAST AFRICA RECONNAISSANCE REGIMENT, THE LOUNGE LIZARDS, were closed up on the border with Italian East Africa. For the past two weeks they had been running patrols across the border. The reports were encouraging. The Italians were in a state of dismay. They seemed to have lost the will to fight.

There were three reasons for the disintegration of the Italian morale

Reason number one: Captain Jack Desmond Bonham, accompanied by his Airedale dog Kim, had succeeded in raising the natives against them. He probably had not achieved the 60,000 he had suggested possible, but there were a lot of angry natives in the desert bush, and the drums were beating in the night. The tribes, still deadly enemies, had put aside their quarrels temporarily. While not united, they were at least concentrating—for the time being—on harassing the universally-hated Blackshirts instead of murdering each other. They clustered around every isolated Fascist outpost and, emboldened by some limited support in the way of six Operational Centers from Force N and weapons and material airdropped out of Camp Croc, were moving in on the large coastal cities.

Reason number two: Captain Mike "March or Die" Mikkalis had broken his 1st "Mercs" Mule Raider Battalion into platoon-sized raiding units. Since he did not have the advantage of mountainous terrain to melt into after an attack, he had to spread his forces out so they could vanish into the shrub brush desert. The result was that his 1st MRB was constantly raiding—hitting and running—creating the impression of a much larger force. The Italians, while they had a few raiding units of their own that had operated into the remote Kenyan Northern Frontier, were not skilled at counterinsurgency. They did not know how to react to the pin-prick raids, so they did nothing. That was a mistake because it only encouraged more of them.

Capt. Mikkalis was beginning to coordinate his operations with the OC-led Patriots—bad news for the Italians living in the Red Sea coastal belt and the desert environs behind it.

The former Legionnaire knew about operating in arid country. He understood the value of the few water sources and the fragile lines of communication connecting remote garrisons to their home stations. The 1st Mercs raided the Blackshirt forts at the wells and ambushed the desert roads constantly. They lurked around the major cities, striking when the opportunity presented itself. No Italian ever felt safe outside of a brigade-sized or larger military installation or a major city.

No one even considered traveling at night.

Reason number three: Captain Hawthorne Merryweather, the irrepressible psychological warrior, was having his finest moment to date in what had been a really excellent campaign for him personally. After relocating his printing press to N-2 he decided that the better idea was for him to move to Camp Croc and set up shop. Initially, he left Lieutenant Pamala Plum-Martin behind to continue her nightly serenades of the remote Italian road-watch garrisons. Then later, when she started piloting her own Walrus, it was decided to have her relocate to Camp Croc and fly shorter missions against the Italians opposite where East Africa Force under Lieutenant General Alan Cunningham would be attacking.

Mrs. Brandy Seaborn and Lieutenant Penelope Honeycutt-Parker, RM were brought in to take over her old duties flying missions into central Abyssinia to play music to the homesick Italian troops. Captain the Lady Jane Seaborn also worked with them rotating nights when she could take a break from her other duties. Y-Service radio intercepts indicated that these psy-ops music missions were wildly successful.

One intercepted message read, "Intensely moving, we have to admit, to hear music from great familiar voices floating down to us from invisible loudspeakers in the heavens at night. The songs produce pleasure, which turns into deep despair."

The lonely Italian boys loved the sexy British women in the airplanes serenading them. The troops eagerly awaited their visits. Some flashed proposals of marriage in Morse code at the sky with their flashlights. It is never good for the opposition when some of their troops have a crush on some of your troops.

The small printing press Capt. Merryweather had at Camp Croc soon proved unequal to the task of printing propaganda leaflets in the volume required for the entire country. But it worked well on small runs mounted on the back of a truck traveling with the South African Air Force. Lady Jane made arrangements with the newspaper in Nairobi to print the bulk of his propaganda. No Amharic or Arabic print was available, so type had to be reproduced by lithograph process from picture and line drawings. The leaflets were also printed in Italian.

The SAAF initially resisted "wasting their time dropping toilet paper" when Capt. Merryweather approached them with the idea. But when they saw Y-Service intercepts indicating that the Italian High Command feared the (mostly accurate) world news contained in the leaflets was "sowing despair and a spirit of imminent defeat" among their troops, the Air Force assigned aircraft to the mission.

Over one million leaflets were dropped.

Line crossers carrying Capt. Merryweather's printed surrender forms—the Italians could fill them out in advance—soon started arriving. Enemy personnel were coming in to the advanced East Africa Force units closed up on the border, waving the leaflets as instructed.

"Our officers tried to prevent your printed material from being passed around," one Blackshirt soldier said. "But it read like the truth; we knew our struggle was hopeless and our death not worth the cause."

The most effective one was short and simple: "Have you been paid recently?" The answer was a problem for the Italians—everyone knew Force N troops were being paid regularly in Maria Theresa silver dollars. Abyssinian deserters arrived volunteering to fight against their former Italian masters if they too could be paid in "Fat Ladies."

When he learned that, Capt. Merryweather quickly printed up and dropped leaflets showing the 1 Guerrilla Corps (Parachute), Force N pay scale.

COLONEL SIR TERRY "ZORRO" STONE WAS FEELING GOOD ABOUT HIS command. The blue-blooded, sublimely confident Yeomanry of the single squadron Lancelot Lancers Regiment had assimilated well with the native Abyssinian troops from the No. 5 Parachute Company he had been training to be in his 2nd Mule Raider Battalion before it had been disbanded.

A company of Rhodesian engineers had been attached to evaluate bridges and effect immediate repairs as necessary. The hush-hush Phantom radio unit gave him a communications capability unknown in military circles until now. The truck-mounted navy three-pound fast firers had proven equal to the task of keeping up with the armored cars. The South African Air Force had a detachment from No. 40 Air-Cooperation Squadron in a Rhino armored car attached. And the Rolls Royces, though museum pieces, had turned out to be excellent for the terrain in which they were operating. Particularly after the fitters had removed the turrets and added additional machine guns.

When the attack kicked off, East Africa Reconnaissance Regiment would be leading the way in advance of the 11th African Division driving straight for the port city of Kismayo. The main battle would be fought on the River Jubba. The Italian defenses were based on the "Jubba Line."

An opposed river crossing against an entrenched enemy who has had time to prepare his defenses and is expecting you is one of—if not *the*—most difficult of all military operations.

Col. Stone's assignment was to lead the 11th African Division cross-country to the Jubba River, liberate Kismayo en route, locate a crossing and force the river. All the while maintaining contact with the 12th African Division that would be attacking on a parallel axis north through Lisoi, Heweina and Afmadow before sending one brigade south to hit Kismayo from the flank. If—and that was a big if—East Africa Force could break through the Jubba Line, the idea was to advance up the coast taking in turn Modun, Merca and Mogadishu with East Africa Reconnaissance Regiment, the Lounge Lizards out front.

It was a mission he had been training for all his life.

THE HUDSON WAS FLYING THROUGH THE PREDAWN SKY, HAVING TAKEN off from Camp Croc after refueling and picking up Waldo Treywick, who had been attending a short course at the parachute school outside Nairobi. The old ivory poacher was sporting shiny new parachute wings on one of the tailor-made soft green bush jackets he had pilfered from Brigadier John Randal, who was also onboard. Waldo would not have wanted anyone to know how proud he was to be wearing the wings.

Also on the aircraft were Major General James "Baldie" Taylor, Rita Hayworth and Lana Turner.

The plane was en route to Lieutenant General William Platt's Headquarters outside Keren.

"The Rases ain't comin' in," Waldo explained to Maj. Gen. Taylor in response to his question on the subject. "One did—to test the water—but he wasn't real serious so the Brigadier shot 'im.

"Who's comin' in is the *tillik saus*. The Big Shots want to join up with Force N so they can establish their bona fides with their Emperor, hopin' for a royal title when he gets back on the throne. The Rases, well, they're keepin' their options open."

"Any chance the Rases will ever commit?"

"Don't count on it, General. They'll play both ends against the middle to the bitter end, always hopin' to make a better deal. They ain't on anybody's side but their own selves. Any promises of help fightin' Italians would be subject to change if the other side upped the ante."

"We're better off with the *tillik saus*," Brig. Randal said.

"Yeah, the Big Shots is makin' pretty good soldiers," Waldo agreed. "Know they got to distinguish themselves fightin' to have a shot at a title down the line. And, they don't resent the brigadier comin' in and takin' charge the way the Rases do—see it as a career opportunity workin' with a new man."

"Railroad approaching dead ahead, General," the pilot announced.

"Come up front, Brigadier, I want to show you something," Maj. Gen. Taylor said.

The two men entered the cockpit and looked out the windscreen as the sun came up—blazing hot from the moment it peeked over the horizon. Coming in to view was one of the strangest things Brig. Randal had ever seen. Up ahead was an elevated railroad with gondolas dangling from cables. It looked like a giant ski lift.

"Called the 'Ropeway.' Apparently it was easier to construct like that through this rough country," Maj. Gen. Taylor explained. "The railroad spur runs from Massawa to Keren. The Ropeway stops at Asmara where the Italian troops and material are off-loaded onto regular rail cars. The Air Force has tried and failed to knock it out."

"I've never seen anything like it," Brig. Randal said.

"That's what I wanted to show you," Maj. Gen. Taylor pointed toward a big black mountain looming in the distance. "Keren, the Italian stronghold. The Kaid has been attacking it head on, and he is stuck like a bug on flypaper. The 4th and 5th Indian Divisions have been fighting to scale the razor sharp ridges to get at the fortress on the top, but it has been a bloodbath right out of the last war.

"The dead of both sides are piled up between the lines and hyenas eat them at night. Our troops attack and take a ridgeline, then the Italians counterattack behind a cloud of their little Red Devil hand grenades and take it back. Never let anyone try to tell you the Italians are not excellent soldiers when they choose to be. This seesaw battle has been going on for six weeks now.

"Platt has to take Keren with the troops he has. General Wavell has no reinforcements to send—they have been frittered away on a forlorn hope in Greece at the insistence of the Prime Minister. Now the Germans are rattling their sabers at Crete, so it gets first priority on reinforcements. To make matters worse for Middle East Command, a general named Rommel has recently turned up in the desert with the first German troops of what they called the 'Afrika Korps.' "

"Why fight for the mountain at all?" Brig. Randal asked.

"There's no way around. Platt has to go through Keren to reach the ultimate objective on the coast—Massawa. Putting even more pressure on the Kaid, the President of the United States has privately let it be known he is willing to bend the rules on Lend Lease.

"As soon as Platt takes Massawa, Roosevelt will declare the Red Sea safe for U.S. merchant convoys—even though that will not be entirely true."

"Why not demonstrate at Keren with one division to pin the Italians in place?" Brig. Randal said. "Pull the other back to the Sudan, regroup, then send everything we can scrape together straight at Massawa overland from there?"

"No one thought of it," Maj. Gen. Taylor said. "General Platt has been fixated on Keren from the beginning."

"Force N has one principal we live by," Brig. Randal said, " 'Never fight the bad guys when they want to fight you.' "

"Too bloody late now," Maj. Gen. Taylor said. "General Platt is going to lift the restriction on Force N operating to his front. He wants to tell you himself."

"What's the man think we can do at this point?"

"Let's let the Kaid explain," Maj. Gen. Taylor said. "If you feel Force N is not in a position to comply with his request, simply say so. I know you will not be bashful."

22
HATE IT WHEN THAT HAPPENS

LIEUTENANT GENERAL WILLIAM PLATT'S HEADQUARTERS WAS located in a tent city not more than three miles from the mountain battle taking place at Keren. Artillery was firing intermittently, and the occasional bomb blast rattled the canvas tents. Currently there were no ground attacks in progress on the mountain. The Kaid was rethinking the battle.

The exhausted British and Indian troops were clinging to what ground they had taken.

The Blackshirts were equally spent. However, they were fighting for their lives. Every man knew if Keren was taken, the war was lost. It would simply be a matter of time before they would have to surrender.

The great fear was in the event they became prisoners, the Italians would be turned over to the Patriots. The last time an Italian Army was captured and at the mercy of Abyssinians, the prisoners had been castrated.

If that were not incentive enough to fight to the last man and last bullet, many of the Fascist officers and men had wives, daughters or mistresses in-country—and some had wives, daughters *and* mistresses. What horrific outrages would the women be forced to endure if they fell into the cruel hands of the Patriots?

Rape was not considered much of a crime under normal circumstances in Abyssinia. Much less when it was committed on the wife, daughter or mistress of a hated occupying enemy soldier. The Blackshirts had reason to be concerned.

So the Italian defenders, while battered, were highly motivated. The British attackers were bloodied but not beaten. And Lt. Gen. Platt was searching for a Plan B.

Waldo peeled off to talk to Major Jack Merritt at his command post. Gazelle Force had been disbanded. No. 9 Motor Machine Gun Company had been reassigned as the palace guard. Having distinguished itself in the campaign thus far, No. 9 MMG Co.'s task now was to protect the General Headquarters (GHQ) while awaiting developments— hoping for the pursuit to pick back up again sometime soon.

Major General James "Baldie" Taylor and Brigadier John Randal with Rita and Lana in trail walked into the Operations Center. The two girls silently took up station just inside the door of the tent. Brig. Randal studied a large wall map of Keren while Lt. Gen. Platt and Maj. Gen. Taylor conferred.

Staff officers clutching papers hurried past. Field phones clanked. The atmosphere in the tent was tense. The heat was oppressive.

"Brigadier," Maj. Gen. Taylor motioned.

The three senior officers moved over to another large wall map—this one showing all of Italian East Africa.

"We are here," Lt. Gen. Platt tapped the map with his flywhisk. "Force N operates in this general area over here. The Italians have recently begun reinforcing the fortress here at Keren from Addis Ababa by trucking troops north and looping the long way around your AO to avoid you and your band of cutthroats.

"Need to put an immediate stop to that, Brigadier."

"Sir, I was ordered …"

"If I rescind the order prohibiting Force N from operating on my front, can you prevent the Duke from sending more reinforcements to Keren by the northern route—and if so, how quickly can you act?"

"Sir, I can have a Mule Raider Battalion—approximately 250 picked men plus an additional 400 to 500 ahh … Patriots … in the area ready to commence operations within five days. I can have an additional two companies … my personal Escort Company and the Force Raiding Company with another 500 Patriots arrive two days later."

"Can you stop the Italians from reinforcing?"

"That's mountainous terrain, General," Brig. Randal said. "The Blackshirts have only the one strategic road through there. We can make 'em fight for it every inch of the way."

"Brigadier Randal was in that part of the country recently," Maj. Gen. Taylor said. "He parachuted in with a team and knocked out a dozen Caproni 133s slated to be attacking your troops."

"I was informed the South African Air Force destroyed those bombers. I personally decorated more than a few of the pilots."

"The SAAF strafed already-damaged airplanes," Maj. Gen. Taylor said. "The brigadier and the two slave girls standing by the door infiltrated the airfield, stole an all-terrain three-tonner, drove to the flight line, clipped the tails off the Capronis parked there and then made a clean getaway in the truck."

"That true ... you did that?"

"Not much choice, sir," Brig. Randal said. "My original plan wasn't working out."

"I hate it," Lt. Gen. Platt said, "when that happens.

"Besides ambushing the strategic road north of Addis Ababa is there anything else you might think of your guerrillas could do to help take the pressure off us here? We can use all the support we can obtain."

"Loan me Jack Merritt's No. 9 MMG Co., sir," Brig. Randal said, "and, we'll knock down the elevated Ropeway behind Asmara— isolate Keren for you."

"When?"

"Take about a week to set up, sir."

"No. 9 is yours Brigadier; sooner is rather better than later."

As they were climbing back on the Hudson for the return flight, Maj. Gen. Taylor asked, "Remember Brigadier Slim—from the battle at Gallabat?"

"Good man having a bad day."

"Africa has not been kind. Friendly fire incident couple days ago," Maj. Gen. Taylor said. "Slim got shot in the ass."

"Nothing friendly about that."

ON THE KENYAN BORDER, THINGS HEATED UP AFTER THE GEOGRAPHICAL Survey Section divined water where there was thought to be none. A section of South African engineers sank a well and struck a 600 gallon-per-hour gusher at 356 feet. This and another 400 gallon-per-hour water well dug a few miles away freed up enough trucks from hauling water to the troops that Lieutenant General Alan Cunningham sent by hand of officer a penciled note to his boss, Field Marshal Sir Archibald Wavell, indicating he was now ready to launch his attack toward the port of Kismayo.

Colonel Sir Terry "Zorro" Stone received his marching orders. He put the East Africa Reconnaissance Regiment on the road at once, even though it was the middle of the night. Despite reports of banda activity in the area, he insisted on leading the way in his personal command car. The regiment crossed the border before sunrise. Kismayo was the initial target. Unfortunately for the Italians, it was located on the wrong side of the Jubba River, which made it difficult for them to incorporate in their master defense plan.

Kismayo was a minor port town of little consequence. The real objective was to capture a bridge or crossing over the Jubba River.

The Lounge Lizards were tasked with passing through Kismayo and securing a place on the river where the 11th African Division could cross, attack and breach the Jubba Main Line of Resistance on the far bank.

In the distance, there was a glow in the sky that seemed larger than the average spectacular African sunrise. Garish explosions pulsated. The Italians were blowing their ammunition dumps and oil storage tanks prior to abandoning the city.

When the Lounge Lizards rolled into the outskirts of Kismayo, instead of resistance they found the place in a wild orgy of celebration—a scene not unlike Times Square on New Year's Eve, Carnaval in Rio or the Rape of Nanking. Starving dogs and cats were roaming the streets, looters were hard at pillaging and virtually the entire populace was partying in the street. Toward the center of the city a conga line with hundreds of dancers snaked its way through downtown.

Dead Italian soldiers were sprawled like broken dolls in the gutters, stripped of their weapons and valuables. A number of men and women were hanging dead by the neck from lampposts. From time to time, gunshots crackled like firecrackers, then died out. The crowd, clearly intoxicated and potentially volatile, welcomed the Lounge Lizards as liberators.

No one had expected that to happen.

Col. Stone's Rolls Royce came around a turn in the road and screeched to a halt. A dozen or more shot-up cars and light trucks lined the boulevard with windscreens spider-webbed, chassis pocked with holes, and dead Italians slumped inside them riddled by bullets.

A man was standing in the right-of-way, his face obscured by the brim of his bush hat. He did not look like he intended to move.

"Shall I squirt the cheeky bastard, sir?" The Yeomanry gunner on the pedestal-mounted, twin Vickers K machine guns asked tersely. He had yet to fire a round in anger and was looking for an opportunity.

"Stand down," Col. Stone barked. "Point your weapon up!"

The man in the road walked toward the car.

"Fancy meeting you here, old stick," the Lounge Lizards' commander drawled as he climbed out of the car.

"What took you so long?" Brigadier John Randal said.

"We expected to have to fight our way in," Col. Stone said. "Never counted on finding a street party—what happened?"

With the column halted, the troops began dismounting to brew up tea while the two senior officers studied a map spread out over the hood of the command car. Single gunshots rang out from time to time in the distance. Someone was extracting payback—old grudges being settled.

"Jack Taylor raised a lot more guerrilla fighters than anyone thought he could," Brig. Randal said. "They decided to come to town last night. The banda troops stationed here in Kismayo mutinied and started shooting their Italian officers. The place went crazy—everyone's armed and drunk."

"My orders," Col. Stone said, "are to push on through town and secure a river crossing for an attack on the Jubba MLR tomorrow or the next day."

"We've already done that," Brig. Randal said. "You need to get to the dock and cordon off the million gallons or so of gasoline and high octane aviation fuel in the fuel storage tanks. Mike Mikkalis is there now fighting the Italian demolition engineers who are trying to blow it."

"You captured a bridge?"

"No, the bridges are all down, but there's a low-water crossing about fifteen miles upriver."

Brig. Randal pointed to the location on the map. "We watched a column of Italian trucks cross yesterday on our way here—only hub deep. It's not defended on either side."

"Perfect," Col. Stone said. "I shall want to go inspect it straight away after we secure that fuel—what a prize!"

"Which one—the crossing or the fuel?"

"If East Africa Force can put itself across the river in strength, that's it for the Duke of Aosta. Your low-water crossing may be the war winner, John. Once over the Jubba, we shall drive up the coast road to Mogadishu with the Royal Navy sailing along on our right flank with their 16-inch guns, merrily shelling anything that dares oppose us."

"Consider it a present," Brig. Randal said. "I'm just passing through."

"You should try to be more careful in the future," Col. Stone advised. "My machine gunner nearly shot you."

The Yeomanry gunner looked up from where he was squatting beside the Rolls Royce brewing his tea and gave a toothy grin.

"Really," said Brig. Randal reaching up and touching the brim of his cut-down bush hat with his left hand.

Rita Hayworth and Lana Turner materialized behind him in the road with their 9mm MAB-38A submachine guns. Waldo stepped out holding the 12-gauge Browning A-5 straight up by the pistol grip with the chopped-off barrel resting against his right shoulder. On the roofs of the houses lining both sides of the streets heavily-armed Patriots stood up looking down on the column.

There appeared to be hundreds of them.

Clearly the Lounge Lizards had driven unawares into the killing zone of a perfectly prepared ambush—as the dead Italians in the wrecked vehicles had the misfortune to discover.

"If I were you, Colonel," Brig. Randal said. "I'd think twice about letting my men take a smoke break this deep in Indian County."

"Yes, sir!" Col. Stone said to his best friend. "Point taken."

"Don't be a hero, Terry. You know a regimental commander doesn't have any business pulling point. You're no good to anybody dead."

"Keep that in mind yourself, John. I may be on the sharp end, but you are out in *front* of the tip."

COLONEL HUGH BOUSTEAD, LIEUTENANT RANDY "HORNBLOWER" Seaborn and their guest, Major Edwin Chapman-Andrews, who was over visiting the Frontier Battalion from Colonel Orde Wingate and the Emperor's Patriot column, were sitting in canvas camp chairs eating small slices of a white cake specially prepared for the occasion. The three were in the field on a bald ridge overlooking a major Italian base. Behind them a short distance away, their soldier servants were holding their saddle mules.

Down below a platoon of the Frontier Battalion was moving into position against the Blackshirt fort. The mortar section was being set up farther along the ridge. The odds against them were staggering. However, Col. Boustead was maneuvering his tiny force with the skill of a field marshal. He was the consummate professional fighting commander of native troops, and he had the situation well in hand.

Maj. Chapman-Andrews said, "The camels are dying at the rate of nearly a hundred per day. It is almost as if they are staging a protest with their lives."

"Should not be happening," Col. Boustead replied. "We have camels supporting the Frontier Battalion—only lost the odd animal... broken leg and whatnot."

"At this rate, by my calculations there will be no camels left by the time we reach Addis Ababa—terribly depressing to be a witness to," Maj. Chapman-Andrews said.

"Wingate blames the deaths on the poor quality of animals supplied him, tainted feed, stock, etc. The handful of experienced cameleers in the column who actually know what they are doing blame Wingate for overloading the camels and not resting them properly."

"Orde Wingate," Col. Boustead sneered. "What an ass."

"There is great dissention in the ranks of the Europeans marching in the Patriot column. We are bickering our way ever onward into the heart of darkest Abyssinia. At night, if Wingate shows up at one of the campfires to chat, the other people gradually start to drift away until he is left at the fire all alone. No one likes Orde—and even worse, no one respects the man. The officers are not bashful about letting him know it, either.

"No. 1 Operational Center—the hard-drinking Australians who were the original volunteers to serve with Wingate—sent a message out to their HQ complaining there was no organization, no tactical plans and not enough rations. They claimed the column was simply blundering along trusting to luck—and that from men who are supposed to worship Wingate.

"Even the Emperor has privately instructed me to restrict Wingate's personal access. The King of Kings has had his fill of the imposter. Orde made a big mistake not letting him bring his Royal Umbrella."

A Sudanese messenger rode up and handed Col. Boustead a message. After scanning it he responded, "Tell Bimbashi Johnson to open at his pleasure."

The messenger galloped off. Within minutes the sound of mortars began thumping, followed moments later by the *CRUUUUUUPH, CRUUUUUUPH, CRUUUUUUPH* of rounds detonating. From where the trio of officers sat, now sipping from small cups of piping hot tea, the rounds could be observed exploding within the Italian base.

Shortly, a white flag was run up.

"Congratulations, sir," Lt. Seaborn admired. "Nicely done. How do you propose we handle the prisoners?"

"You and I shall ride down there in a moment, Randy, and negotiate a withdrawal. The Wops outnumber us twenty or thirty to one. Since we have no provisions to care for POWs and not enough men to guard them anyway, we shall simply let them march out with their personal arms at the slope. No need to have the poor lads slaughtered by the shifta, what?"

"But they will simply fall back on the next fort, sir," Lt. Seaborn protested, "to fight another day."

"In that case, Randy," Col. Boustead said unperturbed, "when we arrive at their new front gate they shall already have the drill down—makes the next retreat all the easier."

23
FIRE IN THE HOLE

THE CONSOLIDATED MODEL 31, *AKA* THE PREGNANT GUPPY, ROLLED IN on its final approach to the Initial Point – flying low and slow through enemy skies east of Asmara, deep in Italian East Africa. On loan to 1 Guerrilla Corps (Parachute), Force N from the Consolidated Company, the American crew was there to demonstrate the virtues of the world's newest and most versatile amphibian in action, though technically they were mercenaries. To date, not a single Model 31 had been sold to any military service.

The Americans were making a lot of money flying missions out of Camp Croc.

The red light came on in the dark of the troop compartment.

"TEN MINUTES!" Brigadier John Randal shouted at the thirteen paratroopers seated in the bench-style canvas seats running along the outboard sides of the aircraft.

Captain "Pyro" Percy Stirling, the third jumper in the stick, gave him a thumbs-up.

Up ahead on the ground in the semi-arid desert a giant letter "N" was burning brightly in the fifty-five gallon barrels that had been cut in half and filled with oil to form the signal.

Brig. Randal braced his rubber-soled, canvas-topped raiding boots on either side of the open door, grabbed the metal ridges that ran around it with his fingertips and arched his body outside the aircraft. He spotted the "N" and swung back inside.

The blond crewcut Load Master was chewing bubblegum and talking into a headset. He looked up, made eye contact and nodded his head.

"SIX MINUTES!"

Rita Hayworth and Lana Turner were sitting number 1 and 2 next to the open door. The two girls were going to follow Brig. Randal out the door. Capt. Stirling and his band of saboteurs would be right behind them. The Railroad Wrecking Crew had one more mission ahead of it.

Back in the Force N Area of Operations their work on the railroad was done. You can only blow up one rail line so many times – and they had. From Addis Ababa to Harar nothing was moving by train. Seldom, if ever, in any war had one young officer paralyzed an entire country's rail system. But the effort had not been without its tribulations, as Capt. Stirling would attest.

"STAND UP!"

The Load Master and one of his assistants were muscling a door bundle into position behind Brig. Randal. The men clipped its snap hook on the steel cable static line that ran the length of the fuselage. They would kick it out seconds after the last man in the stick went out the door.

"HOOK UP!"

Brig. Randal hooked his snap link on the steel cable, made sure it was set, and threaded a safety pin into the small hole below the hook. Then he bent the wire down flat on the far side.

"CHECK YOUR STATIC LINE!"

The jumpers all rattled their static lines vigorously to make sure they were hooked up correctly.

"CHECK YOUR EQUIPMENT!"

This was a redundant command – they had all checked their equipment a hundred times. But in the military during wartime for a paratrooper getting ready to jump behind enemy lines, redundancy is a good thing.

"SOUND OFF FOR EQUIPMENT CHECK!"

"OK... OK... OK..." came racing forward from the back of the stick like a string of falling dominoes. Rita stuck her palm out flat, "All OK!"

For Brig. Randal, this was about the longest conversation he had ever had with either of the girls. He gave Rita a wink. She stared back expressionless – Zār priestess cool.

"CLOSE ON THE DOOR!"

The stick of jumpers all shuffled forward, pressing up hard against each other. The idea was a quick, tight exit would get them all on the drop zone close together. No one wanted to drift off the DZ on a night combat jump in Africa.

Brig. Randal arched back outside the door looking forward at the burning "N". Timing it by guess, he swung back inside the aircraft.

"ONE MINUTE!"

Then he shuffled forward until the sole of his lead right boot was halfway outside of the airplane. He reached outside and slapped his palms flat on both sides of the door. He was watching the jump light burning bright red.

The light flashed to green.

"LET'S GO!"

Then he was outside the aircraft in a tight body tuck – head down, chin tight on his chest so the static line could deploy his X-Type parachute over his shoulder. Both eyes open, everything at this point seemed to be going in slow motion. He was buffeted and tossed by the prop blast from the airplane's monster-sized engines but managed to maintain his body position.

The parachute cracked and he looked up and saw it was open – no blown panels, no lines over the canopy. Everything was copasetic, as paratroopers like to say when things look good. It was a beautiful night.

He dropped the bag he had clutched between his knees down on its sixteen-foot lowering line. His 9mm MAB-38A submachine gun was inside it, disassembled. It dangled down, tied to his left ankle.

The ride did not last long. He took up a good prepare-to-land position. Then out of the corner of his eye something blazed and he knew the ground was coming up. Nothing was going in slow motion now.

WHAAAM! His toes, pointed down, hit the ground as he was coming in backwards. He landed on the balls of his feet, swiveled as fast as a cat, fell on to the outside of his calf, thigh, buttocks, small of the back – the five points of contact of the parachute landing fall. The momentum carried him all the way over. He flipped and landed back on his feet.

You are not supposed to do PLFs like that but it made for one of the fastest landings and recoveries he had ever experienced. Brig. Randal popped his quick release and the parachute harness fell to the ground.

"Nice jump, sir," Major Jack Merritt said. "Welcome back."

There were no hard fast rules since parachute operations, even for small-scale raids, were still in their infancy. But most commanders would have elected to jump a nice, safe distance from the objective – meaning thirty or forty miles (far enough away that the enemy would not be able to hear the sound of the airplane's engines); make a careful approach to their target – in this case the Ropeway aerial rail system – traveling by night and hiding by day; execute the mission; then conduct a forced march cross-country to rendezvous with their extraction element.

Brig. Randal did not like that technique and had never employed it. He preferred to drop close to the target, carry out his mission as quickly as possible and have an extraction plan where his team was picked up virtually on the objective. Hit and run before the enemy could react.

Brig. Randal realized he was in the minority with that line of thinking. However, he did not really care what anyone else would have done in his place or if there was an *approved* school solution. He planned tonight's operation as a quick in-and-out.

No. 9 Motor Machine Gun Company had already reconnoitered the Ropeway, left a small stay-behind party to keep the objective under observation then selected the drop zone. Maj. Merritt had set up the "N" signal on the DZ, collected the door bundle of explosives when it landed and was prepared to transport the demolitions team to the target immediately.

His gun-trucks would provide security while the explosive charges were placed. Then Maj. Merritt was to drive Brig. Randal's raiding party overland to an isolated straight stretch of road some sixty miles distant (one of his platoons was there now keeping it under observation) where the Pregnant Guppy would land the following night and fly them out.

The plan followed Raiding Forces Rule No. 2 – 'Keep it Short and Simple.'

Plan B was if the extraction site was compromised and the Consolidated Model 31 unable to land, No. 9 MMG Co. would drive the raiding party overland back to friendly lines outside Keren.

The night was hot and dry. After a quick check to make sure all the jumpers and equipment had been policed up, the Railroad Wrecking Crew boarded the trucks for the short three-mile ride to the target. The demolitions men were keen to get to work.

There were two types of structures to be blown.

The Ropeway was a cable car rail system. Fifty-foot tall metal towers that looked not unlike miniature Eiffel Towers supported its cables. Blowing down a tower was a simple demolitions task for trained explosive experts. Prepared cutting charges would be set against three of the tower's four legs.

The original ground rail line, built before the turn of the century, ran parallel to the Ropeway though it had not been used in years. Strangely, considering the Italians were legendary for their prowess as railroad operators, the ground rail system had been allowed to fall into a state of disrepair. By all reports it was unusable.

Brig. Randal was not taking any chances. The Blackshirts really were excellent railroad men and they might be able to affect repairs in time to continue to support their forces fighting in the Keren mountain fortress. He had ordered Capt. Stirling to develop plans to take out a mile of track and blow up a railroad trestle that crossed an intermittent stream in the target area.

For purposes of planning and navigation, the bridge had become the objective.

The charges were all prepared, packed and airdropped in the door bundle. In addition, Maj. Merritt brought demolitions in his gun-trucks as back up. Before the night was over, Brig. Randal was confident all the explosives would be used. Capt. Stirling was not called "Pyro" without cause – he was a 'Death or Glory Boy' and he liked to blow things up.

When No. 9 MMG Co. reached the vicinity of the target area, a halt was called while a foot patrol went forward to contact the stay-behind party who were observing the Ropeway and bridge. After a short wait, the patrol returned and the main body continued on. The semi-arid desert was very quiet. With the moon out three-quarters full, the brush was bathed in plenty of light for them to do their work.

One of the advantages of operating in remote, desolate terrain is that the enemy cannot defend everywhere. There were not enough men in Italy to have guarded the rail line. It was not patrolled at night.

When the gun-trucks came into sight of the cable towers, Brig. Randal felt the old familiar shiver of excitement he always experienced when he saw his objective for the first time.

Cap. Stirling's men had rehearsed this mission. Every man knew exactly what he was supposed to do. The demolitions party went into action like a well-honed demonstration team. By this time in the campaign the Railroad Wrecking Crew were highly experienced.

They made the job look easy.

It had been estimated that if one tower could be brought down, the Italians would not be able to repair the damage until after the issue at Keren had been decided. The plan tonight called for five of them to be taken out.

Why take a chance?

When Brig. Randal and Capt. Stirling walked the rail line they saw it was in a worse state than initially believed.

"No way the Italians could possibly get this up and running in less than a month – if then, sir," Capt. Stirling estimated.

"Skip blowing the track – give you some extra explosives to play with," Brig. Randal ordered. "Go ahead and knock down the bridge though. Never hurts to play it safe."

"Sir!"

"Try to not blow me up tonight – for once."

"Not setting the charges on the tracks will save time," Capt. Stirling said, hoping to change the subject. "Two hours at least, sir."

He felt remorse about killing Parachute.

At 0220 hours Capt. Stirling reported to Brig. Randal that the placing of explosives was complete. "Would you care to inspect the demolition charges, sir?"

"Let's do it," Brig. Randal said. "Jack, this won't take long – be ready to get the hell out of Dodge as soon as we get back."

"With your permission I shall pull in my security elements now," Maj. Merritt replied.

"Go ahead."

Brig. Randal, trailed by Rita and Lana, who as usual did not want to miss anything, followed Capt. Stirling as he led them down the line of towers pointing out the placement of the explosives. Then they walked out on and across the bridge, which was a simple wooden trestle approximately thirty feet high and about 400 yards long. Then they walked back. The inspection was a courtesy to his demolitions officer – it was not necessary.

When Capt. Stirling blew something up he really blew it up and it stayed blown up.

"How're you planning to set it off?" Brig. Randal asked

"Timed fuse, we can be long gone or close by when it blows," Cap. Stirling said. "Your prerogative, sir."

"I want to see it."

"Yes, sir."

No. 9 Motor Machine Gun Co. moved off approximately 500 yards. Brig. Randal and Maj. Merritt broke out cigars and waited for Capt. Stirling to join them after his men lit the fuses. There was no need to be stealthy at this point. Rita and Lana twittered like canaries. The girls were clearly enjoying themselves waiting for the fireworks.

The gun-truck carrying Capt. Stirling and his men rumbled through the scrub brush.

"Fire in the hole!"

The string of explosions, when they came, sounded anti-climactic. The result was not. In semi-slow motion the cable car support towers teetered then toppled over with three of their legs blown out from under them. All five towers went down.

The wooden railroad bridge made for an even more spectacular show. When the first charges went off, the support beams left standing could not support the weight of the tracks. The trestles started popping and toppling like a string of dominoes. The bridge was totally destroyed,

"Nice job, Pyro," Maj. Merritt said. "Italians shall not be using this line any time soon and you did not scare twenty years off the lifespan of anyone we know."

Brig. Randal said, "Roger that."

24

MAN-EATER

"WE HAVE INTELLIGENCE INFORMATION," BRIGADIER JOHN RANDAL said to the assembled officers and NCOs of Captain Harry Shelby's 5th MRB *aka* Harry's Hellraisers, Captain Lionel Chatterhorn's Escort Company and Lieutenant Butch Hoolihan's Force Raiding Company. He had parachuted in to take direct command of the 1 Guerrilla Corps (Parachute), Force N operations north of Addis Ababa.

"Two reinforced Italian battalions will be departing the capital at daybreak tomorrow, heading north. They will be taking the long, roundabout route to Keren. Our mission is to prevent them from reaching there.

"Here's how we're going to do it," Brig. Randal said as he pointed the tip of his Fairbairn knife to a location on the map that Lana and Rita were holding up for the group to see. "Lieutenant Hoolihan will set up a company-sized ambush along the road in this area.

"Immediately to his right flank, Captain Chatterhorn will set up a company-sized ambush with Escort Company. To his right flank Captain Shelby, you will set up a series of company-sized ambushes here, here, here, etc. with your five companies.

"The purpose of the exercise is to make the Italians pay a price for every inch of road. We probably can't stop 'em... at least at first... so we'll plan to make 'em run a gauntlet. Butch, as soon as they fight past you pull out, swing around behind Escort Company, leapfrog Harry's battalion and set up another ambush on his far right flank. Lionel, Escort Company will do the same thing as will each of Harry's companies in turn after they have executed their ambush.

"Make maximum use of your 81mm mortars and your Boys .55 Anti-tank Rifles. Each company has one tube while Force Raiding Company has three. Butch, you keep one tube with you and drop the other two off with Escort Company when you relocate. Sergeant McDonald – when Lieutenant Hoolihan pulls out, leave one of your mortars with Force Raiding Company and take command of the other two mortar teams being attached to Escort Company. Continue relocating straight up the road going from company to company with your two tubes so there will always be three 81s supporting each individual company ambush.

"This is a far ambush. Do not assault the killing zone until I order it. There's a possibility we're never going to be strong enough to tackle this convoy straight up. Shoot, move, and do it again.

"T-C, you'll be responsible for flank and rear security using the Patriot forces.

"This concludes my briefing. What are your questions?"

"Where would you like me to position myself, sir?" Captain Harry Shelby, MC asked.

"You fight your battalion," Brig. Randal said. "I will initially be with Force Raiding Company, then Escort, then you."

"Any other questions?" Brig. Randal looked around the semi-circle of guerrilla leaders. "OK then, you can count on the bad guys having armor and air support. So be it.

"Our troops fighting at Keren are in a death struggle – we're not letting any Italian reinforcements get through. We'll keep leapfrogging up the road, fighting all the way until we kill 'em all or they turn back.

"Commanders, take charge of your units," Brig. Randal ordered. "Fight hard."

Cheap Bribe, Kaldi, Waldo Treywick and Lieutenant Jeffery Tall-Castle were waiting for him as the briefing broke up.

"We got us a situation," Waldo said. "A big *tillik sau* up here is ready to sign on – says he can bring in a couple 'a thousand men."

"He is willing to subordinate to Gubbo," Lt. Tall-Castle added, "provided we do him one favor."

"What's the man want?"

"He's got a bad cat problem. Man-eater done run up a big score," Waldo said. "Say's we take out his kitty, he'll jump right in and go to killing Wops – up the Emperor, he's a loyal man."

"OK."

"In that case, I'll get one of the Bimbashis to shoot the cat," Waldo said. "Cap'n Shelby has a couple experienced big game hunters in his crew."

"Negative," Brig. Randal said. "You make arrangements for the set up tonight, Mr. Treywick. Shelby's officers will be busy reconning their ambush sites and getting their troops ready for tomorrow – you and I can kill this cat."

"I thought you said an airdrop was coming in this evening," Waldo said hopefully. "Ain't that gonna' require your personal attention?"

"Don't need me for that."

"Just when I thought we was out 'a the huntin' business for good," Waldo griped, "I get drug back in. Supposed to be a real talented people-eater. We're gonna' fool around and be the Blue Plate Special yet."

"Move out, Mr. Treywick," Brig. Randal ordered. "Get this show on the road."

"The most important rule to remember about huntin' killer cat," Waldo said, "is quit when you're ahead."

THE EAST AFRICA RECONNAISSANCE REGIMENT SLIPPED ACROSS THE Jubba River in the dark at the ford Brigadier John Randal had pointed out to Colonel Sir Terry "Zorro" Stone on the map. A brigade of South Africans under Brigadier Dan Pienaar came charging after it at sunrise and immediately engaged the Italian Main Line of Resistance to the left and right of the crossing, sealing it off. The Italians were taken completely by surprise.

11 African Division rolled up, its engineers threw a pontoon bridge across the Jubba and the division poured across. The division fought a series of company-sized actions. While not the single big battle

the Italians had anticipated, it was enough to defeat the much heralded Jubba River Defense Line – at least at the point where East Africa Force needed to penetrate it.

Assaulting a defended river crossing is one of the most difficult of all military operations. The Jubba River Defense Line was the Italian's great hope in the south. It was expected to stop East Africa Force in its tracks.

Rivers make excellent defensive barriers. There is, however, one problem associated with defending them. Generally, a river is fairly long so it requires a lot of troops to man the line along one. To be successful a river defense has to stop the attacker at the water's edge or in the water while attempting the crossing.

If a mobile attacking force can cross the river by force or by stealth and punch through the hard crust of the fortifications on the far side they are out in the open running free. And the result is there are a lot of enemy soldiers wasting their time manning defensive lines along the riverbank where they will never be attacked.

East Africa Force was the first completely mechanized army in history. It was highly mobile. Col. Stone's reconnaissance regiment was the most nimble unit in the EAF. They were over the river quick and through the defenses before the Italians realized what was happening. The Lounge Lizards broke loose from the belt of jungle that bordered the Jubba and raced up the coast of the Indian Ocean, strafing the odd unsuspecting Italian unit as they rolled past.

Three days and 250 miles later the Lounge Lizards were closing on Mogadishu. No unit in history had ever covered as much ground so fast against opposition. Not even the German Panzers in the early blitzkrieg days in France. In his wildest imagination, Col. Stone had never imagined a hell for leather cavalry ride like this.

Most Italians the Lounge Lizards encountered chose not to stand and fight. When some recalcitrant Blackshirt commander tried, Col. Stone deployed his Yeomanry armored car squadron on line with their Vickers Model K .303-caliber machine guns to establish a base of fire. Then he brought up the fast-firing 3-pounder crewed by the Royal Navy and had the truck-mounted parachute infantry company maneuver around behind the enemy position, dismount and make a demonstration.

In nearly every instance once their line of retreat was threatened the Italians evacuated.

Col. Stone never allowed his regiment to become committed to a prolonged firefight. If the situation required a position be assaulted, he simply struck his tent, had his troops mount back up then drove around the Blackshirts and continued to race up the coastline. Fighting was not his mission – covering ground was.

11ᵗʰ African Division, traveling along in his wake, was responsible for mopping up pockets of resistance. When the 1ˢᵗ South African Brigade under Brig. Pienaar leading the division came up, they made quick work of the holdouts. The division had two sure-fire ways to deal with Italians who did not choose to fall back or surrender.

Number 40 Air-Cooperation Squadron, South African Air Force would be summoned, fly over in their Pretoria-built Hartebeest dive-bombers and bombard the target. That always worked.

Or even better, the Royal Navy would cruise offshore, unlimber their massive guns and pound the Fascist opposition into dust. Word spread about the price of resistance and soon very few Blackshirts wanted to experience firsthand the East Africa Force combined arms firepower.

Before long, when the Lounge Lizards rolled up on an enemy position the National, Colonial or Banda troops inside would mutiny and either run up a white flag or abandon the post. The Duke of Aosta's defenses in the southern part of Italian East Africa were crumbling. No one on either side had foreseen that happening.

The 23ʳᵈ Nigerian Brigade replaced the 1ˢᵗ South Africans at the head of 11 African Division. Everyone liked the cheerful Nigerians, especially the British officers who commanded them. The Nigerians loved to tease the other troops, particularly the South Africans – by claiming to be cannibals… then invite them over "for a meal."

A platoon of 23ʳᵈ Nigerian Brigade Field Security Police raced ahead and linked up with the East Africa Reconnaissance Regiment.

The British lieutenant in command reported to Col. Stone, "Mogadishu has been declared an open city, sir. My orders are to travel with you and station my policeman at key points in town to prevent damage by looters."

"Move up and fall in behind my lead element," Col. Stone ordered. "My orders are to secure the fuel dumps in the dock area. You happen to have any intelligence information on the storage tanks, per chance?"

"Sir, I have no intelligence on anything – war is moving too fast. My original assignment was traffic control in Kismayo – 250 miles back."

"Hang on, Lieutenant," Col. Stone warned. "If you thought things were moving fast before, you've not seen anything yet."

The Lounge Lizards pulled onto the paved *autostrada* for the final 100-mile run to Mogadishu. They threw caution to the breeze now that they knew there was not going to be a fight for the metropolis. The important thing was to get to the fuel storage facilities. The petrol was needed for the next leg of the operation.

Night was falling when the lead Rolls Royce armored cars sped into Mogadishu. The city was devoid of troops. The Italian 102nd Division defending the city had pulled out on orders from the Duke of Aosta. He had wanted to "spare" it from the Royal Navy gunfire.

As the regiment rolled in, it took snappy salutes from Italian military policeman still on duty and civilians wearing the blue brassards of the special police. Unlike the reception at Kismayo, there was no party atmosphere. The streets were lined with silent civilians who seemed stunned at the sudden fall of the city.

Bells tolled from the church cathedrals to announce the defeat. As the Lounge Lizards pulled up to the Governor's Palace, which had served as the 102nd Division's Headquarters, Italian officers began to voluntarily lead their own men who had not fled the city into prisoner of war cages (originally built to hold the troops of East Africa Force). The Field Security Police lieutenant dropped off a detachment of a corporal and two men to guard the palace then went off in search of the telephone exchange and other strategic points that needed to be secured.

"Don't cook anyone," Col. Stone said to the corporal, getting a big white-toothed grin and a razor sharp salute in response. As he trotted up the steps to try to find someone inside who could give him information about the location of the fuel tank farms in and around the city, he noticed a Rolls Royce armored car parked at the curb. It was not one of his.

The building was abandoned. There was a light burning in the commanding general's office. He went to investigate. Inside, sitting behind the general's desk with her boots propped up was Captain the Lady Jane Seaborn.

"What are you doing here?"

"Waiting for you," Mrs. Brandy Seaborn said from a bat-winged chair just inside the door. "We want to hitch a ride to Harar, Terry."

"That's a thousand miles north!"

"Seven hundred forty-four to be exact. Located at the foot of the central highlands – Force N's Area of Operations," Lady Jane said. "Come on, let's go get John."

BRIGADIER JOHN RANDAL AND WALDO TREYWICK WERE SITTING IN THE dark waiting to kill a man-eating lion. The men had done this many times before. When Force N Advanced Party had parachuted in to raise a guerrilla army, the parachute carrying the team's radio experienced a complete malfunction... a Roman Candle... which meant the radio had shattered into a million pieces. Since they could not radio for money to be dropped in to pay them, the only way to win the support of the natives had been to eradicate man-eating lions that were a plague on the countryside since the Italian Invasion of Abyssinia five years earlier.

For sport Italian soldiers routinely shot people at random from their passing convoys, leaving them where they lay and the Regia Aeronautica soaked the countryside in poison gas from time-to-time. The unintended consequences of these practices was that a lot of big cats had acquired a taste for human flesh from eating the dead bodies lying around. When lions graduated from scavenging dead bodies to live ones, they learned how easy it was to kill and eat people as compared to trying to pull down a buffalo, which was sure to fight back – the man-eater problem became epidemic.

Hunting lions is considered dangerous. Hunting man-eating lions on a regular basis is suicidal. Unless the hunter can get in a tall tree stand with a big bright spotlight and a heavy caliber rifle, the lion has all the advantages.

Tonight the two lion hunters did not have their powerful spotlight and there were no tall trees in the area. Brig. Randal and Waldo were sitting at the bottom of a tall rock face with their backs against it, just outside a village that had been experiencing nightly man-eater attacks for months. The remains of the lion's last victim were about fifty yards down the slope.

The plan was when the big cat came back to finish his meal they would shoot it. Tonight Waldo had borrowed Lieutenant Butch "Headhunter" Hoolihan's .45 Thompson submachine gun in case it came down to a fight. The ex-ivory poacher had a bad feeling about this hunt – the lion had a fearsome reputation.

"Wake me up when he gets here," Brig. Randal said.

"Are you crazy?" Waldo shrieked in a high-pitched whisper. "A killer cat out there, he knows we're here, and you're gonna' take a nap?"

"Long day tomorrow."

There was the sound of bones cracking. The lion had arrived and was munching on the leftovers of yesterday's kill. The man-eater had to know they were there.

The big cat was indifferent. He would eat them later. That's what happens when a lion loses its natural fear of man – it holds them in contempt. Sitting fifty yards (or maybe less – it had been hard to judge in the twilight) away from a hungry man-eater… that's not a good thing.

Waldo was quivering. Brig. Randal was alert but it seemed to Waldo that he acted bored. In the old army scout's estimation there were two words in the English language that did not belong together in the same sentence under any circumstance – "man-eater" and "bored."

"Ready?" Brig. Randal asked, bringing a stubby weapon out from under his sand green parachute smock. Since he had been carrying his .30 M-1903 A-1 Springfield with the ivory post sight for dark work, Waldo had expected that to be the weapon of choice tonight. In fact, other than his pistols he never traveled without, Waldo had not even realized the brigadier had another weapon with him. In the pitch black he guessed it was the sawed-off Browning A-5 12-gauge shotgun.

"As I'll ever be," Waldo said.

Brig. Randal turned on the flashlight taped to the short barrel of his weapon. It put out a dim yellow beam that illuminated a pair of monster-sized orbs staring at them. Waldo felt a chill go down his spine as he heard a soft *BLOOOOP* followed almost instantaneously by a tremendous *KAAAAABOOOOOM* explosion that rocked the night and echoed through the canyons.

A 45mm mortar round detonating within fifty yards (in this case, maybe less) makes a big boom at night when you're high in the mountains and not expecting it.

"Are we alive?"

"I think I got him."

"What the hell does it matter," Waldo clutched his chest. "I'm probably in cardiac arrest over here or maybe wounded. Damn... sure in pain."

"Shine your light down there, Mr. Treywick."

"What's the burstin' radius on a 45mm?" Waldo asked, fumbling for the flashlight he had dropped when the round detonated. "I'm pretty sure I heard shrapnel ricocheting off the rock behind us. You think we're hit? I don't feel nuthin'. But that's what you're supposed to feel when you're dyin'... nothin'."

"Not sure exactly – we'll have to ask somebody. I heard some too."

"Don't you think it's a little late to be checking up on details like that? You're supposed to know that nomenclature *before* you touch her off."

"I've never fired at anything less than a hundred yards or so," Brig. Randal said. "Shine the light."

When the flashlight came on, the beam was too weak for them to see much of anything. "That's probably a good sign," Waldo said, not sounding too confident. "If you didn't kill the son-of-a-bitch he ain't ever gonna' be seen in this district again. Bet he done lost his appetite."

"I'm pretty sure I hit him."

"For the record, I ain't ever goin' huntin' with you anymore, Brigadier. This is the end of our cat-killin' relationship – all she wrote for me. Twenty years scoutin' for the army with P.J. Pretorius, poachin' Portuguese ivory and being a captured slave was kindergarten compared to what I've had to go through backin' you in the last six months.'"

"Let's go check it out."

"OK, I'm right behind you – take the Tommy gun. I'm shakin' too bad to hit anythin' with it. I don't think we're gonna' have to bother with any Big Cat Down Shoot Again Procedure tonight. If that cat ain't dead, he sure ain't gonna' be hanging around to see what'll happen next."

As they crept down the slope Waldo said, "When I was in parachute school Lady Seaborn used to come out and jump with me – helped to keep my courage up but you don't have to tell her that. You know she offered me a job when this is all over?"

"Good."

"Now I understand all the commotion over the woman. Drop-dead gorgeous is right. You know what I'd 'a done if I was you when I found out the man I'd rescued from the Nazi Germans was her dead husband?"

"What's that, Mr. Treywick?"

"Taken and hauled his ass back to the Nazis. Between huntin' bad cat and failed matrimony, you're a babe in the woods, Brigadier. Somebody needs to go along and hold your hand full time.

"In the future it ain't gonna' be me. I'm probably gonna' take that job."

They found the lion. Not that there was much of it left to find. The 45mm mortar round had struck the animal squarely in the chest. A lucky shot, but by then Brig. Randal had put over a thousand rounds through the little shoulder-fired mortar.

The cat was one dead man-eater.

"You sure used enough gun. Too bad that ain't your main competition laying there," Waldo observed, looking down at the still smoking remains of the cat. "We could 'a said it was a huntin' accident."

25

AMBUSH

THE DUKE OF AOSTA SENT TWO MOTORIZED INFANTRY BATTALIONS north out of Addis Ababa as reinforcements for the mountain fortress at Keren, taking the long, "safe" route around the 1 Guerrilla Corps (Parachute), Force N Area of Operations to the south. The battle of Keren was going well for the Italians. The British Forces striking out of the Sudan had been stopped and were pinned down on the piping hot mountainside, being slaughtered in their exposed positions. Every time the British and Indian troops fixed bayonets, attacked up the mountain and gained any ground, they were counterattacked and thrown back.

The key to victory at Keren was that the Italians could reinforce. Lieutenant General William Platt, the Kaid could not. The British were all in.

The Italian troop convoy to Keren was escorted by a company of tankettes and a regiment of armored cars. The tankettes, armored cars and trucks had made this run three times previously and encountered no enemy contact. They were not expecting any trouble.

The convoy was nearly two miles long.

Brigadier John Randal issued orders for Force Raiding Company and Escort Company to allow the Italians to pass and for Captain Harry Shelby to initiate the ambush when the convoy was fully in the killing zone of the first company in his battalion. The idea was to catch all the lorried infantry in the ambush so the troops would not be able to dismount, assault up the mountain ridge, flank the Force Raiding Company and roll up the ambushers from left to right. He wanted the Italian infantrymen pinned down.

By this point in the guerrilla campaign, the Force N troops were highly experienced at the art of ambush. When the Blackshirt convoy, oblivious to what was about to happen, motored into their sights, Brig. Randal's men let them pass. Green and tan mottled Caproni 133 bombers swept down the road at low level from time to time ahead of the column, giving the Italians a false sense of security.

At 1000 hours Brig. Randal was with Force Raiding Company watching the convoy roll by 300 yards below. The mountainsides along this stretch were sheer, almost straight up, and there was a 1,000-foot drop-off on the far side of the road. The Force N ambush site had been carefully selected with these two terrain features in mind.

Once the ambush was initiated, the Blackshirt cavalcade would have only two options—continue driving forward on the road or back up, turn around and go home. If the convoy attempted to fight their way through, they were going to be under fire until they drove out of the highlands. Unfortunately for the Italians, the mountains went all the way to Keren, 200 miles away as the crow flies—a lot farther by the single-lane curving road they would have to travel.

As the ambush was initiated and the firing broke out at the head of the column, the trucks back down the line closed up for security and kept going. That was a mistake. They should have maintained their interval. Bunching up a convoy does not provide security. It creates a bigger target.

Lieutenant Butch "Headhunter" Hoolihan threw a Mills bomb as hard as he could. Due to the great height of the ambush site, the grenade flew most of the distance, then bounced and rolled the rest of the way down to the road. It blew up with a loud resounding *BOOOOOM!*

The men of Force Raiding Company engaged immediately.

The battery of three 81mm mortars under Sergeant Jock McDonald went into action. Machine gunners began hosing down the trucks with streams of .303-caliber fire. The Green Jackets on the Boys .55 plinked the truck's engines and aimed for exposed petrol cans. Lovat Scouts Munro Ferguson and Lionel Fenwick began sniping at the open-topped tankettes, taking out the vehicle commanders and gunners.

Force Raiding Company was working the bolts of their M-1903 A-1 Springfield rifles with a passion. The men were still miserable shots despite the months of training expended by Lt. Hoolihan and the almost constant guerrilla fighting. So, although a lot of noise was being generated, the indigenous troops were not hitting much.

Moving along the ridgeline, Brig. Randal rained 45mm mortar shells down on the bunched-up, thin-skinned vehicles, firing the Brixia M-35 with both eyes open. In the daylight it was possible to watch the round in flight. He adjusted his aiming point using Kentucky windage for the next round from where the last one hit—the mortar did not have any sights.

Firing the Brixia M-35 reminded him of shooting the Red Rider BB gun he had when he was a boy. The difference was the satisfying *KERCHUUUMH* when the 45mm mortar detonated. His BB gun had not made that noise.

When one of the 45mm rounds slammed into a truck, the blast could be spectacular if the fuel tank went up. On occasion he got a secondary explosion from ammunition being transported in one of the truck's beds.

Twice he managed to drop rounds down the open-topped turret of a tankette with gratifying results. The little armored vehicles erupted like volcanoes when the mortar shell set off the AP and HE rounds stored in their ammunition lockers.

Brig. Randal was having the shoot of his life—fish in a barrel.

The ambush was a one-sided slaughter—but too good to last. Caproni 133 bombers roared over, bombing and strafing along the top of the ridgeline. This contingency had been anticipated. The troops were dug in, so little damage was done. However, nearly everyone in Force N was taking cover, not fighting—which gave the Italians down below the chance to recover and reorganize.

Properly led and inspired Italians are excellent soldiers. Leadership of the troops in the ambush was open to question, but the soldiers were highly motivated. The Blackshirts fell to with a will, shoved the burning and destroyed vehicles out of the way or over the cliff, cleared obstructions, then mounted up and drove on with all guns blazing.

"Shift your position, Butch," Brig. Randal ordered.

In a moment of inspired improvisation, Lt. Hoolihan had his men light a number of small fires to give the Capronis something to aim at after they pulled out. First the heavy weapons teams packed up and moved, then the men legged it down the backside of the ridgeline to the picket line where the mules were tethered. Within minutes Force Raiding Company was riding to the next ambush location.

Waldo was waiting there when they arrived to guide them into position.

Escort Company waved off Sgt. McDonald's mortars. He continued on to the next company. The Italian convoy had already cleared Escort's ambush location. Captain Lionel Chatterhorn would be pulling out and relocating as soon as Force Raiding Company passed behind his company.

Everything was going like clockwork. The Capronis were expending their ordnance on the fires in the abandoned position. The Italian trucks and their armored escorts drove straight into the next series of ambushes. There was very little return fire from the Blackshirts caught in the killing zone.

The life of a guerrilla was good.

When he received word the relief convoy was under attack, the Duke of Aosta reacted violently.

The hopes of the Italian High Command were pinned on Keren (the full implication of the collapse of the Jubba Line had not set in). If Keren fell, it was thought in Addis Ababa, the war was lost.

It is one thing for a European power to lose a war to a signer of the Geneva Convention. It is an entirely different matter to surrender to a semi-civilized African Army with a history of rape and castration who has never heard of the Geneva Accords.

To complicate the situation, there were many Italian civilians accompanied by their dependents in Addis Ababa. A lot of military wives, daughters, mistresses and casual girlfriends were there also. The women could not fall into Abyssinian hands any more than could the Italian military men. They would be considered dessert.

Desperation was beginning to set in. The senior Blackshirt commanders could no longer see any way to win. Yet they could not afford to lose.

The Duke immediately ordered another battalion of motorized infantry north to reinforce the embattled convoy with additional armored cars and tankette escorts. He called in the Regia Aeronautica commander and demanded full air support—which was immediately dispatched. No one had to explain the situation to the Air Force.

Additionally, a regiment of field artillery was ordered to move north up the road into range of the beleaguered convoy and provide fire support—no reluctance on the part of the Chief-of-Artillery either. He dispatched his brightest colonel to oversee the operation.

Orders went out to the Italian troops, "Fight through to Keren or die—retreat and you will be shot."

The fighting was all Force N's way until approximately 1500 hours when the tide began to turn.

The intensity of the Regia Aeronautica air strikes had been increasing all morning. Most of the Caproni 133 bombers were decoyed away from the actual Force N ambush positions by using Lt. Hoolihan's method of building small fires where they would do no harm. And the Force N machine gunners firing on the convoy were ordered to remove the tracer rounds from their magazines to prevent the pilots from spotting their actual firing positions. The constant bombing and strafing was having an effect on the Force N guerrilla troops.

Around 1600 hours the artillery brigade from Addis Ababa managed to get a battery up and running. The howitzers began ranging the Force N position. Forward observers linked up with the convoy to adjust their rounds.

As additional Italian batteries came up, they contributed more and more guns to the fire missions. By 1630 hours Force N was being hammered with aerial bombs and artillery. The Blackshirts had now achieved fire superiority.

Being a guerrilla was no longer quite so good.

The Abyssinians surprised Brig. Randal. The men did not break and run. The more the Italians shelled, the more obstinate the indigenous troops became. There was, however, a limit on what the guerrillas could be expected to take. His soldiers were raiders not storm troopers.

Shortly after 1700 hours, Captain "Geronimo" Joe McKoy rode in with two companies of his 6th MRB. They had been riding around the clock. He found Brig. Randal with Rita and Lana mounted on their mules on the reverse slope of the ridgeline behind where the battle was raging. Incoming cannon shells were thundering in the mountains.

"What are you doing here?" Brig. Randal said.

"Heard you'd jumped in up here to pick a big fight," Capt. McKoy said. "So, I grabbed a couple of companies of good men and we lit out to see if you'd let us get in on the action, John. We been in the saddle for three days."

"How'd you find us?"

"Easy, we been riding to the sound of the guns like ol' Napoleon told his marshals. You boys stirred up a real hornet's nest. Where do you need us?"

"Place your troops up on the line with Force Raiding Company and Escort Company. I want you with me," Brig. Randal said. "I'm designating you my second-in-command."

"You sure about that?"

"Harry's dead; Butch has been wounded. They're bringing him down now."

"What do you want me to do first?" Capt. McKoy did not waste time on remorse or commiserations. Personal feelings had no place in a firefight. Those could and would be expressed later.

"Knock out that artillery," Brig. Randal ordered. "Or at least interdict it. I was planning to send Sergeant McDonald out with an escort and a mortar to try."

"No problem," Capt. McKoy said. "Frank's a heavy weapons man. Claims he can drop an 81 down a pickle barrel at a mile—that right, Leatherneck?"

"Semper Fi," the former U.S. Marine growled, his eyes staring out from under the flat rim of his campaign hat.

"Pick you out a platoon as security, Frank. Go get those guns. Look for the landlines … the artillery spotters must-a run back to their guns. Cut the wire and shell the batteries. You'll be in command."

"I'll take Ringold's boys."

"Round him up, I'll make sure Bimbashi Ringold understands who's in charge," Capt. McKoy said.

"Frank, you can have an extra mortar team if you want," Brig. Randal offered.

"I'll take it, sir," The ex-Devil Dog said, striking a match on the checkered walnut stock of the big Bergman-Maynard 9mm Largo in his chest holster and lighting the stub of the cigar he always had clamped between his teeth. "Tell McDonald to give me his best crew."

"Roger," Brig. Randal said. "Move when you're ready."

After briefing Bimbashi Ringold, Capt. McKoy rode off to inspect the ambush lines with Waldo.

Mr. Big Shot was summoned. Brig. Randal ordered Kaldi, "Tell him Rita and Lana need three or four drum players—they're planning to do their mumbo jumbo on Butch."

The *tillik sau's* eyes grew when he learned the two girls were Zār Cult priestesses—highly respected and much feared.

Brig. Randal took out his map and showed it to Mr. Big Shot, pointing with the tip of his Fairbairn knife, "Kaldi, I want him to ride out and attack every one of these farming projects. Burn 'em down if he can or strafe 'em and drive off their livestock if he can't.

"Raid everything in a twenty-mile circle—I want Italian farmers screaming bloody murder to Addis Ababa for help."

The Abyssinian smiled when he heard the orders.

"Tell the man if he does well, we'll put in a good word with the Emperor for him."

Mr. Big Shot began bowing and would have prostrated himself if Kaldi had not physically restrained him. He was an opportunist who lived by his wits and realized he had been handed the opportunity of a lifetime. A license to murder, pillage, rape and steal with a chance to advance his career thrown in on the deal.

And he would be able to get far away from the awful bombing and shelling.

LIEUTENANT RANDY "HORNBLOWER" SEABORN WAS HANDED A NOTE BY the Phantom radio operator. He read the message.

"I must present this to the Emperor immediately," he said to Colonel Hugh Boustead.

"Take a platoon as an escort, lad."

The distance between the Frontier Battalion and the Patriot column had narrowed to less than ten miles as they moved deeper into Abyssinia. Colonel Orde Wingate had pulled in close behind the Frontier Battalion for protection. Lt. Seaborn covered it as fast as the platoon of Sudanese could travel on their mules.

Major Edwin Chapman-Andrews scanned the message and said, "Wait here."

He was back in five minutes. "Inform Brigadier Randal the Emperor has sanctioned his request."

Lt. Seaborn rode back to the Frontier Battalion at the trot.

COLONEL SIR TERRY "ZORRO" STONE WAS IN HIS FIELD HQ, AN abandoned girl's school on the outskirts of town, preparing to roll out of Mogadishu with his regiment. His orders were to, "Go to Harar." The commander of the Phantom Detachment traveling with the Lounge Lizards, "Major Jones" walked in and handed him a flimsy.

Major David Niven was not fooling anyone with the full beard he was wearing in an attempt to remain incognito.

"Thanks, Jones," Col. Stone said, fighting a grin.

"Don't thank me yet, old chap."

He read the content of the radio message. "Jane."

Captain the Lady Jane Seaborn was in conversation with Brandy Seaborn and Lieutenant Penelope Honeycutt-Parker on the other side of the room.

"John is in a battle north of Addis Ababa attempting to stop a convoy of reinforcements from getting through to Keren. The Italians are throwing everything but the kitchen sink at him to break through his roadblock," Col. Stone informed her, not mincing words.

"Harry Shelby is KIA and Butch wounded … no information on how seriously."

"Anything else, Terry?"

"Here's the message—pretty bare bones."

"Force N does not have a doctor, much less a surgical team," Lady Jane said grimly. "I'm off to Nairobi; contact Bunny to have a plane for me at the airport here."

"Jane, this once … try not to do anything foolish."

"Expect me to link back up with you in Harar. Look after Brandy and Parker."

"Not to worry," Col. Stone said. "The ladies shall be traveling with … ah … Major Jones."

"Perfect," Lady Jane said. "Going to war with a movie star."

AT 2345 HOURS BRIGADIER JOHN RANDAL AND WALDO TREYWICK WERE standing on the Drop Zone. A giant letter *N* was burning. They were preparing to receive an ammunition drop. The Force N guerrilla troops were using up ammo at a high rate of speed. The fighting had been nonstop. None of the Abyssinians had ever been in a battle like this. Not even the former NCOs who had served in the King's African Rifles.

"What's the report on Butch?" Waldo asked.

"Rita and Lana were still doing their magic act when I tried to check on him—wouldn't let me in," Brig. Randal said. "Wound was a through and through gunshot. Bullet didn't hit any ribs."

"Yeah," Waldo replied, "but we don't know what it went *through* when it went through."

"Roger that."

In the distance, the faint sound of an approaching airplane could be heard. Captain "Geronimo" Joe McKoy had pulled a platoon of Force Raiding Company men off the line to put out the signals and retrieve the bundles. The men began to assemble, ready to run down the parachutes. They had performed this task many times before and knew the drill.

The big Consolidated Model 31 leveled out low and slow and parachutes began to spill out. First door bundles and then paratroopers. Jumpers had not been expected.

Brig. Randal was there to greet the first parachutist to touch down, Captain "Pyro" Percy Stirling.

"Sorry about Harry …"

"I brought my Bimbashis and Lieutenant Pip Pilkington of the Kent Fortress Royal Engineers, assigned to Raiding Forces out from Seaborn House," Capt. Stirling reported, clearly not wanting to discuss the death of his best friend.

"A dozen men from the Railroad Wrecking Crew too, sir."

"We can use the help."

"My team shall halt your convoy for you sir—dead in its tracks."

"Oh, we've got it stopped, Percy," Brig. Randal said. "Problem is what to do *now*. These guys don't want to just roll over—and there's a lot of 'em."

"Give my lads twenty-four hours to work our magic, sir," Capt. Stirling vowed. "Then stand back—all your troubles will disappear in a puff of smoke—hey, presto."

"Can do," Brig. Randal said. "How far do you recommend I stand back?"

26

TAKE A NUMBER

BRIGADIER JOHN RANDAL HAD NOT EXPECTED TO SEE LIEUTENANT Butch "Headhunter" Hoolihan up walking around when he came into camp from the Drop Zone with Captain "Pyro" Percy Stirling and his party of demolition men.

"What do you think you're doing, Butch?"

"Going back to my company, sir. They need me up there."

"Are you nuts?"

"No, sir," the young Royal Marine officer said. "Rita and Lana put a magic hex on me. I'm not cured, but I feel fine—a little sore, maybe."

The two Zār priestesses had changed back into their normal garb and were looking on with worried expressions. The girls had not intended for Lt. Hoolihan to jump off his pallet right after their ceremony and head straight back into the fight.

"Be worth taking another bullet, sir," Lt. Hoolihan said, slinging his Thompson submachine gun over his shoulder, "if I could see that show again—what a night! Was it like that, sir, when the lion got you?"

"No," Brig. Randal said. "What did you two girls do in there? One of you stays with Butch at all times until this is over, is that clear?"

"You didn't pay 'em, did you Butch?" Waldo demanded.

"Not a cent, Mr. Treywick."

"Well don't."

"Percy," Brig. Randal said, turning to another issue. "Can Lieutenant Pilkington handle the demolitions without you?"

"Pip's a qualified man, sir," Capt. Stirling said. "He was going on Commando-type raids to France blowing up oil storage facilities to prevent them from falling into Nazi hands before there even *were* any Commandos."

"In that case, you take over Harry's old outfit," Brig. Randal said.

"Yes, sir!" Capt. Stirling was a cavalryman, 17/21 Lancers—the Death or Glory Boys. Command of a Mule Raider Battalion was a dream assignment come true. "Someone else can blow things up for a change."

"Yeah," Brig. Randal said. "We'll all probably rest easier with you handling troops instead of high explosives."

MOGADISHU HAD BEEN CAPTURED ALMOST INTACT EXCEPT THE PORT had been blocked by British magnetic mines during the blockade. Not to worry, the parachute company of East Africa Reconnaissance Regiment had liberated 200 British prisoners, officers and men of the Mercantile Marine held in a POW camp for six months. They volunteered to help clear the obstructions. Over 350,000 gallons of petrol was discovered in storage. Lieutenant General Alan Cunningham realized he now had enough fuel to continue the attack without having a logistical pause—the dream of every commander who has ever had his enemy on the run.

The Lounge Lizards were augmented with two companies of 2 Nigerian Regiment and a motorized detachment of machine gunners from the 1/3 King's African Rifles. Colonel Sir Terry "Zorro" Stone was given his marching orders. "Go to Jijiga"—600-plus miles due north through the bush country to the escarpment of the Abyssinian Central Highlands—the southern tip of 1 Guerrilla Corps (Parachute), Force N's Area of Operations.

The 23rd Nigerian Brigade under Brigadier C.C. "Fluffy" Fowkes, 11th African Division, would be following some 100 miles to his rear.

East Africa Reconnaissance Regiment with attachments, now identified simply as "Lounge Lizard Force" (LLF) by Lt. Gen. Cunningham's senior staff on their operations maps, rolled out within two hours. LLF raced up the paved Strada Imperiale with armored cars in the lead. Two days and 220 miles later through inhospitable desert, they took the small Regia Aeronautica airstrip at Belet Uen and, without firing a shot, captured the three water wells located there.

Planes from the South African Air Force flew in and were landing same day.

Col. Stone studied his map and ordered, "Take on water for three days."

Degehabur, approximately 350 miles farther north straight up the road through the Ogaden Desert, was his next objective. From there he could develop plans for the final dash to Jijiga. After that it was only 100 miles or so to Harar—the maps being unreliable. Different ones gave different distances ... towns, lakes, rivers etc. were all spelled differently, too.

If they could take Harar, Col. Stone realized, the final dash to the capital of Addis Ababa and victory was only 400 miles northwest through the mountains with the guerrillas of Force N supporting them the entire way—which could be a good thing... or possibly not.

THE FIGHTING IN THE MOUNTAINS HAD REACHED A FEVER PITCH. THE Italians were battling their way up the road despite the best efforts of 1 Guerrilla Corps (Parachute), Force N to stop them. Captain "Geronimo" Joe McKoy formed Force Raiding Company, Escort Company and the two MRB companies he had brought with him into an ad hoc battalion. He took personal command in addition to remaining Brigadier John Randal's deputy.

The two Force N battalions, his and Captain "Pyro" Percy Stirling's, were constantly leapfrogging each other, company by company, at least one company always on the move to its next location to set up a new fighting position.

Italian artillery came in waves. Mercenary soldier Frank Polanski had been able to locate the Italian batteries and engage them with his two

81mm mortars. His counterbattery fire silenced the guns—but only temporarily.

Then the Italians would shift position or the ex-U.S. Marine would have to relocate his. Either way, the Blackshirts always managed to bring their guns back into action. Frank Polanski was playing a deadly cat-and-mouse game. If the Italian artillery observers ever managed to spot his 81s with line of sight to the tubes, the big guns could end the contest with a few well-placed rounds.

Frank kept a team patrolling the road to the south cutting the wire strung from the gun batteries to their forward observers. The Italians sent out repair teams to repair the cuts. The former Devil Dog dispatched another team to ambush the cuts and kill the repairmen.

The Regia Aeronautica was out in force, bombing and strafing. The air strikes were having a demoralizing effect on the guerrilla troops. They were used to melting away, not standing and taking a pounding.

Lieutenant Pip Pilkington divided the Railroad Wrecking Crew into two parties—both with a Bimbashi in command. With a platoon each of bearers carrying the heavy bundles of explosives, the demolition teams disappeared into the mountains in different directions. Lovat Scout Munro Ferguson went with one, and Lovat Scout Lionel Fenwick went with the other to guide them.

Brig. Randal had promised Lt. Pilkington twenty-four hours, and he intended to give it to him.

He spent as much time as he could up on the firing line plinking Italian trucks with his shoulder-fired Brixia M-35 45mm mortar. However, as necessary as it was for Brig. Randal to be seen up front fighting alongside the men, it was even more important to be available to his subordinate commanders when they needed him. The trick was to be in the right place at the right time—and provide guidance as needed, but not too much.

"I don't know which is worse," Waldo said. "Huntin' bad cat or takin' incomin' artillery."

"What?"

"Ya' know it's coming for ya'— ya' never know when you're gonna' get got."

Lana rewarded Waldo with a forced smile. The artillery crashing in was clearly grating on the girl's nerves.

Casualties were mounting. Already Force N had lost more men since they had been fighting the convoy than it had in the past six months of irregular guerrilla operations. Brig. Randal had suffered more casualties to British Raiding Forces personnel assigned to Force N in this single battle than he had in all the Commando units operations combined since its inception.

The only bright spot, if you could call it that, was the Regia Aeronautica was not capable of flying at night. If the Force N troops could hold out until sundown, their chances of hanging on long enough for Lt. Pilkington to do his stuff dramatically improved. The hands on Brig. Randal's Rolex were locked in place—for once when he looked at the black-faced watch he was not thinking about Lady Jane.

Time was standing still—combat is like that when things do not seem like they are going your way. The best that could be said was Force N was giving better than it was taking—not much consolation considering all the bombing, strafing and incoming artillery.

Brig. Randal had standing orders to never become committed to defending a fixed position that could result in a climactic battle. The worst mistake a guerrilla commander can make is to allow his troops to become ensnared in a battle they cannot melt away from. The exception was a roadblock—but only so long as he did not allow the enemy to fix him in place.

There were three things, Brig. Randal reasoned, that exempted this particular convoy ambush from falling under the parameters of his orders: 1) he did not have his entire command present—defeat would not result in the total destruction of Force N; 2) he had the advantage of terrain. The Italians would find it difficult to get up into the mountains in order to come to grips with his troops; and 3) this battle was strategic— the fate of the British Forces in front of Keren rested on the Italians being refused the means to reinforce their troops.

In short, the two battalion element of Force N in contact was expendable. This was a fight to the death. Both sides understood the situation.

Capt. McKoy came along leading a file of Force Raiding Company troops that were relocating to their next ambush location as artillery thundered up the mountain. He stepped out of the column and stood with Brig. Randal as Lieutenant Butch "Headhunter" Hoolihan continued on with his company.

"How's it going, Butch?" Brig. Randal called.

"Fine, sir."

"Lootenant," Waldo said, paying his highest compliment of calling an officer by his rank instead of his name—something he almost never ever did.

Rita dropped off, and Lana took her place in the column going along to look after Lt. Hoolihan.

After Force Raiding Company passed by, Brig. Randal went up the mountain to troop the Escort Company line plinking trucks. Capt. McKoy, Waldo and Rita moved up to wait for his return. Capt. McKoy would lead Escort Company part way to their next position when it was time for them to withdraw and leapfrog to the far right flank. The two officers planned to keep this routine up until Capt. McKoy had his entire battalion relocated.

After that, the silver-haired cowboy would stay with his troops while Brig. Randal repeated the process with each company of Capt. Stirling's battalion.

Brig. Randal was angry with himself. The Force N troops were shooting and moving, but they were not hitting and running. He realized too late that he had made a major tactical error in the conduct of this battle. What Force N should have done, he now understood, was ambush the convoy, then pull out and move rapidly three to five miles up the road and ambush it again—repeating the process as necessary until the Italians turned back or were all dead.

He had failed to follow his own directive to his officers to stay mobile—hit and run. Now the troops under his personal command were paying the price. Force N was having its finest hour, but Brig. Randal was not having his and he knew it.

"Watch, John," Capt. McKoy advised. "He's been hard at it a long time now—ain't getting much rest in this fight."

"Naw, the brigadier's doin' fine," Waldo said. "We even squeezed us in a little time the other night to go huntin'—killed a cat."

THE PREGNANT GUPPY LEVELED OUT OVER THE FORCE N DROP ZONE AT 0135 at an altitude of 800 feet. Brigadier John Randal, Rita and Waldo were on hand to observe the resupply drop. The first parachute to deploy was a jumper, not a bundle.

The parachutist drifted in, slipped into the wind and made a graceful stand-up landing—which was against King's regulations.

"Didn't anyone tell you you're not supposed to make stand-up landings, soldier?" Brig. Randal barked. The last thing he needed was someone else injured.

"Court martial me," Captain the Lady Jane Seaborn laughed as she unstrapped her jump helmet and shook out her thick walnut-colored hair. "Nice to see you too, John. Hello Rita."

"Jane, what the hell ..."

"Clear this drop zone as rapidly as possible," Lady Jane interrupted. "Squadron Leader Wilcox will be landing a Walrus here in a few minutes. He's strafing the Italian convoy right this minute burning up his remaining fuel and waiting for us to set up lights to mark a landing strip."

"He can't bring in an airplane here," Brig. Randal said. "This ground barely works as a drop zone—it's crisscrossed with ravines."

"Paddy intends to crash land," Lady Jane said. "He has a surgical team onboard—the only way to get them here. None of the medical personnel are parachute-qualified."

"Neither was I my first jump," Waldo said.

"The doctor and his two assistants are not volunteers, Mr. Treywick. Inspector McFarland is on board holding a pistol on them since he had to take the handcuffs off for the flight."

Brig. Randal knew she wasn't making this story up. "Mr. Treywick, inform Captain McKoy he needs to have the drop zone cleared in ten minutes—make that five minutes.

"Put out a series of small signal fires fifty yards apart for a half mile."

"Ain't gonna' work, Brigadier."

"Get those fires in place—do it now."

Capt. McKoy picked out the best part of the DZ he could in the dark and marked it with small bonfires as directed—but it was not a half mile.

Up in the sky, the Walrus turned on its landing lights and lined up on the improvised airstrip. When Squadron Leader Paddy Wilcox made his approach, he was almost at stalling speed. He was the acknowledged best rough-landing bush pilot in Canada, which meant the world. His plan tonight was to put the plane down just before it quit flying and pancake it—a long skid he suspected would most likely result in disaster.

Controlled crashes are not for the faint of heart—what he was attempting was virtually suicide—at least for any pilot less talented than he was.

When the Walrus came in, it did not bounce or skid. The little pusher plane smacked down and crunched. It stayed put.

Brig. Randal, Capt. McKoy, Lady Jane, Waldo and a group of native troopers rushed the airplane to pull the passengers out in case they had been stunned by the impact or it caught on fire. Before they could reach it, the doors flew open and people started spilling out. No one was seriously hurt, but the medical team seemed in a state of shock.

Sqn. Ldr. Wilcox climbed out of the wreckage and shouted, "YEEEEHAAAAAH!"

"I'm pressing charges against you for kidnapping," the doctor threatened when he saw Lady Jane. "See you in prison, you crazy bitch."

"Watch your mouth Doc," Waldo snarled. "Anybody ever tell you what Abyssinians do to captives? Did, huh? Speak to Lady Seaborn like that again, and we'll lose you in these mountains … guaranteed."

"Take a number, doctor," Lady Jane said. "Brigadier Randal has already threatened to have me court-martialed for performing an illegal PLF."

The doctor had no idea what a PLF was. However, he saw the Force Raiding Company troops that had rushed to help him draped in bandoleers, wicked-looking knives and wearing Tom Mix hats, misinterpreted their intent, and shut up like a clam.

The knives were particularly threatening.

Inspector McFarland added menacingly, "I'll certify you missing—parts of you certainly will be—case closed."

"I've got a lot of badly wounded men," Brig. Randal said. "Only way you're getting out of here is to save every last one of 'em. Get an attitude adjustment, mister—is that clear?"

"Quite."

"Let's go," Brig. Randal ordered. "Rita, you're on Lady Jane. Don't let her out of your sight."

Under his breath he said to Lady Jane, "He ain't wrong—you are crazy."

LIEUTENANT PIP PILKINGTON RODE UP TO WHERE BRIGADIER JOHN Randal was sitting on his mule talking to Waldo and Captain "Pyro" Percy Stirling. The battle was raging behind them at the top of the mountain. Capt. Stirling's troops were fighting hard. The Italian artillery was quiet for the moment. The Regia Aeronautica had left a temporary gap in their air patrol, which allowed the Force N troops the luxury to come out of hiding and pour fire into the trucks trapped in the killing zone of the ambush below.

Brig. Randal glanced at his watch—1425 hours.

"How goes it, Pip?"

"We have our demolitions set on the far side of the ambush— managed to make better time placing our charges than anticipated. We can detonate them now or wait until our other party is ready then set them off simultaneously.

"What are your orders, sir?"

"Blow it now—cut the road to Keren—that's the priority," Brig. Randal said.

"Let me go up to the top of the ridgeline to send up the signal flare to my lads to execute, sir," Lt. Pilkington said. "Would you care to ride over and inspect our handiwork?"

"Love to."

When Brig. Randal, Lt. Pilkington and Waldo rode up on a promontory overlooking the scene of the demolitions eight miles north of the ambush site, what they saw was beyond belief. Half of a mountain had been neatly sliced off. A massive pile of rubble had slid down across the road, burying it for approximately a half mile. No way over or around the obstruction.

Reinforcements would not be getting through to Keren anytime soon.

"So," Brig. Randal said taking out a thin cigar and lighting it with his battered 26th Cavalry Regiment Zippo, "you work for me now?"

"Yes, sir. I have been carrying out classified operations for Commodore Seaborn out of Seaborn House. Sorry, but I'm not authorized to discuss them with anyone— including you, Brigadier. A condition of my deploying to Africa, sir."

"Really?" Brig. Randal said. "I can see I'm going to like having you on board. Nice job, stud."

"Cut looks like it was made by a surgeon," Waldo said. "You're a maestro with explosives, Lootenant. Do as good at the tail end and those Wops are doomed. Buzzards 'll pick their bones, that is after Mr. Big Shot's shifta get through takin' trophy, torturin' and murderin' 'em."

"Our loyal patriotic allies would do that?"

"Them's the ones."

Later that afternoon, Lt. Pilkington's second team set off their charges. The result—half a mountain deposited on the road to the rear of the enemy column. The Blackshirt convoy was trapped.

Rearmed, refueled Caproni 133s returned to the battle. When they flew over and saw the two colossal piles of boulder-strewn debris blocking the road cutting off the motorized column, the pilots turned around and returned to base. No sense wasting their time.

Captain "Geronimo" Joe McKoy rode out to conduct his own road damage survey. His estimate of the situation: "We're done here."

27
CHARGE OF THE LOUNGE LIZARDS

FIELD MARSHAL SIR ARCHIBALD WAVELL ARRIVED AT LIEUTENANT General William Platt's headquarters. The field marshal was a man known for ponderous silence interspersed with periods when he said almost nothing. The commander in chief, Middle East Command had a lot on his mind. And he did not have much time to waste on a campaign that had already become a sideshow. He was fighting Italians in the desert, a German general named Rommel had recently arrived in Egypt with the first Nazi ground troops called the Afrika Korps, Ultra intercepts indicated the Germans were preparing to invade Crete, he was winding down a fighting withdrawal and naval evacuation of the Expeditionary Force to Greece … the list went on and on.

FM Wavell was not pleased with the progress of the attack on Keren. The Kaid had attempted to force one flank or the other time and again—only to fail miserably despite a magnificent effort by the 4th and 5th Indian Division troops. What had *not* been attempted was a direct assault on the mountain—up the valley head on.

"Go straight at them," FM Wavell said, tapping the wall map with his walking out stick.

"Precisely what we plan to do, sir," Lt. Gen. Platt said.

This was news to his operation's officer.

At that moment, almost identical communiqués arrived in Lt. Gen. Platt's and Lieutenant General Nicolangelo Carnimeo's Headquarters. The British signal was a Y-Service intercept of the Italian message. The news was the convoy of reinforcements out of Addis Ababa en route to Keren had been ambushed, trapped and annihilated by 1 Guerrilla Corps (Parachute), Force N guerrillas.

Lt. Gen. Platt's reaction when he read the intercept was a sense of relief—his staff was euphoric.

The Lt. Gen. Carnimeo on Keren, already reeling from the shock of having the rail line to Massawa cut, was demoralized by the dispatch. Now the fortress was completely isolated from the outside world. The Duke of Aosta signaled the suggestion they might consider attempting to hold out until General Rommel's Afrika Korps drove the British out of Africa—easy for him to say.

BRIGADIER JOHN RANDAL WAS RIDING IN THE BACK OF THE PREGNANT Guppy headed south, having been picked up on a straight stretch of road north of the site of the ambush. On board were the wounded plus Captain "Geronimo" Joe McKoy, Frank Polanski, Waldo, Captain the Lady Jane Seaborn, Rita, Lana, Kaldi, the Lovat Scouts Lionel Fenwick and Munro Ferguson, Captain Pip Pilkington and his two Bimbashis, Lieutenant Jeffery Tall-Castle and Ras Gubbo Rekash. Major General James "Baldie" Taylor had a map spread out over a crate.

"Colonel Stone's Lounge Lizard Force is preparing to lead the drive on Jijiga. Captain Mikkalis has been making a forced march across the Ogaden Desert to get up into the mountains behind Harar to link up with your southernmost battalion commanded by Captain Corrigan. The problem is going to be here at Marta Pass. Some of our own people say it's impregnable. East Africa Force has to go over it to reach Harar in order to launch the final leg of the attack through the mountains to Addis Ababa."

"So," Brig. Randal said, "the decision has been made to capture the capital?"

"Purely political," Maj. Gen. Taylor said. "Concern for the safety of the Italian nationals—men and women. There is a large population of

Italian Americans in the U.S. who would not be pleased if we British stood idly by and allowed Italians to be raped and murdered by the Abyssinians—which everyone knows is going to take place given the chance."

"It sure is," Brig. Randal said.

"The Duke of Aosta is nobody's fool—using that threat as a bargaining chip. Claims he cannot guarantee the safety of his own people. Setting us up to take the blame if the Abyssinians seek revenge for all the people the Wops have slaughtered the last five years."

"I don't know anything about Marta Pass," Brig. Randal said. "But, I have plans to support an attack up the road to Addis Ababa from Harar."

"Jijiga," Maj. Gen. Taylor said, "and the Marta Pass are the keys to victory."

"Roger," Brig. Randal looked at the map. "We'll drop Captain McKoy off at N-1—link up with the remainder of your battalion and take it south to Harar, Captain."

"Wilco, John."

"I'll take Waldo and the girls, we'll in-flight rig and jump in to link up with Captain Corrigan's battalion," Brig. Randal said, "recon the Marta Pass and see what we can do to help.

"The idea is for most of the rest of Force N to shift south. The MRBs will step up the tempo of the raids on the isolated DCP model farms and small company-sized outposts—overload the Italian Command with demands for security.

"Pip, you jump with me. We'll drop off your two Bimbashis at N-1. They can pick up the rest of the Railroad Wrecking Crew and head south.

"I've ordered Captain Stirling to operate in the Addis Ababa area," Brig. Randal said. "However, Force Raiding Company, Escort Company and Captain McKoy's two companies are en route to link up with Force N Rear. We'll send them orders to continue south.

"I should have most everyone in place within the next six to eight days, General."

"Outstanding!"

"Lieutenant Tall-Castle, you and Ras Cheap Bribe disembark at N-1 also," Brig. Randal said. "Take Kaldi with you; work your way down to where Captain McKoy and Captain Mikkalis will be north of Harar. Bribe's men will be coming down with Captain McKoy's. That'll give the Ras some time to organize the local Patriots until they arrive. We're going to need as many in the field as you can raise—Bad Boys too. I'll give you the word when to unleash 'em."

"Yes, sir."

"Where do you want me, sir?" Lieutenant Butch "Headhunter" Hoolihan inquired.

"You're ..."

"The hospital in Nairobi," Lady Jane said, cutting Brig. Randal off in a take-no-prisoners tone.

"I'm fine, Lady Seaborn," Lt. Hoolihan insisted. "Now is not the time for me to be out of the field just when we are getting ready to take down the Italians hard."

Ignoring him, Lady Jane said, "I shall contact Pamala. We will start flying nightly lonely hearts missions over Jijiga and Harar immediately. General, I would like you to arrange for Captain Merryweather to work directly with us."

"Consider it done, Lady Seaborn," Maj. Gen. Taylor said. "Your serenades and his leaflets have had a devastating effect—he's a genius propaganda operator."

"Pretty deadly with a bull horn too," Waldo said.

GIDEON FORCE WAS HALTED SHORT OF DEBRA MARCOS AWAITING THE turncoat Hailu, the Ras of Gojjam. The Emperor was eagerly anticipating his arrival. It was expected the Ras was coming to pledge his fealty. With him in the Emperor's camp, the fate of the Italians in the northern sector of Abyssinia was sealed.

The capital was only 320 miles away.

A strange thing happened, typical of Abyssinian politics. The collaborator sent a messenger ahead to demand his meeting be with Colonel Orde Wingate—not the Emperor, which amounted to an insolent summons to talk terms. The request was granted without consulting the King of Kings.

Displaying incomparable cheek, Ras Hailu arrived in a chauffeured Alfa Romeo wearing the uniform of an Italian lieutenant general. He concocted an ingenious story as to why he had aligned himself with the Italians in the Emperor's absence. The Ras was very sure of himself, unbowed and unrepentant.

The Emperor was forced to look on impotently, snubbed by his rebellious subject as the Ras swept regally into Col. Wingate's headquarters.

Ras Hailu declared that it was only due to his power and influence that the Italians had retreated before the Patriot column. He claimed he had 6,000 men, the ability to rouse the countryside to civil war against the Emperor, and by implication—the British. All in all it was a typical Abyssinian power play.

Had the traitor tried this tactic on Brigadier John Randal, he might have experienced a terminal result. Col. Wingate caved immediately. He agreed that the Ras could remain in power in Gojjam province. No pledge of his loyalty was required. The Emperor was seething.

Colonel Hugh Boustead said to Lieutenant Randy "Hornblower" Seaborn, "Onion Breath will live to rue this day."

LOUNGE LIZARD FORCE CROSSED THE OGADEN DESERT IN HOT PURSUIT of the retreating Italians with dust devils dancing along and sometimes swirling through the column as high as the clouds in the sky. At times the highway petered out and the reinforced regiment was forced to cut cross-country until they picked it up again. The heat simmered and mirages flickered in the distance. It was hard to tell the real vehicles from the imaginary ones floating on invisible streams that vanished in a poof into the desert.

The word came through Phantom that the Duke of Aosta had flown to Harar and ordered General de Simone to fight to the death. The race was on to Jijiga. From there East Africa Force could begin the assault on Marta Pass and then on to the slave-trading city of Harar.

The concern was that the Regia Aeronautica would put in an appearance. Lounge Lizard Force was very vulnerable to aerial attack. The Italian Air Force never showed.

The South African Air Force claimed they had destroyed the planes at the main Italian airfield at Dire Dawa outside Harar—not the first time in the campaign they had made such a claim.

Lounge Lizard Force, five days out of Mogadishu, debouched on to a rising green plain. Not an enemy was in sight. Abandoned Italian military vehicles littered the track. Abyssinians were lining the road to sell fresh produce to the new occupiers.

Major "Jones" brought another flimsy to Colonel Sir Terry "Zorro" Stone. The Royal Navy, staging out of Aden, had conducted an amphibious landing with two Punjabi battalions at Berba under Cdre. Richard "Dickey the Pirate" Seaborn supported by HMS *Glasglow, Caledon, Kandahar* and *Kingston*. The commodore expected to make an opposed landing, however, that failed to develop. Once ashore he discovered that the 70th Colonial Brigade defending the town had disbanded itself. A tearful Italian colonel and sixty men—all that were left—were drawn up prepared to surrender the town when the first wave came in.

The next day Lounge Lizard Force took Jijiga. The regiment, now with the Nigerian Light Battery attached, had raced forward attempting to cut off the fleeing Italian retreat. No joy—they were running too fast.

The ground elements of No. 40 Army Coordination Squadron, South African Air Force took over the airfield. A squadron of Hurricanes flew in and commenced offensive operations same day.

Now with the addition of No. 1 and No. 18 Field Batteries in addition to the Nigerian Light Battery, a beefed-up Lounge Lizard Force rolled out with the sun well up and headed straight for the imposing Marta Pass. Col. Stone was in the lead with the armored cars carrying out a full-blooded cavalry charge. To all observers, including the Lounge Lizards making the charge, it looked like Balaclava redux—the Charge of the Light Brigade.

Marta Pass was impregnable—everyone knew that.

The pass consisted of twin peaks imaginatively named Marta's Right Breast and Marta's Left Breast—whoever Marta was. The Italians were entrenched on both mountains. the Fascists had been preparing their defense for years, spent six months to make their final dispositions and now had their backs to the wall.

The Lounge Lizard Force charge shocked the Blackshirts, taking them completely by surprise because of the audacity of the LLF. It thrilled the 1ˢᵗ South African Brigade following up the regiment. They stood on the cabs of their trucks for a better view, waving their caps and cheering like mad men.

Col. Stone's three batteries attached needed to be within 5,000 yards to go into action. That meant the Lounge Lizards had to close a six-mile wide gap in the open plain in full view of the Blackshirts defending Marta Pass in order to bring the mobile artillery into range. To achieve that meant LLF would be exposed to the much heavier Italian 105mm cannon fire the entire way.

The regiment raced across the plain. The Italian guns were slow going into action. When they did commence firing, long-range shells began screaming in and exploding, throwing up tall black geysers of dirt and high explosives. The Lounge Lizards pressed on with the charge, ignoring the incoming fire.

Col. Stone was convinced they were all riding to their death. Then, as the armored cars caromed across the wide open plain, the Yeomanry men produced their hunting horns and with artillery screaming in, began sounding the chase.

Out of the corner of his left eye, the LLF commander caught sight of an unarmed armored car pulling up and taking up station on his command car's flank. Brandy Seaborn was at the wheel, and Lieutenant Penelope Honeycutt-Parker was riding shotgun.

They were supposed to be far in the rear. In fact, Col. Stone had intended to order the two women to stay behind, but in the excitement of the moment it had slipped his mind. Brandy had outrun nearly the entire regiment.

"If Mrs. Seaborn passes us, Trevor," Col. Stone shouted at his driver (his second cousin), "I shall transfer you to the infantry, old stick."

The Lounge Lizards pulled into range, wheeled around, and the Nigerians and the South Africans stood to their guns. The howitzers began banging away furiously in full sight of the Italians who had 105mm cannons up on the twin peaks.

The gun crews were in full sight of the enemy and in *advance* of 3 Nigerian Brigade that was coming up to support them with bayonets fixed.

Fortunately, and it was purely chance—the fortunes of war—the Lounge Lizards were so close that the Italian guns mounted on the reverse slope of Marta's Left and Right Breasts could not lower their barrels enough to hit them.

Col. Stone's three batteries got off nearly 100 rounds in three minutes. And the three-pounder fast firers mounted on the three-ton trucks manned by the Royal Navy gun crew got off another 125 rounds.

3 Nigerian Brigade passed through. The troops reached the base of Marta Pass then began advancing up the twin peaks. A half-hearted Italian counterattack was quickly beaten back with fire. To Col. Stone's surprise, there was no climatic battle—no fighting to the death.

When 3 Nigerian Brigade with the No. 9 Abyssinian Company (Parachute) leading the way up the road with the Lounge Lizard armored cars in support reached the top, they found dead and wounded enemy but no resistance. Marta Pass was evacuated—the Italians had cut and run.

When he reached the top of the pass, Col. Stone, traveling on foot with his company of paratroopers, turned and looked back the way they had come. The scene was incredible. It looked like a drill on Salisbury plain—guns, trucks, and formations of troops on the move. The Italians should have been able to hold the place forever.

A Rolls Royce armored car pulled up with Brandy Seaborn at the wheel and her passenger Lt. Honeycutt-Parker. "Hop in, Terry," the blonde adventuress called. "Give you a lift."

The two should not have been there. However, he would appreciate a ride. It had been a steep flog up to the top of the pass on foot—expecting to get shot the entire way.

"I cannot fathom why the Wops would give up so easily," Co. Stone said as he climbed into the back seat, took out his silver cigarette case and tapped a Player's on it.

"Maybe *he* had something to do with it," Brandy said, laughing as the car drove around a hairpin curve on the far side of the pass.

Brigadier John Randal was leaning against a huge boulder, cradling his 9mm Beretta M-38 submachine gun, smoking a thin cigar.

28

HARAR

"THERE'S THREE ROADS TO HARAR FROM HERE," BRIGADIER JOHN Randal said as he pointed to the map that was spread over the hood of Colonel Sir Terry "Zorro" Stone's Rolls Royce armored car.

Brigadier Dan Pienaar, commanding the 1st South African Brigade, which was tasked to pass through and retake the lead from the Nigerians after they had cleared Harar, had come forward to make a personal reconnaissance and was listening in on the briefing.

"Two of them are new Italian strategic roads. The other is an ancient slave trading route that leads to a pass that the Italians may try to defend.

"Might be a good idea to secure the pass, but I recommend you concentrate on pushing down the two improved roads as fast as you can. Close on the Bisidimo River, get across, and Harar is all yours. The native troops are in open revolt. The Italians are afraid they'll be murdered by their own men and also for the safety of their women if they fall into Abyssinian hands. I don't think they'll stand and fight—surrender is their best option."

"We have intelligence Harar may be declared an open city," said Major General Harry Edward de Robillard Weatherall, the commander of 12th African Division, who had recently arrived and now joined the officers studying the map on the hood of the armored car. "However, the Italians have yet to stop firing on our aircraft."

"The war starts here, sir," Brig. Randal pointed to the north side of Harar with the silver tip of his Fairbairn knife. To reach Addis Ababa you're going to have to fight your way up a single hardball that can rise or drop 2,000 feet in a single mile through 350 miles of 5,000-foot mountains stacked wall to wall.

"There's company-sized road watch bases every fifty miles with battalion, brigade and even division-sized forts interspersed at what the Italians consider the most defensible locations to support them. Every inch of this road is good ambush country—so be advised."

"Sounds like bloody stiff terrain to have to fight through," Brig. Pienaar said.

"Against a determined enemy, you wouldn't ever make it," Brig. Randal said. "Force N has been working central Abyssinia for six months now. We have a plan, and if you push up the road, keep the pressure on and never let up, my guess is we can be in Addis Ababa in three or four weeks."

"What do you need from us, Randal?" Maj. Gen. Weatherall asked. "Dan's brigade will be leading the advance when it leapfrogs the Nigerians. His troops will be in contact with your guerrillas."

"Keep Colonel Stone in command of the lead element so I can coordinate my operations directly with him. Get your earth-moving equipment forward—right up with his regiment."

"You believe the Italians will blow the road?" Brig. Pienaar asked.

"If they don't," Brig. Randal said, "we will."

"Force N is going to blow up our only good hardball to Addis Ababa?"

"That's the plan—be ready with your road-building engineers—you'll need bridging capability too. The speed of your advance will depend almost entirely on how fast they can clear obstacles."

"Sounds bloody crazy, but you don't ask much, Randal."

"Just this, once you clear Harar and your South Africans head north," Brig. Randal said, "bring it hard, keep coming and don't stop. Force N will deal with the Italian installations and screen your flanks."

"You can do that … tackle the Wop forts with your irregulars?" Brig. Pienaar asked.

"We think so, but you need to be prepared for prisoners—a lot of 'em. Going to be your biggest problem."

"Why has the Regia Aeronautica been a no-show?" Maj. Gen. Weatherall inquired. "Sending out 1,000-truck convoys as we are, they are our worst nightmare."

"Running out of airplanes, sir. One of my battalions raided the Harar airfield five nights ago, destroyed eighteen on the ground."

"SAAF pilots made the same claim."

"Enemy planes won't be flying in any numbers," Brig. Randal said. "Once you get into the mountains there's only so many places the Regia Aeronautica can land, rearm and refuel, sir. We know where those are. When the Italians land at one of 'em from this point on, Force N guerrillas will be waiting—they're in position now."

"Outstanding," Maj. Gen. Weatherall said. "See you in Addis Ababa, Brigadier."

"No, sir," Brig. Randal said. "I'm not here, so I won't be there."

"How about a lift to the bottom?" Brigadier John Randal said as Rita and Lana materialized beside the road with Waldo.

"My pleasure, old stick," Colonel Sir Terry "Zorro" Stone said.

"Tell me ... how did you manage to bring about getting the Italians to abandon this position? I know our theatrics had little to do with it. If they would have stood and fought, the Wops would have been able to have held this place till kingdom come."

"Yeah, but you looked really good making that charge, Terry."

"How did you do it?"

"Ras Gubbo Rekash shanghaied about 8,000 or 9,000 locals, marched them out last night and ordered each one of them to build seven or eight small fires down at the bottom of the pass—kept 'em at it all night. The villagers melted away back home before first light."

"Clever," Col. Stone said. "Fifty or sixty thousand camp fires, must have looked from up here like the Golden Hoard had the Wops surrounded!"

"We've been experimenting with tactics to deal with the forts," Brig. Randal said. "Discovered the Italians can't stomach the idea of being cut off. If we can make the commander of a fort think his base is encircled, he'll abandon the position every time."

"Interesting—you always have been good at tactics."

"That's it, our plan," Brig. Randal said. "Smoke and mirrors."

"Explain blowing up the only road to Addis Ababa."

"To work we have to convince the bad guys they're cut off and surrounded. First we take out their landline communications to create a sense of isolation. Then, to heighten their fear we cut off retreat to the capital by blocking the road north of the installation," Brig. Randal said.

"You'll be coming up from the south, Terry. Bribe will be out at night in the mountains building fires simulating a vast Patriot army.

"Jane and Pamala will be airborne serenading the scared troops and showering them with surrender leaflets. Between records, the girls are going to describe the outrages Bribe's boys are planning to inflict on prisoners, their wives, daughters and mistresses unless the Italians surrender to you and not the Patriots.

"When they're finished, Paddy will arrive with a flight of Walrus gunships he's modified. He'll bomb and strafe the place the rest of the night.

"At the same time, Force N will be working the position over with mortars and sniping anything that moves with our Boys .55s."

"So, I roll up," Col. Stone said, "direct the flow of prisoners to the rear, have the road builders clear obstructions and/or bridge chasms?"

"You're a quick learner, Terry."

"Think it will work?"

"Hope it does," Brig. Randal said. "Plan B is mountain warfare uphill for 350 miles."

The Rolls Royce armored car arrived at the bottom of the pass, and as Brig. Randal stepped out, Col. Stone said, "Your battle plan makes it sound as if Force N has a whole army, John. By my count you have less than seventy-five Empire officers and men—total of which one third are Raiding Forces men, one third Cavalry Division and Yeomanry volunteers and the rest Colonial hostilities-only personnel.

"None of your MRBs started out with more than 250 men, and they must have had casualties from all the fighting by now.

"Paddy's gunships are Walrus antiques no one else wants, and you only have one 81mm mortar per company.

"Your AO is the size of France—so tell me, how many men exactly are you going to be using to deal with those company and larger-sized Italian forts?"

"A platoon," Brig. Randal said, slinging his MAB-38A submachine gun over his shoulder. "I've got one of Butch's."

"He's been evacuated."

"That's why I have it."

"Let me get this straight," Col. Stone said. "You and I are going to blast our way through a quarter million Italians entrenched in mountainous terrain with one under-strength, indigenous platoon and the world's smallest armored car regiment?"

"Roger that."

"Tell me, why does this sound like less than a brilliant idea?"

"See you, Terry."

Brig. Randal walked over to Brandy's armored car. "Think you or Parker might be able to ride a mule?"

"Seriously, John," Brandy said, "We are both members of the Beaufort Hunt—Parker rode in the Grand Nationals when she was 17. Why do you ask?"

"I have a mission for you," Brig. Randal said, "with Force N. How long will it take you to pack—if you want the job?"

The two adventuresses looked at each other. Lieutenant Penelope Honeycutt-Parker said, "Our bags are always packed—you can fill us in on the details later."

"Good," Brig. Randal said. "Tell Terry he has another armored car. Maybe he'll put guns on it now.

"Brandy, you're going to need a Red Cross armband."

WHITE FLAGS WERE FLYING OVER HARAR. RAIN WAS FALLING AS A FIAT truck with a bed sheet nailed to a bamboo pole drove up the road to signal the surrender. Colonel Sir Terry "Zorro" Stone rolled into town at the head of Lounge Lizard Force with the sirens mounted on their Rolls Royce armored cars wailing. The place was in chaos.

"Got them in the bag," Major "Jones" said. He had come up to ride with the LLF commander.

By midmorning all the Blackshirts had been rounded up by the 23rd Nigerian Brigade and marched off to POW cages.

Col. Stone and Maj. Jones strolled into the only hotel still open to find Italian waitresses still on duty and a bartender who had worked at the Bradford in London still at his station. The radio was playing American jazz.

The bartender said, "Blackstrap, Sir Terry?"

The intelligence officer for Brigadier Dan Pienaar's 1st South African Brigade, who would be taking the lead, did the math. Italian troop losses at Harar, mostly through desertion, were approximately 19,000 men, which made the total in the campaign in the south so far stand at approximately 50,000 dead, wounded, prisoner or deserted.

Lounge Lizard Force was ordered to move out immediately and head north—"On to Addis Ababa and victory."

Col. Stone was on the move before teatime.

THE NEXT DAY THE MOUNTAIN FORTRESS KEREN FELL. THE ITALIANS simply imploded; they had more men than Lieutenant General William Platt; they had commanding positions and military stores laid in to last for months if not years, but they had lost the will to fight. Four days after that, General Erwin Rommel, commander of the Afrika Korps, launched his first attack in the Western Desert.

Field Marshal Sir Archibald Wavell was in desperate need of troops. He felt he could no longer afford to have them tied up in Abyssinia (once Keren fell it was merely a race to the Red Sea port of Massawa and victory—U.S. Lend Lease was assured—Great Britain saved to fight another day). What had been the most important campaign of the war only days before, now had faded into obscurity, overshadowed almost immediately by other rapidly changing world events. Abyssinia had already become a sideshow, and it was quickly becoming a military backwater.

Against FM Wavell's strong opposition, he had been required to send 31,000 men to Greece. The Greek Expeditionary Force had landed then promptly been routed by the Germans, who had intervened on the behalf of the Italians (who were getting their head handed to them by the

Greeks). Now British Forces were in full retreat, conducting a fighting withdrawal, hoping for evacuation by sea.

Ultra was warning Crete was going to be invaded by the Nazis at any moment.

The field marshal ordered 4 Indian Division back to Egypt the day after Keren surrendered. 1 South African Division was alerted to prepare for deployment to the desert in the near future as soon as sea transport was available. FM Wavell toyed with the idea of stopping all offensive operations in Abyssinia. His thought was to let the Italians slowly twist in the breeze, wither and die on the vine in a worthless, now land-locked country harassed by Patriots who killed for sport.

Prime Minister Winston Churchill had no problem with that plan. However, he had international politics to consider. The PM cabled it would be disastrous to British prestige if Empire Forces stood idly by and allowed the Abyssinians to extract the revenge everyone knew they were going to take on Italian National troops and their dependents.

When queried about the situation on the ground, Lieutenant General Alan Cunningham informed the field marshal he anticipated he could take the capital within six weeks. That would be cutting it close time-wise. Gen. Rommel was on a tear, but FM Wavell had no choice—politics trump military necessity.

The race to Addis Ababa was still on.

Unaware of any of the high-level machinations, Colonel Sir Terry "Zorro" Stone's Lounge Lizard Force was headed north to Addis Ababa. Major Jack Merritt's No. 9 Company, Sudan Defense was pounding south to the Red Sea. And Colonel Hugh Boustead and Lieutenant Randy "Hornblower" Seaborn were pondering a Most Secret message ordering them to "Bring the Emperor to Addis Ababa—not to arrive until date specified."

No date was specified.

BRANDY SEABORN AND LIEUTENANT PENELOPE HONEYCUTT-PARKER were peering over the edge of a high ridge approximately 400 yards above the strategic road that ran out of Harar into the central highlands. Brigadier John Randal was lying next to them on his back with his cut-down slouch hat down over his eyes napping in the sun. Down below, a gigantic gypsy caravan of Italian trucks was snaking its way through the treacherous hairpin curves fleeing the advance of East Africa Force.

"Sir," said Lieutenant Butch "Headhunter" Hoolihan.

Brig. Randal was awake instantly, no in between. One second he was sound asleep and the next fully aware. He rolled over with his stubby 45mm Brixia mortar launcher in his arms.

"Let's get 'em," he said, so casual it sounded almost to the women as if one of them had suggested, "Let's go shopping."

Ambushing this convoy was not part of the big picture, but it was too good a target to pass up.

"Jane is really going to be mad when she finds out she missed all this," Brandy said. "And, she is *really* going to be furious when she finds out you checked yourself out of hospital, Butch."

"I'll keep him on light duty," Brig. Randal said. Then he leaned over the ridge and fired a round at the lead truck.

At the sound of the Brixia M-38 discharging, everyone in the ambush position commenced fire. Down below the mortar round slammed into the bed of the dirt-colored Bedford truck leading the convoy and detonated. *KEERCHUUUMPH.* Troops bailed over the side as the truck swerved to the left and ran off the cliff, on fire.

It was nearly 1,000 yards straight down. The Bedford sailed through space with people still flying out of the back for what seemed like a long time before it crashed and exploded. The bottom was so far down the truck was only a little red speck as it burned.

The second truck must have been transporting ammunition. When Brig. Randal's 45mm mortar round landed in its bed, there was an immediate secondary explosion. A smoke ring sailed up in front of where Brandy and Lt. Honeycutt-Parker were watching wide-eyed.

When it blew up, the wrecked truck blocked the narrow road.

A flight of four Hurricanes from No. 40 Ground Coordination Squadron, South African Air Force arrived on the scene unexpected and unannounced attracted by the column of smoke. The fighters strafed the two-mile long convoy until they ran out of ammunition. Oily smoke columns from burning trucks marked the length of the formation. With their execution done, the pilots roared off.

Captain Hawthorne Merryweather went to work with his bullhorn as soon as the Hurricanes cleared the area. He ordered the Italian survivors to cease firing, move to the rear of the convoy, sling their weapons over their shoulders muzzle down and to move south, back in the direction of Harar.

"You have five minutes to depart the area," Capt. Merryweather boomed in fluent Italian. "After that we will launch a ground attack and all surviving prisoners will be castrated."

The movement to the rear, while not a thing of military precision, was by any measure vigorously executed. This convoy was about the same size as the one Force N had ambushed north of Addis Ababa. The difference was it did not have the will to fight back.

Lounge Lizard Force's point pair of Rolls Royce armored cars traveling in advance of the regiment was amazed to encounter an enemy column of fours, 6,000-strong marching down the road behind a flag bearer carrying a pole with an Italian officer's white dress shirt tied to the tip.

"Wops have the wind up, right enough," the Lancelot Lancers Yeomanry captain in command of the point element (Colonel Sir Terry "Zorro" Stone's brother-in-law) said to his driver as he was studying the marching column through his binoculars. "Best get ourselves prepared for a tidal wave of prisoners."

"Reckon there's trophy hunting to be had out of that mob, sir," the driver asked, "after the Patriots had first dibs?"

"Not bloody likely. My guess is the fuzzie-wuzzies will have picked 'em clean."

"Damn guerrillas!"

29
BRINGING IT

THE COMPANY-SIZED ITALIAN ROAD WATCH BASE WAS ABANDONED. Captain the Lady Jane Seaborn and Lieutenant Pamala Plum-Martin had serenaded and papered it with surrender leaflets the night before. Ras Cheap Bribe had 2,000 local villagers out in the hills simulating a vast military force—burning fires, telephone poles, and the favorite Force N trick ... building a huge flaming arrow pointing straight at the Blackshirt position.

Flying out of N-2, Squadron Leader Paddy Wilcox kept a constant rotation of Supermarine Walrus converted gunships overhead from the time the music stopped until an hour before sunrise. The gunships dropped 100-pound anti-personnel bombs. Each Walrus was capable of carrying four of them, and they pickled the bombs one at a time. In between bombing runs, the little amphibians strafed the fort with their ten organic .303-caliber machine guns.

From high in the mountains, Sergeant Jock McDonald dropped 81mm mortar rounds on the fort from time to time carrying out what gunners like to call H&I (harassment & interdiction) fire. What H&I really meant was the Royal Marine was making life miserable for the inhabitants of the fort. And he was good at it.

Before she and Lt. Plum-Martin departed to serenade another Italian base, Lady Jane had informed the commander of the fort over the loud hailer that the road north of his location had been blown. She instructed him to have his men lined up in a formation at 0800 hours the next morning or Force N was going to attack. Surrender and they would be allowed to march south retaining their personal weapons as protection from the shifta. Any women in the fort would be taken under the protection of Mrs. Brandy Seaborn, a "senior representative" of the International Red Cross.

Fail to comply and Force N would overrun the position. Prisoners would face the knife—any women found in the position would be turned over to the Patriots for their pleasure, then sold into slavery.

At sunrise, the two Lovat Scouts, Munro Ferguson and Lionel Fenwick, went to take a look. They discovered the place deserted. Apparently the Italians had marched out on a small trail that wound through the mountains, taking their chances rather than surrender. Possibly the Blackshirts did not believe they would not be handed over to the Patriots once they surrendered.

That was a mistake. Ras Cheap Bribe was prepared for this contingency. The Patriot commander had a band of his shifta waiting five miles out at a perfect ambush site where the trail crossed a swift mountain stream. The Patriots would not be taking prisoners or turning any women over to the "Red Cross."

Brigadier John Randal, Captain Hawthorne Merryweather, Lieutenant Butch "Headhunter" Hoolihan, Brandy Seaborn (wearing a Red Cross brassard on her left shoulder with another pinned to the front of her slouch hat), Lieutenant Penelope Honeycutt-Parker, Waldo, Ras Cheap Bribe, Rita and Lana walked up the road to inspect the abandoned camp. The gate was standing open.

The field phone in the commander's office could be heard clacking. Waldo went inside.

He came back to the door and said, "Who's our best Italian speaker?"

Capt. Merryweather went in to take the call along with Brig. Randal, followed by his entire entourage crowding in, not wanting to miss anything.

"Colonel Razine, the commandant of the next fort up the road, sir. He wants to know the situation here."

"Tell him the entire garrison has been wiped out to the last man by Patriots in the mountains." Brig. Randal said. "We're coming to kill him and take trophy on all his men if he doesn't have a white flag flying and surrender the minute we arrive."

"He says he has a large number of women and children from the plantations in the area that have sought refuge from the incessant guerrilla raids. Colonel Razine is concerned for their safety if he surrenders, sir."

"Put Mrs. Seaborn on the horn," Brig. Randal said.

"Brandy, you inform the colonel that Force N will be there in six hours," Brig. Randal said. "He needs to have his troops prepared to move south down the road within ten minutes after we arrive. Say the Red Cross will guarantee the safety of the women and children on the road march until they link up with Terry."

"But you had Lieutenant Pilkington blow a mountain down on the road between here and there, John."

"He doesn't have to know that," Brig. Randal said.

Brandy gave him a glittering smile and took the receiver of the phone.

"Bribe," Brig. Randal said, "it's all yours. Get your boys to work; make it quick. We're pulling out ASAP."

The word was passed to the Patriots waiting outside the wire. They charged in, eyes glazed … and the sack was on.

"I had no idea," Lt. Honeycutt-Parker said, "guerrilla warfare was so fascinating. War by telephone. Are we going to fight the Italians if they fail to meet your demands?"

"Yeah … but not fair," Brig. Randal said. "Colonel Razine commands the 99th Colonial Brigade, Parker. He has over 12,000 combat troops."

"Oh!"

"Butch," Brig. Randal ordered, "have the Phantom people contact Colonel Stone to come quick. Tell him to be expecting prisoners."

"What about the convoy we ambushed sir? There's 800 to 1,000 abandoned trucks blocking the road."

"Tell Terry he's going to need bulldozers up as well as earth-moving people to shove 'em off the cliff."

"Yes, sir!"

"Bribe," Brig. Randal said, "send word to your boys to hurry up and finish looting those trucks before the Lounge Lizards get there."

Pinned on the wall by the phone was an 8x10 glossy photo of Lady Jane in her swimsuit.

"Either you," Waldo said, "or her husband ought to be real jealous."

COLONEL SIR TERRY "ZORRO" STONE WAS IN HOT PURSUIT, EATING UP large chunks of mileage every day. Lounge Lizard Force, now augmented by a South African company of road-building engineers, was driving on Addis Ababa as fast as the former South African diamond miners could clear Lieutenant Pip Pilkington's landslides and his Nigerian engineers could repair the bridges the Italians destroyed in their retreat—which slowed LLF but had no effect whatsoever on the 1 Guerrilla Corps (Parachute), Force N guerrillas pursuing them.

Enemy opposition was virtually nil. When the Italians did try to ambush the LLF column, to their regret they found it contained three light batteries of 75mm artillery, homemade gun-trucks bristling with a combination of Breda 12.5 and Vickers K model machine guns and Rolls Royce armored cars with up to six extra Vickers K .303-caliber machine guns in twin mounts bolted on.

Col. Stone requested mortar support because the mortar's high angle of fire would allow them to shoot *over* the ridgelines. A platoon of motorized four-inch tubes from the Gold Coast Regiment was rushed forward and attached to LLF for the remainder of the operation. The four-inch rounds hit with the authority of a 105mm cannon.

LLF was the smallest regiment in the British Army, but it packed as much firepower as a conventional brigade of armored cars.

Up in the mountains, elements of 1 Guerrilla Corps (Parachute), Force N and Patriot auxiliaries were pacing Lounge Lizard Force. Ambushes were immediately taken under fire from two directions. The Italians ceased attempting them almost altogether as word spread about what happened to those who did.

Lounge Lizard Force came to a deep gorge with the 800-foot bridge across it blown and lying down in the river below. Col. Stone did not have time to wait for the Nigerian engineers to bring up bridging equipment. He ordered block and tackle broken out and the armored cars were lowered down into the gorge one at a time. Then the block and tackle was divided into individual loads, lowered down by ropes, and porters carried it up the far side of the canyon where it was reassembled.

The armored cars were then winched up, and the chase was back on. The rest of the LLF column had to wait until the bridge was repaired before crossing. Then they were off, racing to catch up.

Lounge Lizard Force was not stopping for anything—no obstacle too great.

BRIGADIER JOHN RANDAL AND HIS ENTOURAGE WALKED UP THE ROAD to the fort—the largest they had encountered thus far. A white bedsheet flag was flying over the garrison as instructed. Over 18,000 troops were rumored to be inside plus dependents, the odd mistress and Italian Nationals from the surrounding countryside who had sought sanctuary from the 1 Guerrilla Corps (Parachute), Force N guerrillas.

The Blackshirts would have been surprised to know that Brig. Randal had only twenty-three people total with him at this point in the campaign.

The Italian garrison commander, a major general in full dress uniform to include a plumed cockade hat, sword and ceremonial chrome-plated MAB-38A submachine gun (no cause for alarm—the Blackshirts had been authorized to retain their personal weapons for protection) strutted out to surrender with his own entourage that consisted of six senior officers sporting acres of gold braid and a flock of bird feathers adorning their sun helmets. The honor guard carried matching ceremonial chrome-plated MAB-38A submachine guns.

Except for the sun helmets, they looked like admirals.

"Peacocks," Brandy said.

The general brought his shiny MAB-38A up, as did the escort with him and said something in Italian.

"What did he say?"

"Drop your weapons," Brandy translated. "You are *my* prisoners."

"Uh-oh!" Waldo said.

Brig. Randal looked confused. "Surrender?" he said softly, talking to himself as if pondering the situation, not knowing what to do.

"Bastard!" Lieutenant Penelope Honeycutt-Parker spat.

Fiddling with the strap of his own MAB-38A submachine gun at sling arms, Brig. Randal said, "Surrender hell," as his submachine gun came off his shoulder and into the general's belly. He let lose a burst, point blank. *BBBBRRRAAAPPP.*

No one on either side could believe he had chosen to fight all the Blackshirts like that.

The general was on his knees, struggling to bring his weapon into action but the shiny chrome barrel was pointed at the dirt when it discharged. The Fascist had an incredulous look on his face as he crumpled over dead.

Brig. Randal's submachine gun fired again—one long continuous burst. The rest of the Italian party went down. Not one of the Blackshirts got off a single round other than those the general triggered, even though they all had their weapons pointed at him while his had still been on his shoulder.

Brig. Randal handed the smoking MAB-38A to Brandy. In full sight of the enemy in the fort he took out one of his ivory-stocked Colt .38 Supers, went around and shot each of the prostrate Blackshirts in the head.

There was a long silence after the last pistol shot rang out.

The gate opened and Italians began marching out with their weapons slung over their shoulders, muzzles down, as per Lady Jane's original instructions—no fight in them. The first man to approach, a colonel, was waving a white towel. He called out in flawless English talking one hundred miles per hour.

"Do not hold us responsible for that arrogant fool's treachery—women and children had nothing to do with this incident, they throw themselves on your mercy. My troops demand the protection promised in the leaflets dropped last night and those guaranteed under the Geneva Accords.

"Rights?" Brig. Randal said. "You don't have any rights!"

"As the senior surviving officer I call on the Red Cross representative present to be witness to our surrender."

The colonel was nervously eyeing the blond woman in the Red Cross regalia, eager for her to intervene and be his savior. Brandy was holding a submachine gun. Red Cross personnel are normally not armed.

"Allah do it," Ras Cheap Bribe threatened, reaching for his rhino-horned knife.

"Lighten up, Bribe," Waldo said. "You done had your chance to be a hero, and like the rest of us you was found wantin.'"

"Move out, Colonel," Brig. Randal ordered. "You'll be met on the road. Don't stop marching south until you are. Weren't any Patriots at the Geneva Convention. I'd keep that in mind if I was you."

Cheap Bribe's men were moving among the Blackshirt ranks relieving the men of their valuables and bandoleers of ammunition. The leaflets had explicitly ordered that the Italians bring only the rounds contained in the magazine of their individual weapon's magazine for purposes of self-defense. Bullets were money.

After today's sack was completed, Ras Gubbo Rekash was going to be filthy rich. Equally important in coming months—as the internal power struggle worked itself out after the Emperor was back on his throne—he was going to be heavily armed, including artillery. Not many Rases had cannons.

"Do that often?" Lt. Honeycutt-Parker asked, taking out a cigarette for Brig. Randal to light as she kept her eye on the Italians trudging past. "Shoot down men aiming guns at you?"

"Second time that's happened to me … a white flag double-cross," the U.S. 26th Cavalry Regiment Zippo flamed. "Never pays to trust Blackshirts, Parker. I forget, you remind me of that."

"Fascinating …"

BRANDY SEABORN AND LIEUTENANT PENELOPE HONEYCUTT-PARKER mounted their mules and moved to the head of the Italian column moving south down the strategic road. Rita and Lana went along to serve as their personal bodyguards. Lieutenant Butch "Headhunter" Hoolihan took charge of a detail of five men from Bimbashi Jack Masters' platoon of his Force Raiding Company and rode up to join them.

A column of prisoners that may have reached 25,000-strong—including civilians, women and children—was being marched south into captivity by Lt. Hoolihan, his page, six 1 Guerrilla Corps (Parachute), Force N indigenous troops and four women.

"Butch," Brandy called when they had traveled approximately a mile down the road, "have the colonel hold up the column."

"Yes, ma'am."

Brandy and Lt. Honeycutt-Parker rode back to the tail of the formation. The civilians and dependents were ordered to do a half left then a half right and continue to march. When the dependents and civilian refugees reached the front, Brandy kept them moving.

"Have your troops fall in behind," Brandy ordered the perplexed Italian colonel. "Women and children shall set the pace."

Prisoners marching south were a problem not only to Colonel Sir Terry "Zorro" Stone; they were causing a logistical nightmare for East Africa Force. The columns of surrendering Italians clogged the road. There was not enough truck transport forward to haul them—fighting vehicles and engineering equipment had priority.

The decision was made to repair the railroad and run trains to the front. The Italians would be transported to Harar, where a giant holding center was being organized to accommodate them.

The hardest-working troops in East Africa Force were the engineers. They had blazed roads through deserts where there were none, drilled water wells, cut through landslides caused by Force N guerrillas, rebuilt bridges, and now they were having to repair damage the Railroad Wrecking Crew had done to the rail system.

An angry South African road building engineer was standing on the road with his fists on his hips looking at what appeared to be "Bloody Mt. Everest blocking *my* road. Showoffs painted a bloody *N* on that rock as if I didn't know who did it."

He was exhausted from a long, hard campaign and mad that his own side was responsible for creating virtually all the work his men were doing.

"Damned guerrillas," the engineer said, to the man in a fur-collared leather bomber jacket standing next to him looking at the roadblock.

"Hate 'em worse than the bloody Wops—up their bloody Patriot cobbers, the wily bastards … playing with bloody dynamite knocking bloody mountains down across *my* perfectly good highway. Get my hands on a couple I'll show 'em some bloody demolitions, mate."

"Yeah, I can see how you might feel that way."

An armored car approached followed by two trucks transporting mules. The animals were unloaded. A gray-haired man appeared from somewhere leading two more mules. Four women, half a dozen native soldiers and a young lieutenant dismounted the vehicles. Everyone mounted up.

"Have a nice day," Brigadier John Randal said to the South African engineer.

Then the group rode around the roadblock up the mountain, their mules carefully picking the way up the steep slope.

BRIGADIER C.C. "FLUFFY" FOWKES' NIGERIANS LEAPFROGGED Brigadier Dan Pienaar's South Africans for the final push into Addis Ababa. There were only a little over 125 miles left to go, but there was one final obstacle: a gorge nearly a mile deep that had to be crossed. Reports from 1 Guerrilla Corps (Parachute), Force N and confirmed by aerial reconnaissance was that the bridge across it had been blown by the fleeing Italians. This was a major obstacle to be crossed.

The canyon was too deep and steep for Lounge Lizard Force to use the block and tackle technique to lower the armored cars down to the bottom and then winch them back up the far side. Besides, there was a swift-flowing river raging in the bottom.

"Fluffy Fowkes is a thruster," Colonel Sir Terry "Zorro" Stone said to the team of civilian mechanics from Rolls Royce. "He's going to want us across and won't take no for an answer."

The team leader, a man who had served in armored cars in Mesopotamia in the last war said, "Lay in all the ropes you can get your hands on, Colonel. Arrange for engineer support to build rafts down in the gorge of a type we can haul back and forth across that river on pulleys. Then stand back and leave the rest to us."

"That's it?"

"We can use a few men with mountaineering experience if you can locate them."

"I shall see what I can do."

30
GETTING THE HELL OUT OF DODGE

MAJOR JACK MERRITT HAD BEEN FIGHTING HIS WAY TOWARD THE PORT of Massawa. Two major battles were behind him since the fall of Keren. No. 9 Machine Gun Company, Sudan Defense Force was leading the way as usual with 4 Indian and 5 Indian Divisions hard on his heels. But it had been tough going at times. The Blackshirts fought desperately when they chose to make a stand.

The minute Lieutenant General William Platt, the Kaid, took the port city, President Franklin Roosevelt was going to announce that the Red Sea was clear for Lend Lease.

The French Foreign Legion's 13ᵗʰ Demi-Brigade, Captain Mike "March or Die" Mikkalis' old outfit commanded by Colonel Ralph Monclar, struck out cross-country and linked up with No. 9 Company. Maj. Merritt received orders to report to Col. Monclar for the remainder of the campaign. His company was now under the operational control of the Free French. His orders: "Go to Massawa."

Now the race to the Red Sea port picked up speed.

The Blackshirts at Massawa were commanded to "fight to the last man and the last bullet." Whether they would actually do so remained to be seen. The Italian High Command had given "die in place" orders before with not a lot to show for it.

BRIGADIER JOHN RANDAL STOOD ON THE FAR SIDE OF THE GORGE. IT WAS a mile to the bottom. Lounge Lizard Force was on the other side, but they were not stopped by the natural barrier. The Rolls Royce mechanics had completely disassembled the nine RR armored cars. (The three LLF South African Dingos could not be broken down into component groups like the RRs.) Volunteers with mountaineering experience from regiments throughout East Africa Force were at the gorge supervising the lowering of the armored car's parts to the bottom of the canyon by stages on ropes.

When each bundle of parts reached the floor, Nigerian engineers who had rappelled down were waiting with log rafts to haul them across the swift-flowing stream at the bottom. As soon as the bundles were loaded, the rafts were drawn across on ropes attached to pulleys manned by other engineers on the far side.

While that was taking place, Abyssinian paratroopers from Lounge Lizard Force's No. 5 company were scaling the cliffs up to where Brig. Randal was standing observing. Behind them, the Yeomanry of the Lancelot Lancer Regiment were waiting their turn at the ropes.

LLF was only going to be able to get its Rolls Royce armored cars across until the bridge was repaired, but Colonel Sir Terry "Zorro" Stone was prepared to make the final run on Addis Ababa with just the nine cars if he had to.

The colonel was driving hard. LLF had their blood up. They were not to be denied being the first to the capital.

Standing next to Brig. Randal, Lieutenant Penelope Honeycutt-Parker was looking through the Force N commander's Zeiss binoculars. "Fantastic, I wish Father were here to see this." Her father had been the regimental commander of the "Shiny Tenth" before the war ... by some accounts the wealthiest cavalry regiment in the army. Nowadays he was in command of a corps in Palestine.

Brandy Seaborn said, "Makes me really proud of Terry."

Brig. Randal said to the two women, "We better get moving or Zorro's going to pass us."

COLONEL HUGH BOUSTEAD AND LIEUTENANT RANDY "HORNBLOWER" Seaborn were studying the latest Most Secret communiqué delivered by Phantom. They were instructed to have the Emperor outside of Addis Ababa by the first week of April. The Elect of God was not—under any circumstance—to be allowed to make entry into the city until such time as authorized by Lieutenant General Alan Cunningham, Commander East Africa Force. Like their last directive, no exact time was stipulated.

By this point in the campaign, Emperor Haile Selassie had endured chancy flights in ancient airplanes, survived a truck crash, seen his men and camels roasted to death by out-of-control signal fires, been betrayed by his own noblemen who were, even at this late date, collaborating with the Italians—protecting them in some cases—and endured being led cross-country by a mad man. The King of Kings had come to loathe Colonel Orde Wingate. He was biding his time to settle the score—still royally displeased with not being allowed to bring his Royal Umbrella on his triumphant return to his rightful throne.

Only, the Conquering Lion of Judah did not exactly see the process of his return as being triumphant. The King of Kings had dreamed of liberating his capital in person. It was clear that was not going to happen. He was a pawn of the British.

By the time the Patriot caravan climbed the escarpment above Addis Ababa, only fifty-three camels were still left alive out of the over 25,000 that had started the expedition. The Emperor was heard to remark in private, "Many camels have sacrificed their lives in the service of their nation."

Col. Wingate claimed the reason so many camels had died was because those provided him had been of inferior quality. The handful of experienced camel handlers said he had made the beasts carry excessive loads, did not give them time to rest or adequate forage.

It was possible to count on one hand the number of camels Col. Boustead's Frontier Battalion (covering the same ground during the same time period) had lost.

The only major action the column had fought during the entire journey had been a chance meeting engagement of the 2nd Abyssinian Battalion with a superior Italian force, which Col. Wingate called "Boyle's Blunder." Even though Major Ted Boyle's troops had given a good account of themselves, the major was rewarded for his efforts by being relieved of his command.

Col. Wingate had previously threatened to sack Col. Boustead for some imagined ineptitude—he wanted to fire somebody simply to show he could.

"You can't relieve me," Col. Boustead said.

And that was the end of that.

ALL OVER THE CENTRAL HIGHLANDS OF ABYSSINIA THE MULE RAIDING Battalions of 1 Guerrilla Corps (Parachute), Force N were on a rampage. Brigadier John Randal issued orders for the MRBs to break down into platoon-sized elements and go all out. He wanted Force N spread out to cover a wider area than it ever had before.

Brig. Randal concluded the Duke of Aosta was expecting him to concentrate his forces along the strategic road from Harar to Addis Ababa to attack the forts clustered along it. He believed that the Italians wanted him to do just that. If he did, the Blackshirts would try to crush Force N in one blow.

Therefore he did the opposite, spreading the MRBs all over his Area of Operations. This had the effect of placing an even greater strain on the High Command in Addis Ababa. The Duke of Aosta's Headquarters was inundated by pleas for help from hundreds of isolated installations, plantations and bases that, under normal operational circumstances, would have been ignored by the guerrillas because they were of little or no military value.

The tidal wave of hysterical pleading from the isolated Italians out in the countryside was taking its toll on the Duke of Aosta and his staff's morale. They were powerless to do anything. The High Command imagined who knew what indignities their fellow countrymen were enduring at the hands of the evil Patriots ... men debased, women despoiled, children sold into slavery. And they could picture the same outrages happening to them one day soon.

The deadly cat-and-mouse game Brig. Randal had been playing with the Duke of Aosta from day one when he parachuted into Abyssinia had shifted so that the roles of who was the cat and who was the mouse had been reversed.

Brig. Randal ordered the Bad Boys to Addis Ababa. Random acts of sabotage became endemic. The letter *N* appeared everywhere.

Mysterious fires were seen in the mountains surrounding the city—tens of thousands of them every night. The wives and mistresses of the officers and public officials trapped in Addis Ababa were becoming hysterical. The Italian National civilian population was panic-stricken. The native population within the walled city was turning surly.

Millions of Patriots were out there sharpening their knives— everyone knew that was a fact, and it was clear the Italians were powerless to do anything about it.

Captain Hawthorne Merryweather was not helping in the Italians' moment of doubt and despair. He was papering Addis Ababa nightly with leaflets describing Patriot atrocities—complete with lurid photos (fake) of women being violated and men desecrated.

The situation was spinning out of control for the Duke of Aosta. He privately initiated back-channels contact with Lieutenant General Alan Cunningham to inform him the native population within Addis Ababa was about to revolt. The Duke declared that if the Abyssinians rose against him he would not be able to guarantee the safety of Italian Nationals or other Europeans in the capital.

Blame for the bloodbath sure to follow would fall on the British—the Duke, not satisfied with Lt. Gen. Cunningham's response to surrender immediately, then went on the radio and stated that publicly.

When that ploy still failed to elicit the desired response, the Duke of Aosta offered to allow East Africa Force into Addis Ababa to take control of the rapidly worsening situation. Then he stole away in the night with as many of his troops as he could muster and headed north into the mountains to set up a final redoubt. His hope was to hold out until General Erwin Rommel could defeat the British in Egypt and come to his rescue.

Reports of Afrika Korps' early successes against British Forces in the Lybian desert gave the Duke of Aosta reason to hope that might not take very long.

COLONEL SIR TERRY "ZORRO" STONE RECEIVED ORDERS TO "GO TO Addis Ababa." He had nine Rolls Royce armored cars and No. 5 Company of paratroops across the gorge. The bridge was a long way from being repaired. Lounge Lizard Force had no way to get additional transport across to carry the paratroops.

Brigadier John Randal came to his rescue. He arrived with enough captured Italian trucks for No. 5 Company. As soon as the last paratrooper climbed on board, Col. Stone set out on a mad dash to the city with the sirens mounted on the armored cars wailing.

He was aided by Captain the Lady Jane Seaborn and Lieutenant Pamala Plum-Martin flying ahead of the small column announcing the humanitarian nature of the mission. The Italians in the forts remaining along the road to the capital were admonished to allow it free passage. Failure to honor the humanitarian nature of Lounge Lizard Force's mission would result in "an immediate attack by Patriot forces with the garrison being put to the knife."

Patriots all along the route came out into the open to intimidate the Blackshirts. Many of these were sunshine soldiers who merely wanted to throw in with the winning side. The general uprising by the Abyssinians was very bad news for the Italians. The natives were not operating under any central control. Most were part-time shifta only out for easy plunder. Mistreatment was assured for any Fascist who fell into their hands.

The Italians who had not had time to fall back on the capital were taken aback by the rapid change of fortune. They no longer had any friends, no safe havens. No place to run.

Long columns of dejected Blackshirts started marching south along the road. They hoped to reach British Forces to surrender and avoid being taken by the shifta.

Ugly reports began circulating that the Patriots liked to throw prisoners off the cliffs into the gorges—one so deep, according to legend, it took a falling man a full day to hit to the bottom.

Italian troops were desperate to contact British lines.

Brig. Randal ordered 1 Guerrilla Corps (Parachute), Force N to start folding in on Addis Ababa. The Mule Raiding Battalions were instructed to rally on the capital city but not slow the pace of their operations. Unrelenting, the MRBs raided every target they came across as the battalions drew in on the capital, leapfrogging from target to target in an orgy of destruction.

Force N pillaged and burned its way to their final Objective Rally Point.

LOUNGE LIZARD FORCE ENTERED ADDIS ABABA ON 6 APRIL 41.

MASSAWA WAS CAPTURED BY THE 13TH DEMI-BRIGADE, SPEARHEADED by No. 9 Motor Machine Gun Company, Sudan Defense Force on 8 April 41. The Italians chose not to fight to the death.

THE EMPEROR WAS ENCAMPED OUTSIDE THE CAPITAL BUT NOT ALLOWED to enter Addis Ababa. He was instructed to wait until "additional" East Africa Force troops could arrive "to guarantee his safety" and a formal ceremony be staged. Finally, the Conquering Lion of Judah took matters into his own hands and marched on the city, defying Colonel Orde Wingate who had his orders not to let him. No one was going to shoot the King of Kings at this point.

There was not anything Colonel Hugh Boustead or Lieutenant Randy "Hornblower" Seaborn could do but go along.

Dignitaries flew to the capital. Rases that had been treading with the Italians and, in some cases, aiding them in their escape to the redoubt, now flocked to Addis Ababa to be on hand to pledge fealty when the Emperor arrived to reclaim his throne. An impromptu parade was scheduled.

Col. Wingate arranged for a white horse for the Emperor to ride in his triumphant entry. The Kings of Kings flatly refused. He chose a captured Alpha Romeo limousine as more befitting a modern ruler—his personal body slave rode on the running board.

Snubbed and left holding an empty horse, Col. Wingate climbed in the saddle and rode at the head of the Patriot column. When Lieutenant General Alan Cunningham saw him, he ordered, "Get Wingate off that horse!"

Photographs showed a skinny, bearded man in a ridiculous, oversized sun helmet riding a malnourished white horse at the head of a formation of barefooted Abyssinians. Generated by the corps of reporters who had traveled with the column, headlines worldwide blared, "Wingate and the Patriots liberate Abyssinia."

And the photos were there to prove it.

AT A DESERTED AIRFIELD SOUTH OF ADDIS ABABA, BRITISH PERSONNEL of 1 Guerrilla Corps (Parachute), Force N were assembling. Only there were not as many of them as had jumped in. Over forty percent had been killed, wounded or evacuated due to illness. The British officers and NCOs of Force N were not taking part in the festivities in the capital. However, the native guerrilla troops of the five mule raiding battalions were all there under the command of the Abyssinian officers. They were soon to become a regular unit of the Abyssinian National Army.

The Consolidated Model 31 "Pregnant Guppy" and two South African Air Force Junkers JU-52 transports were waiting with their motors ticking over. Their departure was imminent. Major "Jones" had already flown out with all the Phantom men from the Frontier Battalion, Lounge Lizard Force and Force N in another Junkers.

Seated on board the Model 31 were the members of Strategic Raiding Forces who had served in Force N. Also, officers and men from the Cavalry Division and those from the "Hostilities Only" units who had been selected to volunteer for permanent duty with Raiding Forces.

The remainder, who planned to return to their units, were aboard the other two SAAF aircraft. They would be flying out first. Brigadier John Randal and Captain the Lady Jane Seaborn boarded each of the Junkers JU-52s. The Force N commander went down the aisle and shook hands with every officer and man, congratulating them on a job well done. He took his time.

When he and Lady Jane exited, the SAAF transports took off flying south. The next stop was Nairobi and—for most—a thirty-day furlough.

Ras Cheap Bribe was standing by the ramp to the Pregnant Guppy, looking particularly spiffy in his (actually, Brig. Randal's) Pembrook's tailored uniform, Ray-Ban aviator glasses and captured Italian hat with the gold scrambled eggs on the bill crushed down over his beehive hairdo and black eye-patch. He was impatient to get to the city and have his moment with the Emperor. It was to be their first official meeting. In fact, Ras Rekash had never ever even laid eyes on the King of Kings ... not even from a distance.

Kaldi was already in Addis Ababa. Emperor Haile Selassie, it was now learned, was his uncle—a fact kept secret until today. He would make the introduction. Ras Gubbo Rekash was well-connected, it turned out.

Lady Jane handed Brig. Randal a long, thin box. He motioned Ras Cheap Bribe around the side of the airplane, where no one could see what was taking place, and handed the box to the ex-bandit. Inside was an exact replica of the Force N commander's ivory-handled horse tickler, except his had "GR" engraved on the silver cap instead of the Emperor's royal crest and there was no lion's tail attached.

The Patriot's one good eye bugged out when Brig. Randal showed him the concealed button to punch that released the thirteen-inch, razor-sharp stiletto blade that was concealed inside.

Then Brig. Randal and Lieutenant Butch "Headhunter" Hoolihan followed Lady Jane up the ramp—the two were first in, last out. Everyone on board, recognizing the significance, stood up and cheered.

Squadron Leader Paddy Wilcox, flying co-pilot today, came up on the intercom and said, "Force N, prepare for takeoff."

"Yeeehaaaa!" shouted the troops, giving the old Raiding Forces Comanche Yell.

Major General James "Baldie" Taylor had seats saved next to Lieutenant Penelope Honeycutt-Parker, who was sitting next to her husband, Captain Lionel Honeycutt-Parker; and Lieutenant Pamala Plum-Martin, who had come along to escort the troops home. Rita Hayworth and Lana Turner were already buckled in.

Lieutenant Randy "Hornblower" Seaborn was seated next to his mother, Brandy—not surprised to learn she had seen more action than he had.

GG was onboard. Lady Jane had arranged to have him employed by Special Operations Executive, at least on paper.

Conspicuously absent, Captain "Geronimo" Joe McKoy, Waldo Treywick and the ex-U.S. Marine, Frank Polanski. At the last minute, Capt. McKoy informed Brig. Randal, "We've got us some unfinished business to attend to, John."

Waldo gave him a weak grin.

Brig. Randal said, "Getting ready to do something stupid, Captain—sure about this?"

"We'll see you when we see you."

"Don't make me have to come back and get you."

The Model 31 was taxiing when the brakes locked, and it came to a tire-screeching halt.

"An armored vehicle has pulled out on the runway and is blocking our takeoff," the pilot announced over the intercom.

Tension in the back of the airplane ratcheted sky high.

Pounding came from outside the jump door at the tail of the aircraft.

"Open it," Brig. Randal ordered, fingering the ivory grip of the Colt .38 Super in his chest holster.

A canvas duffel bag came sailing through the opening as Colonel Sir Terry "Zorro" Stone swung in.

"Father showed up with my brother. Reginald is to take the parade with the Lancelot Lancers. I'm back with Raiding Forces."

"Welcome aboard," Brig. Randal laughed. "Only you could get relieved of command at your own victory parade."

"Crank it up," Lady Jane called to the pilot who had come back to check on what was taking place.

"Roger, we'll be airborne in zero five."

"No more delays, Captain," Lady Jane ordered, "Time for us to get the hell out of Dodge."

"LADIES AND GENTLEMEN," THE PILOT CAME ON THE INTERCOM, "WE have departed Abyssinian airspace."

The cabin erupted with cheers and Comanche yells.

Reaching up and unbuttoning the epaulets on his bush jacket, Major John Randal pulled off the cloth brigadier insignia and tossed them to Major General James "Baldie" Taylor.

"You can have these back, sir."

Maj. Gen. Taylor reached up and removed his own insignia. "I'm a civilian, Major. Don't call me sir."

————————

To be continued in Necessary Force – book XI in the Raiding Forces Series

————————

The Raiding Forces series continues…all the way to VE Day.

————————

To be on our notification list for the next book, contact phil@philward.com

ABBREVIATIONS
ORDERS & AWARDS

Bt	Baronet
CB	Companion of the Bath
CMG	Companion of the Order of St. Michael & St. George
DCM	Distinguished Conduct Medal
DFC	Distinguished Flying Cross (Royal Air Force)
DSC	Distinguished Service Cross (Royal Navy)
DSO	Distinguished Service Order
GC	George Cross
GCB	Grand Cross in the Order of the Bath
GM	George Medal
KBE	Knight Commander of the Most Excellent Order of the British Empire
KCVO	Knight Commander of the Royal Victorian Order
LG	Lady Companion of the Order of the Garter
MC	Military Cross
MM	Military Medal
MVO	Member of the Royal Victorian Order
OBE	Order of the British Empire
VC	Victoria Cross

GUERRILLA COMMAND
ACRONYMS

AT – Anti-Tank

CP – Command Post

DCP – Democratic Colonization Project

DZ – Drop Zone

EAF – East Africa Force

GHQ – General Headquarters

H&I – harassment & interdiction

HLI – Highland Light Infantry

HMG – heavy machine gun

IEA – Italian East Africa

LD – Line of Departure

LLF – Lounge Lizard Force

LLY – Lancelot Lancers Yoemanry

LMG – Light Machine Gun

LZ – Landing Zone

MMG – Motor Machine Gun

MRB – Mule Raider Battalion

OC – Operational Center

ORP – Objective Rally Point

PLF – Parachute Landing Fall

RR – Rolls Royce

GUERRILLA COMMAND
LIST OF CHARACTERS

Amedeo Umberto Isabella Luigi Filippo Maria Giuseppe Giovanni de
    Savoia-Aosta, Viceroy of Italian East Africa, the Duke of Aosta
Bimbashi Cord Granger
Bimbashi Jack Masters
Bimbashi Airey McKnight
Brandy Seaborn
Brig. C.C. "Fluffy" Fowkes
Brig Dan Pienaar
Brig. William "Bill" Slim
Capt. Jack Desmond Bonham
Capt. Mickey Duggan, DCM, MM, RM
Capt. Douglas Gray
Capt. Lionel Honeycutt-Parker
Capt. "Geronimo" Joe McKoy
Capt. Hawthorne Merryweather
Capt. Mike "March or Die" Mikkalis, DSM, MM
Capt. Jeb Pelham-Davies, MC
Capt. Roy "Mad Dog" Reupart
Capt. the Lady Jane Seaborn, OBE, RM
Capt. Harry Shelby, MC
Capt. "Pyro" Percy Stirling, MC
Capt. Jack Desmond Taylor
Cdr. Mallory Seaborn, RN
Cdre. Richard "Dickie the Pirate" Seaborn, VC, OBE, RN
Chief Inspector Ronald McFarland
Col. Hugh Boustead, MC
Col. Frank Messervy
Col. Ralph Monclar
Col. / Brig. Dan Sanford
Crown Prince, the Duke of Harar
Frank Polanski
FM Rodolfo "Butcher" Graziani
Gen. Orlando Lorenzini, Lion of the Sahara
Gubbo Rekash *aka* Cheap Bribe
Guido Grazinni, *aka* "GG"

Haile Selassie, His Imperial Majesty, Emperor, Lion of Judah, King of
   Kings, Elect of God
Kaldi, *Interpreter*
Lana Turner, *slave girl*
Lovat Scout Lionel Fenwick
Lovat Scout Munro Ferguson
Lt. Ralph Brothers
Lt. Dick Courtney
Lt. Penelope Honeycutt-Parker, RM
Lt. Butch "Headhunter" Hoolihan, MM, RM
Lt. Charles "Bomber" Kearey
Lt. / Maj. Jack Merritt, MC, MM
Lt. Karen Montgomery, RM
Lt. Pip Pilkington
Lt. Pamala Plum-Martin, OBE, RM
Lt. Randy "Hornblower" Seaborn, DSC, RN
Lt. Jeffery Tall-Castle
Lt. Dirk Van Rood
Lt. Gen. / Maj. Gen. William "the Kaid" Platt
Lt. Gen. Alan Cunningham
Lt. Gen. Erwin Rommel
Lt. Gen. / FM Sir Archibald Wavell
Maj. Jack Black
Maj. Ted Boyle
Maj. Edwin Chapman-Andrews
Maj. RFC "Rhino" Fosdick
Maj. David Niven, *aka* Maj. Jones
Maj. / Brig. John Randal, DSO, MC
Maj. / Col. Sir Terry "Zorro" Stone, KBE, MC
Maj. / Col. Orde Wingate
Maj. Gen. George "Daddy" Brink
Maj. Gen. A.J. Goodwin-Austin
Maj. Gen. Louis "Piggy" Heath
Maj. Gen. James "Baldie" Taylor, OBE
Maj. Gen. Harry Edward de Robillard Weatherall
Plt. Off. Gasper "Bunny" Featherstone, DFC
PM Winston Churchill
Ras Hailu, Ras of Gojjam
Ras Kassa

Ras Yaqut Morjan
Rflmn. Ned Pompedous
Rita Hayworth, *slave girl*
Sgt. Jock McDonald, RM
Sgt. Maj. Matthew Clive
Sgt. Maj. Maxwell Hicks, DCM
Sqn. Ldr. Paddy Wilcox, DSO, OBE, MC, FC
VAdm. Andrew Cunningham
Waldo Treywick

1
GOLDEN SQUARE

THE WOMAN CAME INTO THE ROOM. SHE WAS CARRYING A BIG KNIFE with a curved blade. Major John Randal was not as sound asleep as he appeared. His fingers tickled the ivory grip of his Colt .38 Super under the covers next to his leg.

A shadow appeared behind the woman. From the dock where the Nile houseboat was moored a lamp beamed through the porthole creating a yellow glow which materialized into the distinctive slim silhouette of a pistol barrel. The question in Maj. Randal's mind was which one did he shoot?

Quick as a cat the woman turned and stabbed the person behind her.

Maj. Randal's Colt .38 Super spoke two times.

Flashlights came on. Armed policemen swarmed the boat. Someone blew a whistle. A sawed-off police captain with a toothbrush mustache wearing an ill-fitting off white linen suit shouted, "Are you OK, Major?"

"What took you so long, Sansom?" Maj. Randal said as he swung out of bed pulling on his pants and Blood's slip-on boots.

"Events did not go strictly according to plan," Captain A.W. Sansom said. "Not anticipating a second party to show up."

"Well, neither was I."

"Fatima is, or I should say *was* an operative for the Golden Circle – that much we know. The man she knifed is an unknown - Abwehr, Muslim Brotherhood or perchance a freelance… who is to say."

"You're supposed to know the players."

"I spy spies, I don't read crystal balls," the policeman said. "If you had been a little quicker on the trigger and shot the miscreant before Fatima went for him maybe she wouldn't have felt compelled to kill you too."

"Right," Maj. Randal said. "If I had, he'd have turned out to be one of *your* boys."

"Had we wanted Fatima dead, Major, we could have killed her ourselves. The plan was for you to pass out. Then, as the lady in question photographed the classified documents about the Abyssinian guerrilla operation contained in your briefcase, we break in and nab her red-handed. Couldn't stick to the script, eh, lover boy."

"One thing led to another," Maj. Randal said.

"Have to give it to you Major, you make first-rate bait."

"I've had practice."

"So we hear," the Chief of Cairo's Counterintelligence Department said. "Remember, you were not here tonight. This never happened."

"Tell that," Maj. Randal said, "to the sporting set at the Kit-Kat Club."

"Quite right," Capt. Sansom said. "You shot the best belly dancer in Egypt."

MAJOR JOHN RANDAL WAS LAYING ON A LOUNGE AT THE POOL OF THE Gezira Club soaking up sun next to the leggy brunette Lieutenant Penelope Honeycutt-Parker, RM. Her husband, Captain Lionel Honeycutt-Parker was inside making reservations for dinner.

"Hot date last night?" Lt. Honeycutt-Parker asked. "You look tired, John."

"No," Maj. Randal said. Not that he would tell her if he had. She was a longtime friend of Captain the Lady Jane Seaborn, RM – worked for her in the Raiding Forces Women's Royal Marine detachment.

The truth was there had not been any dates. Last time he had been in Cairo, women were literally throwing themselves at him. It had helped to have Special Operations Executive supplying female operatives to sleep with him to see if he would reveal military secrets.

This trip women would not come anywhere near him, that is except Fatima – and she had an agenda.

No books had been published about his latest military adventures this time around either. In fact, Maj. Randal never heard the Abyssinian campaign mentioned at all. It was as if it never happened. The talk was about the calamity in Greece, the threatened invasion of Crete and the German general named Rommel in Libya.

Except for the Honeycutt-Parkers, he did not know hardly anyone in Cairo

Lady Jane was away in England. Her dead husband, Lieutenant Commander Mallory Seaborn, RN, had turned out not to be so dead when Maj. Randal rescued him on the first MI-9 mission to the Continent before coming out to Africa. Since he was engaged to Lady Jane at the time, to say that his love life was complicated would be a major understatement.

When Force N, meaning Maj. Randal and Lieutenant Butch "Headhunter" Hoolihan, RM, went missing in Abyssinia, Lady Jane abandoned her husband to come out to Africa to help organize a rescue operation. She stayed for the entire campaign, which did nothing to untangle their relationship.

Rita Hayworth and Lana Turner, the slaves he had liberated in Abyssinia, had gone to England with Lady Jane. Now they were members of her Royal Marine detachment. The girls were scheduled for complete medicals and then who knew what Lady Jane had in store for them. Maj. Randal was surprised at how much he missed the girls. Rita and Lana had been his constant companions, shared every danger he had faced for the past six months. He wondered what the two Zār priestesses were up to.

Lt. Hoolihan was off on a course in England. The school he was attending was designed to initiate him into the mysteries of being a Royal Marine officer. Lady Jane had mentioned a visit to Chatterley's Military Tailors. The young Royal Marine lieutenant was her pet project.

Maj. Randal had been Lady Jane's pet project once upon a time. It was good to be her pet project.

Major Sir Terry "Zorro" Stone was home on leave too. His exact rank was in question (he had been an acting colonel). He was no longer commanding officer of the Lancelot Lancer Yeomanry Regiment *aka* Lounge Lizards. His brother had resumed command in Addis Ababa following the conclusion of the Abyssinian Campaign. Maj. Stone had led the longest, fastest, most successful armored cavalry advance in modern history – over 1,700 miles. Nothing the Germans had done on any of their blitzkriegs had even come close. Only his father, the Duke, had wanted his eldest son Reginald to command – and it *was* the family regiment.

Major Jack Merritt was staying in command of No. 9 Motor Machine Gun Company, Sudan Defense Force. Maj. Merritt had been nominated for an immediate Distinguished Service Order for his brilliant leadership during the run up to the Battle of Kern and then the race to the strategic Port of Massawa on the Red Sea. There was a rumor the Free French also had plans to award him the Legion of Honor. No. 9 MMG Co. was being detached from the Sudan Defense Force to be trained by the Long Range Desert Group in deep desert operations. The plan was that it then be assigned to Raiding Forces, Middle East.

Mule Raiding Battalion commanders Captain Taylor Corrigan, Captain Jeb Pelham-Davies, and Captain Pyro "Percy" Stirling were on home leave.

Lieutenant Randy "Hornblower" Seaborn, RN had returned to Seaborn House with the naval contingent that had traveled with Lounge Lizard Force to operate the three-pound fast firers for the Lancelot Lancer Yeomanry. His boat, MGB 345, was back from its refit.

Captain Mike "March or Die" Mikkalis had gone on leave somewhere in Africa. He had informed Maj. Randal that his temporary rank was only temporary. He did not intend to remain an officer. The job he wanted was Sergeant Major of Raiding Forces, Middle East.

Lieutenant Pamala Plum-Martin, RM was away going to flight school, Maj. Randal was not sure exactly where but it was in the Middle East somewhere. Because she had amassed so many hours flying combat missions for Psychological Warfare Executive (PWE) over Abyssinia in a Supermarine Walrus she was going to be able to place out of most of the training. There was a possibility the aviatrix might be awarded her wings and the Distinguished Flying Cross on the same day.

Squadron Leader Paddy Wilcox had gone along with Lt. Plum-Martin to be available to tutor her on the finer points of the written examinations. He had taught her to fly at Seaborn House. And it had been his idea to allow her to fly combat missions over Abyssinia. The Canadian pilot wanted to make sure the Vargas Girl look-alike Royal Marine received her wings.

Brandy Seaborn was with her husband, Commodore Richard "Dickey the Pirate" Seaborn. Cdre. Seaborn was going to get his wish at long last, command of a capital ship – a cruiser. Brandy had originally come out to Egypt to serve with Colonel Dudley Clarke in A-Force but now with Raiding Forces, Middle East being organized she was thinking about doing something with it instead. She and Maj. Randal had always been very close.

One thing was certain – she was not going to be a Royal Marine. Brandy marched to her own drum.

Missing were Captain "Geronimo" Joe McKoy, Waldo Treywick and ex-U.S. Marine Frank Polanski. The three had stayed behind to carry out a private enterprise the day Force N flew out of Abyssinia. No word of their whereabouts had turned up yet.

Maj. Randal was growing bored in Cairo. He was ready to go to work reorganizing Raiding Forces. He had been in talks with Capt. Honeycutt-Parker. The Royal Dragoons officer had proven to be a superb organizer. He was either going to take command of Raiding Forces, Europe located at Seaborn House or become deputy to Maj. Randal. There were a lot of possibilities for raiding to be had – he simply had to put the pieces of the puzzle together.

A blonde in a two-piece swimsuit that appeared to be made out of three Band-Aids and a couple of bootlaces strolled over to where Maj. Randal and Lt. Honeycutt-Parker lay sunning. The woman was tanned pure gold and had white platinum hair the color of ice (even paler that Lt. Plum-Martin's, if that could be possible). It was pulled straight back in a long ponytail. There were a dozen thin gold bangles on her left wrist.

She looked vaguely familiar.

"Are you Major Randal?" the woman asked with a slight accent. She could not avoid staring at the scars on his chest from being mauled by a lion.

"That would be me," Maj. Randal said. "Who might you be?"

Lt. Honeycutt-Parker had raised her sunglasses to check out the golden girl.

"Rikke Runborg. My friends call me Rocky."

"Nice to meet you, ah, Rocky."

Actually we *have* met, Major." Rocky had an impressive set of white teeth when she smiled... which it seemed like she did a lot. She was very supple.

"Really?"

"I was with Mallory," Rocky said, "the night you saved us. Never had the opportunity to thank you properly – things happened so quickly after the gun battle and the mad dash to the boat."

"Didn't recognize you," Maj. Randal said, "with your clothes on."

"Mallory failed to mention he was married," Rocky said. "When I discovered the truth I came to Cairo to work with the Norwegian Legation. Call me."

"Fascinating," Lt. Honeycutt-Parker said as she watched Rocky ripple her way back to her lounge. "I would not make that telephone call if I were you, John."

"No?"

"Have you noticed women avoiding you?"

"As a matter of fact, Parker..." Maj. Randal said.

"Before she flew out, Jane passed the word over the 'old girl network' you had spent the last six months behind the lines in Abyssinia," Lt. Honeycutt-Parker said. "Every woman in Cairo knows the VD rate there is eighty percent or better. Get the picture, hero?"

"I hope you're making that up."

CAPTAIN LIONEL HONEYCUTT-PARKER RETURNED TO THE POOL AREA. "Who was that?"

"Mallory's ex-girlfriend," Lieutenant Penelope Honeycutt-Parker said. "John rescued her from the Nazis."

"Vichy French Police," Major John Randal said.

"She wants him to phone her."

"I would advise against that call," Capt. Honeycutt-Parker said. "Mallory has damned fine taste in women, credit him that."

Jim "Baldie" Taylor walked out to the pool. "Who was that smasher you and John were chatting with, Parker?"

"Rikke Runborg, friends call her Rocky. She was with Mallory the night John brought the two of them out of France for Norman Crockett's MI-9 – dropped by to ask him to call her so she can thank him properly."

"I am going to do you a favor, Major," Jim said. "We can take off this afternoon for the RAF base at Habbaniya. Pam is graduating from the flying school there in a couple of days. Let's fly up to see her awarded her wings.

"Take along a couple of those long-range Springfield 7mm-06s you brought back from Abyssinia. Get in some White Oryx hunting. The place is a paradise in the desert."

"Am I invited?" Lt. Honeycutt-Parker asked. "Lionel is leaving for England to check on Raiding Forces operations at Seaborn House. I am at loose ends."

"Absolutely," Jim said. "Habbaniya is the home of RAF No. 4 Service Flying Training School. It's a man-made oasis where they send pilots who need rest. Said to have the best swimming pool in the service, golf, polo, riding... you name it. Have ourselves a nice quiet holiday.

"Besides, Major, you do not want to place *that* phone call."

ABOUT THE AUTHOR

PHIL WARD IS A DECORATED COMBAT VETERAN COMMISSIONED AT AGE nineteen. A former instructor at the Army Ranger School, he has had a lifelong interest in small unit tactics and special operations. He lives in Texas on a mountain overlooking Lake Austin.

Other books in the Raiding Forces Series:

Those Who Dare

Dead Eagles

Blood Wings

Roman Candle

Necessary Force

Desert Patrol

Private Army

Africa 1941

The Sharp End

Raiding Rommel

Strategic Services

Tip of the Sword

Always So Few

Made in the USA
Columbia, SC
07 April 2023

14923454R00169